Sir William D´Avenant

# The dramatic works

## Vol. 2

Sir William D´Avenant

**The dramatic works**
*Vol. 2*

ISBN/EAN: 9783337304713

Printed in Europe, USA, Canada, Australia, Japan

Cover: Foto ©Andreas Hilbeck / pixelio.de

More available books at **www.hansebooks.com**

# THE DRAMATIC

# WORKS OF SIR WILLIAM D'AVENANT.

## WITH PREFATORY MEMOIR AND NOTES.

### VOLUME THE SECOND.

MDCCCLXXII.

EDINBURGH: WILLIAM PATERSON.
LONDON: H. SOTHERAN & CO.

# CONTENTS.

# THE
# PLATONIC LOVERS.

*The Platonick Lovers. A Tragi-Comedy. Presented at the Private House in the Black-Fryers, by his Majesties Servants. The authour, William D'Avenant, servant to her Majestie. London, Printed for Richard Meighen, next to the Middle Temple in Fleet Street, 1636, 4to.*

*The Platonick Lovers.—London, Printed for Gabriel Bedel, and T. Collins, and are to be sold at their shop in the Middle Templegate in Fleet Street, 1665, 12mo.*

*The Platonick Lovers. A Tragi-comedy. In the collected works of Sir William D'Avenant. 1673, folio.*

In one of the amusing letters, addressed by James Howell to his friend Philip, afterwards Sir Philip, Warwick, who was then residing in Paris, dated from Westminster, the 3d June 1634, he gives him all the scandal of the Court, and mentions that there were " little news at present, but that there is a Love call'd Platonick Love which much sways there of late. It is a Love abstracted from all corporeal, gross impressions and sensual appetite, but consists in contemplations, and ideas of the mind, not in any carnal fruition. This Love sets the Wits of the Town on work, and they say there will be a Masque shortly on it, whereof her Majesty and her Maids of Honour will be a part."

Although the name of D'Avenant is not given, it may be inferred that this intended Masque was no other than the Temple of Love, in which, as has already been shewn, the Queen and the Ladies of her Court appeared as Masquers, the entertainment itself being given at their own charge. The subject of the Masque is Platonic Love, of which one of the characters thus treats:

> " They raise strange doctrines, and new sects of Love,
> Which must not woo. or court the person, but
> The mind ; and practice generation not
> Of bodies but of souls."

The present comedy of " The Platonic Lovers," represented two years afterwards, evidences the fact that this ideal passion was then still popular.

The duodecimo edition of the Platonic Lovers, printed in 1665, is merely a reprint of the preceding edition, with the dedication. It forms the second of " Two Excellent Plays ; The Wits, a Comedie ; The Platonick Lovers, a Tragi-Comedie. Both presented at the Private House in Black-Friers by His Majesties Servants." Each of these has a separate title-page, but the pagination is continuous throughout.

The dedication is :—" To the most noble Mr Henry Jermyn. Sir, I have boldly fix'd your name here, to shew the world where I have settled my estimation and service; and expect it should add much to my judgement that I have made so excellent a choice. When you have leisure, and can a little neglect your time, be pleas'd to become my first reader. If it shall gain your liking the severe rulers of the stage will be much mended in opinion ; and then it may be justly acknowledg'd you have recover'd all the declining fame, belonging to

Your Unfortunate Servant,

WILLIAM D'AVENANT."

Henry Jermyn, Esq., was the second son of Sir Thomas Jermyn of Rushbrook in the county of Sussex, who, trying his fortune at Court, was so successful as to obtain from his Royal Master, in January 1643, the Barony of Jermyn of Bury in the county of Suffolk, and in 1660 his Majesty, Charles II., created him Earl of St Albans, by letters patent dated at Breda.

Jermyn was much esteemed by the Queen, and attended her abroad. It was rumoured that her Majesty was privately married to him. Sir John Reresby in his Memoirs says, "I had three cousins in an *English* convent of *Paris*, one of them an ancient lady, and since Abbess of the House. Hither the Queen was wont often to retire for some days: and the Lady would tell me that Lord Jermyn, since St Albans, had the Queen greatly in awe of him, and indeed it was obvious that he had great interest with her concerns; but that he was married to her, or had children by her, as some have reported, I did not then believe, though the thing was certainly so."*

If true, this curious fact would indicate that whatever opinion Henrietta Maria may have originally entertained in favour of Platonic Love, it had, during the latter portion of her life, suffered considerable modification.

After the Restoration, Lord St Albans was created a Knight of the Garter, and constituted Lord Chamberlain of the Household. He died in the year 1683 when the Earldom of St Albans became extinct, an event which enabled Charles II. to confer on his natural son, by Nell Gwyn, the Dukedom of St Albans.

* London 1735, 8vo, p. 4.

The Barony of Jermyn, in consequence of a remainder in the patent, devolved on Thomas, the nephew of the Earl, who, obtaining the appointment of Governor of Jersey, died in 1703 without male issue, whereby the Barony became extinct. He left several daughters, descendants from whom still exist.

Mr Halliwell reprinted, in 1850, for the Percy Society, a collection of songs from a black-letter copy in his own possession, supposed to be unique. It is titled " The Loyal Garland, or a Choice Collection of Songs highly in request, and much esteemed in the past and present times." Lond. 1686. In that collection are two songs, bearing upon our present subject, one named " Platonick Love,"—the other " The Platonick Lover." Of these we subjoin the first, on account of its own merit:—

> Fond lovers, what do you mean,
>   To court an idle folly?
> Platonick love is nothing else
>   But meerly melancholy;
>   'Tis active love that makes us jolly.
>
> To dote upon a face,
>   Or court a sparkling eye,
> Or to believe a dimpled chin
>   Compleat felicity,
>   'Tis to betray your liberty.
>
> She cares not for your sighs,
>   Nor your lamenting eyes;
> She hates to hear a fool complain,
>   And cry, he dyes, he dyes;
>   Believe she loves a close surprize.
>
> Then be no more so fond
>   As to think a woman can
> Be satisfied with compliments,
>   The frothy part of a man;
>   Oh no, she hates a Puritan.
>
> Then venture to embrace,
>   'Tis but one or two,
> I'm confident no woman lives,
>   But sometimes she will do;
>   The fault lies not in her, but you.

# PROLOGUE.

' Tis worth my smiles to think what enforc'd ways
And shifts, each poet hath to help his Plays.
Ours now believes the Title needs must cause,
From the indulgent Court, a kind applause,
Since there he learnt it first, and had command
T'interpret what he scarce doth understand.
And then, forsooth, he says, because 'tis new
'Twill take ; and be admir'd too by a few :
But all these easy hopes I'd like t'have marr'd,
With witnessing his title was so hard,
'Bove half our city audience would be lost,
That knew not how to spell it on the post.*
Nay, he was told, some critics lately spent
Their learning to find out, it nothing meant :
They will expect but little, he replies,
From that which nought or little signifies.
Well, I, your servant, who have labour'd here
In Buskins and in Socks this thirty year,
I'th truth of my experience, could not chuse
But say, these shifts would not secure his Muse
Then straight presented to his willing fear,
How you are grown of late, harsh and severe.
Excuse me that I am so bold to speak my mind
I'the dark, of what so publicly I find.
But this hath made him mourn ; I've left him now
With's limber hat, o'ershadowing his brow,
His cloak cast thus—to hinder from his ear,
The scorns and censures he may shortly hear :
Such as shall teach, despair, lead him the way
Unto a grove of Cypress, not of Bay.

* The bill of the play for the night was, in London, at the
time, placed on the several posts in the vicinity of the Theatre.

# THE PERSONS OF THE PLAY.

THEANDER, *A young Duke, lately a General.*
PHYLOMONT, *A young Duke that borders by him.*
SCIOLTO, *An old Lord, Friend to Theander.*
FREDELINE, *Creature to Theander.*
CASTRAGANIO, *Creature to Fredeline.*
GRIDONELL, *A young Soldier, son to Sciolto.*
BUONATESTE, *A generous Artist.*
ARNOLDO,⎱ *Attendants on Theander.*
JASPERO, ⎰
EURITHEA, *M^{ris} to Theander, Sister to Phylomont.*
ARIOLA, *M^{ris} to Phylomont, Sister to Theander.*
AMADINE, *Woman to Eurithea, Sister to Castraganio.*
ATTENDANTS, &c.

*The Scene :*

SICILY.

# THE PLATONIC LOVERS.

## Act I.  Scene I.

*Enter* Sciolto, Arnoldo, Jaspero, *Attendants.*

Scio. What ho! Arnoldo, Jaspero! Dispatch,
Dispatch!   You move like great fat Burgers that
Had newly din'd.  Cripples would stir more nimbly
To a whipping.   Are all things prepar'd?
    Arn. My Lord, there's time enough: the Duke
        will not
Be here till night.
    Scio. From whence, pray, that intelligence?
    [Jasp.] From the Gazet,* brought hither by a mule
From Paris, Sir.
    Arn. Your Lordship receives yours,
I think, in a little letter tie'd to
A Tartarian arrow.
    Jasp. Or 'bout the neck of a Barbary pigeon.
We know he'll not be here till night.
    Scio.                              You know?
Your knowledge, Sir, will scarce prefer a clerk,
To dine upon the ear of a tythe pig.
Death! my good serving gentleman,
Did not I leave him a league off, and with
Him too, Duke Phylomont? their train enough
To famish our whole Sicily, were not
Nature bounteous to us in our good corn.

---

* The Gazette, a paper of public intelligence and news of
diverse countries, was first printed at Venice about the year
1620, and was so called, according to some accounts, because
*Una Gazetta*, a small Venetian coin, was paid for the privilege
of perusal.—*Nouv. Dict. Hist.* Others derive the name from
the Italian word for magpie—*gaza*—*i.e.*, chatterer.  A Gazette
was printed in France in 1631.

ARN. Hath sprightly Phylomont encounter'd with
Our Duke Theander by the way too ?
   SCIO. 'Light ! your business is to ask questions,
      Sir ?
A court examiner ?   Are all provisions made
Of furniture and meat ?
   JASP.               All, all, my Lord !
   SCIO.  The inner room's new hung, and th'garden
      gallery
Adorn'd with Titian's pictures, and those frames
Of Tintoret, last brought from Rome ?
   ARN. Yes, Sir, and tables spread with napery
Finer than Poppea's smock.*
The cupboards crack with studded plate
And crystal vials thick enough t'endure
A fall or hammer, Sir.
   JASP.             Our kitchens smoke so,
That the steam blown o'er a town besieg'd,
Would cure the famine in't ?
   ARN. The cellars too  so  fill'd that they would
      make
A Danish army drunk.
   SCIO.          Arnoldo ! Rogue !
With good pure muskaden of Crete ?
I'm old, and must be nourished with
My morning sop, like matrons that want teeth.
   ARN. Your  Lordship  shall  not  fail  to have it
      spic'd.
   JAS. And,  when  'tis  noon,  your  malamucko
      mellon of
An amber scent serv'd in a grotto, Sir,

* Poppea Sabina, daughter of Titus Ollius, of great beauty
and elegance of form.  She became wife of Rufus Crispinus, a
Roman knight, from whom, Otho, then one of Nero's favourites, carried her away and married her.  Nero, in turn, lured
her from Otho, repudiated his wife Octavia, on the plea of
barrenness, and also married her ; but behaved so cruelly to her,
that she died of a kick while pregnant, A.D. 64.  She bathed
daily in asses' milk.

To cool your Lordship's wishes, not your blood ;
For that, we guess, hath not these many years
Been feverish towards women.

    Scio.                          A merry knave !
Go, good boys both.  Call all the waiters, and
The grooms, t'attend upon their several charge :
The Dukes will instantly arrive.  Our brave
Theander sent me for dispatch before,
To take command of the whole house.  Look to't !
I shall be bounteous, but severe.

    Arn. My Lord, we love your government and
        will make haste.

                      [*Ex. Jaspero, Arnoldo.*

     *Enter* Fredeline, Castraganio.

    Fred. Walk our horses near the park gate until
A gen'ral care be given for all the troop.

    Within.                        I shall, sir.

    Fred. My Lord Sciolto, your good horseman-
        ship
Hath put us to some trouble to o'ertake you.
Let me prefer this gentleman unto
Your knowledge.  He will deserve them both.

    Scio. I thank you for him, signior Fredeline ;
No friendship of your choice can deserve less ;
How is he call'd?

    Fred. Castraganio.  'Tis he,
Whom with your kind consent, I would prefer
To our Duke's chamber : and the brother to
The witty Amadine, whom late I plac'd
Chief woman to Eurithea
Our grand master's mistress.

    Scio. Signior, give me your hand !
I love not courtship, but I will promise
To befriend you, and perform it too.

    Cas. Your Lordship hath just power o'er my
        belief.

FRED. He's lately posted from Vienna, Sir,
And can present you with a letter.

[*Cas. gives Sciolto a letter.*

SCIO. I hope from the noble Colonel, my son's
Governor.

CAS. His name, Sir, is subscrib'd to it,
And straight you will behold your son.
The situation of this house hath but a while
Employed his eyes without.

SCIO. Fredeline, the boy comes
As I were master o'er my wish. 'Tis now
Full thirteen years, since first of tender growth,
I sent him to the camp. This letter, sir,
My better leisure shall survey. But pray,
How is he bred? My peevish humour gave
A strange direction to his governor:
That he should never learn to write nor read,
Nor never see a woman.

CAS. My Lord, you are obeyed in both. He is
A good soldier, and by his learning will
Sooner confute the foe, than a philosopher.
As for women, th'are things he ne'er heard nam'd;
Nor can the camp present him any, but
Coarse sutlers' wives, creatures of so much dirt,
That, shovel'd well together, they will serve
To make a trench ere they are dead, more fit
To heave the stomach, than to stir the blood.

FRED. I know 'em perfectly! They wear no
smocks
But cut out of an old cast tent, and bind
Their hair in horses' girths* instead of phylliting.

SCIO. Such I dare allow him.

FRED. Yet, with the freedom of your Lordship's
leave,

---

* This allusion to the sutler's wives, and their mode of binding their hair, is introduced throughout these plays more than
once. For instance, see vol. i., p. 29.

These are but homely principles to give
For education of a son and heir !
Not write nor read, nor see a woman !
   Scio. I will endure the hazard of a new
Experiment, and try how nature will
Incline him.   Learning, I find, doth make men
Saucy with their Maker, and false unto  ·
Themselves ; and women make us all fools.

*Enter* Gridonell

   Cas.                Here comes your son.
Practise your reverence, sir! there stands your
     father.
   Grid. Well, which is he ?
                     [*Stands still, gazing about.*
   Cas. There, sir, with the grey beard.
   Grid. A comely old fellow, by this hand, sir.
I am glad to see you, with all my heart !
   Scio. If you stand upon these points, sir,—and
     I you !
   Cas. Go, ask blessing !
   Grid.            Does the old man look for't ?
   Scio. Not I, introth ! for though the custom be
Devout enough, it shows methinks
Too like a compliment.
   Grid. You are in the right, sir,
And I hate compliment as much as you.
   Fred. My Lord, his governor hath follow'd your
Directions to the shadow of a hair.
He's rarely bred to make a favourite
In the French Court.
   Scio. Go, prick your ears, good signior, if you
     like
It not ; 'tis music unto mine.   But son,
How e'er these manners are not much in use,
You can be dutiful ?
   Grid. Sir, I am taught my father is my officer,

I must perform my duties, and obey him :
Besides, I love you more than a good sword.
   Scio. Why, I thank you, sir ; there is no love lost.
   Fred. For me, exc'lent courtship ! Just like the
       parley
'Twixt Mounsier Hobbynol and Colin Clout.
   Grid. I pray a word ! I'm told I should expect
Certain duties from you too.
   Scio. May't please you, son, I shall be glad to
      learn.
   Grid. You must allow me still new choice of
      armour,
Brave horse for service, and high pric'd gennets
To curvet i'th' streets ; and rich cloaths.
   Scio. Heaven forbid else !
   Grid. Jewels and money too.
   Scio. O son, I shall know my duty.
   Grid. And when the time conspires with my
      necessities
To call you to't, you must make haste and die.
   Fred. My Lord, how like you that ? This
      breeding's right :
Nor is it altogether new, or strange.
   Scio. I'd rather ever find it on his tongue,
Than once believe it in his heart : a rough boy !
I must keep him still from the sight of the ladies:
It will continue him in's innocence. Hold, sir !
This key will lead you through the terrace that
O'erlooks the orchard walk, and then you pass
Into an armoury. Spend there your time
A while : and take your choice. I know the Duke
That owns it will make good my gift. Will you
      walk, sir ?
   Grid. I pray, sir, lead the way !
   Scio.             Nay, I beseech you, sir.—
   Grid. I know 'tis fit I give place to my elders.
   Scio. But I have business here. Do you think, son,

I'd be so much uncivil else, as not to wait upon you?
 GRID. Well, take your course. I love to see good
  armour.           [*Exit.*
 SCIO. If I can keep him from the ladies, I
Am happier than king Priam that had fifty sons,
But sure not one like this.   [*Flourish afar off.*
 FRED. My Lord, this summons shews the Dukes
  are come.
Sir, stand you here! I'll find a time for your
Address.        [*Leads Cas, aside.*

*Enter* THEANDER, PHYLOMONT, ATTENDANTS.

 WITHIN. Make way, there! Ho! bear back,
  bear back!
   [*Theander embraces, and whispers Phylomont.*
 FRED. This is Theander, sir, whose present sway
Palermo owes allegiance to ; rich in
His mind and fame, as in his large extent
Of land ; and, to augment his wealth, he comes
Loaden with spoils of frequent victories.
Though but i'th' blossom of his life, he hath
Already done enough to fill a history,
And is deriv'd from th' old Sicilian kings.
Him I have chosen to prefer you to.
 CAS. If I could double all my faculties,
You have obliged them wholly to your use.
What is the other signior, whom he seems
To court with such a fervent show ?
 FRED. Duke Phylomont, that neighbours to his
  government,
And rules the western borders of this Isle :
All that the rich Mazara* yields. He equals Duke
Theander in the best of's virtues, and his fate ;
And now brings too, though from a climate more
Remote, the triumphs of a war. But yet,
If midnight howlings heard in cities sack'd

<hr>

* A river in Sicily.

And fir'd, the groans of widow'd wives,
And slaughter'd children's shrieks can pierce the
        ears
Of Heaven, the learned think their glorious ghosts
Will have a dismal welcome after death.
However, in this world, 'tis good to follow 'em
I would not fright your nice and pious mind
T' unprofitable fears.
    CAS. Kind signior, doubt me not.
    THEA. Thou breath'st into me, mighty Phylo-
        mont,
No other soul but mine.   My better thoughts
Are moulded in thy breast, and, could we grow
Together thus, our courteous hearts would not
Be nearer, nor yet more entire.  I gratulate
Thy victories in Spain : thou hast undone
A nation with thy noble deeds, and taught
Them how to fight, by seeing frequent conquests on
Themselves, when brave examples come too late
To imitate, and they are left no land
To fight for, or defend.
    PHYL.                        Renown'd Theander !
What delight can wise historians have
To mention me ?   Whilst Naples keeps the sense,
Or memory to mourn, thou art the argument
Of all just praise.   Alas ! my battles will
Be thought, when thine are nam'd,
But village-quarrels, that poor herdsmen make
To keep their common from their landlord's sheep.
My ensigns not deserve to hang
As curtains at thy shrine, when thou shalt lye
Ador'd, and styl'd the wars' first saint,
That taught thy armies how to cleanse, not sack
The cities thou hast won.
    THEA.                                  No more !
Be these embraces ever hearty and
Renew'd, till time shall lay us both asleep

Within one tomb.

PHYL. I am no more alive.   When these
Shall cease, or thou absent'st thyself by death.

THEA. Sciolto! where's my sister, fair Ariola?
Methinks her welcomes are so slow, they scarce
Commend her love.

SCIO.                        Your Excellence will find
She'll bring such an excuse with her, as soon
Shall be receiv'd : the Princess Eurithea
Whom she's gone t'entreat, to honour this
Solemnity.   They'll instantly appear.

THEA. That's joy indeed !  The music of her name
Salutes the ear, with sounds more cheerful and
More full of triumph than the shouts of victory !

PHYL. As much doth fair Ariola surprise
My sense with gladness, wonder, and with love.
                        [*Fred. takes Theander aside.*

FRED. This is the gentleman to whom your grace
Vouchsaf'd to promise entertainment at
My humble suit.

THEA. He shall be well receiv'd :
Sir, you had skill to know your business needs
Must thrive, when you chose Fredeline your advo-
        cate.

CAS. I am the creature of your Excellence.

*Enter* EURITHEA, ARIOLA.

THEA. Brave Phylomont, entreat my sister to
Forgive a while the tend'ring of my love,
Till I have breath'd it into thine.

PHYL. The like request, Theander, to my sister
        make,
Till thine have first receiv'd the righteous vows,
And offerings of my heart.
                [*Eurithea runs cheerfully to embrace Theander.
                Ariola seems to retreat a little at Phylomont's
                salute.*

CAS. Sir, our Theander and his mistress meet,
Methinks, with more alacrity and free
Consent, than Phylomont and his Ariola ;
She wears him at a careful distance from her eyes.
FRED. Right, Sir. The first are lovers of a pure
Cœlestial kind, such as some style Platonical ;
A new court epithet scarce understood ;
But all they woo, sir, is the spirit, face,
And heart : therefore their conversation is
More safe to fame. The other still affect
For natural ends.
CAS.                              As how, I pray ?
FRED. Why such a way as libertines call lust,
But peaceful politicks and cold divines.
Name matrimony, Sir ; therefore although
Their wise intent be good and lawful, yet
Since it infers much game and pleasure i'th' event,
In subtle bashfulness she would not seem
To entertain with too much forwardness,
What she perhaps doth willingly expect.
Sir, this is but my guess, and I beseech
It may remain a secret unto you.
CAS. Signior, my lips are seal'd.
THEA. O do not strive t' afflict thy tenderness
With unkind thoughts. 'Tis not the fortune of
A day, the victor's glory, when he toils
To humble others' pride, that he may swell
His own : nor yet to lead a nation cold
And naked forth, then bring them home, gay and
Fantastic in their silks, sweating in furs
Pontifical, as they had sate
Like civil Judges to redress those men
Whom for their own relief they slew.
No, Eurithea, these were not the charms
That have so long betray'd me from thy sight.
EU. Then I have cause to fear your weariness
Of love, and that would poison my weak faculties
B

With a disease, that can admit no ease
To soothe my willing hope, nor cure, but death.
   THEA. Old pilots, when benighted, have more
     cause
To doubt their star's direction to their card,
Or th' adamant's true friendship to their steel,
Than thou the loyalty of my strong faith.
   EU. Three summers absent from your native land
And me, as many tedious winters too,
To make up time more sorrowful and long !
How can you fashion an excuse so well
As to expect belief ?
   THEA. Truth wants no power.
I went in search of virtuous fame, to make
Myself more fit in noble worth
For the encounter of thy love.
   EU.                         Alas !
How are you certain of my modesty,
That you should give me such continual cause
To blush ? I should find courage sure
To chide you for't, but that I'll minister
No cause to hasten your remove from hence,
Where I have hope my prayers and innocence
Shall keep you long.
   THEA. Else I should lose such a felicity,
As he that hopes for better in the other world
Must fast and live severely to attain't.
   PHYL. The rugged fashion of the war hath dull'd
My understanding and my speech, or else
Your ears, Ariola, have lately lost
Their wonted tenderness.
   ARIO. Sir, you do willingly mistake in both :
But 'tis because you know, you have as great
A privilege to injure me, as to abuse your self.
   PHYL. Shall I be heard then when I speak, and
     cheerfully
A little list'ned to. that by degrees

I may recover my sick hope?
    ARIO. You cannot lose your virtue, Sir, and then
I'm sure my courtesy will never fail :
To promise more would make me seem too
    prodigal
Of what you can't in nobleness receive.
    PHYL. The favour of your hand I may—
[Offers to kiss it.
    ARIO. That not becomes your dignity—
    PHYL. Indeed my bold ambition rather would
Advance me to the sweetness of your lip——
    ARIO. That worst becometh mine——
    PHYL. Forgive me, kind Ariola.   I thrive
My chastisement, and mean to sin no more.
    THEA. Methinks, since yonder building on the
    mount,
And that large marble square was turretted,
The house looks pleasant, and would tempt us to
Enjoy the summer in't.  What says my Phylomont?
Shall we forsake the toils o' th' peace and here
With triumphs celebrate the camp ?  That, we
Have [surely] purchas'd and deserv'd.
    PHYL. I'm here, Theander, govern'd by your
    laws,
And must consent ; but they are such I like.
    THEA. Come, Eurithea ! let me hasten to
Begin my happiness.   Lead to the myrtle walk !
[Exeunt all but Fred., Cas., Sciolto.
    FRED. My lord !  Make me indebted to your ears
A while before you go.  This Gentleman
May safely share with us i' th' privacy.
    CAS. You do me honour with your trust.
    FRED. How worthy 'tis of grief, a Prince so
    young,
Endow'd with all the helps that nature, art,
Or fortune need to make up perfect man,
Should wear away the happiest season of

His strength, in tedious meditation thus,
Severe discourses, and a cold survey
Of beauty that he loves, yet fears to use !
   Scio. Oh Signior !
It hath forc'd me make a very spunge
Of my pillow; I've wept at midnight for 't.
It is a thought too dangerous for one
Of's grey-hair'd friends to bear in memory.
   Fred. His name, if he continue ignorant
O' th' use of marriage thus, must perish with
Himself, and all his glorious conquests have
Achiev'd be left without a heir.
   Scio. Right, sir, for I believe those babies he
And Eurithea do beget by gazing in
Each other's eyes, can inherit nothing,—
I mean by th' custom here in Sicily.*
As for Plato's love-laws they may entail
Lands on ghosts and shadows, for aught I know :
I understand not Greek.
   Cas. How, Sir, is she inclin'd ?
   Fred.            As coldly as himself.
   Cas. Is there no way to tempt their simple
     loves
To the right use ?
   Fred. My lord, I have conceiv'd a remedy
In my own thoughts ; 'tis an experiment
Which, if your lordship's judgment can allow,
May meet with glad success.
   Scio.            I'm bound to hear't.
   Fred. There lives within Mesina, three leagues
     hence,
One Buonateste, a physician and
A sad philosopher, who though his wealth
Not makes him eminent, yet he is rich
In precious vellum, and learn'd manuscripts
Yellow'd with age ! In old disjointed globes,

* [and] Ed. 1665.

And crooked mathematic instruments,
Enow to fill a brazier's shop, which with
His magazine of coles,* and still of glass,
For chymick purposes is all he hath.
   SCIO. A very rich alderman philosopher.
   FRED. Believ't, my lord, this kingdom will
      receive
More future fame by being honoured with
His birth, than by our Æschylus, our Diodore,
Our Gorgias, and Empedocles, Euclid,
And our Archimedes, who all took here
Their knowledge, and their lives.
   SCIO. Well, sir, wherein consists our present
      benefit ?
   FRED. This man by art shall make him marry
      whom
He now so ignorantly courts.
   SCIO. That would incline much near a miracle.
   FRED. Reward my care, but with your patience,
      and
Observe. I'm no protector of their silly faith
Who think, forsooth, that phylters mixt with
      herbs,
Or min'rals can enforce a love. Those, sir,
Are fables, made to comfort distressed virgins,
That want estates to marry 'em.
   SCIO. How then, signior ?
   FRED. I say my reason thinks it possible,
With long endeavour'd art, where love is fixed
And interchang'd already, by a free
Consent, to heat their bloods into desire
And natural appetite ; and these desires
They both may exercise, being married, sir,
With leave of custom and our laws: you apprehend ?
   SCIO. With little labour, sir. Give me your hand,
And let me thank you for't ; for, as you said,

* Herbs.

Though art cannot enforce a mutual love
When it hath found a lover out, it can
Provoke and warm him to do notable feats.
But by what subtle means is this perform'd?
    FRED. He hath a rare elixir.
    SCIO. Well, sir, you give much reason, and some
        hope:
But in my greener years I thought no elixir
Like powder'd beef, and good round turnips to't,
If eaten heartily and warm.
    CAS. My Lord, I'm your disciple.
    SCIO. Nay, I have found an humble bee, pickled,
Can do as much as your cantharides.
But who will you employ unto this man
Of art? It must be secretly design'd.
    FRED. Castraganio! You, sir, shall straight take
        horse;
My former trust emboldens me to make
No fitter choice. This letter will insinuate
Our plot, which, with five hundred crowns that
        purse
Contains, may speed him hither e'er't
Be night.
    CAS. My care shall make me worthy of your love.
    FRED. Farewell! Be swift and prosperous.
    SCIO. I'll in, and wait the duke's commands.
            [*Exeunt Sciolto, Castraganio, severally.*
    FRED. This fellow hath a wondrous little skull;
And, sure, but half a soul, easy and fit
To knead and manage in all forms my dark
Contrivements shall design; but for
My hum'rous lord, that his old gouty feet
Should stumble too into my snares, hath in't
As much of fortune, as of mirth. Down, down,
The secret troubles of my breast! I have
Not long to mourn, if all my arts prove safe.
My midnight purposes are new and strange,

But heavy headed mules tread in the plain
And beaten path ; the fat dull porpoise still
With danger on the open water plays ;
Wise serpents creep in crook'd and hidden ways.

[Exit.

---

## ACT II.—SCENE I.

Enter FREDELINE, CASTRAGANIO.

CAS. Sir, he is come! I have divorc'd him from
His books, and found his eyes employed to reconcile
Old hieroglyphics by their shape, and then
T'interpret blind half eaten characters,
Deform'd as locksmiths' or as carvers' tools.
FRED. Hath he considered our request, and gives
Some hope we may find remedy in art ?
CAS. With an industrious and exact survey ;
But in his mighty science slights our fears,
As 'twere a thing most easy to be done.
FRED. My joys, dear sir, will grow too great
      for my
Discretion to conceal.
CAS. There's your money !
FRED.        How ! would he not receive't ?
CAS. He says he likes your nature well, that
      you
Could freely part with trifles of such high esteem.
And for that cause he came, but will not sell
The labours of his mind : besides, profess'd
Those gilded counters are not things he loves.
FRED. A noble fellow ! these philosophic
Blunt book-gallants, have oft their genty* tricks

* Courteous. In Scotland this adjective was in use to signify
neat, limber, and at the same time of elegant formation—
      White is her neck,
       Saft is her hand,
    Her waist and feet's fu' genty.
Ramsay's Poems, ii. 226.

Of nice honour, as well as favourites,
Whom kings make wanton with their sudden
　　wealth.
Where have you now dispos'd him unto rest?
　Cas. Within your chamber, sir, and he expects
Your visitation will be straight perform'd.
　Fred. I am all speed, dear sir; my tongue is
　　much
Too little to express my thanks.  My select friend,
Lord of my functions and my life, wear me
With what title your indulgent memory
Shall please, so you will wear me long.　　[Exit.
　Cas. This Fredeline's a very saint, so meek,
And full of courtesy, that he would lend
The devil his cloak, and stand i'th' rain himself.
Sure I have suck'd some Sybil's milk ; I could
Not be thus lucky else t'enjoy his love.

Enter Sciolto.

　Scio. So soon return'd?  Your haste foretels
　　good news.
　Cas.  All will succeed, my lord, I hope, as if
You had the certain skill to make
Your wishes prosperous.  He is with Fredeline,
And they expect your interview; but look !
Here comes my sister, and your son.  He never saw
A woman until now; it will be sport
Worthy your stay, t'observe how he demeans him-
　　self.
　Scio.  She's old and poor.  He may safely enough
　　converse with her.

Enter Amadine and Gridonell, he gazing at her.

　Amad.  This gentleman wants money, brains, or
　　sleep.
Do you know him, brother?
　Cas. Sweet Amadine, contain thy wit a while:

He never saw a woman.   Use him gently.
  GRID.                         This is a rare sight !
One of the angels sure, and a great gallant among
      'em.
Had it but blue wings on the shoulders, it
Could not be of less degree than an angel.
  SCIO.  I perceive nature inclines men to wonder,
And makes 'em somewhat relish too o'th' fool.
  GRID. An angel of the better sort: some lieutenant
Colonel in heaven, I take't;  it can't be less.
  SCIO.  Will he not speak to her ?
  GRID.  Sure it hath wings, and they are made, I
      think,
Of cambric and bonelace.
  SCIO.                 A pox upon him !
He looks as he had stol'n a silver spoon, and it
Was found sticking in his wrist.
  GRID.                 If she would fly
Aloft, methinks I should so peep under her.
  SCIO.  All these are documents of nature still.
  GRID.  Sure those, I think, are petticoats !  I've
      heard
Of such a word.  'Tis a fine kind of wearing.
The new colours have just taffeta enough
To fashion such another; would t'were made,
That I might practise how to walk in't.
  SCIO.  I'd beat him, but that the villain's roughly
      bred,
And perhaps would strike again.
  CAS.             Speak to him, Amadine.
  AMAD.  I'm mortal, sir ; no spirit, but a maid.
Pray feel me, I am warm !
  GRID.  Indeed forsooth!  I never felt a maid.
  AMAD.  Heaven keep him from pepper and
      tobacco,
For's brains are grown so loose in's head, they'll run
Through's nose next time he chance to sneeze;

And dancing too will shake 'em out. It is
An exercise too violent for that
Disease. Sir, do you use to dance?
    GRID.              What's that, forsooth?
    AMAD. To dance, sir, is to move your legs, as
        thus——
    GRID. We use i'th' wars to march and make a halt,
And sometimes we double our paces.
    AMAD. Fresh straw and a strong chain! The
        gentleman
Is mad. Look to him, brother!         [*Exit.*
    SCIO. If I'd another son, I'd hardly trust
Nature again with his breeding.
    GRID. She said she was a maid: and I've been told
A maid's a kind of woman.
    SCIO.             She is a woman, son.
    GRID. If women be such things, 1 wonder th'
        enemy
Do never bring their wives against our camp,
To give us battle. Sure we should all yield.
    SCIO. Belike then, you have a month's mind
        to her.
    GRID. O sir, she hath the prettiest pinking eyes;
The holes are no bigger than a pistol bore.
    CAS. An excellent simile for a painter,
That would draw a good face.
    GRID. Her fingers are so small, and longer than
A drum-stick. Ah, how they'd bestir themselves
Upon a phiph.
    SCIO. Then you could leave the wars, and live
        with her?
    GRID. So she would still sit by and let me gaze
Till my eyes ache.
    SCIO. Still he's innocent: one of Plato's lovers.
    GRID. Pray what was he?
    SCIO. An odd Greek fellow that could write
        and read.

Grid. O, belike some clerk of a company.
Scio. If he continue's wonder thus, and ignor-
    ance
To ev'ry woman that he meets, I may
Entail my land upon the poor.   He'll not
Be able to beget an heir, as big
As my thumb.   I must think upon some course.

*Enter* THEANDER.

The. My Lord Sciolto, I had thought your white
And rev'rend head had held this season fit
For sleep ; night takes her swarthy mantle up
As she would wear it straight.   What gentleman
    is this ?
Scio. Your grace may please to own him for
    my child.
His mother, sir, would justify as much,
Were she alive.
Thea. What, Gridonell !   Men speak him of a
    great
And daring heart, and skilful how to vex
The foe, though he be young.
Scio. Faith if the foe put but an apron on,
Or get his corslet edg'd with Flanders purl,*
He'll do him little hurt.
Thea.               You are accus'd,
My lord.   They say you bred him to no use
Of books : he cannot write nor read.
Scio. 'Twill keep him, sir, from ent'ring into
    bond.
Thea. Let us begin acquaintance, sir.   The day
May come when you shall lead my ensigns forth,
And though you bring them shot and ragged home,
Yet they'll be crown'd with wreaths.
Grid. Strike up your drums to night then, if
    you please ;

* A fringe, in twist-work of gold and silver.

If th' moon be froward, sir, and will not shine,
We'll fire small towns to light us as we march.
    Scio. Mass! I thank nature for that yet he has
Good mettle in him.
    Thea.    His meaning's straight and smooth,
Though's words be rough.
I like him well: you must bestow him on me.
    Scio. Most gladly, sir, and let me tell your
            Grace,
You'll find him one of the most exquisite
Platonic lovers this day living.   He will
So innocently view and admire a lady!
    Thea. Still fitter for my use.  Soldier, good-
            night !                                    [Exit.
    Scio. I must to Fredeline, and the philosopher.
                                                [Exit.

    Cas. This woman was my sister, Gridonell.
    Grid. And did one father make you both ?
    Cas. Ay, Sir, and with a very little pains.
    Grid. My father's old and lazy now, if he'd
Take pains he'ld soon make such another too
For me.   But I shall see her, Sir, again ?
    Cas. Yes, when you please : she must be gently
            us'd.
    Grid. Alas, I cannot choose.   Would you bring
Her to my chamber in the dead of night ?
    Castr. You must excuse me, Sir : farewell.
            Each hour
I' th' day she may be yours.
    Grid.                            I shall so dream.   [Exeunt.

*Enter* Ariola, Rosella, *with tapers.   A table with
            Night-linen set out.**

    Ario. Prithee unpin me, wench !  If I were given

* In the original 4to, Phylomont is, by mistake, marked to
enter with them ; his entrance, again marked, not being necessary until after their short dialogue.

Enough to pray'r or cares I could not be
Thus incident to sleep.    Take heed ! you hurt me.
    ROSEL.  Your Ladyship is tenderer on the breast
Than you were wont ; I would your heart were so.
    ARIO.  I'll wear my Tuscan raile * to-morrow ;
            smooth
It out.  But whence comes that wish, Rosella ? You
Are still complaining on my poor heart.
    ROSEL.  Madam, these two long hours the noble
            Duke
Hath waited at your chamber door.
    ARIO.                          Who ! my brother ?
    ROSEL.  Duke Phylomont, who vows t' inhabit
            there,
Unless you let him in.
    ARIO.  Heaven comfort his sick soul !
What does he mean ? Here, lock these pendants up !
The wonder of him makes me sick.  I'll use
No powder now.   Alas, what shall I do ?
I dare not let him in : the season is not fit.
    ROSEL.  He vows his visit shall be so precise
And civil, that you need not counsel him,
Nor check him with a frown.
    ARIO.                          Ay, but at night,
Men's busy and officious tongues will talk.
    ROSEL.  In troth, your Ladyship's too strict, when
            you
Consider too your marriage is design'd ;
If my opinion, Madam, had authority,
No time's unfit to lovers so far gone.
    ARIO.  You'll be his orator ? Go, let him in !


    * A neckcloth of fine linen.  "Rayle for a woman's necke,
crevechief en quarttre doubles."—Palsgrave.
        " And then a good greye frocke,
        A kercheffe and a raile."
                        Friar Bacon's Prophesie, 1604.
A night-rail was different.  It partly covered the head.

*Enter* PHYLOMONT.

PHYL. Methinks, my fair Ariola, you keep
Your beauty overmuch enfolded and
Conceal'd.   You are a flower that would become
The night as sweetly as the day.
    ARIO. You make me  proud with your simili-
        tude ;
But whilst I gain by it, your inference
Must lose ; mary-golds now shut in their leaves.
    PHYL. Alas, poor potage flower !   Ariola
Should imitate the lily and the rose :
They boldly spread themselves still open to
The night, yet yield the sun so fresh and sweet
A sacrifice, that every morn he seems
To blush at's own weak influence, which can
No longer keep them beauteous on their stalks,
But they must drop, and perish with the Spring.
Your precious colour, and your odour too,
My gentle mistress, needs must yield to time.
    ARIO. The loss will not be mourn'd for, Sir,
        since 'twill
Be scarce discern'd.
    PHYL.                        Sweet ! You remove
Your understanding from my words, and make
Them of no use.   Their meaning would persuade
You to enjoy this pleasant treasure, whilst
It lasts.   Why are you still enclos'd thus like
An anchoress, as if our conversation could
Infer a sin ?   Why am I nicely barr'd
Your chamber, when the Priest, b'ing paid for a
Few ceremonious words, must license me
Your bed : your bosom too ?
    ARIO. Our marriage, Sir, may promise much,
        till then
Your Excellence will grant me leave not to
Admit of opportunities, that may give breath

To ill report.

PHYL. Be not so cruel in your bashful care.
My sister makes all hours and seasons fit
To celebrate Theander, and he knows
No wrinkle on her brow, that may be call'd
A frown.  O ! be you kind and free !

[*Offers at her hand.*

ARIO. By your chaste vows, forbear !

PHYL. Theander may embrace my sister's hand,
Until with warmth he melt it from the wrist :
Why should I have less am'rous privilege ?
I have desires as bold, which will be made
As lawful too ere long.

ARIO.                    The meaning of
Their love is only mutual wonder and applause,
And so proclaim'd ; therefore can stir no jealousy
In the severest thought.   Alas, we must
Be married, Sir, which may perhaps enforce
Your inclination to a dangerous hope.

PHY. Where is thy safety then, Ariola ?
This is the dismal silent time when ravishers
Reach forth their trembling guilty hands to draw
The curtains where unpractis'd virgins sleep ;
False Tarquin's hour, when he did hide his torch
From Lucrece eyes, and would not suffer her
Wak'd beauty to eclipse that sickly flame,
Till she had quenched a greater in his blood.
How would thy courage faint, if I should make
Thee subject to my eager youth and strength ?

ARIO. Poor Phylomont !   If thou shouldst so
          forsake
Thy loyalty to love, yet I were still secure,
And can subdue thee with my virtuous scorn ;
For now, though but my cambric helmet on,
Thus thinly harness'd in my lawn, my trivial fan
My shield, I stand the Champion of my sex.
Alas! I fain would see the proudest of

You bearded tyrant men, that durst but hope
To force from me the least of these dishevell'd
          hairs,
Which I will still as bounteous favours wear
For every wanton wind to sport withal,
But not for you.
    PHYL.                      Can you be angry ?
    ARIO. Then you should sigh unto yourself,
And in your own enamour'd ears distil
The soothings of your cunning tongue, whilst I
Enjoy the quiet of my sleep again
Without disturbance.  By those midnight plaints
Your mournful concert at my window made,
Wherein you curs'd the guiltless stars, who seem'd
To smile and wink upon each other in
Their spheres, as if they heedful notice took
Of all your feigned grief.
    PHYL.  Can you be angry, my Ariola,
Or censure aught I spoke with an unkind
Belief ?  Hear but my vows !
    ARIO.                      Good night !
Your Excellence hath greater power
To move my sorrow than my rage.
    PHYL. Remember, gentle love, I have your heart
By sacred plight.  Our nuptials now draw near.
    ARIO. I never knew the way how I might break
My faith ; but, till that hour arrive, we must
Converse no more: no, not at distance, sir.
The cause is hidden in my breast.  Virtue
And peace, my Lord, still govern your desires. [*Exit.*
    PHYL. I shall grow mad with these delays ;
Sh'ath made a vow never to marry me,
Until her brother seal't with his consent.  I'll
          move
It to Theander ere I sleep.  Hymen !
Go light thy fires, and make thy tapers shine,
Or cure me, sacred Love, by quenching thine. [*Exit.*

*Enter* AMADINE *with a Taper, and* THEANDER.

AMAD. Not in her bed, sir, yet.  I left her with
Her lute, whose music, I believe, hath woo'd her to
A gentle sleep.
        THEA.            Tread easy then !
With a slow tim'rous pace ; let's make less noise
Than Time's  soft feet,  or  planets  when  they
    move.
    [*Draws a canopy.  Eurithea is found sleeping on
     a couch, a veil on, with her lute.*
Give me the light !  Now leave us and retire.
    AMAD. This is an odd kind of lover.  He comes
Into my lady's chamber at all hours ;
Yet thinks it strange that people wonder at
His privilege.  Well, opportunity
Is a dangerous thing ; it would soon spoil me. [*Exit.*
    THEA. She lies as in a shady monument,
Secure as pious votaries that knew
They were forgiven ere they died.
    EU.  Who's there ?  my lord, the prince ?
    THEA.  O, sleep again, and close those eyes that
    still
Enlighten mine, till I have merited
The beauty of their beams, by blessings such
As Love's religious priests do give.
This sacred office would become me well :
'Tis not a robe of lawn, a hallow'd verge,
Nor flow'ry chaplets nicely wreath'd, can add
Prosperity to prayers, or to vows.
No formal pomp or ceremony needs
To wishes that are clean and humbly made.
    EU. Theander, sit! Where have you been so long?
'Las, wherefore do I ask, since I
So lately found you in my dream ?
    THEA. Unveil, my love !  When this is but dis-
    play'd,

C

Thou open'st like a fragrant bud before
The morning's eye, whilst all that's near thee is
Perfum'd.   Thy breath converts me to a flower :
Wear me within thy bosom, virgin friend,
And I shall last in odour all the year.

    Eu. Thou art Theander, and that name includes
The sweetness of the Spring and Summer's wealth.

    Thea. Thou art not Eurithea, but my rose,
My sober bashful flower, and I
Thy wanton woodbine that must grow about
Thee in embracements thus, until thou art
Entangled with chaste courtesies of love.

    Eu.  This is a happiness too great to last !
Envy or fate must lessen it, or we
Remove 'mongst the eternal lovers, and
Provide our habitation near the stars !
My wonder grows upon me like my joy.
O Theander !

    Thea.  What says my Cherubine ?

    Eu.  How shall I give my estimation words,
When it would value thee that art the wars'
Chief soldier, best example and delight ?
So bold, thou dar'st seek danger in a storm
When all the winds prepare to quarrel in
The Baltic sea ; yet thou art milder than
A captive saint, so pitiful that I
Have seen thee weep o'er the distress'd, till thou
Mightst give a name to rivers as their spring.

    Thea.  And thou, my love, art sweeter far
Than balmy incense in the purple smoke ; *
Pure and unspotted, as the cleanly ermine ere
The hunter sullies her with his pursuit ;
Soft as her skin, chaste as th' Arabian bird, †

* The incense in common use does not emit purple smoke.
Such a property exists in sandal wood and some of the more
choice gums.

† The Phœnix. See footnote, vol. i., p. 48.

That wants a sex to woo, or as the dead
That are divorc'd from warmth, from objects,
And from thought.
Still, Eurithea, I could multiply thy praise,
Yet still prove loyal unto truth ;
When I embrace thee thus, I straight forget,
As weak delights, the days of victory,
And glories of the war.
    EU.                      But when you hear
The drum, and the shrill trumpet call,
You'll mount your angry steed again, and haste
To live confin'd in trenches ; to exchange
Your marble palace for a tent, whilst I,
Like a distress'd sad turtle, am ordain'd
To mourn without a mate.
    THEA. Do not afflict me with thy jealous fears.
I'm come to tell thee, love, to-morrow in
Th' adjoining grove I'll meet thee like
A shepherd, such as fair Arcadia bred,
That, with variety, our old delights
May still seem new.
    EU.                    A lover's wish
Can imp the hours' short wings, and hasten time.
Look up, Theander ! it is day.
    THEA.               Where should I look ?
Thou dost mistake the sphere and residence
O' th' morn : let early village labourers
And dull benighted seamen do their homage to
The East for light : the region of our day
We seek like lovers in the fairest eyes.
    EU. If you should look in mine, 'twill still seem
        night.
    THEA. To bed, to bed ! methink I hear the lark,
The morning's merry officer ; and see
Him shake his dewy wings, as he would strive
To climb high as his cheerful voice.
    EU. The best that poets' wishes can invent,

Or lovers' prayers procure ; thy sleeps enjoy !
   THEA. And thine, that precious harmony that
      dwells
With quiet hermits in their narrow cells.
                [*Ex. several ways.*

   *Enter* BUONATESTE, SCIOLTO, FREDELINE, *and*
         CASTRAGANIO.

   BUON. I say, my lord, your business doth
      concern
The blood, and not the eyes ; and, since 'tis late,
It were abuse of time to read long lectures
Of the Optics, to tell you their consent
And unity, or show you through a perspective
How Amorists,* oppos'd in level to
Each others' sight, unite and thrid their beams,
Until they make a mutual string on which
Their spirits dance into each others' brain,
And so begin short journeys to the heart.
Or to reveal the shape and colour of
Those spirits too, that were a miracle
Worthy sublime and powerful art !
   SCIO. Their colour's orange tawny, Sir, as I
      conceive.
   BUON. Your lordship can conceive no more,
      than your
Weak knowledge will give leave.
   FRED.                To him, doctor !

---

  * A wooer. "An Amorist is a man blasted or planet-
strooken, and is the dogge that leads blind Cupid. He is
never without verses, and musk comfects, and sighs to the
hazard of his buttons ; his eyes are all white, either to weare
the livery of his mistris complexion, or to keep Cupid from
hitting the black. . . . He answers not, or not to the purpose ; and no marvell, for he is not at home. He scotcheth
time with dancing with his mistris, taking up of her glove,
and wearing her feathers, is confined to her colour, and dares
not passe out of the circuit of her memory."—*Characters in Sir
Thomas Overbury his Wife.* 12mo. 1664.

BUON. Nor do I think it can concern you much,
Whether the nerval conjugations be
But seven, and, of that mystic number too,
Whether the Opticks be the chief.
    SCIO. For your seven conjugations, sir, you
        shall
Excuse me ; but, believ't, "the seven wise masters"
Is a volume I read much in my youth.
    BUON. Your lordship gives good proof of't in
        your age :
But yet you never heard, sir, of the fam'd
Antipheron,* whom once the learned Stagirite
Admir'd so for the self-reflection that
He wore like to his perfect image
Still where he mov'd.
    SCIO. No more, my good wise friend, thou hast
My wonder, that's enough ; my understanding
Shall come after, but not till I am dead,
For then they say we shall know all things
Without paying for our books.
    BUON. There is the powder, sir.
    FRED.                Give it to my care.
    BUON. The Duke must take it in his draught to-
        night.
To-morrow, as the sun increaseth in
His power, it works ; at noon you'll see pure
    miracles.
    FRED. My lord, 'tis fit our Castraganio give
It him : he takes a rouse † of Corsick wine

---

  * Aristotle, styled by Ælian "an inhabitant of Stagira," who
saw his own image before him wherever he went.—*Sen.*
  † An excess of liquor, from the German word " rusch," half
drunk.
      " No jocund health that Denmark drinks to-day,
        But the great cannon to the clouds shall tell,
        And the King's rouse shall bruit it back again,
        Bespeaking earthly thunder."    *Shakspeare.*
Shakespeare, in this sentence, when he mentions cannon,
falls into a sad anachronism.

Still e'er he sleeps.  He, waiting in his chamber,
May fitly mingle and present it to him

                    [*Cas. takes the paper.*

    CAS. I'll use my safest diligence.
    SCIO.                        Where is he now?
    CAS. With Eurithea, sir ; he hath not call'd.
    SCIO. Stays he so long? 'tis now i' th' ken of
        day.
Signior Buonateste, have you no more
Of this rare magical stuff?
    BUON. Another dose ! I came provided, sir.
    SCIO. Pray give it me.
    BUON. Most willingly, but to whom will you
        dispos't ?
    SCIO. Unto no other but my son : I find
He's very much platonically given.
    BUON. My Lord, I still beseech you not to
        wrong
My good old friend Plato, with this Court calumny;
They father on him a fantastic love
He never knew, poor gentleman.   Upon
My knowledge, sir, about two thousand years
Ago, in the high street yonder
At Athens, just by the corner as you pass
To Diana's conduit,—a haberdasher's house,
It was, I think,—he kept a wench !
    SCIO.               How, sir, a wench !
    BUON. I could say more; my friend was lewdly
        given.
    SCIO. But, with your favour, sir, a plump brown
        wench ?
    BUON. Faith, authors differ about that; some
        write
She had a flaxen hair, and others too,
That did not blush to know more private marks,
Say she had a mole under her left thigh :
Others a hollow tooth, that put him to

The charge of cloves, because her breath
Grew somewhat troublesome.
  Fred.       Give me thy hand,
Doctor ; I'll have some share too in thy heart
Ere long. But did not Plato write of love ?
  Buon. Divinely, sir. But not such kind of love
As ladies would have now : they mistake him.
  Scio. He wrote in Greek, doctor.
  Buon·      True, my good lord.
  Scio. Why then belike my son mistakes him
   too.
He understands no Greek ; this dose shall conjure
   him,
I'll give't him straight. Come, sir, the night decays
Apace. Let me direct you to your bed.
  Buon. Your lordship's kindness honours me too
   much.
  Fred. My jolly, dear philosopher, good-night.
        [*Exeunt Scio. and Buon.*
Sir, you have found, with what assur'd and con-
   fident
A soul, I give you interest in all
My business and my thoughts.
  Cas. Signior, I plead no merit but your bounty.
  Fred. And now, under the same protection of
Your friendship and your trust, I must reveal
A secret that doth oft enforce me walk
With arms enfolded thus, still to combine
And fasten in my ribs, lest it should split
My breast ; and you shall know it, sir. I love,—
Curs'd fate that I must utter it,—I love
The princess Eurithea.
  Cas.     Signior ! indeed
This will deserve to be a secret and
Securely kept.
  Fred. So love her, sir, that men
In fierce conspiracy, despair, or want,

Enjoy more quiet sleeps than I ; and, since
I am declin'd much into weakness, and
Unpleasant years, you see what narrow hopes
Are left to give my furious appetite success.
    CAS. Introth, 'tis pity, sir !
    FRED. There you express the charity
And melting nature of a friend, and may
Administer redress, for it will much
Reflect within your power.
    CAS. You cannot want it then ;
But, sir, it seems preposterous
And strange to my dull brain, that since
Your love doth force you wish her to yourself,
You strive by marriage to bestow her on
The Duke, and with such heartiness and care.
    FRED. In this your friendship is again conjur'd.
I do beseech you never seek the end
Of that mysterious cause. Some salt I have
That shews th' Italian humour in my blood.
I not affect to compass my designs
The vulgar way.
    CAS. But how can I redress your grief ?
    FRED. Your sister Amadine
Is, in affection and attendance, near the
Princess' person and her mind. She may,.
By your entreaty, render me in such
A character of cunning praise, as shall
Advance me to her love, perhaps : at least,
To a refreshing of my sick desires.
    CAS. She's bound in conscience, sir, to do good
      offices.
    FRED. But wilt thou charm thy sister with all
      force
Of thy affinity and words, to be my friend?
Endear us so, that I may whisper my
Own cause, and teach her mediate my access !
This must be done to-morrow, for delays

Will make my grief too dangerous to bear.
   Cas. To morrow, doubt it not, my functions
     shall
Entirely be employed to your best use.
   Fred. I had almost forgot the med'cine ; it
Is late, and time 'twere working in his draught.
Farewell ! command me to the loss of fame,
Of treasure, and of life, dear Castraganio.
Be but benign, and chain me as thy slave.
                      *[Exeunt severally.*

   *Enter* Phylomont, Arnoldo, *and* Jaspero
         *with lights.*

   Phyl. I thought t'have found him safe in's
     quiet rest,
With's curtain drawn ere this.   Is it his use to
     stay so long ?
   Arn. The visits he presents unto your Grace's
     sister,
Though at night, are never hastily perform'd.
   Jasp. Time's gouty legs may tire, if he run on
Until such true and faithful lovers
Finish their discourse, as wearisome and long.
   Arn.               Jaspero, that's the morn
Which so inflameth yonder cloud.
   Jasp. Is it your Grace's will we go and try
To hasten his approach ?
   Phyl.              Please you to trust
Me here alone, I'll stay his coming, sir.
My business asks a private conference.
                 *[Ex. Arn., Jasp.*
My sister is so bounteous of her love,
And gives her favours with such bold neglect
Of fame, but that I knew the pure and chaste
Condition of her soul, I should grow vex'd
With jealous fears.   Ariola will not vouchsafe
To use me so.

*Enter* THEANDER.

THEA. My Phylomont, this is a season when
Your visit would import some great affair
That carries haste or wonder in't.
    PHYL. You have a mistress, sir, preserves
Your spirits full of fire ; your glad heart keeps
Eternal triumph in her close warm throne,
Whilst mine encreaseth not in joys but weight.
'Tis heavy, sir ! if it continue so
'Twill break the strings.   Your froward sister—
    THEA. Will she not love ?   I'm sure her beauty
        was
Ordain'd for no felicity but love.
Her sweetness and her forms, though she were less
Allied unto my nature, would proclaim
It to the world.
    PHYL.            Sir, she hath banish'd me.
    THEA. Upon what rock or promont? Was she by
A Scythian nurs'd, that she is grown so cruel ?
It cannot be.
    PHYL. Th' affliction will not long endure,
I hope, because you may repeal the doom.
    THEAN. You are assur'd, my Phylomont, I needs
Must strive to further love.  What shall I do ?
    PHYL. Give your consent that I may marry her.
    THEA. How ! marry her ! Your souls are
        wedded, sir,
I'm sure you would not marry bodies too ;
That were a needless charge. Come, you shall
        save
Your bridal feasts, and gloves.
    PHYL. This mirth, sir, is a little too remote
From th'answer I should have.
    THEA. Blame my conception then ; I under-
        stand
You not. To what purpose would you marry her ?

PHYL. Why, sir? to lye with her, and get
    children.
THEA. Lye with my sister, Phylomont? how vile
And horridly that sounds!   I prithee sleep
A while; 'tis thy distemper, and I pardon it.
    PHYL. This is strange, being married, is't not
    lawful, sir?
THEA. I grant it may be law, but is it comely?
Reduce thy reason to a cleaner sense,
Think on't a noble way.   You two may live,
And love, become your own best arguments,
And so contract all virtue, and all praise:
Be ever beauteous, fresh, and young, at least
In your belief; for who can lessen, or
Defile th'opinion which your mutual thoughts
Shall fervently exchange?   And then you may
Beget reflections in each others' eyes;
So you increase not children but yourselves
A better, and more guiltless progeny;
Those immaterial creatures cannot sin.
    PHYL. But who shall make men, sir: shall the
    world cease?
    THEA. I know not how th'are made, but if such
    deeds
Be requisite, to fill up armies, villages,
And city shops; that killing, labour, and
That coz'ning still may last, know, Phylomont,
I'd rather nature should expect such coarse
And homely drudgeries from others than
From me.
    PHYL. And yet you had a father, sir.
But why do I tell him so? That was
His mother's fault not his.   This is mad doctrine.
I'll bid your Excellence good night, but first
I'll leave this information in your ear;
You'll find your sister of my mind,—she fain
Would marry too.

THEA.                         Oh prodigy ! belike
She understands then what it means.     Wrong not
A lady, sir, whose innocence is such
She wears no blushes for herself, but you.
Leave me ! although our friendship, sir, be great,
My patience is too little to subdue
My rage.    To bed, my gentle Phylomont !
If thou art guiltless, thou wilt sleep.
     PHYL. I'll take your counsel, sir ;
The morning may reclaim us both.        [*Exit.*
     THEA. O poor Ariola ! where hast thou chang'd
Thy bashful virtue for unchaste desires ?
Thy ears are blister'd with lascivious breath,
Thy understanding is become thy crime ;
I shall not know thee when I meet thee next,
Thy very soul is sullied, and thy blood,
That ran so pure, will now grow black with sin,
Till't make thy beauty like an Æthiop's skin.
                                [*Exit.*

### ACT III.   SCENE I.

*Enter* THEANDER, ARIOLA.

     ARIO. Your looks are clouded, sir. I fear your health
Is alter'd, or your mind perplex'd.
     THEA. Your looks, Ariola, will shortly too decay ;
Whilst by their strange and early perishing
Your former beauty must be quite forgot,
Like sullen roses that would wither on
The bough, ere throughly blown, ere gather'd for
The still ; so lose all memory that they
Were ever sweet.
     ARIO. I need instructions what you would infer.
     THEA. Have you no secret sickness in your blood ?
     ARIO. Not that I feel, nor do I think my prayers

So vainly made, that I should perish yet.
  THEA. Have you not heard of late some new
       discourse,
Such as inflam'd you to desire strange practices
Of heat, trials of youth, I know not what
They are? but nature oft doth put odd tricks
On young and curious fools, which still
The bashful may resist.
  ARIO.                              If to be ignorant
Be safe, I am to learn, sir, what you mean.
  THEA. Indeed! look up, and with a virgin con-
      fidence
Contemn the enrag'd severeness in my brow
By urging that for truth without a blush.
  ARIO. Alas! you have amaz'd me, sir, but I
Dare look i'th' face of Heaven, write all my willing
      faults,
And stand unveil'd whilst they are read.
  THEA. Perhaps she is abus'd.   Ariola,
Pray tell me the request you sent by Phylomont;
I know not how I understood it then,
But sure't hath troubled all my powers.
  ARIO. I sent you none but what was good and
      lawful.
  THEA. Are you become so wise
In wickedness, to choose offences that
The laws protect?   Th' ambitious in the world's
First age invented them to gather wild
And wand'ring nations into towns and forts:
And so rais'd Common-wealths for their own pride
To rule.   Those cunning scribblers knew that
      laws
Make subjects, and tame slaves, not virtuous men;
Live thou as not to know or need their use.
  ARIO. I can be further justified, for my request
Was fit and modest too.
  THEA.                          Then you may name't.

  Ario. I gave him leave fairly to question your
    consent,
That we might marry, sir.
  Thea. Do you already know what that word
    means ?
  Ario. Your judgment hath sufficient cause to
    blame
My breeding else. I have been often told
Its sacred institution, and the use
For which 'twas first ordain'd.
  Thea. The use, Ariola ? Sh'ath rarely profited
Since my long absence from her at the camp :
Who read these lectures in your ear ? If't were
A woman, sure, she fastened on her mask
To hide her blushes whilst she talked.
  Ario. In my weak judgment, sir, you are too
    nice,
And make uncomely mystery of that
Which both the learned and the noble have
Allow'd and taught, and such as vestals may
Discourse, yet not be banish'd from their holy
    lamp.
  Thea. But to remain a vestal still, Ariola,
To live in sweet unskilful virginhood,
The angels' life, for they no sexes know,
But ever love in meditation, not in act.
Hah ! is not this a sweetness far beyond
The pleasures that our appetites create ?
  Ario. Sir, it is excellent and free, but, I
Am told, the next degree of happiness,
The married challenge and enjoy.
  Thea. O she is lost ! I will
Go weep into the sea, and sooner hope
To find my unmix'd tears upon my cheek
Again, than her perverted heart reclaim'd
Unto her former innocence. Reach me
Your hand ! you are my prisoner now, and must

Be kept from sight of men.

ARIO. Sir, though I cannot learn m' offence, yet I
Shall soon be taught t'obey.

THEA. If since thy late perversion thou hast left
But one acquaintance in sweet Heaven, that dares
Befriend thy orizons, kneel to him straight.

ARIO. Though you are cruel grown, you cannot
      want
My tender wishes, that your angry thoughts
Be to their peaceful harmony restor'd !
                *[Exit. Theander seems to lock her in.*

THEA. Yet am I not left desolate, to mourn,
With single grief, this ruin'd virgin's fate :
My Eurithea, when she hears of her revolt,
Will sigh her piteous soul away to air.
            *Enter* PHYLOMONT.

PHYL. Theander, I am come to learn if yet
Your temper can with kind, discreet civility,
Return an answer to my suit?

THEA. Sir, y'have undone a noble maid, one
      nurs'd
In such severe behaviour of her mind,
So meek and humble in desires, she seem'd
Much fitter for a cloister than a court ;
But now she aims at liberty and change.

PHYL. What I have taught her, sir, hermits and
      nuns
Might in their dying minutes listen to
Without disquiet to their parting souls ;
And things less chaste, I know, she would not hear.

THEA. Take heed, my princely friend ! Do not
      augment
Thy crime, by owning as thy knowledge, what
Is yet, but the mistake of thy belief ;
I had a hope thy vain conceptions would
Be mended much by sleep.

PHYL.                Well, I'll be brief.

Your sister I would marry, sir, and then
As lords and princes use, that love their wives:
Lye with her.
    THEA. You are too masculine!
Name not those words again : you blast me with
Your breath. Poor ruffians in their drink, that dwell
In suburb alleys, and in smokey lanes,
Are not so rude. Leave me! my anger may
Undo us both.
    PHYL. Theander, can you think
To fright me hence, or is it safe to chide
Me from my business with bold words? I would
Be better used. Tell me, I pray, is this
All the fit answer my demands shall have?
    THEA. All, sir; and more than I can patiently
Allow. Your conversation never could be less
      esteem'd.
    PHYL. I fear your noble reason is diseas'd.
Where I have lov'd affliction makes me pitiful,
And where I pity I can ne'er intend
Revenge. Farewell, injurious prince! but know,
If I can get your sister's kind consent,
I'll not endeavour yours.
    THEA. Go not deluded with that trivial hope:
She is my prisoner lock'd and enclos'd
From all address that force or opportunity
Would make. Thou shalt behold her face no more.
    PHYL. Hah! imprison'd! I sooner would cage up
The little bird, that sung a requiem o'er
My mother's hearse: the sad domestic redbreast, or
The courteous wren, that strew'd with cypress
      leaves
Th'unburied pilgrim in the field. Examine, sir,
Your troubled memory. It cannot be.
    THEA. You'll find it most expedient, and a truth.
    PHYL. Imprison her! her beauty will break forth.
You may as soon in crystal jails confine

The sun's refulgent beams, climb heaven, reach
    down
A star, and in a lanthorn shut it, as
Imprison her!
    THEA.                    This iteration will
But vex us both.   Farewell!   You may believ't
At leisure, sir : time will persuade you to't.
    PHYL. Theander, stay! Mark how I cancel all
Th'affection, merit, and the glorious vows
We interchang'd in war, the parting tears
We shed, when in the day of battle our
Bold troops we did divide against the foe :
And those embraces made, when met again,
Joy'd and exalted with our victory,
Are now eternally forgot.
    THEA. I should lament this loss, had you pre-
      serv'd
Your virtue still, and purity of heart.
    PHYL. Until three journeys of the sun expire,
I'll give thee leisure to repent, but then
Release thy sister to her free converse,
And public view, or I will spread my ensigns
    here,
And 'gainst thy palace fix my cannon, till
I batter it to dust.
    THEA.                    Poor Phylomont!
How I neglect thy fury when it dares
Enkindle mine.   If fate resolve, we that
In foreign climes made others mourn, so soon
Must bleed at home ; yet, ere we part, let us
Salute like civil enemies.   Farewell!
When next we meet, 'twill be in danger, noise,
And sulph'rous smoke ; for Eurithea's sake
Thy fetters shall be silver, and thy bonds of silk.
    PHYL. And for Ariola's if thou shalt fall
Beneath my sword, I will embalm thee with my
    tears. .

D

My eyes grow moist with pity of our fates.
    THEA. And mine with sorrow melt so fast away,
I shall be left in darkness if I stay.

                              [*Exeunt.*

*Enter* CASTRAGANIO, FREDELINE, *and* AMADINE.

    CAS. This Gridonell is young and simple, sir,
Admires all women with tame extacy.
And then my sister Amadine, you know,
Hath a most pure contriving wit.  If we
Could get him marry her, it were a stratagem
Would make us rich and famous.
    FRED. But will you bring her to him now ?
    CAS. That's our design.
    FRED. Hast thou o'erwatch'd thyself? Art mad ?
    CAS. Why, signior ?
    FRED. 'Tis past the time two hours, when, by
        our great
Physician's date, the med'cine 'gan to work.
I do believe, the duke, ere this, hath felt
Some sudden diff'rence in his maiden blood :
And Gridonell, I'm sure, drunk his full share.
'Twill work him to such fury, he will ravish
Thy poor sister, nay eat her up, not leave
A morsel big enough to bear her name,
Or memory that such a creature was.
    CAS. She's old, and tough, and will be sure to
        put
Him, sir, to th' trial of his teeth.   But I
Had quite forgot he took the medicine : we
Must choose some other time.
    FRED. As for your sister's marriage,
Sir, with Gridonell, trust my plots : such I
Have laid as shall join hearts and hands, then
        straight
Bring 'em to bed.  I think, sir, she desires no more.
    CAS. Sir, you oblige us with new benefits.

Fred. Some cause you'll have to say so now :
    read that !
'Tis a commission I procur'd the duke
This morning sign, which gives you a Company
In's regiment garrison'd at Messina :
So you are now my friend and captain, Castraganio.
    Cas. The latter adds to my revenue, sir,
The first to my content.
    Fred.                         Have you employed
Your sister Amadine in my behalf ?
    Cas. Sir, there she stands, ready to execute
All you enjoin, to th' hazard of her life.
    Fred. Sweet Amadine, your kindness can excuse
An old sinner, whose frail, weak flesh, nature
Intending to keep long, a little hath
O'er season'd with her salt.  I would be glad
Sometimes to be refresh'd.  I know you hold
The princess in your power ; will you endear
Me to her fair esteem, procure me such
Address as may be opportune and fit ?
    Amad. Sir, I've already mov'd your praises with
Some vehemence ; it prospers too, as far
As good opinion of your person and your parts.
    Fred. And is there hope we may converse, by
    star
Or moon-light, yet be so maidenly to call
To have the curtains drawn ?
    Amad. This, sir, with good endeavour may be
    done.
    Fred. Then cough and make a noise, till we
Grow witty in our fears, and break small jests,
Laugh out again, and lift the apron up
To stifle laughter, till 't be crush'd into
A grave and silent smile.
    Amad.                         But meaning, sir, no harm ?
    Fred. And whisper close, till, in the dark, the
    lips

Be oft mistaken for the ears, and then,
Laugh out, and wake the posset-eating-nurse.
 AMAD. Still meaning, sir, no harm?
 FRED. None I protest; mine's pure platonic
  love.
 CAS. My sister, signior, is inquisitive,
Guilty of my offence, she ask'd me ere
You came, why you endeavour'd thus to have
The lady married to another, whom you meant to
  love?
 FRED. That's the platonic way; for so
The balls, the banquets, chariot, canopy,
And quilted couch, which are the places where
This new wise sect do meditate, are kept,
Not at the lover's but the husband's charge.
And it is fit; for marriage makes him none,
Though she be still of the society.
 AMAD. And may, besides her husband, have
A sad platonical servant to help her meditate.
 FRED. All modern best court authors do allow't.
 AMAD. You give good light into the business, sir.
 FRED. Were Eurithea married, I would teach
Her the true art: she is unskilful yet.
 AMAD. Hymen may burn his taper to a snuff
Before we see her wedding day; there's nothing
  comes
So seldom in Theander's thought.
 FRED.        But are you serious?
 AMAD. I've newly dress'd her like a shepherdess;
And he, i' th' old Arcadian habit, meets
Her straight, to whine and kiss. That's all they do.
 FRED. How? 'Tis two full hours since the pre-
  fix'd time
Our artist did prescribe his charm should operate;
I hope he hath not us'd us thus. Castraganio!
Captain, I'd forgot. Dear sir, hasten, and see
How it doth work with Gridonell.

You, gentle mistress, shall conduct me to
Some covert in the grove, where I may best
Observe Theander and his talk.  It will concern
Me much.                        [*Exeunt.*

*Enter* ARNOLDO, JASPERO, GRIDONELL.

ARN. This creature you so admire is but
The princess' woman, sir.

JAS. A very creature, and doth serve.

GRID. Would I might serve her, gentlemen.  I
    long
To wear a fan.  I have a tossing feather
In my chamber, as broad as a sycamore tree ;
It will make two dozen of fans.

ARN. But for what uses could you serve a
    woman ?

GRID. Instead of rearing a square sconce, I'd
    learn
To raise up paste ; and then for push o' pike,
Practise to poke a ruff.

JAS. These qualities will make your wages, sir,
At least four marks a year.

GRID. My corp'ral shall serve too.
It is an honest fellow, and a lover ;
He may wash bucks,* and scour dishes, instead
Of armour.

ARN.                     Is he a lover too ?

GRID. O, ay ! he loves women ; dares talk and
    handle 'em :
And would tell such pretty tales of a
Fine gentle damsel that he knew.

JAS.                   What was she ?

GRID. I never saw her, sir, but she boil'd
    chestnuts,

---

* Wash dirty clothes.
  " Of late, not able to travel with her furred pack, she washes
bucks here at home."— *Shakespeare.*

And sold bloat herring in the Leaguer.
 ARN. There are ways left for you to compass
  Amadine,
Better than service : you should woo and win her.
 GRID. Pray, gentlemen, how do they use to woo ?
 ARN. Why, with fine language.
 GRID. What's that, sir, French ?
 JAS. French is indeed the smoothest and most
  prosperous.
 GRID. Alas ! I can speak none but a few words
We use i' th' war, as at our Court *de guard*,
We cry, *Que va la.*
 ARN.      That, sir, will serve
When you shall meet your mistress in the dark.
 GRID. And then after a battle, *Randee rous.*
 JAS. This may be us'd, sir, when she's obstinate,
And will not yield to love.
 GRID.    This is all my fine language.
 JAS. Women are woo'd with music too.
 GRID. Will the drum and trumpet serve, with
  sad songs
Set to 'em, to the tune of a dead march ?
 ARN. Yes, at the fun'ral of a General's wife.
But there is yet another means : they oft
Are woo'd by letters elegantly penn'd.
 GRID. Ay, you are happy that can write and
  read.
I was taught once to set my mark to a shoe-
  maker's bill.

*Enter* CASTRAGANIO.

 CAS. Arnoldo ! does this soldier's humour last ?
 ARN. Still more.　He's grown demurer than
A young Geneva bride ; commits Idolatry
To every laundress in the house, and dares
Not speak to 'em, but with his hat in's eyes.

Cas. Belike the med'cine hath not wrought.   I'll
  lead
Him to my sister.   Follow, sir ! this is
The blessed hour, wherein you shall behold
Fair Amadine, and court her too.
  Grid. Good gentleman, pray go and bear me out !
But teach me how to wear my cloak, and when
I should pull on my gloves.                [*Exeunt.*

*Enter* Fredeline, Sciolto, Buonateste.

  Fred. We are undone ! I found him lying in
A poplar shade, with colder thoughts about him
Than old Carthusians have when they are sick ;
Less apt for our venereal love than Muscovites
Benighted when they travel on the ice.
  Scio. And works so little with my son, he stands
Moping and fix'd, as he were to be sold
To a stone-cutter for a marble statue.
  Buon. My lord, I'm lost in my astonishment !
Some envious spirit checks my art : it was
Not wont to fail the strictest minute given,
To make the virtue and effect appear.
  Scio. This is the powder that you priz'd so high,
As 'twere a grated carbuncle, or that
Long diamond pounded which the Sultan wears
Upon his thumb.
  Fred. Where's your philosophy, your strong
  deep art,
That, piercing through the centre, would look down
To hell ; there number all the fiends, and take
Account, how many load of coals is every year
Allow'd for their expense ?
  Scio. Yes, sir, and when the sun
Is blown out by a strong northerly wind,
You'd undertake again to light him with
A torch heav'd up by a long Jacob's staff.
  Buon. My Lord, I smile at these vain injuries

You do to art, not me : 'tis fitter for
Your wonder than your mirth.   But, take your
        course.
    FRED.  Since your great Master Aristotle died,
Who fool'd the drunken Macedon out of
A thousand talents to buy books, what have
The multitude of's learn'd successors done ?
Wrote comments on his works ; 'light !  I could beat
You all.   Have you so many ages toil'd
T' interpret what he writ in a few years ?
Is there yet nothing new, to render benefit
For human life, or strengthen reason* for
Our after hopes ?  Why do we build you colleges ?
    SCIO.  Yes, and allow 'em pensions too, that they
May scribble for no end, but to make paper dear.
    BUON. For one unlucky scape† in knowledge must
I suffer all this tyranny ?
    SCIO.                        You study physic too ?
    FRED.  He knows to cure sick chickens o'th' pip.
    SCIO.   I'ld fain see one of that profession live
Five hundred years without loss of a tooth.
    FRED. No, sir.   They'll suffer ruin and decay
In their own bodies for examples' sake,
That others may fall sick and make 'em rich.
    SCIO. Right, Fredeline, for notwithstanding all
Their min'rals and their herbs, we must be fain
At last to betake our selves to the wide yawn,
Grinning, and the long stretch.
    BUON.                        You make all knowledge
But deception, sir ; and cheaters of the learn'd
        philosophers.

    * Strength in reason.—*Folio.*
    † Deviation.
            " No natural exhalation in the sky,
                No scape of nature, no distemper'd day,
                But they will pluck away its nat'ral cause,
                And call them meteors, prodigies, and signs."
                                        *Shakespeare.*

FRED. 'Troth, little less. The merry fop of Thrace
That always laugh'd, pretending 'twas at vanity ;
Alas, 'twas his disease !  Going to steal
Mushrooms for his supper, the blue mouth'd
     serpent skulk'd
Under a dock leaf, and bit him by the thumb,
From whence he took that laughing malady.
    SCIO. And his antagonist would ever seem
To weep, out of a pious cause.  A fine
Dissembling fellow : 'twas not sorrow made him
     weep.
    BUON. No sir ? make that appear.
    SCIO.          I'll show a manuscript,
Now kept i' th' Vatican that proves
He had nine years a fistula in's eye.
    FRED.          Mere coz'ners all !
    SCIO. As for Diogenes, that fasted much
And took his habitation in a tub,
To make the world believe he lov'd a strict
And severe life, he took the diet,* sir,
And in that very tub sweat for the French disease.
    FRED. And some unlearn'd apothecary since,
Mistaking's name, called it Cornelius Tub.
    BUON. My noble friends, make much still of your
     spleens,
Tickle your selves with straws, if you want sport ;
I shall have my revenge ere long.
    SCIO. I think y' have poison'd the Duke, and
     my son too :
If it be found I'll cut your throat so wide
Open, that, when you take your morning's draught,
You shall go near to spill your drink.
    BUON. My Lord, I scorn your calumnies.
I'll to Messina, and contemn you both.     [*Exit.*

    * "I commend rather some diet for certain seasons, than fre-
quent use of physic ; for these diets alter the body more, and
trouble it less."—*Bacon.*

Scio. My fears misgive me, Fredeline : if he
Should now take horse, and leave us here to own
His treacherous fact, that were a fine philosophy.
    Fred.    Unless he have the subtle art to fly ;
We'll overtake him.  He shall not stir until
We know his med'cines' quality.            [*Exeunt.*

        *Enter* Theander *like a noble shepherd.*

    Thea. Three weary circuits of the sun expir'd
Fierce Phylomont and I shall meet,
To know the diff'rence of our stars : till then
I'll practise rites of love.  My Eurithea must
Not know our anger, nor the cause.   Come forth,
My princely shepherdess ! and leave thy lambs
Less gentle than thyself, whilst we a while
Grow pensive in this gloomy shade.

        *Enter* Eurithea *like a shepherdess.*

    Eu.    Why should we hide our selves, Theander,
            from
The free discoveries of the light, that know
Not guiltiness to cause a bashful fear ?
    Thea. This  green and fragrant palace tempts
            our stay.
Here sit, where nature made the sharper scented
            briar,
And luscious jes'mine meet to qualify
And reconcile their diff'ring smells within
The honey woodbine's weak and slender arms.
Sit nearer ! we are too remote.
    Eu. How, my Theander, am I still subdu'd
With thy chaste victories upon my heart ?
Would heaven had ne'er begun these joys, till it
Had kindly promis'd they should never end.
    Thea.   Yet whilst they last, we'll strive to make
            the strict
Example of our love an easy law

Unto the vain fantastic world.
EU.                              The nimble dwarf,
And lazy eunuch then, which are the spies
And messengers of their blind god, might rest
Upon their quilts at home, for all their toils
And simple business upon earth should cease.
    THEA.  And that small god himself, who ne'er
            could tempt
Wise poets to increase his stature, or
To mend his eyes, as knowing what
A useless deity they made, might soon
Go shake his quiver, and unplume his shafts.
The influence with which his fond idolaters
Are giddily inspir'd, is incident
To falsehood and to change.
    EU.  But our affection, time nor sad distress
Have power to alter or destroy.
    THEA.  Yet, say, the fury of some sudden war
Should lead us captive to a cruel land,
Could'st thou endure the frowns of destiny,
And be thus beauteous still ?   When scornful men
Shall ask, where now are all those Persian looms
Your lover's flowing wealth employ'd to weave,
Your vestments ever new, when you appear'd
Like gaudy April in Sicilian meads,
Or various tulips in the Ides of May ?
    EU. Fear not, my love, the homely weeds spun by
The coarse and heavy finger'd people, that
Reside i'th' neighbour vale, should well become
My beauty then, since humbled by my thoughts.
The brisk pert linnet in his russet feathers flies,
As warm as any bird of paradise
With all his painted and his gilded trim.
    THEA. But, oh! methinks I hear thy mourning, and
The saucy foe demand, where are those fumes
Of sweet Assyrian Nard,* wild Cypress boughs,

                * Spikenard.

And sifted Amber of the Southern sea,
Which ever as you mov'd, Theander burnt,
Pretending sacrifice?   But 'twas to hide
You in those costly mists, from rivals' eyes.
    Eu. Then with my wiser scorn I shall reply,
For sweets, behold yond' bed of violets,
That lean and hang their heads together, as
They seem'd to whisper and consult how to
Preserve their odour to themselves ; whilst near
Each chrystal brook the primrose stands
Triumphing on his stalk, as he disdain'd
His hidden root, ambitious to be worn
Within a chaste, although a captive's breast.
    Thea. Still, still, methinks, this rugged conqueror
Derides thee with his wit, and asks
Where are the whispers of your amorous lute,
That sooth'd you into slumbers till your dreams
Became your greatest sin?
    Eu. When I shall music need, I'll say each tree
Doth entertain a quire at nature's charge.
And what is he dares touch the Tuscan lute,
Whilst in the night he hears the bird begin
Her pensive notes ; whose feather'd ancestor
The fiery Tereus wrong'd?*
    Thea.   And whilst thy days of bondage last,
        thou shalt
With artful needle draw, in silken imag'ry,
The stories of our fatal love, and learn
T'outwork that mystic nursery of minds
The Phrygian Sibyl taught.†
            [Theander *gazing on her, rises and starts.*

* Tereus, a King of Thrace, forced his wife's sister, Philomela.   Philomela, as every school-boy knows, means the nightingale.—*See Ovid's Metam.*
† The Phrygian Sibyl (of Ancyra) is said to have been the
ninth, out of the supposed ten prophetic women, who foretold
the Advent.   Phrygia vestis is a garment wrought with needle-
work, or made of cloth of Baudkin.   Phrygian, an embroiderer.

Eu. Ay me ! what sudden terror shakes you thus
Into a wild demeanour of your looks ?
Thea. Such fire as this I have not felt before,
It boils my liver and it burns my heart :
My blood runs flaming till my scorched veins
Together curl, like broken treble strings.
   Eu. Tell me, the best of princes! what's your
      grief ?
Thea. 'Tis strange ! Come Eurithea, let us walk.
   Eu. Will you divide your troubles from my
      breast ?
Shall I not know your grief, which, though
My pity cannot remedy, my prayers may ?
   Thea. It is a fire kindled and bred in hell :
For it persuades and warms me to a guilt,
As strange and distant from my knowledge, as
My will. Move on ! my gentle love. Oh stay ! go
      back !
Go back a while till I've subdu'd my thoughts.
   Eu. Help him, sweet Heaven ! Preserve his
      reason safe.
   Thea. Nay, do not weep; those wat'ry obsequies
Serve to lament,* not quench such fun'ral fire
As mine.
   Eu.                   A funeral fire ?
   Thea. O yes ; 'twill burn me after death,
      though thou
Could'st drop more showers than April weeps
      when March
Hath blown the ruder winds into his eyes.
Though every tear thou shed'st were swell'd into
A wave, thou couldst not quench this secret fire.
   Eu. Dear Theander !
   Thea.            Hide, hide thy beauty ere
Thou speak'st ! Put on thy veil ! nay, closer yet.
                    [*She veils herself.*

* Qu. foment ?

EU. You careful angels that reside above,
Can you have business of more grace or need,
Than to consider such a change as this?
Theander, speak! what may it mean?

   THEA. To name it were such impudence, as
       bawds
And ravishers cannot attain till they
Are grown long exercis'd, and old.

   EU. These words are newer than the wondrous
       cause
That gives them breath.

   THEA. Bold devil! Thou imperious flame,
Sure I shall stifle thee at last. Now come
My Eurithea, let's move on! thy strong
O'ercoming beauty clouded thus we may
Converse, and safely too I hope. Alas,
Why dost thou weep? O sad, sinister change!
I am resolv'd; for if my tainted veins
Still harbour this disease, I will not need
Thy anger, Phylomont, to make me bleed.

[Exeunt.

ACT IV.   SCENE 1.

Enter BUONATESTE, SCIOLTO, FREDELINE.

   BUO. Where is the honour of my science now?
Are my assertions true? I told you, though
Their cold unpractised constitutions might
For two short hours be an impediment
To our fierce hopes, it could not fail to work.

   SCIO. Magnanimous Rabbin, thou hast conquer'd
      us:
We yield to thy philosophy. I would
Kneel down for expiation of my mis-belief,
But that my joints are old, and it were troublesome
To rise again. My fine magical Mounsier,

Be courtly in thy learning! embrace us, and
Forgive our heresy.

BUO. But are you reconcil'd, with pious thoughts,
Unto the ancient sages, and believe
Their knowledge of some use?

SCIO. They are right worshipful,
I rev'rence all their ghosts; but for the old fellow
That walk'd with's lanthorn to find honest men,
Introth he did an ancestor of mine
A private wrong, sticks in my stomach yet.

FRED. My lord, it needs must be so long ago
Your goodness should persuade your memory
To blot it out. But pray, what wrong could poor
Diogenes afford your ancestor?

SCIO. Why, meeting him in a blind lane, he
       denied
To lend him that lanthorn, which you know, signior,
To a gentleman in silk stockings, and white shoes,
Was a discourtesy.

BUO. Your lordship's subtle in antiquities,
And have kept a very nice intelligence.

SCIO. Well, Fredeline, this lucky plot was ours;
We've done enough: we now may comb
Our heads, stroke 'em, strew 'em o'er with nutmegs
To gratify our brains, then lay 'em up
To sleep. Hast thou convers'd with the good Duke
Since he did feel the med'cine in his blood?

FRED. O, sir, the ice is melted that hath kept
       his veins
So frozen and condens'd. He must find out,
That nature made a woman for some use
More consequent than to converse with and
       admire:
Besides, this our belov'd and knotty sophister
Hath fill'd me with such potent arguments,
Divine and moral: to persuade the rites
Of marriage, wise, and seemly too, as he

Shall needs consent in's reason and his will,
That he was once begotten, and must now beget.
    Scio. Th'ast drawn this circle with my own
        compass,
And rais'd a spirit in't Agrippa's self,
Were he alive, could not allay.
    Fred. Nay more, by my appointment, sir, there
        waits
A priest, at th' chapel door, who just upon
The nick of his conversion may appear,
And tie that mystic knot; which Eurithea, though
She pick it with her little fingers and
Her bodkin, hardly will unloose again.
    Scio. Exquisite Fredeline! I hear, the dose
I gave my son hath turn'd him from a tame
Soldier to a town bull.  I will go seek
Him straight, and find some means t'appease
His am'rous wrath.                          [Exit.
    Fred. Philosopher, we two must seal a brother-
        hood.
Come, let me shake thy Hebrew and thy Greek
Transcribing fist: not all thy leathern, nor
Thy vellum friends, those dead companions on
Thy shelves, shall be more faithful to thee than
Thy humble Fredeline.
    Buo.               Though my own studies, Sir,
Be solemn and profound, I honour a
Good wit, and can be tickled with pure fancy,
As well as youthful poets in their wine;
Yours I have plac'd in my first choice.
    Fred.                        Ah, my philosopher!
If thy almighty art could do one courtesy
In my behalf, I'ld fill thy standish with
My heart blood, ere thou shouldst want ink to
        write,
And leave thy wisdom to the world.
    Buo.                        But name it, Sir;

We, that are rich in treasure of the mind,
Like others wealthy in their gold, do oft
Preserve the best and chiefest part conceal'd.
   FRED. Couldst thou, by some rare subtle com-
      pound, work
On nature so, that whom I lov'd might be
Enforc'd to make return of an affection hot
And violent as mine? Methinks I see
A cheerful answer in thy looks. Be kind!
And speak some comfort ere I faint.
   BUO.                 This may be done.
   FRED. How, how! my sage immortal friend?
   BUO. You are in love!
   FRED. Platonically, Sir: no other ways.
   BUO. Fie! fie! profess a friendship, and presume
To gull me with a lady's paradox!
Do not I know what that imports?
   FRED. Well, Sir, you, that have skill t' interpret all
The eastern tongues, may manage my weak words
Into what sense you please.
   BUO. If you expect redress, the mistress whom
You love must grow familiar to my sight,
That I may study her complexion, and
Her years; then mark which way her soul's inclin'd.
   FRED. I know, 'twill be as safe a secret in
Your knowledge as in mine. 'Tis Eurithea!
   BUO. I thank you much, not for the trust you put
Into my breast, but for your brave ambition, sir,
For I affect great spirits like great wits.
But give me leave to ask——
   FRED. I will prevent you, Sir, for I presume
You'll but demand what others, privy to
My bold design, have question'd twice; why I
Thus toil to make Theander marry her,
Since by my hopes prescrib'd for mine own bed?
   BUON. You guess my wonder to the full.
   FRED. My other instruments I thought too thick

E

And heavy soul'd, to merit knowledge of
This mystery.  But you have reason, Sir,
And shall be satisfied.
    BUON. Signior, I wear your praise as my best
      dignity.
    FRED. Pray, listen then!  If I should think
      t' enjoy
Her by the tame and formal title of
A wife, I were but simply gull'd by my
O'erweening and too saucy ignorance,
As knowing well my birth, my fortune, and
My years make me unfit for such a hope.
Yet it is apt she marry too ; and why ?
That she may taste man : for, sir, in this cold
And frozen life of her virginity,
There is no means to prosper my desires ;
But when she comes to relish man, whose warm
Contaction makes her thaw, then like a spring,
Too long imprison'd in her ice, she'll spread
Into a lib'ral stream, that every thirsty
Lover may carouse, until his heat be quench'd.
    BUON. 'Tis subtly said.  But signior, now sup-
      pose
The wedding past, have you no other means
To prosecute your love ?
    FRED. More cunning and sublime !
My deep designments have contriv'd, before
His bridal kisses cool upon her lips,
He shall grow jealous of her chastity.
This, Sir, is certain as the night's
Succession to the day, and, well you know,
She that finds that her husband's jealous without
      cause,
Will lye perdu until she give him one.
    BUON. Thy bold ambition and thy wit, endear'd
Thee first unto my thoughts, but now I find
Thee deeply read in lovers' politics ;

The lustful priests of Paphos might have been
Disciples to thy skill.   How I affect
Mischief, when managed by a brain can lead
And usher it in new untrodden ways!
   FRED. But will you make this compound, Sir?
   BUON. It shall be straight prepar'd, which ere
      you sleep
You must receive into your nostril by a fume
Made on a little fire of Cassia roots; then gaze
On her to-morrow but two minutes' space,
Until your am'rous optic spirits, by
A secret transmutation, steal into
Her eyes, and straight the work is crown'd.

Enter THEANDER.

   FRED.  I am oblig'd to sacrifice my life:
The Duke is come!  Away!  It is not fit
Your friendship should be yet begun; go to
Your lymbeck, dear philosopher.     [_Exit Buon._
   THEA. Leisure, and drowsy sloth did first beget
These crooked and abortive thoughts: they are
The progeny of ease.   What do I here?
When I had business in the camp they ne'er
Durst tempt me in my idlest dreams: but oh!
They have o'ercome my nature, and my strength!
If there be remedies, I'll chuse the best.
   FRED.  This morn your Excellence was pleas'd to
      think
My counsels learn'd and requisite; I wish
Your wise opinion may not change her faith.
There waits a priest within will give a sweet
And sudden cure to your disease.
   THEA. I thank you, Sir!  Have you acquainted
      Phylomont
With my desire of peaceful conference?
   FRED. He will obey you, Sir.   Look, where he
      comes!

*Enter* PHYLOMONT.

PHYL. Sir, I am told, you wish'd me here on some
Affair may much concern us both, and that
Our meeting should be full of equal courtesy.

THEA. Sir, I have done you wrong, and made
    mine eyes
Severe inquisitors to find your faults,
But veil'd them when they look'd upon mine own.
I'm grown less temp'rate than yourself: something
I feel, which to extenuate with civility
I'd name, unruliness of youth, though I
Was wont to call 't a sin.

PHYL. O, is it come to this? I'll cashier my new
    levied troops,
We'll kill no soldiers, Sir: there's hope we may beget
Some now.   Theander, speak ! shall we preserve
Our ensigns folded and proclaim a peace ?

THEA. My sister, you shall marry Phylomont.

PHYL. I thank you, Sir, most heartily !  You, if
You please, shall marry mine, and then do with
Her what you list ; for I'll make bold with yours.

FRED. This Duke is one of Plato's heretics.

THEA. Howe're our inward inclinations are
Most sulphurous and foul, let us, I pray,
Enforce a little virtue from hypocrisy,
And hide it from external view.

PHYL. Theander, I was bred under as chaste
And modest discipline as any prince alive ;
And can affect a lover's tenderness
And decency of speech ; but not to know
The order and the course of things were fond
Unmetal'd ignorance.   It's not the custom, Sir,
That we must marry first and then to bed.

THEA. To bed, that is to sleep.

PHYL. Right, if the bridegroom, Sir, be mad,
    sleep is
His med'cine then ; I'm sober, I thank heaven,

And know my business.   Your sister shall find it.
  THEA. All this is news to me, either thou
    knowest
Too much, or I have thought a virtue what
More pregnant men may term a dull mistake;
It cannot be, I have a strange instinct
That gives me pleasure in my former faith.
  PHYL. Enjoy it still.  Your life and motion, Sir,
You can preserve by immaterial fire:
We, that are forc'd to keep our spirits warm
In flesh and blood, must be content to live
As other mortals do.
  THEA. I prithee let's dispute it bashfully.
Yet I would learn, is custom grown so bold?
First marry Phylomont, and straight to bed!
  PHYL. To bed, that's as you said to sleep; and
    then
'Tween sleep and waking, Sir, to touch, as 'twere
By chance, not purpose, and so fall into—
You guess the rest.
  THEA.          Enough! I'll hear no more.
  PHYL. But where's your sister?  I would fain
    dispatch.
  THEA. Conduct him to her, Fredeline; this key
Will open you the way.  If I shall need
Her pardon to excuse m' unskilfulness,
Entreat it for me, Sir.
  PHYL.          It shall be easily attain'd.
  FRED. This is a service I have much desir'd to do
Your Excellence.
  PHYL. Signior, you have deserv'd my thanks.
                [*Exeunt. Phyl. Fred.*
  THEA. This noble youth was by the general voice
Held most exact and heavenly in the whole
Demeanour of his life.  His judgment is
Of late defil'd, or what I feel is no
Rebellion of my reason, but my strength .

Not a disease, but some odd sauciness
Of health, which he doth merrily commend.

*Enter* EURITHEA *veil'd.*

Behold, my fair Carthusian now appears,
Whose purer thoughts and beauty soon will turn
This new opinion to an heresy.
    EU. I was persuaded, Sir, thus veil'd, to wait
On your commands.
    THEA. 'Tis now, sweet Eurithea, in thy power
To shew a mercy that may save my life.
Slaves, that are chain'd unto the heavy oar,
Who labour till they chafe the restless waves
Into a foam, are not enthrall'd like me.
    EU. Can you believe, my Lord, your griefs are so
Contracted to your self, so slow and lame
With their sad weight, that in this tedious space
They ne'er could travel to my heart ?
Know they have made a visit here, here they
Are lodg'd ; and I could wish, though strangers
        much
Unwelcom'd at the first, they never would
Return from whence they came.
    THEA. Thou art too pitiful ! but be so still
That I may flatter my oppressions with
Some hope, if not with remedy.  Grant a
Request which I unwillingly must urge,
And thou shalt faintly hear.
    EU. Why do I languish with delays ? Call't not
Theander, a request, but a command,
And justly confident reveal it straight.
    THEA.                        O, that we could
Exchange intelligence with our dumb thoughts,
And make our meaning known ere it should need
The tongue ! I cannot, dare not name't.
    EU. You wrong th' unblemish'd virtue of your
        soul.

Your contemplation never could create
A business so deform'd, as not deserves
To be deliver'd by your voice!   I sigh,
And mourn until I hear't.
   THEA. If I must speak, I would some northern
      frost,
That purifies the morn's infected mists, would purge
My breath, ere it arrive unto thine ear.
Poor Eurithea! you must marry me.
   EU. Is't this that so hath vex'd your utterance?
More willingly than I would leave the black
And sooty caves, where fiends reside, to walk
I'th' fragrant dwellings of the blest? lead on!
Be cheerful, and recall your health; your own
Domestic Priest, with ceremonious rites,
Will quickly perfit your desire.
   THEA.                             So willingly!
Stay, Eurithea! can you guess th' intent
Of what you would perform, of many new
And undiscover'd trials you shall make
Of things we had not courage yet to learn?
Dark deeds, and practis'd in the night, which
      when
Our hasty youth shall ask our wisdom leave,
May seem perhaps convenient, but not good.
   EU. Why should I make my meditation judge
Of what your better knowledge hath resolv'd?
Thus I unveil, to tell the world I dare,
I'th' open interview of light, approve
And justify your worst and secret thoughts.
Theander, lead the way!
   THEA.                             O cruel stars!
I shall betray a virgin now, whose innocence
Is so extreme it yields, and turns to guilt!
   EU. Why do you stay, my Lord, and strive
      to make
Or find new sorrows, ere the old are lost.

THEA. Leave me, my gentle love! I will not go,
Nor tell the cause.  Would thou were't wicked as
My self awhile, that thou might'st know't: my eyes
Grow sick ; 'tis not secure to wear
Thy beauties thus display'd.

EU. Alas, these are but coz'ning forms, there is
No truth in your delays ; I know you spoke
In the sincereness of your soul, when you
Profess'd our marriage would assist your mind's
Recovery.  Theander, come !

THEA. Dull fate ! where is the vigour that I
      shew'd
When our loud cannon seem'd to stifle the
Affrighted day with smoke, and rivers flow'd
Themselves into a new extent, swelling
Their tides with human blood?  In lovers' soft
And simple war I'm weaker than a child.

EU. Still more delays ! you kill me if you stay.

THEA. She is resolv'd ! her better angel sure
Is ever by her side ; no danger then
Can harbour where she goes.  And yet I blush
As I should need her veil to hide my shame
Ere I commit the sin.  Lead you the way !

EU.  This is a strange command ! Here, follow,
      sir.

THEA. Thou little, though imperious, God of love,
Warmly enthron'd within my mother's lap,
How wilt thou sit and smile when thou shalt see
To sooth thy wantonness, and swell thy pride,
The bridegroom woo'd, and usher'd by the Bride?
                                        [*Exeunt.*

*Enter* GRIDONELL, CASTRAGANIO, ARNOLDO,
            JASPERO.

GRID.  I will not follow a Platonic Duke !
So tell him, Sir, I am inspir'd, and know
The meaning of the word.

Cas. Be not so furious, Sir! I'm of your sect.
Unless he suddenly recant, I am
Resolv'd sooner to serve the great Turk.
    Grid. The Turk! Is he platonically given?
    Cas. Troth, Sir, not much; he hath some seven
        hundred
Of those taff'ty creatures you admire so, in's
Own house.
    Grid. Would I were the great Turk
But for one month; yet 'tis a chargeable place.
He can't spend less than a Colonel's pay
In pins among these damsels, besides muffs,
And fine white gloves! Poor gentleman, he lives
At a great rate.   Castraganio, a word——
                                [*Takes him aside.*
    Cas. Be not so boisterous, Sir: the powder
        works strangely.
    Grid. Fetch me your sister hither straight.
    Cas.                    But for what purpose?
    Grid. What's that to you? I've occasion to use
        her.
Something I must do, I know not what 'tis,
But I begin to feel she will be very
Convenient for me at this time.
    Cas. If you'll agree upon the wedding hour.
    Grid. How long then must I stay?
    Cas. Till a license be brought from Palermo,
And the Priest have done his office.
    Grid. I have not patience to expect till then.
Go bring her hither straight; dispatch!
Or I'll wear out my fist upon your smooth coun-
        tenance.
    Cas. You are too rude! I'll leave you, Sir. [*Exit.*
    Grid. Deny me such a poor request! 'tis an
I'll-natur'd rogue! Come hither, Jaspero. Have you
        a sister?
    Jasp. Yes, and a pretty one, I thank my stars.

GRID. Fetch her to me instantly, I cannot stay!
JASP. You must have patience till her nurse
    have made
Her ready, Sir.
GRID. Her nurse, what does she with a nurse?
JASP. She is at suck, and hardly six months old.
GRID. At suck! nay if she lye at that poor ward,
Tippling of milk, she is not for my turn.
Arnoldo? prithee fetch me thine.
ARN. I would be glad to do my friend a
    courtesy.
Would you had spoke in time, for, Sir, introth
    she's dead.
GRID. I do not like a dead commodity.
Well, gentlemen, you must each stand sentinel
Close at the laundry door, and bring me the
First prize. No words! it must be done.
ARN. Gladly! We love th' employment, Sir.
JASP. This soldier has din'd with the devil lately,
And fed on sea-coal cakes, he's vildly alter'd!
                  [*Ex. Jasp., Arnold.*
GRID. I'm wondrous hot within, my guts are
    dried
To a bundle of match; and I breathe gunpowder.
What have I done of late, where have I been?
Let me consider it.

*Enter* SCIOLTO.

SCIO. Hah! melancholy, son; thy corporal would
Look merrier when he sees his feather worn
I'th' enemies hat and's knapsack without bread.
Tell me, what dost thou want?
GRID. Something that you may help me to; you,
    Sir,
Are old, and well experienc'd in the world.
SCIO. And thou shalt have it then: tell me what
    is't?

GRID.                              Why, sir, a wench.

SCIO. How ? boy ! make me your pimp,
Do not vex me, you shall know I could fight in
     my youth.

GRID. Ay, Sir, any man will fight for a wench.

SCIO. You will provoke me. Get you in, and give
Attendance to Theander's marriage rites,
'Tis straight to be perform'd.

GRID.                              Alas, I dare
Not go ; there is a cause not fit to be told.

SCIO. You know what's fit, y' had best to tell
     it me.
Speak ! what's the cause you dare not go ?

GRID. Sir, I should ravish the bride.

SCIO. Are you so eager bent ? rare philosopher!

GRID. If I but see a priest, and a maid by,
Though her dowry be but a silver thimble
And a skein of silk, I shall beat him, sir,
Unless he do his office straight, and marry us.

SCIO. Hah ! 'tis high time to wear mine eyes
     open.
He may chance, in this mad fit, contract himself
To some inheretrix that's landed on
The high-way; whose father sells fine crab-sticks,
And hazle-nuts to riding citizens.
Come, son, this key must lock you up ! you shall
Remain a prisoner in my chamber till
You grow more tame.

GRID. I'll not be taken prisoner, sir, by any
     man alive.

SCIO. Nor yet obey your father, you? You'll not
Enforce me draw my sword ?

GRID.                    No, sir, you had not best.

SCIO. D'you threaten, boy: not best to draw my
     sword ?

GRID. No, sir, for fear you sprain your arm ;
     these weak

Old fellows know not what's good for 'em.
   Scio. Sirrah, go in! one disobedient word,
And I will dis-inherit thee.
    Grid. My Lord, I'll yield! but if you would but
      lock
Fair Amadine a prisoner i' th' same room——
   Scio. Thou traitor, get thou in!
   Grid. Perhaps she would be willing, sir.
   Scio. Go in, I say!            [*Exeunt.*

*Enter* PHYLOMONT *and* ARIOLA.

   Phyl. Let me a while contain thee in mine arms,
Belov'd Ariola, the force of Indian winds
That shake the aged cedar from his root
Shall not divide us now.
   Ario.                  Here I would stay,
My valiant Phylomont, till death should wave
His dart, and beckon us to follow him
Unto the hidden shades, till he should make
By angry power these kind embraces cold.
   Phyl. How sad and dismal sound the farewells
      which
Poor lovers take, whom destiny dis-joins,
Although they know their absence will be short!
And, when they meet again, how musical
And sweet are all the mutual joys they breathe!
   Ario. Like birds, who when they see the weary
      sun
Forsake the world, they lay
Their little pensive heads beneath their wings,
To ease that weight which his departure adds
Unto their grief.
   Phyl. 'Tis true my love : but when
They see that bright perpetual traveller
Return, they warm and air their feathers at
His beams, and sing until their gratitude
Hath made them hoarse.

ARIO. My brother I request
May be forgiven, and call not my restraint
His cruelty, 't hath mended me within,
And fill'd me with such bless'd designs,
As will deserve your wonder and your thanks.
Forgive him, Phylomont!
    PHYL.                Our friendship is
Restor'd, which thus I will confirm with vows
Upon thy sacred hand, but surely it
Were better ratified upon thy balmy lip,
Which, after absence, decent custom will
Allow to those, who are delighted when they meet.
    ARIO. Your virtues have such great and safe
Authority, they cannot ask what's fit to be denied.
                                *[He kisses her.*
    PHYL. This seems, methinks, a new
Demeanour. She is alter'd much, more free
And kind than she was wont.
    ARIO. Why dost thou ruminate aside, as if
Thy meditation were too guilty, or too great
To be reveal'd?
    PHYL. Give me, thou precious darling of my
        heart,
The privilege to doubt a little, and
Resolve me straight; why are thy courtesies
So great now, and so easily attain'd,
Which heretofore thou didst deprive me of
With frowns, and strict behaviour of thy brow?
    ARIO. It shall be ever thus. My passion, and
My thoughts are chang'd; as Eurithea with
My brother lives, so shall our conversation take
All liberty, and our salutes be far
More amorous and bold, though virtuous still.
    PHYL. This bounty had been excellent, when
        you
Had privilege to give, or to deny ; but now
Your charter's out of date, and mine

Begins to rule : the priest attends below
To celebrate our nuptial rites, which is
The happy hour that both advance
The husband's government.   Come to the chapel,
        love.
    ARIO.  A little pause; what need we marry, sir?
I lately was instructed to a clearer choice
Of our felicity : is it not better to live thus,
In a perfection that we know, than to attempt
New joys, which our unskilfulness should
Make us doubt ?   This is the angels' life ;
My brother told me so, and then he breath'd
Such holy lectures as have prosper'd much
Upon my soul.
    PHYL.  Not marry, my Ariolo?  Is that the fatal
        word ?
Take heed how you are sooth'd into a strange and
        fond belief.
    ARIO.  Your caution, sir, is only needful to
Your self.   Can you desire a blessing more
Exact than this we may possess, to live
In everlasting confidence of what
We do, yet still embrace, and love, although
In persons not conjoin'd, united in our souls ?
    PHYL.  These are but trivial documents, alas !
I'm hardly taught thus rashly to renounce
What all the wiser world have taken so
Long leisure to approve ; besides, Ariola,
You much mistake your brother, for just now
I saw him married : the deed's past, these hands
Gave and presented him to Hymen's use,
And he's preparing for my sister's bed.
    ARIOL.  Your sister's bed ! gentle my lord,
        beware
How you confer a calumny, which all
Your orizons, and mine to help them, can't
Excuse to Heaven.

PHYL. Let me conduct you to him, and your eyes
Shall witness my assertion for a truth.
  ARIO. No, sir, if he be guilty grown, I shall
Not wish to see him so ; can he recant,
Thus soon, the fair religion he did preach
With all the fervency of mind ?
  PHYL.                         Do not lament.
Th' example you should rather follow than
Accuse : come, my Ariola, like him,
We'll marry too, our wisdom shall persuade us to't.
  ARIO. Some wicked spirit strives, sir, to betray
Us both : make trial of this new
Unusual happiness awhile, live, and
Converse beneath the spreading poplar for
Our shade, and for variety we'll sit
On yonder river's flowery banks.
  PHYL. There whisper till we court him to delay
His journey to the sea, and swell, until
He leave his scaly deaf inhabitants
Upon the shore, as tribute to our loves.
  ARIO. Ay, Phylomont, these are the guiltless
    sports
  PHYL. Fine holy dreams indeed, but cannot last.
You and I must marry, 'tis resolv'd.
  ARIO. Banish that thought, or I will take my
    leave,
And be estrang'd for ever from thy sight.
But when reclaim'd seek me i' th' myrtle grove.
  PHYL. Stay, fair Ariola! my reason sure must
    laugh
At this subjection of my faith, but I
Will on, freedom and kind addresses she
Hath still assur'd.  Come, follow me! like an
Unwilling proselyte I slowly move
To try the pleasures of Platonic Love.
                              [*Exeunt.*

*Enter* AMADINE, FREDELINE, *with a paper, and*
                CASTRAGANIO. .

AMAD.  Dispatch, sir! it grows late! my lady will
Expect I wait on her to bed.   Th' intelligence
I bring is full of certainty and truth :
Make your advantage of 't with your best skill.
      FRED.  Wilt thou adventure, Amadine? 'tis but,
At worst, the forfeiture of thy poor service,
Which I'll requite with giving thee young Gridonell
To be thy husband, and to rule.   My plots
Have so design'd, why did I order 't else
That he should take the med'cine which hath forc'd
Him to such feminine attempts ?
      AMAD.  Indeed he's grown more bold with me of
            late,
And will come fairly on in time.
      FRED.                              O, doubt it not !
Can my experienc'd head study in vain ?
Captain, my endear'd friend, will you forsake
Me now, when such a ripe occasion shews
It self, to give success unto my hopes ?
Your sister is content to hazard all.
      CAS.  'Tis full of danger, sir !
      FRED. I will be there my self, and stand between
Your person and his wrath.
      CAS.  'Tis certain loss, sir, of my company.
      FRED.  How ?  What's a company that brings as
            frail
Revenue, and uncertain, as our purchases
At dice ? who'd live, and be maintain'd by others
            deaths ?
Look here, just now I caus'd him sign this grant,
The Provostship of Necosia newly void,
Which, being under's hand and seal confirm'd,
No new relapse of favour can recall
The gift.  You see your name here, sir ; carv'd out

In Roman characters : the feat but done,
I'll put it in your hand, then straight you may
Take horse, ride post unto your government,
Your sister with you, on some parsons strong
Tall double gelding, sir, kept in my stable for
That use ; and then laugh at your patron till
He sicken at your mirth.

   AMAD. But shall my husband elect follow us ?

   FRED. And ride as swiftly as a Scythian from
A battle lost.

   AMAD. In my weak judgment, brother,
Our rewards are fair. I am resolv'd to venture it.

   CAS. Early i' th' morning, Sir ?

   FRED. Just at the first appearance of the light.
The door I told you of must be the place.

   CAS. You will be there protected with your
     sword ?

   FRED. A captain, and raise doubts, that sound
     like fears !
Come, sir, all shall be safe. You to your lady.
Let's meet i' th' upper lobby two hours hence,
And there consult. My chymick fume I have
Already ta'en; if that succeed, and this
Plot thrive, I will require no more from my
Uncertain fate, nor art, whose usual scope,
Is but to pay learn'd industry with hope. [*Exeunt.*

   *Enter* THEANDER, EURITHEA, *a table, stools, and
     lights set out.*

   THE. Husband, and wife, we have a calling now ;
Shews it not strange, disquieting thy tender ears
With sounds th' are unacquainted with ? Titles,
Methinks, that yet we know not how to wear,
We should be taught behaviour, and some forms
Of gravity: are they not useful, Eurithea ?

   EU. My lord, I am more ignorant than you :
If we have ventur'd upon errors, we'll

F

Conceal them, and forgive our selves.

THE. Her beauty kindles in my breast new fires,
Before the old are quench'd.   Wise Fredeline
Told me, our marriage would procure my remedy.
Alas! the cure's to come, and now I must
Require't as custom or a duty from her;
In my nice thoughts 'twill teach her impudence.
O curs'd disease! what shall I do?

EU. Theander, you are still perplex'd.   I thought
The holy priest had a mysterious power
To make these troubles cease.   Did you not vow
Our nuptials was the means to save your life?

THE. To bed, my Eurithea! it is late.
They say the married pair are incident
To cares, 'tis fit they should sleep.   Prithee
To bed; shall I go call thy woman?

EU. My lord, you are not kind: the tedious hours
I could contract to minutes in your company,
And waste them faster than our village girls
That dance in meadows all the month of May.
I'll take my leave, yet boldly too,
With all the solemn sweetness of a bride.   [*Kisses.*
My lord, good night!

THE.                                    I am inflam'd again.
Did she not take her leave, and say
Good-night? then whither must I go?
One bed I thought kind Hymen had allow'd
To both, since by his God-head we are made
But one; thus it is generally receiv'd:
Stay Eurithea, we must talk.

*Enter* AMADINE.

AMAD. Madam, your bed's prepar'd! shall I
    undress
Your ladyship, or the bridegroom first?
I' th' province where I liv'd, we us'd to call
A dozen apron squires t'uncloath the husband,

Then sew him in a sheet, and lay him on his pillow,
Tamely to expect the bride two hours before she
   came.
   Eu. Wench, thou art mad! D' you understand
    her, sir?
   The. A little, Eurithea. Do not you?
   Eu. She talks as it were fit we two—
   Amad. Should lye together, that's my meaning,
    madam.
   Eu. Hence! and leave us, immodest fool.
   Amad. I knew 'twould come to this—Fredeline
    will
Find my words true; the morning may, perhaps,
Make you both melancholy.         [*Exit.*
   Eu. This wench, Theander, hath been fam'd for
    wit;
I doubt she hath experience too in things
Not decent for th' observance of a maid.
   The. Alas, she talks but what she hears, and in
Her understanding seems proper and fit!
   Eu. That we should sleep together in one bed.
   The. Indeed it sounds most strangely to us yet,
But use will dull those scruples to the ears.
It must be done, custom will be obey'd.
   Eu. Never by us. We'll live to be examples,
Not, sir, to follow those we cannot like.
   The. Consider, gentle love, ere you believe
Your own opinions best. Why did we marry?
   Eu. That's easily resolv'd, I thought, Theander,
Some wild sad jealousy had vex'd thy heart
With fear of rivalship; and, by this sacred band,
Thou would'st secure and tie me to thy self,
More safely to destroy another's hope,
Though these were needless doubts. I never gave
You cause to hold my love in your suspect.
   The. Thou dost mistake my griefs, it hath a cause
More foul, which I'd acquaint thee with, if it

Were comely to reveal't, but since I have
Betray'd and led thy guiltless feet into
This sacred snare, 'tis fit t' avoid the scorns
Which singularity and overbashful
Niceness will beget; we'll live as others do,
As much i' th' practices of night as day.

　　Eu. O Theander! the sweetness of thy soul
Is sour'd, like Cretan wines that are too excellent
To last.　My blood thou hast to water turn'd,
And I shall soon consume it all in tears.

　　The. Go, Eurithea, to thy bed! sleep like
A virgin, not a wife : be by thy own
Embraces warm'd, enjoy thy bosom to
Thyself, away ! haste to thy bed, I to
My grave, and let my coffin lye
Ungarnish'd in the earth.　Come not to strew
It o'er with flowers : I am so pestilent,
That I should blast thee after death.

　　Eu. Theander stay ! who knows but heaven may
　　　give
Such mighty blessings to my speech that straight
I may persuade thee from thy guilty thoughts ?

　　The. Never ! my breast is now become
The burning prison of the fiends, it is
So sulphurous and hot, methinks they find
Their punishment increas'd, and would, to cool
Themselves, return unto their former hell.

　　Eu. O direful extacy ! can I hear this and live ?

　　The. I'll tell thee more, to make thee fly
With some kind angel's borrow'd wings, from this
Infected region where I breathe.　Know all
Our married vows (which certainly were first
Ordain'd for holy use) I merely took,
As formal helps to my pernicious lust.

　　Eu. Yet stay ! in this short tyranny of time,
Thou canst not be so sinful grown, as to despise
My pity and my prayers too !　O, stay !

THE. I dare not, for thine eyes augment my
    smart,
Each small neglected beam they shed
I gather up in flames, and quite pervert
Their virtuous influence to a lustful fire.
    EU. Thou lost remainder of the noblest prince,
The active war or wiser courts e'er knew,
How do I blush to find my groans and sighs
Have left me breath enough to speak my last
Farewell.
    THE. How far is it to heaven, that yet
This lady's mournings are not heard? for, if
They were, my sufferings and my guilt would
    cease;
Or cannot our petitions climb, and get
Access as nimbly as our faults? O this
Is it that so emboldens vex'd humanity,
Makes us complain, those undiscern'd
Immortal governors are often in
Their bounty slow, in justice too severe,
And give not what we beg, but what we fear.
                          [*Exeunt.*

## ACT V. SCENE I.

*Enter* THEANDER, FREDELINE.

THE. My gladness doth o'ercome me, Fredeline.
Some kind celestial power hath physic'd me
With immaterial balm, the sickness of
My blood is gone, my hot and eager thoughts
Grow temp'rate now, my veins are cool within,
As silver pipes replenish'd from a spring.
    FRED. It seems the philosopher's dose hath done
Working: 'tis well he is already married.
    THE. O, I am light, more nimble than a dove,
Or empty eagles in their morning's flight.
Methinks this sinful vestment of my flesh

Shows clean and new upon my soul: now I
Shall sleep again, and have such guiltless dreams.
As I may tell my mother when I wake.
    FRED. 'Tis strange the operation should decay
So soon ; some few hours hence my subtle fume
Will govern in mine eyes : and there I hope
Continue longer than his lust hath done with him.
    THE. I'm thinking, Fredeline, how Eurithea
        will
Rejoice, when she shall find what mastery
Her holy friends above have wrought in my behalf.
    FRED. 'Tis now near birth of day, and, as I told
You, sir, to find her pensive in her bed,
To draw her curtains, and reveal yourself
Quite alter'd and recover'd in your mind,
Will by the sudden wonder much augment
Her joy.
    THE. It must be full of pleasure.   Shew the way.
    FRED. That's her chamber, sir, but through a
        back door
(Unless her careful women hinder us)
By a strong bolt, I can convey you to her
Without noise ;
Make me your guide, and move to your right hand.
    THE. I shall be welcom'd and admir'd, as I
Had made my visit from a region so
Remote, that my return would be no more
Believ'd, than from the grave.
    FRED.                              Here I enjoin'd
My captain and his sister stand conceal'd.
If he should prove too cowardly for such
A guilt, I were undone.   Sure that's his voice.

    *Enter* CASTRAGANIO (*in a night Gown unready*)
            *and* AMADINE.

    CAS. They both are come.   Speak louder,
        Amadine,

He cannot hear us else.

THE.                     Hah! who are these?

FRED. They come from Eurithea's chamber, sir,
Let's retire to the Arras, and listen to their talk.

AMAD. Brother, take heed how you discourse
And boast of your access. Theander would
Go near to kill us both, if he but knew
Of this night's revelling.

CAS. Dost think I wear my tongue so slipp'ry in
My mouth? These are not pleasures fit to be
Reveal'd: Away! w' have said enough.

                  [*Ex. Cas. and Amad.*

FRED. They have observ'd your language I pre-
    scrib'd
To the strictness of a syllable.

THE. Sure he did urge my name! and spoke as it
Concern'd my justice to destroy 'em both.
Who are they? thou know'st 'em, Fredeline?

FRED. My endear'd friend; can you be guilty of
Such close night exercise?

THE. Who is thy friend? death on thy cour-
    teous fears,
Why dost conceal't so long? What is he call'd?

FRED. Were he my brother, and thus injur'd you,
My secrecy should never make him safe.
'Tis Castraganio and his sister Amadine:
She that attends upon your wife.

THE.                    My wife!
That title's new, and will grow horrid now!
Her chamber was their sphere of revelling:
They came from thence.

FRED. Can you think so, my lord?

THE. Why dost thou strive to lessen my belief,
With wearing such disguises on thine own?
Thou saw'st they came from thence.

FRED. Sir, if they did, that can infer no cause
To make your reason so disquieted;

Are there not many of these tiffany*
Young kerchief people that will have their lovers in
Their lady's chamber whilst she sleeps ?

    THE. Her lover, Fredeline ! thou wouldst beguile
My jealousy with hopes impossible ?
It is her brother, think on that.

    FRED. Can incest seem so strange to your conceit ?
The sooner, sir, for by that means th'are sure
T' increase th' alliance of those children which
They get, and make them more akin unto them-
      selves ;
But if the gentle Eurithea you
Suspect, (as be it far from my dull thoughts
To raise a saucy fear), let me kill him !

    THE. Go, follow straight ! bring me his heart,
      that I
May see it pant and bleed within my hand.
Kill him ! his sister too : Yet stay, stay Fredeline :
'Tis not the custom of my soul to be
Reveng'd by deputy, or fix my anger where
There is not equal strength and valour to
Encounter it.

    FRED. But, sir, if he should live
To prattle in his wine, and boast what he hath
      done ?

    THE. Go then, take care thou see him straight
      embarqu'd,
And let some cunning pilot steer him to
A coast so wild and distant from this clime,
That's language never may be understood.
Not to secure my fame, but in a piteous tenderness
To Eurithea's sex.   False Eurithea !
When I had purg'd my memory of all
My raw unwholesome thoughts, could'st thou defile't
Again with acting what I but unwillingly
Desir'd ?

    * A kind of fine flax or linen, like cambric or lawn.

FRED. 'Tis worth my poor vexation too,
When I consider how the scornful, that
Malign'd the pure celestial sect of
Lovers which you mutually conspir'd
To raise, will smile when they shall hear of this,
And say, 'twas but an old Platonic trick.
    THE. Leave me, and see him suddenly im-
       barqu'd.
    FRED. Sir, your command shall be obey'd; but I
Beseech you not proceed to danger, on
These weak unlucky doubts.
    THE. This was the cause she did dissuade me
       from
Her bed, that she might make another room,
Most virgin-like pretending 'twas a crime to ask
A husband's privilege.   Prithee, leave me !
    FRED. I dare not yet, my noble injured Prince.
[ Exeunt.

Enter CASTRAGANIO and AMADINE.

    CAS. I'm glad the danger's past. It had been
       hard
To teach me venture it, but that the Provostship
Was a most powerful bait.
    AMAD.                          And then to make
The rich young Gridonell my husband too,
For all his plots are sure.
    CAS.                          But that which perfected
My confidence, was thy assurance of
The lady's easy inclination to
Forgive.   For, as thou told'st me, if the worst
Succeed, and we should be constrain'd to tell
The truth, she'll pity young beginners that
Are forc'd to hazard a little honesty
To make 'em rich, and is able to
Procure Theander's pardon as her own.
    AMAD. You may presume it and rejoice, for I

Have felt her breast; 'tis soft and tender as a
    pelican's.

    *Enter* FREDELINE, *with a parchment writing, and*
        *pocket inkhorn.*

    FRED. My noble captain, and my precious friend,
I will not name what lasting gratitude
Your cares and courage have obliged me to.
Men that are hearty and sincere come late
With promises, and early with their deeds.
    CAS. I hope, sir, though our dialogue were short,
We utter'd your meaning in your own words?
    AMAD. My voice was valiant too, and loud
    enough.
    FRED. All was exacter than my hopes desir'd :
And now (just dealing, sir, doth strengthen love)
There is the patent for your Provostship.
Pray put it in your pocket safe, make choice
Of all my horses, straight to hasten you
Unto your government.
    AMAD. And shall my husband follow us?
    FRED. Just now he's drawing on his boots, he'll
    ride
Half naked with his legs, for out of haste
He hath forgot to put his stockings on.
    AMAD. Were he quite naked, he should be wel-
    come, sir.
    FRED. Friend, I implore I may by ev'ry post
Have letters of thy business, and thy health ;
And, pretty Amadine, when you have children
(As heaven no doubt, will send you store), pray keep
Them warm, and let 'em eat no fruit, nor fish.
You go unto a cold raw clime, and I
Desire all your posterity might thrive.
    AMAD. It is the kindest gentleman.
    FRED. We'll meet i' th' stable straight, there
    have

A parting tear or two, and so farewell.
Mischief on my frail memory!   I had
Forgot a written schedule here, to which
I must entreat your hands.

       *[Draws out a paper, pen, and ink.*

CAS. How! what is it, sir?

FRED. Only a short certificate, that justifies
You lay with Eurithea, sir; and Amadine
Must needs subscribe, as witness, that she saw
You in her bed.

CAS.       You shall excuse me.

FRED. Can you deny me this?

AMAD. What w' have already done can raise
  but his
Suspicions.   This will make him mad.

FRED. Speak! will you write?

CAS. Our other crime, if it be found may be
Forgiven, but once consent to this, he'll grow
Too wise, sir, to be merciful.

FRED. Well, I must seek for friendship among
  beasts;
There is no melting courtesy, no honesty
In men.   Determine straight! will ye subscribe?

CAS. You have our answer, signior; pray receive't.

FRED. Dear friend, I take my leave.  Sweet
  Amadine,
Farewell!   I'm sorry we must part, as blind
Men do, never to see each other more.

CAS. Believe not so unkindly of our destinies.

FRED. Never, I fear: for I, suspecting you'ld deny
This small request, was fain to hire
Two shaggy ill-look'd gentlemen, a brace
Of massy hilted rogues, who wait below
To cut your throats.

CAS. Y'are not in earnest, sir.

FRED. Dear friend! when did you find I was in
  jest?

However, if you'll fix your names in writing here,
You may go on with safety to your government.
Shall they come up?

   AMAD. No, no sir, if they be rogues,
And have such shaggy looks.  Brother, I find
He's mischevious.

   CAS. Give me the paper, sir!

               [*He writes, and gives it Amadine.*

   FRED. Gentle mistress, your name too—
So, now ye are kind, let me embrace you both.
And pray look on the patent, sir, I gave
You to assure the Provostship.

             [*Cas. takes it out and opens it.*

   CAS. Hah! here wants the Duke's hand.

   FRED. Right; to what purpose, pray, should it
     be there,
When th' office is not fall'n.

   CAS. I'm gull'd! led by the nostril like an ass.

   AMAD. And shall I have no husband, signior?

   FRED. Introth I have been busied much of late,
And never spoke unto the gentleman;
Besides, I thought y' had been inclin'd to the Pla-
   tonic way.

   AMAD. I would my nails were long enough,
     villain,
I'ld fley* thee into rags.

   FRED.            Alas, I smile at injuries.

   CAS. Peace! do not anger him.  Come, sister, we'll
Unto my garrison.  I've a commission for
A company: I hope you'll speak unto
The Duke I may enjoy't.  I'm sure his hand is to't.

   FRED. But yet you'll find a willing small
Mistake too in that grant; the captain is
Not dead that had the place.

   CAS. Would I had spirit but to beat my self.

---

  * Here meant to signify "scratch," although, more properly,
"scourge."

FRED. You are a Florentine; one of the subtle
    tribe,
That think your neighbours have no brains, but
    what
They meet serv'd in with sage and vinegar,
To a calf's head. I pray, believe you found
A dull Sicilian once, that could out-wit
A Tuscan gentleman.
    CAS. Y'are master of your pleasure, sir. Whither
    shall we go?
    FRED. You must to sea.
    AMAD.           To sea! I'll drown here first,
Or ask pardon and confess all.
    FRED. Not one word more, on forfeiture of life.
    CAS. My wonder makes me dumb. I need no
    threats.
    FRED. You shall to the Bermudas, friend, and
    there
Plant cotton, whilst your sister learns to spin.
It is the Duke's command, and till I can
Provide a ship, I must enclose you in
A garret safe, where you may weep and meditate.
No howling now, nor crying loud, for fear
My ill-fac'd blades below o'erhear't, and straight
To qualify your voices, cut your throats ;
Nor do not grumble curses out, I hold
Them much unwholesome in a morning ere
I break my fast.           [*Exeunt.*

*Enter* PHYLOMONT, BUONATESTE, ARIOLA.

PHYL. I'm weary of this cold Platonic life :
D'you think that I'll sit sighing thus, Ariola,
Under a poplar tree, or whining by
A river side, like a poor fisherman
That had lost his net ? Either consent to marry,
Or I will straight take horse, ride to my province
And seek some downright virgin out, that knows

Nature's plain laws, though not the art of love.

ARIO. Can you complain I am unkind, or the
Sweet freedom which I give, is not so much
As either's virtue might allow?

PHYL. It is enough! men that are satisfied
With wind and air may keep chameleons company:
I'm of another diet.   Ay, my learned
New acquaintance here, laughs to conceive
What Hercules and's fifty mistresses
Would have thought of a Platonic lover.

BUON. He would have beaten's brains out with
his club.

PHYL. Will you consent to marry?   Speak!

ARIO. If I am powerful with thee, Phylomont,
Let me but woo thee to the woods again,
And try how my persuasions can subdue
Thy mind, unto our former temperate love.

PHIL. No, I thank heaven; I'll sooner go thither
To rob poor squirrels of their nuts.   My sage
And learned author, shall I humble you
So much as go to bid my followers
Prepare for my departure hence?

BUON. Stay a little, sir!   The lady may relent.

PHYL. My hopes grow cold.   I'll instantly away!

ARIO. Stay, Phylomont! I do command thee stay,
By the religion of thy sacred vows!

PHYL. One hour I will! upon condition too
You walk aside with my philosopher,
And listen reverently to his advice.

ARIO. My reason's fortified!   Let him come in.

PHYL. Away! Use all the force of your capacity.

BUON. Plato shall lose one fond disciple, sir,
Or I'll go burn my books and singe my beard
Off in the flame.                               [*Exeunt.*

*Enter* THEANDER *and* EURITHEA, *at several doors.*

THE. In this coarse Pilgrim's weed I shall enjoy

That quietness, which, though great princes have
The power oft to preserve in others, yet
Can ne'er command unto themselves.

    EU. Alas, my lord, what have I done,
That you should leave me to suspect
My innocence ?   Why will you thus become
A holy wanderer, to seek that happiness
In other lands, which here you scornfully
Forsake ?   What have I done ?

    THE.                                        Is thy offence
Grown up to be thy glory now ; dost love
To hear it told?   Or art thou sooth'd with silly hope
It is conceal'd ?   The stars are witnesses !
They all grew weary of the night, and wish'd
For clouds to hide their radiant eyes, from what
Unwillingly they saw.

    EU. Ease my amazement quickly, or I die.

    THE. Thou, Eurithea, and the world are grown
Too false and subtle for the easy dull
Sincereness of my heart.   I will retire
To desarts and to rocks, there feed the winds
With my continual sighs : until I raise
A storm shall nightly shake this palace towers,
And give thy flattering conscience cause to fear,
Though I am gone, still my revenge dwells here.
                                    [*Exit.*

    EU. Oh ! I would follow, but my griefs are grown
So burdensome, they bow me to the ground.
                                    [*She falls.*
How various are the changes of our fate !
Now must I lose him, when he's safe restor'd
To all his chaste and noble thoughts.   Which way
Could I consent to an offence ? I am
By some conspiracy betray'd.

       *Enter* FREDELINE.

    FRED. This fellow and his sister must be sent

To sea with speed, for fear some watchful accident
Discover all.  Eurithea! the most
Illustrious princess of this isle, look up !
Fair virgin-wife : alas, why do you weep ?
    Eu. I am forsaken ! lost ! Theander is
Unkind, o'ercome with jealousy and scorn.
    Fred. Madam, I think, I partly know the cause.
Believe't, there are more villains in the world,
Than will appear so in the face, though it
Be wash'd, and shav'd, then view'd with open lights.
    Eu. But, sir, know you what thus disturbs my lord ?
    Fred. Your woman's false ! her brother such a
        knave,
As, were he sent to hell, the fiends would crowd
Together t' avoid his company.
    Eu. She and her brother false to me ?
    Fred. Rise up, I do beseech your excellence !
And, having wip'd away those liquid pearls
From off your beauteous eyes, read this and wonder.
                [*She rises and takes a paper from him.*
    Eu. O dismal ! horrid treachery.
    Fred. There ! you perceive, he doth affirm he did
Enjoy your bed, and Amadine subscribes
To witness what he certifies.
    Eu. Though they are cruel, I forgive them both.
    Fred.  That's heavenly said : yet  mark their
        impudence.
This note they sent to me, t' entreat me give
It to the Duke, but when I do,
Let the quotidian gout seize on my hands,
Until my fingers grow more knotty than
A maple root.
    Eu.                         Sir, I believe you'll strive
Rather to lessen his suspicion, than
By new contrivements give it growth.
    Fred.  D' you think I am of human race ?  This
        room

Is much too public for your miseries.
I pray retire within, and we'll consult
How to dispel all these enchanted clouds.

EU. You are become the treasure of my hope,
And will oblige me, when my fortune smiles
Again, unto a gratitude, that shall
Be great and suffer no decay.

FRED. Already she is very kind: I hope
My fume begins to work. I'll gaze upon
Her still until mine eyes melt into hers.   [*Exeunt.*

*Enter* JASPERO, GRIDONELL, ARNOLDO.

JASP. Your father sent us to release you, sir.
You have the house at liberty again.
He says, he may trust you with women now,
For there is such a blemish found in one
Of the fairest of the sex, as, he presumes,
Will teach all men to fly their company.

GRID. Indeed, my danger towards women's past,
For whether 't be with fasting without
My supper twice, or walking gently in
My shirt whilst the moon shin'd, I cannot tell;
But I am strangely alter'd, grown so cold
Within, as I had lain a whole night *perdu*
O' top o' th' Alps.

ARN. But you were very hot before?

GRID. O, Arnoldo, thou may'st be glad thy sister
Was dead: I had so maul'd her else.

JASP. 'Twas happy mine was at suck too.

GRID. Th'art i' the right; for had she been but old
Enough to wear a bongrace* on her brow,
And nibble gingerbread, sh'ad serv'd my turn.

ARN. 'Twas a miraculous fever you was in.

GRID. Well! shall I tell you, gentlemen? believ't,
I had eaten some strange odd meat, the pickled
   kidney of

* A forehead cloth.

A goat, or the rump of a devil broil'd.
But have you heard of a fair lady that had got a
    blemish ?
   JASP. Our brave new duchess, sir ! sh'ath
    troubled all
The house, and in her very bridal night, they say,
Play'd the adultress.
   GRID.                How, gentlemen ?
Pray hear me speak ; I've judgment in these things.
I will be hang'd if sh' hath not dipp'd her finger
In a French pie, some kickshaw made of sev'ral
Strange bits ; just such as I encount'red with,
And there devour'd the kidney of a goat.
Come, let's go seek my father out !    [*Exeunt.*

   *Enter* PHYLOMONT, SCIOLTO, *and* BUONATESTE.

   PHYL. Though I esteem Theander at a rate,
As if I valu'd all his victories,
And all the civil honours he hath won,
By conqu'ring the mysterious sense of books.
And add to this our loves begotten in
Our infancy, our noble friendship of
A better growth.   Yet Eurithea is
My sister, and the chiefest of my blood,
One whose virtue and perfection I'm so well
Experienc'd in, that neither can admit
My least suspicion or my fear ; th' are both abus'd.
But if my friend will grow too credulous,
I'll learn to use him as my enemy.
   SCIO. For my part, sir, I want instructions what
I should believe, and words to utter half
The dismal wonders I have heard : but sure
He doth proceed on grounds so relative,
As would persuade the wisest to a jealousy.
Yet on my soul she's clear.
   PHYL. Then there is treachery.  Let it be found !
If he permit my sister's honour bleed,

Without full arguments to warrant his
Suspect, ere yet the circuit of one moon
Be added to my age, I'll give
The people of this province cause to curse
Their prince's negligence.
   BUO. Your grace hath found I've been a little
      prosperous
Of late in your affair, trust me with this.
Be pleas'd to tarry here a while conceal'd,
You both shall find I will untie these magic knots,
And straight restore the innocent to such a light,
As shall have force to make their virtue shine.
   SCIO. My man o'medicines, if thou perform this,
Although old Æsculape had but a cock
Allow'd him for a cure, thou every meal
Shalt have a brace of fat cram'd capons at
Thy board, each of 'em larger than a dragon.

*Enter* THEANDER, *like a pilgrim.*

   THE. I seek thee, Phylomont, and, like a friend
Whose kindness grows upon him near his death,
I come to give thee legacies. The arms I won
At Capua are thine, and those Sardinian horse
I chose for our last war ; my glories are
Eclips'd, and I will go where there's no need
Of policy or strength, unto some dark
And empty wilderness, where fame can put
Her trumpet to no use, where all my danger is
Leanness and cold, but I shall live secure
From ladies that are fair and false.
   PHYL. Were I so cruel to believe the cause
Of thy calamity a truth, I would
Invest me too in such a homely weed,
And wander with thee where the sun,
In's universal journey, should not find
Us out. But thou art govern'd by mistakes.
Some treacherous practice hath subdu'd thy sense ;

For both our safeties think my sister such
As I pronounce of thine.   I must not find
Her in thy doubts.
　　THE.　　　　　　　　O Phylomont! I have
Not blood enough to use in blushes, should
I name her crime.
　　PHYL. Thy passions I forgive again! but mark
How much they are misled.   This learned gentle-
　　　man
Will free disguised truth out of that labyrinth
And dismal shade where she resides, then give
An instant remedy to all our griefs.
　　BUON. But you must promise patience, sir, and
　　　when
I give the sign, retire to th' arras
All silent and conceal'd.
　　THE. Such blessings as you promise seldom come
From heaven; I'm sure no human help can do't.

　　*Enter* FREDELINE, *creeping in, as he were sick.*

　　BUON. Away, listen and hide yourselves! There
　　　stands
The conjurer that I must first out-charm.
　　FRED. How am I planet-struck, how suddenly
Depriv'd of strength.   I breathe faintly and short;
Like wearied coursers when the race is done:
My sinews shrink, and bear me crooked when
I move, as I had been their load a hundred years.
Palsies and agues have possess'd my joints,
I quiver like a naked Russian in the snow;
And my dim eyes begin to glare and wink,
Like to a long neglected lamp, whose oil
Is wasted to a drop.
　　BUON. The generous Fredeline!   How do you
　　　sir?
　　FRED. Villain, th'ast poisoned me! the minerals
　　　which

Thou gav'st me in thy fume were full of death!
   Buon. I must confess they were not very whole-
     some.           [*Fredeline offers to draw.*
Nay, be not angry, sir! You draw a sword,
You draw a knitting-needle or a rush.
'Las, poor weak gentleman! but if you could,
Here at my old friend Archimedes' ward
I'ld stand! We mathematic monsieurs have
Our lines revers'd, and our stoccatoes too.
   Fred. This scorn will bring a worse disease into
My gall, than what's already in my blood.
   Buon. You have been bred in cities, courts, and
     camps,
And weighed the hearts and brains of men in your
Own scales; would fool the wisest conclave too,
Though they went fasting to consult; so wise,
You'ld make the devil oversee at cards,
And then persuade him's horns hung in his light.
You had your plots, but we dull bookmen have
Our counterplots.
   Fred.           Sir, 'tis confess'd too late.
   Buon. It was not in the power of art to make
That fume I promis'd you, else you had had
It, sir, but this will serve your turn as well:
'Twill end your lust, and give it ease at once.
   Fred. Have pity on my languishment and pains.
   Buon. Y'are now within the arms of death;
     but I've
A cordial that may prove restorative,
If you will justly answer what I ask.
   Fred. All, sir, and not disguise an article.
   Buon. How did you raise this jealousy in the
Offended Duke? I've heard he found two at
His lady's chamber door, where they discours'd
Such language as inferr'd Eurithea false.
   Fred. Sir, they were planted there by me, and
     what

They said was counterfeit, such as I then
Appointed them to speak.
    THE. O damn'd infernal slave !
    PHYL. I held him for a sober saint.
    SCIO. Contain yourself, my lord : you shall hear
      more.
    BUON. Where have you hid those pious instru-
      ments ?
    FRED. 'Twas Castraganio, and his sister Ama-
    dine ;
Th' are lock'd i'th' garret near the turret leads !
    THE. Give way to my revenge, that I may kill
Him with my foot! spurn out his monstrous soul—
    PHYL. Theander, hold ! your anger was not won
To stoop so low.
    THE. Your counsel's timely, sir.
I give you thanks. Sciolto bear him from
My sight : let him and's cursed instruments
Be safely kept.
    SCIO. Do you grin now ? A pox o' your mild
      looks.
You took a precious care o' th' Duke's posterity ?
    FRED. I'm an unfortunate Platonic gentleman.
    BUON. Keep him for justice, sir. The physic
      which
He took will quickly cease its violence.
                [*Exeunt Sciolt., Fred.*

*Enter* ARIOLA, EURITHEA.

    ARIO. Where is Theander, that hath vex'd the
      best
And gentlest lady in the world to such
Astonishment, that she is drown'd in tears ?
    THE. Kind Eurithea, pardon me ! thy fate
Decreed, that thou, who hast so long preserv'd
My life, shouldst by thy mercy now have privilege
To give it too.

EU.  Restore me to your love, my Lord, and then
Your bounty is so great, that all I can bestow
Will be declin'd, and not seem worthy of
Your thanks.
   THE.  Things are reveal'd, thou'lt hear of horrid
      miracles;
But sure, henceforth I shall not dare to trust
My heart within mine own inconstant breast ;
It must be lodg'd in thine.
   EU.  I shall be tender how I give it cause
Of a remove, 'less mine go with it too.
   PHYL.  Ariola, my philosopher says
His lectures pierc'd quite through your tender ears.
   ARIOL.  Well, sir, y'had best to take me whilst
My new religion is i'th' fit.   He has
A mighty reason, and a fluent tongue.

*Enter* SCIOLTO *and* GRIDONELL.

   PHYL.  To th' chapel then ! my business will lie
      there.
   SCIO.  The villain is imprison'd, sir, and his
Confederates acknowledge all that he
Reveal'd for an unhappy truth.
   THE.  My Eurithea must become their judge,
And my provincial laws shall sleep awhile.
   EU.  That will but hearten others to do wrong.
For mine will be an easy doom.
   SCIO.  Pray, sir, be known to my philosopher.
   THE.  I must embrace him for my friend.
   SCIO.  Well, he hath done strange feats.   You
      took a powder,
And my son too ; there was no harm intended.
You shall hear all within, perhaps find cause
To swaddle my old hide.
   GRID.                    By this hand, sir,
Were you not my father, I would begin.
I thought y'had powder'd me ; 'tis well the heat

Is past.   Lord, how I dream't of taffity
Kirtles, French gowns, and fine Italian tires,
That hung, methought, by my bed side.
　　SCIO.  Son, I'll requite thee with a wife.   My
　　　　friend
Hath so behav'd himself for th' credit of
The arts, that I'll be at charge of a primmer,
And a fescue * till thou learn to read.
　　PHYL.  Theander, my advice is good.  When you
Possess your lady's bed yourself, y'are the
Best sentinel to hinder th' onslaught of the enemy,
Whining and puling love is fit for eunuchs,
And for old revolted nuns.
　　THE.　　　　　I shall incline in time.
　　PHYL.  And when I'm married, sir, I straight
　　　　command
You hear this brisk philosopher one hour
Upon that theme.
　　BUON.  Wise nature is my mistress, sir.  I shall
Demean my self most stoutly in her cause.
　　THE.  Then surely I must yield : Come, Phylomont!
Your nuptial rites perform'd let's all enjoy
The treasure of his knowledge, and his tongue.
Yet we, my Eurithea, have a while
So rul'd each other with nice fears, that none
Hereafter will in civil kindness doubt

　　　　There are Platonic-lovers, though but few
　　　　The sect conceal'd, and still imagin'd new.
　　　　　　　　　　　　　　　　[*Exeunt omnes.*

* "Primmer" and "Fescue": "Primer" or Child's First Book;
" Fescue," a small wire by which teachers point out the letters.
　　" Teach them how manly passions ought to move ;
　　　　For such as cannot think can never love ;
　　　　And since they needs will judge the poet's art,
　　　　Point them with *fescues* to each shining part."
　　　　　　　　　　　　　　　　*Dryden.*

# EPILOGUE.

Unto the masculine I can afford,
By strict commission, scarce one courteous word:
Our author hath so little cause to boast
His hopes from you, that he esteems them lost,
Since not these two long hours amongst you all
He can find one will prove Platonical.
But these soft ladies, in whose gentle eyes
The richest blessings of his fortune lies,
With such obsequious homage he doth greet,
As he would lay his laurel at your feet :
For you, he knows, will think his doctrine good,
Though't recreate the mind,* and not the blood.


    * " will think that doctrine good,
Which entertains the mind," &c.—*Folio*.

# THE WITS.

THE WITS.

*The Witts: a Comedie. Presented at the Private House in Blacke Fryers, by his Majesties Servants. The Authour William D'Avenant, Servant to her Majestie. London: printed for Richard Meighen, next to the Middle Temple, in Fleet Street. 1636, 4to.*

*Reprinted in Malone's Edition of Dodsley's Old Plays, 1780; in John Payne Collier's Edition of the same, 1825; and in Sir Walter Scott's Ancient Drama, 1810.*

*The Wits, London, Printed for Gabriel Bedel, and T. Collins, and are to be sold at their shop in the Middle Templegate in Fleet Street, 1665, 12mo. Printed with the Platonick Lover.*

*The Wits—Works of Sir William D'Avenant. London, 1673. Folio.*

THE comedy of "The Wits" was licensed by Sir Henry Herbert upon the 19th January 1633-4, and was performed at "the private house in Blacke Fryers, by his Majesty's servants, in 1636." It was revived after the Restoration, admired for its smartness, and continued to be performed at intervals for many years.

Editors sometimes attribute a higher degree of excellence to those authors whose works they conceive should be regarded with more general favour than former readers have accorded, and it is not unlikely that many may dissent from the opinion now expressed, that "The Wits" of D'avenant is the most perfect comedy as regards plot, character, and language that appeared during the latter portion of the reign of Charles I. or the earlier part of that of his son. A footnote in the reprints of Dodsley's Old Plays says that "Sir William D'avenant *seems* to have borrowed the hint of the plot from Beaumont and Fletcher's Wit at Several Weapons." This statement is not warranted in any one particular, as the two dramas differ in every respect. There is no resemblance whatever between the leading characters in Beaumont and Fletcher's play, Sir Perfidious Oldcraft and Sir Gregory Fop, and the elder Pallatine and his friend Sir Morglay Thwack in that of D'avenant, as is asserted by the "Biographia Dramatica," an assumption borrowed from Langbaine's* casual remarks, that "*possibly* the two knights were the models" from which Pallatine and his friend were taken. The only character at that date bearing affinity to Sir Perfidious is Sir Giles Overreach in Massinger's "New Way to Pay Old Debts;" but there is this difference—Sir Giles is a splendid villain, whereas the other is a low grovelling rascal, who condescends to the most debasing acts to raise himself in the world. It is not impossible that Macklin may have

* Oxford 1691, p. 216.

had remembrance of the account given by Sir Perfidious to his son, when, in his " Man of the World," he causes Sir Pertinax Macsycophant to disclose to Egerton the means by which he had attained wealth and position. With all his " booing," the Scotch baronet is a gentleman in comparison with the English knight. Sir Gregory Fop is a mere fool, and it is an insult to compare him to the humorous old knight, Sir Morglay Thwack. The elder Pallatine, who was young and " richly landed," left his estate to try his fortunes as a wit in London. His character, his brother's, Sir Morglay's, Lady Ample's, and Lucy's are admirably depicted, and the interest never flags throughout the entire piece. The scenes in which Mistress Queasy, Snore the Constable, and his wife come on the stage are remarkably droll, and must have told well with the audience.

Little is known as to dramatic representations during the reign of Charles I., so that there is no notice of the original representation of " The Wits," or of its reception. We learn from Pepys that, upon 15th August 1661, " he walked to the wardrobe and dined with my lady. . . . I find my Lord Hinchingbroke better and better, and the worst past. Thence to the Opera, which begins again to-day with ' The Wits,' never acted yet with scenes, and the King, and Duke, and Duchesse were there (who dined to-day with Sir H. Finch, reader at the Temple, in great state), and indeed it is a most excellent play and admirable scenes."

So charmed was the Secretary of the Admiralty, that on the 17th of the same month he again mentions having visited " the opera, and saw ' The Wits,' which I like exceedingly. The Queen of Bohemia was here brought by my Lord Craven. Troubled in mind that I cannot bring myself to mind my business, but to be so much in love of plays." Delighted with the drama himself, Pepys resolved that his wife should participate in his pleasure, and a few days afterwards he " took her to the opera, and showed her ' The Wits,' which I had seen already twice, and was most highly pleased with it."*

Lord Craven was William the first Earl, a Privy Councillor, and Colonel of the Coldstream Guards. He

* Pepys' Diary, 3d edition, 1848, p. 262-3-5.

was supposed to be married to the Queen of Bohemia. He died 1697, aged 88, and the Queen of Bohemia 12th February 1661-2.

In 1667 "The Wits," it would seem, had been enlarged and corrected, for Pepys has this entry 18th April: " With my wife to the Duke of York's house, and there saw ' The Wits,' a play I formerly loved, and is now corrected and enlarged ; but, though I liked the acting, yet I like not much in the play now. The Duke of York and W. Coventry gone to Portsmouth makes me thus go to plays."

The last entry by Pepys in his Diary in relation to " The Wits " is on the 18th January 1668-9, when he records, that having given a hasty invitation to dinner, which had been accepted by Mr. Sydney Montague and Mr., afterwards Sir Henry Sheres, to whom he had just paid one hundred pounds " for his pains in drawing the plan of Tangier fortifications, after 'a handsome' sudden dinner, and all well pleased, the three gentlemen and Mrs. Pepys went to the Duke of York's play - house, and there saw ' The Wits,' a medley of things, but some similes good, though ill mixed."

The present text is based upon the original small quarto of 1636, with a few notes of emendations in the folio edition of 1673. Geneste, in his account of the English stage, mentions the names of the principal performers. The elder Pallatine was assigned to Betterton ; his brother to Harris ;* Sir Morglay Thwack, Underhill ; and Lady Ample was represented by Mrs. Davenport.† It is said " that this comedy was well acted in the other parts, and performed eight days successively." It is a pity that the names of the representatives of Lucy, Engine, Snore and his wife, and the worthy Mrs. Queasy were not also preserved. The same writer is mistaken in asserting that at the revival in 1661 it was performed

---

* Joseph Harris was an excellent performer and agreeable companion. See Pepys, vol. iv., page 316. In the Pepysian Library, Cambridge, there is a mezzotinto of him as Cardinal Wolsey. He was bred a seal-cutter.

† She was taken off the stage by the Earl of Oxford, but did not remain with him more than a year.

with alterations, and that "the dialogue is considerably improved and two short scenes added."

Pepys was present *thrice* in the year 1661, when it was revived, and says nothing then about alterations and additions, but in 1667 and 1668, when he again witnessed its performance, he complains of its corrections and alterations, and, lastly, calls it a medley of things, with some similes good, but ill mixed. These alterations and the additional scenes are in the folio edition of D'avenant, and, as it is believed that they were not the work of his hands, have not been embodied in the play itself; but, the scenes more especially, are separately given at the end, in illustration of the (improved?) taste of the times.

"The Wits" is stated to have been reproduced at the Theatre, Lincoln's Inn Fields, upon the 19th August 1726, but with what success is not mentioned.

Endymion Porter, the friend of D'avenant, to whom the Comedy of the Wits is dedicated, was born in the year 1587, as appears from a medal executed by Varin, dated in 1635, whereon he is stated "æt. 48."

Porter by his marriage with the Honourable Olivia Butler, one of the daughters of John Lord Butler of Bromfield, whose wife Elizabeth was a sister of George Villiers, Duke of Buckingham, by his influence obtained not only the appointment of a gentleman of the bed-chamber to James I. and his son, but was, with Sir Francis Cottington, selected as companion of Charles and the Duke, to accompany them in the well-known romantic Spanish journey, by means of which it was imagined that his royal highness would be rewarded with the hand of the Infanta. This appointment was a prudent one, for as Porter had been bred at Madrid he had no doubt acquired such a knowledge of Philip of Spain and his courtiers, as might materially assist the Prince and Buckingham in dealing with the monarch and his ministers.

Endymion Porter was an amiable as well as an accomplished gentleman. He was a great patron of literature, and, as one of the personal friends of D'avenant, addressed him in verses of no inconsiderable merit, in praise of his poem of Madagascar. On the back of the title there is this inscription :

If<br>
These poems live<br>
May<br>
Their memories<br>
By whom<br>
They were cherished,<br>
Endim. Porter<br>
H. Jermyn,*<br>
Live with them.

Amongst the miscellaneous poems of the Laureate are several addressed to Porter, from one of which we learn he had been so seriously ill that his recovery was for some time doubtful. There is an address "for the Lady Olivia † Porter; a present upon a new year's day," which commences thus—

> Goe ! hunt the whiter Ermine, and present
> The wealthy skin as this days tribute sent
> To my Endymion's love ; though she be fair,
> More gently smooth, more soft than Ermine are.
> Goe ! climb that rock, and when thou there hast found
> A star, contracted in a diamond,
> Give it Endymion's love ; whose glorious eyes
> Darken the starry jewels of the skies, &c., &c.

The remaining lines, like those that precede them, are of a similar inflated character, but they show the great intimacy subsisting between the poet and his patron.

Amongst the miscellaneous poems in the folio volume, will be found one addressed to Porter on the subject of the present Comedy, which, as a suitable accompaniment, may not inappropriately be reprinted here :

To Endimion Porter when my Comedy called the Wits<br>
was presented at Black-Fryers.‡

> Hear, how for want of others grief, I mourn
> My sad decay, and weep at mine own urne !

---

* Subsequently Lord Jermyn, and, after the Restoration, Earl of St Albans, K.G.

† Banks, in his Dormant Baronage, calls Porter's wife "Olivera," vol. III. p. 119. She had five sisters, four of whom married noblemen, a circumstance indicating the desire of those about the court to be connected with the all powerful Villiers.

‡ Davenant's Works 1673, p. 235.

H

The hours that ne'er want wings, when they should fly
To hasten death, or lead on destinie,
Have now fulfilled the time, when I must come
Chain'd to the muse's barre, to take my doom ;
When ev'ry term some timrous poet stands,
Condemn'd by whispers, ere repriev'd by hands.
I that am told conspiracies are laid
To have my muse, her arts, and life betray'd,
Hope for no easie judge, though thou wert there
T' appease, and make their judgments less severe.
In this black day, like men from thunder's rage ;
Or drowning showers, I hasten from the stage ;
And with myself, some spirit, had within
Those distant wandring winds, that yet have been
Unknown to th' compass, or the pilot's skill :
Or some loose plummit sunk so low until
I touch where roots of rocks deep bury'd be ;
There mourn beneath the leafeless coral tree
But I am grown too tame, what need I fear,
Whilst not to passion, but thy reason clear ?
Should I perceive, thy knowledge were subdu'd
T' unkind consent with the harsh multitude
Then I had cause to weep, and at thy gate
(Deny'd to enter) stand disconsolate,
Amaz'd and lost to mine own eyes ; there I
Scarce griev'd for by myself, would wink and die.
Olivia then, may on thy pity call
To bury me, and give me funeral.

During the civil wars Porter adhered steadily to the
cause of the king and was so obnoxious to the members
of the commonweal, that one of the conditions in 1642,
insisted on by Parliament, was his exclusion from about
his majesty's own person and the queen's, and from both
their courts. With him were named Mr William Murray,
of the king's bed-chamber, Mr John Winter, and Mr
William Crofts, afterwards Lord Crofts, " being all
persons of evil fame, and disaffection to the public peace,
and prosperity of the kingdom, and instruments of
jealousy and discontent, between the king and the
parliament."*

This notice respecting Porter occurs in Wood iii. 1.

" Virescit Vulnere Virtus. England's Wound and
Cure," printed 1628, [Bodl. 4to, L. 71, Art.] Which
being by many persons of known worth esteem'd an excellent piece, was by the author dedicated to that great

* Clarendon, vol. II. p. 167. Oxford 1826.

patron of all ingenious men, especially of poets, Endimion Porter, Esq., whose native place (Aston under Hill, commonly called Hanging Aston, near to Campden in Gloucestershire), tho' obscure, yet he was a great man and beloved by two kings, James I., for his admirable wit, and Charles I. (to whom as to his father, he was a servant), for his general learning, brave stile, sweet temper, great experience, travels, and modern languages."

During the civil war he was extremely active in secret services for the king, and so obnoxious to the parliament on that account, that he was one of those always excepted from indemnity, and his friends were compelled to pay £1500 composition for him.

Through his exertions and interest Mytens obtained the office of painter in ordinary (or as the warrant calls it, " picture drawer "), to the king.

Though there is no engraved portrait of him (for that which bears his name is an evident forgery, see Granger, ii. 284), yet Vandyke painted an excellent picture of him, with his lady and three sons.

He died at the foreign court of his royal master, Charles the Second, before the Restoration.

## MR. WILLIAM D'AVENANT'S PLAY.

IT hath been said of old, that plays are feasts,
Poets the cooks, and the spectators guests,
The actors waiters: from this simile
Some have deriv'd an unsafe liberty,
To use their judgments as their tastes ; which choose,
Without controul, this dish, and that refuse.
But Wit allows not this large privilege ;
Either you must confess, or feel its edge :
Nor shall you make a current inference,
If you transfer your reason to your sense.
Things are distinct, and must the same appear
To every piercing eye, or well-tun'd ear.
Though sweets with your's, sharps best with my taste
    meet,
Both must agree this meat's or sharp or sweet :
But if I scent a stench or a perfume,
Whilst you smell nought at all, I may presume
You have that sense imperfect : so you may
Affect a merry, sad, or humourous play.
If, though the kind distaste or please, the good
And bad be by your judgment understood :
But if, as in this play, where with delight
I feast my epicurean appetite
With relishes so curious, as dispense
The utmost pleasure to the ravish'd sense,
You should profess that you can nothing meet
That hits your taste either with sharp or sweet,
But cry out, 'Tis insipid ; your bold tongue
May do it's master, not the author, wrong ;
For men of better palate will, by it,
Take the just elevation of your wit.

T. CAREW.

Bless me, you kinder stars! how are we throng'd!
Alas! whom hath our long-sick Poet wrong'd,
That he should meet together, in one day,
A session, and a faction at his play?
To judge, and to condemn: for't cannot be,
Amongst so many here, all should agree. *
Then 'tis to such vast expectation rais'd,
As it were to be wonder'd at, not prais'd:
And this, good faith, Sir Poet (if I've read
Customs, or men) strikes you and your Muse dead.
Conceive now too, how much, how oft each ear
Hath surfeited, in this our hemisphere,
With various, pure, eternal wit; add then,
My fine young comic sir, y' are kill'd again.†
But 'bove the mischief of these fears, a sort
Of cruel spies, we hear, intend a sport
Among themselves; our mirth must not at all
Tickle, or stir their lungs, but shake their gall.
So this, join'd with the rest, makes me again
To say, you and your lady Muse within
Will have but a sad doom; and your trim brow,
Which long'd for wreaths, you must wear naked now;
'Less some resolve, out of a courteous pride,‡

* Your expectation, too, you so much raise,
   As if you came to wonder, not to praise,
   And this Sir-Poet, if I ere have read
   Customs or men, &c.—Folio ed. of *D'avenant's Poems*.
† Young comic sir, you must be killed again,
   But, to out-do these miseries a sort.—*Ib.*
‡ Unless some here, out of a courteous pride,
   Resolve to praise what others shall decide,
   So they will have their humour too: and we,
   More out of dullness than civility,

To like and praise what others shall deride :
So they've their humour too ; and we, in spite
Of our dull brains, will think each side i' th' right.
Such is your pleasant judgments upon plays,
Like parallels that run straight, though sev'ral ways.

Grow highly pleased with our success to-night,
By thinking both perhaps are in the right.
　　　　　Folio ed. of *D'arenant's Poems.*

TO

## THE CHIEFLY BELOV'D

OF ALL THAT ARE INGENIOUS AND NOBLE,

# ENDYMION PORTER,

OF HIS MAJESTY'S BEDCHAMBER.

---

SIR,

THOUGH you covet not acknowledgements, receive what belongs to you by a double title: your goodness hath preserv'd life in the Author; then rescu'd his work from a cruel faction; which nothing but the forces of your reason, and your reputation, could subdue. If it become your pleasure now, as when it had the advantage of presentation on the stage, I shall be taught to boast some merit in myself; but with this inference, you still, as in that doubtful day of my trial, endeavour to make shew of so much justice, as may countenance the love you bear to

Your most oblig'd and thankful

humble servant,

WILLIAM D'AVENANT.

## DRAMATIS PERSONÆ.

PALLATINE *the Elder, richly landed, and a wit.*
PALLATINE *the Younger,* { *a wit too, but lives on his*
                          *exhibition in Town.*
Sir MORGLAY THWACK, *a humorous rich old knight.*
Sir TYRANT THRIFT, *guardian to the Lady Ample.*
MEAGER, *a soldier newly come from Holland.*
PERT, *his comrade.*
ENGINE, *steward to Sir Tyrant Thrift.*
SNORE, *a constable.*


The Lady AMPLE. { *an Inheritrix, and Ward to Sir*
                  *Tyrant Thrift.*
LUCY, *Mistress to the younger Pallatine.*
GINET, *women to the Lady Ample.*
Mistress SNORE, *wife to the constable.*
Mistress QUEASY, *her neighbour.*
WATCHMEN, *&c.*


*The Scene:* LONDON.

# THE WITS.

## ACT I. SCENE I.

*Enter* YOUNG PALLATINE, MEAGER, PERT.

Y. PAL. Welcome o' shore, Meager! Give me thy
    hand :
'Tis a true one, and will no more forsake
A bond, or bill, than a good sword ; a hand
That will shift for the body, till the laws
Provide for both.
    MEA. Old wine, and new cloathes, sir,
Make you wanton. D' you not see Pert, my
    comrade ?
    Y. PAL. Ambiguous Pert ! hast thou danc'd to
    the drum too ?
Could a taff'ta scarf, a long estridge wing,
A stiff iron doublet, and a brazil* pole,
Tempt thee from cambric sheets, fine active thighs,
From caudles where the precious amber+ swims ?
    PERT. Faith! we have been to kill, we know not
    whom,
Nor why : led on to break a commandment
With the consent of custom and the laws.
    MEA. Mine was a certain inclination, sir,
To do mischief where good men of the jury,
And a dull congregation of grey-beards
Might urge no tedious statute 'gainst my life.
    Y. PAL. Nothing but honour could seduce thee,
    Pert !
Honour ! which is the hope of the youthful,
And the old soldier's wealth, a jealousy

    * Dyed red.                   + See note at end of play.

To the noble, and myst'ry to the wise.
    PERT. It was, sir, no geographical fancy,
'Cause in our maps I lik'd this region here
More than that country lying there,—made me
Partial which to fight for.
    Y. PAL.                True, sage Pert.
What is't to thee, whether one Don Diego
A prince, or Hans van Holme, fritter-seller
Of Bombell, do conquer that parapet,
Redoubt, or town, which thou ne'er saw'st before ?
    PERT. Not a brass thimble to me ; but honour !—
    Y. PAL. Why, right ! else wherefore shouldst
        thou bleed for him,
Whose money, wine, nor wench, thou ne'er hast us'd ?
Or why destroy some poor root-eating soldier,
That never gave thee the lie, denied to pledge
Thy cockatrice's * health, ne'er spit upon
Thy dog, jeer'd thy spur-leather, or return'd
Thy tooth-pick ragged, which he borrowed whole ?
    PERT. Never, to my knowledge.
    MEA. Comrade ! 'tis time—
    Y. PAL. What, to unship your trunks at Billings-
        gate ?
Fierce Meager ! why such haste ? do not I know,
That a mouse yok'd to a peascod may draw,
With the frail cordage of one hair, your goods
About the world ?
    PERT. Why, we have linen, sir.
    Y. PAL. As much, sir, as will fill a tinder-box,
Or make a frog a shirt. I like not, friends,
This quiet, modest posture of your shoulders.
Why stir you not, as you were practising
To fence ? or do you hide your cattle, lest
The skipper make you pay their passage over ?
    PERT. Know, Pallatine, Truth is a naked lady,
She will shew all. Meager and I have not--

* A lewd woman.

Y. Pal. The treasure of Saint Mark's* I believe, sir;
Though you are as rich as cast serving-men,
Or bawds led thrice into captivity.

Pert. Thou hast a heart of the right stamp;
    I find
It is not comely in thine eyes, to see
Us sons of war walk by the pleasant vines
Of Gascony, as we believ'd the grapes
Forbidden fruit; sneak through a tavern with
Remorse, as we had read the Alcoran,
And made it our best faith.

Mea. And abstain flesh, as if our English beef
Were all reserv'd for sacrifice.

Pert. Whilst colon † keeps more noise
Than mariners at plays, or apple-wives
That wrangle for a sieve. ‡

* The treasure of Saint Mark's, was that secured in the mint at
Venice. Coriat, 1608, says: "I was in one higher roome of
this mint, where I saw fourteene marvailous strong chests
hooped with yron, and wrought full of great massy yron nailes,
in which is kept nothing but money, which consisteth of these
three mettals, gold, silver, and brasse. Two of these chests were
about some foure yardes high, and a yard and more thicke,
having seven locks upon them. Which chests are said to be
full of chiquineys. In the outward gallery, at the entrance of
the chamber, I told seventeene more of such iron chests, which
are likewise full of money. So that the number of all the money
chests, which I saw at the mint, is one and thirty. Also in two
chambers, at the Rialto, I saw two and forty more of such chests
full of coyne, the totall summe whereof is threescore and thirteene. So that it is thought, all the quantity of money con-
tained in these threescore and thirteene chests doth not amount
to so little as forty millions of duckats."—*Cradities*, p. 191.

† The greatest and widest of all the intestines, about eight or
nine hands' breadth long.—
        "Now, by your cruelty hard bound,
            I strain my guts, my colon wound."—*Swift*.

‡ A kind of basket used by market-gardeners. There are
sieves and half-sieves.
    See also Act 3.—
    "Remember thy first calling; thou sett'st up
    With a peck of damsons and a new sieve,
    When thou brok'st at Dowgate corner, 'cause the boys
    Flung down thy ware."

MEA. Contribute, come!
    Y. PAL. Stand there, close, on your lives! Here,
        in this house,
Lives a rich old hen, whose young egg, though not
Of her own laying, I have in the embers.
She may prove a morsel for a discreet mouth.
If the kind Fates have but the leisure to
Betray the old one.
    PERT. Pallatine, no plots upon generation : we
        two
Have fasted so long, that we cannot think
Of begetting any thing, unless, like cannibals,
We might eat our own issue.
    Y. PAL. I say, close! shrink in your morions;
        go!
    MEA. Why hidden thus? a soldier may appear—
    Y. PAL. Yes, in a suttler's hut on the pay-day.
But do you know the silence of this house,
The gravity and awe? Here dwells a lady,
That hath not seen a street, since good king Harry
Call'd her to a Masque : she is more devout
Than a weaver of Banbury, that hopes
T' entice Heaven by singing, to make him lord
Of twenty looms.*   I never saw her yet ;
And to arrive at my preferment first
In your sweet company, will, I take it,
Add but little to my hopes.   Retire! go!
    [*They step aside, whilst he calls between the hangings.*
    PERT. We shall obey ; but do not tempt us now
With sweetmeats for the nether palate! do not.—
    Y. PAL. What Lucy! Luce! now is the old
        beldam
Misleading her to a cushion, where she

---

* Banbury was chiefly inhabited by Puritans.  Ben Jonson
in his Comedy of Bartholomew Fair, introduces "Zeal-of-the
land-Busy," a Banbury elder, to whose other virtues he adds
that of inordinate gluttony, which inflamed the whole horde of
" Banbury Saints."

Must pray, and sigh, and fast, until her knees
Grow smaller than her knuckles.   Lucy ! Luce !
No hope ! she is undone ! she'll number o'er
As many orisons, as if she had
A bushel of beads to her rosary.
Lucy ! My April love ! my mistress, speak !—

*Enter* LUCY.

LUCY.  Pallatine, for Heaven's sake, keep in
    your voice ;
My cruel aunt will hear, and I am lost.
    Y. PAL.  What can she hear, when her old ears
    are stuff'd
With as much warm wax as will seal nine leases ?
What a pox does she list'ning upon earth ?
Is 't not time for her t' affect privacy,
To creep into a close dark vault, there gossip
With worms, and such small tame creatures as
    Heaven
Provided to accompany old people ?
    LUCY.  Still better'd unto worse ! but that my
    heart
Consents not to disfigure thee, thou would'st be torn
To pieces, numberless as sand, or as
The doubts of guilt or love in cowards are.
    Y. PAL.  How now, Luce ! from what strange
    coast this storm ! ha ?
    LUCY.  Thou dost out-drink the youth of Norway
    at
Their marriage feasts, out-swear a puny gamester
When his first misfortune rages out quarrel,
One that rides post, and is stopt by a cart :
Thy walking hours are later in the night
Than those which drawers, traitors, or constables
Themselves do keep ; for watchmen know thee
    better
Than their lanthorn.  And here's your surgeon's bill :

Your kind thrift, I thank you, hath sent it me
To pay, as if the poor exhibition
My aunt allows for aprons would maintain
You in serecloths.*——        [*Gives him a paper.*
   MEA. Can the daughters of Brabant
Talk thus when Younker-gheck† leads 'em to a
   stove ?
   PERT. I say, Meagre, there is a small parcel
Of man, that rebels more than all the rest
Of his body; and I shall need, if I
Stay here, no elixir of beef to exalt
Nature, though I were leaner than a groat.
   Y. PAL. This surgeon's a rogue, Luce ; a fellow,
Luce, that hath no more care of a gentleman's
Credit, than of the lint he hath twice us'd.
   LUCY. Well, sir, but what's that instrument he
   names ?
   Y. PAL. He writes down here for a tool of injec-
   tion,
Luce: a small water-engine, which I bought
For my tailor's child to squirt at 'prentices.
   LUCY. Ay, sir, he sins more against wit than
   Heaven,
That knows not how t' excuse what he hath done.
I shall be old at twenty, Pallatine,
My grief to see thy manners and thy mind,
Hath wrought so much upon my heart.

> * " She that is fayre, lustye, and yonge,
>     And can comon in termes wyth fyled tonge,
>     And wyll abyde whysperyno in the eare,
>     Thynke ye her tayle is not lyght of the seare ?"
>                 *Commune Secretary and Jalousye.*" N.D.
> † A young, lusty, foolish fellow—
> "See how the morning opes her golden gates,
>     And takes her farewell of the glorious sun :
>     How well resembles it the pride of youth,
>     Trimm'd like a *yonker* prancing to his love."—*Shakespeare.*
> " Why have you suffered me to be imprisoned,
>     And made the most notorious *geck* and gull
>     That ever invention played on !"—*Ib.*

Y. Pal. I'd as lieve keep our marriage supper
In a church-yard, and beget our children
In a coffin, as hear thee prophecy.
Luce, thou art drunk, Luce ; far gone in almond-
        milk : *
Kiss me !
    Pert. Now I dissolve like an eringo.
    Mea. He's ploughing o' the Indies ; good gold,
        appear !
    Y. Pal. I am a new man, Luce; thou shalt find me
In a Geneva band, that was reduc'd
From an old alderman's cuff ; no more hair left
Than will shackle a flea : this debosh'd† whinyard
I will reclaim to comely bow and arrows,
And shoot with haberdashers at Finsbury ;
And be thought the grandchild of Adam Bell.‡
And more, my Luce, hang at my velvet girdle

* The Latin *amigdolatum* is translated by *almond mylke* in MS. Bodl. 604, f. 43.—*Halliwell.*

" *Ryse of flessh.* Take ryse and waishe hem clene, and do hem in erthen pot with gode broth, and lat hem seeth wel. Afterward, take almannd mylkt, and do thereto, and color it with safroun and messe forth." Note, " Almannd mylke con-sisted of almonds ground, and mixed with milk, broth, or water." —*Warner's Antiquitates Culinariæ.*

Almonds are productive of a diametrically opposite effect to that suggested in the text, for " Dioscorides saith that the sweete almond helpeth the stomack if it be eaten new with the skinne, but it grieveth the head, and norisheth dimnes, and kindleth the seruice of Venus, and breedeth sleepe, and letteth dronkennesse."—*Batman on Bartholeme.*

Again : "The eating of six or eight bitter almonds fasting, is said to staye a man from drunkenness that day."—*Dodoneus.*

† The 4to and folio read *debash'd : debosh'd* has the same meaning as *debauch'd.* The word occurs in *The Wandering Jew*, 1640.

"The more I strive to love my husband, the more his *de-boish'd* courses begets my hate."

Again, in *Fennor's Compter's Commonwealth*, 1617, p. 27.

"—— for most commonly some knave or *deboisht* fellow lurch the fooles their sona," &c.

It is also used in our author's " Prince d'Amour."

‡ So late as 1753 targets were erected in Finsbury Fields, during the Easter and Whitsun holidays.

A book wrapped in a green dimity bag,
And squire thy untooth'd aunt to an exercise.*
   LUCY. Nothing but strict laws and age will tame
     you.
   Y. PAL. What money hast thou, Luce?
   LUCY. Ay, there's your business.
   Y. PAL. It is the business of the world. Injuries
Grow to get it; justice sits for the same end;
Men are not wise without it, for it makes
Wisdom known; and to be a fool, and poor,
Is next t' old aches and bad fame; 'tis worse
Than to have six new creditors, they each
Twelve children, and not bread enough to make
The landlord a toast, when he calls for ale
And rent. Think on that, and rob thy aunt's trunks
Ere she hath time to make an inventory.
   PERT. A cunning pioneer; he works to th' bottom.
   LUCY. Hast thou no taste of heav'n? wert thou
     begot
In a prison, and bred up in a galley?
   Y. PAL. Luce, I speak like one that hath seen
     the book
Of fate: I'm loath, for thy sake, to mount a coach
With two wheels, whilst the damsels of the shop
Cry out, a goodly straight chined gentleman!
He dies for robbing an attorney's cloak-bag
Of copper seals, foul night-caps, together
With his wife's bracelet of mill-testers.†
   LUCY. There, sir!　　　　　*[Flings him a purse.*
'Tis gold! my pendants, carcanets,‡ and rings:

---

* An act of divine worship. "Good Sir John,
  I'm in your debt for your last exercise;
  Come the next Sabbath, and I will content you."
                    *Shakespeare.*

† Mill-sixpences.—Milled coin was introduced into this country during the sixteenth century, "Fortie mark mill-sixpences." *Citie Match.* 1639.

‡ A necklace set with stones or strung with pearls. From the old French word *carcan*, whose diminutive was *carcanet.*

My christ'ning caudle-cup and spoons *
Are dissolved into that lump.   Nay, take all!
And, with it, as much anger as would make
Thy mother write thee illegitimate.
See me no more ! I will not stay to bless
My gift, lest I should teach my patience suffer
Till I convert it into sin.            [*Exit.*
   Y. PAL. Temptations will not thrive.   This
      baggage sleeps
Cross-legg'd, and the devil has no more power
O'er that charm, than dead men o'er their lewd heirs.
I must marry her, and spend my revenue
In cradles, pins, and soap : † that's th' end of all
That 'scape a deep river and a tall bough.
   MEA. Pallatine, how much ?
   PERT. Honourable Pall !
   Y. PAL. Gentlemen, you must accept, without
      gaging
Your corporal oaths, to repay in three days.
   PERT. Not we, Pall, in three jubilees ; fear not!
   Y. PAL. Nor shall you charge me with loud
      vehemence,
Thrice before company, to wait you in
My chamber such a night ; for then, a certain
Drover of the south comes to pay you money.
   MEA. On our new faiths!

* It was once the custom for the sponsors to offer as a
present to the child *apostle spoons ;* so-called, by reason of the
figures of the apostles being carved on the handles.  The more
wealthy or ostentatious gave the whole twelve ; others less so
contented themselves with the four Evangelists; or with presenting one spoon only, which figured any saint whom the child
was named after.

  These apostle spoons are still to be found in the cabinets of
the curious, and when they occur for sale, usually, if well preserved, realize large sums.

  † So in *The Lover's Progress*, A. 4.
                        " Must I now
   Have sour sauce after sweet meats ! and be driven
   To levy half a crown a-week, besides
   Clouts, *sope*, and candles, for my heir apparent."

PERT. On our allegiance, Pall!
Y. PAL. Go then—shift, and brush your skins
     well : d' you hear?
Meet me at the new play, fair and perfum'd :
There are strange words hang on the lips of rumour.
    PERT. Language of joy, dear Pall !
    Y. PAL. This day is come to town,
The minion of the womb, my lads,
My elder brother, and he moves like some
Assyrian prince ; his chariots measure leagues :
Witty as youthful poets in their wine ;
Bold as a centaur at a feast, and kind
As virgins that were ne'er beguil'd with love.
I seek him now ; meet and triumph !

    MEA.   }
            King Pall !——       *Exeunt omnes.*
    PERT. }


## SCENE II.

*Enter* Sir MORGLAY THWACK, ELDER PALLATINE,
   *new and richly cloathed, buttoning themselves.*

    ELD. PAL. Sir Morglay, come ! the hours have
     wings, and you
Are grown too old t' overtake them.   The town
Looks, methinks, as it would invite the country
To a feast.
    THWACK. At which sergeants and their yeomen
Must be no waiters, Pallatine, lest some
O' the guests pretend business. How dost like me?
    ELD. PAL. As one, old women shall no more avoid
Than they can warm furs or muskadel.
    THWACK. Pallatine, to have a volatile ache,
That removes oftner than the Tartars' camp,
To have a stitch that sucks a man awry,
'Till he shew crooked as a chesnut bough,
Or stand in the deform'd guard of a fencer ;
To have these hid in flesh, that has liv'd sinful
Fifty long years, yet husband so much strength

As could convey me hither, fourscore miles,
On a design of wit and glory, may
Be register'd for a strange northern act.
  ELD. PAL. I cannot boast those noble maladies
As yet; but time, dear knight, as I have heard,
May make man's knowledge bold upon himself.
We travel in the grand cause.   These smooth rags,
These jewels too, that seem to smile ere they
Betray, are certain silly snares, in which
You lady-wits, and their wise compeers-male,
May chance be caught.

Enter YOUNGER PALLATINE.

  Y. PAL. Your welcome, noble brother,
Must be hereafter spoke, for I have lost,
With glad haste to find you, much of my breath.
  ELD. PAL. Your joy becomes you; it hath
    courtship in't.
  Y. PAL. Sir Morglay Thwack! I did expect to
    see
The archer Cymbeline, or old king Lud
Advance his falchion here again, ere you,
'Mongst so much smoke, diseases, law, and noise.
  THWACK. What your town gets by me, let 'em
    lay up
For their orphans, and record in their annals.
I come to borrow where I'll never lend,
And buy what I'll never pay for.
  Y. PAL. Not your debts?
  THWACK. No, sir, though to a poor Brownist's
    widow;*

* The Brownists at this time seem to have been the constant
objects of popular satire.   The founder of the sect was Robert
Browne, a knight's son of Rutlandshire, and educated at Cambridge.   He was afterwards Pastor of Aychurch in North-
amptonshire, and spent great part of his life in several prisons,
to which he was committed for his steady adherence to the
opinions which he entertained.   He died in jail at Northampton,

Though she sigh all night, and have the next
    morning
Nothing to drink but her own tears.
  ELD. PAL. Nor shalt thou lend money to a sick
    friend.
Though the sad worm lie mortgag'd in his bed
For the hire of his sheets.
  Y. PAL. These are resolves
That give me newer wonder than your cloathes.
Why in such shining trim, like men that come
From rifled tents, loaden with victory?
  ELD. PAL. Yes, brother, or like eager heirs new
    dipp'd
In ink, that seal'd the day before in haste,
Lest parchment should grow dear.  Know, youth,
    we come
To be the business of all eyes, to take
The wall of our St. George on his feast-day.
  THWACK. Yes, and then embark at Dover, and do
The like to St. Dennis : all this, young sir,
Without charge too, I mean, to us ; we bring
A humorous odd philosophy to town,
That says, pay nothing.
  Y. PAL. Why, where have I liv'd?
  ELD. PAL. Brother, be calm, and edify ; but first
Receive a principle ; never hereafter,
From this warm breathing, till your last cold sigh,
Will I disburse for you again ; never!
  Y. PAL. Brother mine, if that be your argument
I deny the major.
  THWACK. Resist principles?
  ELD. PAL. Good faith, though you should send
    me more epistles
Than young factors in their first voyage write

in the year 1630, or, according to others, 1634, when he was
not less than 80 years of age.  See also the notes of Dr. Gray
and Mr. Steevens, to *Twelfth Night*, A. 3. S. 2.

Unto their short-hair'd friends ; than absent lovers
Pen near their marriage week, t' excuse the slow
Arrival of the license and the ring,
Not one clipp'd penny should depart my reach.
   Y. Pal. This doctrine will not pass ; How shall
     I live ?
   Eld. Pal. As we intend to do, by our good wits.
   Y. Pal. How, brother, how ?
   Eld. Pal. Truth is a pleasant knowledge ;
Yet you shall have her cheap.   Sir Morglay here,
My kind disciple, and myself, have leas'd
Out all our rents and lands for pious uses.
   Y. Pal. What, co-founders! give legacies ere
     death !
Pallatine the pious, and Saint Morglay !
Your names will sound but ill i'th' kalendar.
How long must this fierce raging zeal continue !
   Eld. Pal. 'Till we subsist here no more by our
     wit.
Then we'll renounce the town, and patiently
Vouchsafe to re-assume our mother earth,
Lead on our ploughs into their rugged walks
Again, grope our young heifers in the flank,
And swagger in the wool [that] we shall borrow
From our own flocks.
   Thwack. But, ere we go, we may,
From the vast treasure purchas'd by our wit,
Leave here some monument to speak our fame.
I have a strong mind to re-edify
The decays of Fleet-Ditch ; from whence I hear
The roaring vestals late are fled, through heat
Of persecution.
   Y. Pal. What a small star have I,
That never yet could light me to this way !
Live by our wits !
   Eld. Pal. So live, that usurers
Shall call their monies in, remove their bank

T' Ordinaries, Spring-garden, and Hyde-park,
Whilst their glad sons are left seven for their
    chance,
At hazard,* hundred,† and all made at sent ; ‡
Three motley cocks o' th' right Derby strain,
Together with a foal of Beggibrigge.§
    THWACK. Sir, 1 will match my Lord Mayor's
        horse, make jockies
Of his hench-boys, and run 'em through Cheapside.
    ELD. PAL. What beauties, girls of feature, govern
        now
I'th' town ? 'tis long since we did traffic here
In midnight whispers, when the dialect
Of love's loose wit is frighted into signs,
And secret laughter stifled into smiles ;

* *At hazard, sir : a hundred, and all made at sent.*] Folio
edit.

Hazard is a game played with dice. "Seven 's the *main*—
the caster throws five and that's his *chance*, and so hath five to
seven ; if the caster throw his own chance he wins all the money
was set for him, but if he throw seven which was the main, he
must pay as much money as is on the board ; if again, seven be
the main, and the caster throws eleven that is a *nick*, and sweeps
away all the money on the table ; but if he throws a *chance*, he
must count which will come first ; lastly, if seven be the main,
and the caster throws *ames-ace*, *deuce-ace*, or *twelve* he is out, but
if he throw from four to ten he hath a chance, though they are
accounted the worst chances on the dice, as seven is reputed
the best and easiest *main* to be flung." — *Cotton's Compleat
Gambler*, Lond., 12mo, 1710.

† Meaning, perhaps, Piquet, a game at Cards—"the usual
set is an hundred."—*Ib.*

‡ *at sent.*] Query *cent*, a game mentioned in *The Dumb
Knight*. A. 4. S. 1. vol. IV. and corruptedly written *saint*. S.

This game is frequently mentioned in ancient writers, and is
usually spelt *saunt*, probably the manner in which the French
word *cent* was then pronounced. In Gervas Markham's *Famous
Whore : or, Noble Curtezan*, 1609, 4to. Sign. D 4. it is called
*mount cent*.

    "Were it *mount cent*, primero, or at chesse
        I wan with most, and lost still with the lesse." C.

§ The fol. reads *peggibrige*. Perhaps the name of some
famous horse. S.

When nothing's loud, but the old nurse's cough.
Who keeps the game up, ha ! who mislead now ?
   THWACK. Not sir, that if we woo, we'll be at
      charge
For looks ; or if we marry, make a jointure.
Entail land on woman ! entail a back,
And so much else of man, as nature did
Provide for the first wife.
   ELD. PAL. I could keep thee,
Thy future pride, thy surfeits, and thy lust,
I mean in such a garb as may become
A Christian gentleman, with the sole tithe
Of tribute I shall now receive from ladies.
   THWACK. Your brother and myself have seal'd
To covenants. The female youth o' th' town are his;
But all from forty to fourscore mine own.
A widow, you'll say, is a wise, solemn, wary
Creature.  Though she hath liv'd to th' cunning
Of dispatch, clos'd up nine husbands' eyes,
And have the wealth of all their testaments,
In one month, sir,
I will waste her to her first wedding-smock,
Her single ring, bodkin, and velvet muff.
   Y. PAL. Your rents expos'd at home, for pious
      uses
Must expiate your behaviour here.  Tell me,
Is that the subtle plot you have on heaven ?
   THWACK. The worm of your worship's conscience
      would appear
As big as a conger ; but a good eye
May chance to find it slender as a grig.
   Y. PAL. Amazement knows no ease, but in
      demands.
Pray tell me, gentlemen, to all this vast
Designment which so strikes my ear, deduct
You nought from your revenue, nought that may,
Like fuel, feed the flame of your expense ?

ELD. PAL. Brother, not so much as will find a
    Jew
Bacon to his eggs : These gay tempting weeds,
These eastern stones of cunning foil, bespoke
'Gainst our arrival here, together with
A certain stock of crowns in either's purse,
Is all the charge that from our proper own
Begins or furthers the magnifique plot ;
And of these crowns not one must be usurp'd
By you.
    THWACK. No relief, but wit and good counsel !
    ELD. PAL. The stock my father left you, if your
    care
Had purpos'd so discreet a course, might well
Have set you up i' th' trade ; but we spend light,
Our coach is yet unwheel'd.   Sir Morglay, come,
Let's suit those Friesland horse with our own
    strain.
    Y. PAL. Why, gentlemen, will the design keep
    horses ?
    THWACK. May be sir, they shall live by their
    wits too.
    Y. PAL. Their masters are bad tutors else. Well,
How you'll work the ladies, and weak gentry here
By your fine gilded pills, a faith that is
Not old may guess without distrust.   But, sirs,
The city, take't on my experiment,
Will not be gull'd.
    THWACK.  Not gull'd ! they dare not be
So impudent : I say they shall be gull'd ;
And trust, and break, and pawn their charter too.
    Y. PAL.  Is it lawful, brother, for me to laugh,
That have no money ?
    ELD. PAL. Yes, sir, at yourself.
    Y. PAL. You that have tasted nature's kindness,
    arts, and men ;
Have shin'd in moving camps ; have seen

Courts in their solemn business, and vain pride ;
Convers'd so long i' th' town here, that you know
Each sign and pebble in the streets ; for you,
After a long retirement, to lease forth
Your wealthy, pleasant lands, to feed John Crump,
The cripple, widow Needy, and Abraham
Sloth, the beadsman of More-dale ! Then, forsooth,
Persuade yourselves to live here by your wits !

    THWACK. Where we ne'er cheated in our youth,
To cozen in our age we [now] resolve.

    ELD. PAL. Brother, I came
To be your wise example in the arts
That lead to thriving glory, and supreme life ;
Not through the humble ways wherein dull lords
Of lands, and sheep do walk ; men that depend
On the fantastic winds, on fleeting clouds,
On seasons more uncertain than themselves,
When they would hope or fear : But you are warm
In another's silk, and make your tame case
Virtue, call it content, and quietness !

    THWACK. Write letters to your brother, do ; and
Be foresworn in every long parenthesis,
For twenty pound sent you in butcher's silver.

    ELD. PAL. Rebukes are precious, cast them not
        away.         *[Exeunt Elder Pallatine, Thwack.*

    Y. PAL. Neither of these philosophers were born
To above five senses ; why then should they
Have hope to do things greater, and more new
I' th' world, than I ? This devil, plenty, thrusts
Strange boldness upon men. Well, you may laugh
With so much violence, till it consume
Your breath. Though sullen want, the enemy
Of wit, have sunk her low, if pregnant wine
Can raise her up, this day she shall be mine.* [*Exit.*

    * See alteration from folio edition at end of the play.

## ACT II.   SCENE I.

*Enter the* LADY AMPLE, ENGINE, GINET.

AMP. My guardian hors'd ! this evening say'st
    thou, Engine ?

ENG. It's an hour, madam, since he smelt the
    town.

AMP. Saw'st thou his slender empty leg in th'
    stirrup ?
His ivory box on his smooth ebon staff
New civetted, and tied to's gouty wrist ?
With his warp'd face close button'd in his hood,
That men may take him for a monk disguis'd,
And fled post from a pursuivant ?

ENG. Madam, beware, I pray ! lest th' age and
    cunning
He is master of, prepare you a revenge,
And such as your fine wit shall ne'er entreat
Your patience to digest.   To-morrow night
Th' extremest minute of your wardship is
Expir'd ; and we, magicians of the house,
Believe this hasty journey he hath ta'en
Is to provide a husband for your sheets.

AMP. And such a one as judgment and mine
    eyes
Must needs dislike, that 's composition may
Grow up to his own thrifty wish.

ENG.                                   Madam,
Your arrow was well aim'd : I call him master
But I am servant unto truth, and you.

AMP. He choose a husband, fit to guide and
    sway
My beauty's wealthy dowry, and my heart !
I'll make election to delight myself :
What composition strictest laws will give,
His guardianship may take from the rich bank

My father left, and not devour my land.

GIN. Your ladyship has liv'd six years beneath
His roof, therefore may guess the colour
Of his heart, and what his brains do weigh.
But Engine, madam, is your humble creature.

AMP. I have bounty, Engine;
And thou shalt largely taste it, when the next
Fair sun is set, for then my wardship ends.

[*Knocking within.*

That speaks command, or haste. Open the door!

*Enter* LUCY.

Lucy! weeping, my wench? melting thine eyes,
As they had trespass'd against light, and thou
Would'st give them darkness for punishment?

LUCY. Undone, madam, without all hope,
But what your pity will vouchsafe to minister.

AMP. Hast thou been struck by infamy, or com'st
A mourner from the funeral of love?

LUCY. I am the mourner, and the mourn'd;
Dead to myself, but left not rich enough
To buy a grave. My cruel aunt hath banish'd me
Her roof, expos'd me to the night, the winds,
And what the raging elements on wand'rers lay,
Left naked, as first infancy or truth.

GIN. I could ne'er endure that old, moist-ey'd
    lady;
Methought she pray'd too oft.

AMP. A mere receipt
To make her long-winded, which our devout
Physicans now prescribe to defer death.
But, Lucy, can she urge no cause for this
Strange wrath, that you would willingly conceal?

LUCY. Suspicions of my chastity, which Heaven
Must needs resist as false, though she accus'd me
Even in dream, where thoughts commit
By chance, not appetite.

AMP. What ground had her suspect?

LUCY. Young Pallatine, that woo'd my heart
Until he gather'd fondness where he planted love,
Was fall'n into such want, as eager blood
And youth could not endure, and keep the laws
Inviolate. I, to prevent my fear,
Sold all my jewels, and my trifling wealth,
Bestow'd them on him : and she thinks a more
Unholy consequence attends the gift.

AMP. This, Luce, is such apostacy in wit,
As nature must degrade herself in woman to
Forgive. Shall love put thee to charge? couldst
Thou permit thy lover to become thy pensioner?

ENG. Her sense will now be tickled till it ache.

AMP. Thy feature and thy wit are wealth enough
To keep thee high in all those vanities
That wild ambition, or expensive pride,
Perform in youth ; but thou invert'st their use :
Thy lover, like the foolish adamant,
The steel, thou fiercely dost allure, and draw
To spend thy virtue, not to get by it.

LUCY. This doctrine, madam, is but new to me.

AMP. How have I liv'd, think'st thou? E'en by
     my wits.
My guardian's contribution gave us gowns ;
But cut from th' curtains of a carrier's bed :
Jewels were wore, but such as potters' wives
Bake in the furnace for their daughters' wrists :
My woman's smocks so coarse, as they were spun
O'th' tackling of a ship.

GIN. A coat of mail,
Quilted with wire, was soft sarsnet to 'em.

AMP. Our diet scarce so much as is prescrib'd
To mortify : two eggs of emmets, poach'd,
A single bird, no bigger than a bee,
Made up a feast.

GIN. He had starv'd me, but that

The green-sickness took away my stomach.

   AMP. Thy disease, Ginet, made thee in love with
     mortar,
And thou eat'st him up two foot of an old wall.

   ENG. A privilege my master only gave
Unto her teeth, none else o' th' house durst do't.

   AMP. When, Lucy, I perceiv'd this straiten'd life,
Nature, my steward, I did call t' account,
And took from her exchequer so much wit
As has maintained me since. I led my fine
Trim-bearded males in a small subtle string
Of my soft hair; made 'em to offer up
And bow, and laugh'd at the idolatry.

   GIN. A jewel for a kiss, and that half ravish'd.

   LUCY. I feel I am inclin'd t' endeavour in
A calling : madam, I'd be glad to live.

   AMP. Know, Luce, this is no hospital for fools !
My bed is yours, but on condition, Luce,
That you redeem the credit of your sex ;
That you begin to tempt, and when the snare
Hath caught the fowl, you plume* him till you get
More feathers than you lost to Pallatine.

   LUCY. I shall not waste my hours in winding silk,
Or shelling peascods with your ladyship.

   AMP. Frosts on my heart ! what, give unto a
     suitor !
Know, I would fain behold that silly monarch,
Bearded man, that durst woo me with half
So impudent a hope.

   ENG. Madam, you are
Not far from the possession of your wish.
There is no language heard, no business now
In town, but what proclaims th' arrival here,
This morn, of th' elder Pallatine, brother
To him you nam'd, and with him such an old

* Latham says, it "is when a hawk ceaseth a fowle, and
pulleth the feathers from the body."

Imperial buskin knight as th' isle ne'er saw.

AMP. What's their design?

ENG. They will immure themselves
With diamonds, with all refulgent stones
That merit price: ask 'em, who pays? why, ladies.
They'll feast with rich Provençal wines; who
　　pays?
Ladies.　They'll shine in various habit, like
Eternal bridegrooms of the day; ask 'em
Who pays?　Ladies.　Lie with those ladies too,
And pay 'em but with issue male, that shall
Inherit nothing but their wit, and do
The like to ladies, when they grow to age.

LUCY. My ears received a taste of them before.

AMP. Engine, how shall we see them?
Bless me, Engine, with thy kind voice.

ENG. Though miracles are ceas'd,
This, madam, 's in the power of thought and time.

AMP. I would kiss thee, Engine, but for an odd
Nice humour in my lips; they blister at
Inferior breath.　This ring, and all my hopes
Are thine : dear Engine, now project, and live.

GIN. I'd lose my wedding to behold these
　　Dagonets.*

AMP. My guardian's out o' town.　Let us triumph
Like Cæsars, till to-morrow night; thou know'st
I'm then no more o' th' family.　I would,
Like a departing lamp, before I leave
You in the dark, spread in a glorious blaze.

ENG. Madam, command the keys, the house, and
　　me.

* Sir Dagonet was the Squire of King Arthur, in the old
romance of *Morte D' Arthur.*　See the notes of Mr Theobald, Dr
Johnson, Mr Warton, and Mr Steevens on *The Second Part of
King Henry IV.*, A. 3, S. 2.

" Dagon " has been used by Chaucer and others in the sense
of " a slip or piece of blanket."—Hence, " Dagonet " may have
been in use to signify " an adventurer, clothed in rug."

AMP. Spoke like the bold Cophetua's* son.
Let us contrive within to tempt 'em hither :
Follow, my Luce, restore thyself to fame.
               *[Exeunt Engine, Ample, Ginet.*
   [*Young Pallatine beckons Lucy from between the*
           *hangings, as she is going.*
Y. PAL. Luce ! Luce !
LUCY. Death on my eyes ! how came you hither ?
Y. PAL. I'm, Luce, a kind of peremptory fly,
Shift houses still to follow the sun-beams :
I must needs play in the flames of thy beauty.
   LUCY. Y' have us'd me with a Christian care;
     have you not ?
   Y. PAL. Come, I know all. I have been at thy
Aunt's house, and there committed more disorder
Than a storm in a ship, or a cannon bullet
Shot through a kitchen among shelves of pewter.
   LUCY. This madness is not true, I hope.
   Y. PAL. Yes, faith ; witness a shower of malm-
     sey lees, dropt
From thy aunt's own urinal on this new morion †
   LUCY. Why, you have seen her then ?
   Y. PAL. Yes, and she looks like the old slut of
     Babylon
Thou hast read of. I told her she must die,
And her belov'd velvet hood be sold
To some Dutch brewer of Ratcliffe, to make
His *yeu frowe‡* slippers
   LUCY. Speak low ! I am deprived

* Though the name of this monarch is known to us, I believe
we are all ignorant respecting his royal progeny. S.

   This line gives additional support to the conjecture that there
must have been an old play upon the subject of King Cophetua
and the Beggar Maid, besides the old ballads, one of which is
to be found in Percy's *Reliques* i. 202. edit. 1812. Cophetua's
son was perhaps one of the characters in the Play. C.

   † Morion properly means a helmet.

   ‡ This ought to be spelt *Jongerouw*, which in Dutch means a
young woman. C.

By thy rash wine of all atonement now,
Unto her after legacies or love.
    Y. PAL. My Luce, be magnified ; I am all plot,
All stratagem ! My brother is in town :
My Lady Ample's fame hath caught him, girl :
I'm told he means an instant visit hither.
    LUCY. What happiness from this ?
    Y. PAL. As he departs
From hence, I have laid two instruments, Meager
And Pert, that shall encounter his long ears
With tales less true than those of Troy ; they shall
Endanger him, maugre his active wits,
And mount thee, little Luce, that thou may'st reach
To dandle fate, to soothe them till they give
Us leave to make or alter destinies.
    LUCY. You  are  too  loud ;  whisper  your  plots
        within.                              [*Exeunt.*


*Enter* ENGINE, ELDER PALLATINE, THWACK.

    ENG. You call and govern, gentlemen, as if
Your business were above your haste ; but know
You where you are ?
    ELD. PAL. Sir Tyrant Thrift dwells here :
The Lady Ample is his ward ; she is
Within, and we must see her.   No excuses ;
She is not old enough to be lock'd up
To sey* new perukes, or purge for rheum.
    THWACK. Tell her, that a young devout knight,
        made grey
By a charm, t'avoid temptation in others,
Would speak with her.
    ENG. I shall deliver you both.
These tigers hunt their prey with a strange nostril.
Come unsent for so aptly to our wish.—      [*Exit.*

* To *essay*, to try on.

ELD. PAL. But this, Sir Morglay, will not do ;
In troth you break our covenants.
   THWACK. Why, hear me plead.
   ELD. PAL. From forty to fourscore ; the written
     law
Runs so : this lady's in her nonage yet,
And you to press into my company,
Where visitations are decreed mine own,
Argues a heat that my rebukes must cool.
   THWACK. What should I do ? wouldst have me
     keep my chamber
And mend dark lanterns ? invent steel mattocks,
Or weigh gunpowder ? solitude leads me
To nothing less than treason : I shall conspire
To dig and blow up all, rather than sit still.
   ELD. PAL. Follow your task ! you see how early I
Have found this young inheritrix : go seek
The aged out ; bones unto bones, like cards
Ill pack'd ; shuffle yourselves together, till
You each dislike the game.
   THWACK.               'Tis the cause I
Come for : a wither'd midwife, or a nurse
Who draws her lips together, like an eye
That gives the cautionary wink, are those
I would find here, so they be rich and fat.

*Enter* GINET.

   GIN. My lady understands your haste, and she
Herself consults now in affairs of haste :
But yet will hastily approach to see
You, gentlemen, and then in haste return.   [*Exit.*
   ELD. PAL. What's this, the superscription of a
     packet ?
   THWACK. Now does my blood wamble. You !
     sucket-eater !*
        [*Offers to follow her, Pallatine stays him.*

* Eater of sweetmeats.

K

ELD. PAL. These covenants, knight, will never
    be observ'd ; ·
I'll sue the forfeiture, leave you so poor,
'Till, for preferment, you become an eunuch,
And sing a treble in a chauntry, knight.

*Enter* LADY AMPLE, LUCY, GINET : *Elder Pallatine,
and Thwack, address to kiss them, and are thrust
back.*

AMP. Stay, gentlemen.  Good souls ! they have
    seen, Lucy,
The country turtle's bill, and think our lips,
I' th' town and court, are worn for the same use.
  LUCY. Pray how do the ladies there ? poor
    villagers,
They churn still, keep their dairies, and lay up
For embroidered mantles against the heir's birth.
  AMP. Who is begot i' th' Christmas holidays.
  ELD. PAL. Yes, surely, when the spirit of
Mince-pie reigns in the blood.
  AMP. What ? penny gleek* I hope's
In fashion yet, and the treacherous foot
Not wanting on the table frame, to jog
The husband, lest he lose the noble, that
Should pay the grocer's man for spice and fruit.
  LUCY. The good old butler shares too with his
    lady
In the box, bating for candles that were burnt
After the clock struck ten.
  THWACK. He doth indeed.

---

* Gleek : A game at cards. The number of persons playing
must be three, neither more nor less, and most frequently they
play at farthing, half-penny, or penny Gleek, which in play
will amount considerably. The ace is called *Tib*, the knave
*Tom*, the four of trumps *Tiddy*. A *mournival* of aces is eight,
of kings six, of queens four, and a *mournival* of knaves two
apiece. A *gleek* of aces is four, of kings three, of queens *two*,
and of knaves one apiece from the other two gamesters."—
*The Compleat Gamester.*

Poor country madams, th'are in subjection still ;
The beasts, their husbands, make 'em sit on three
Legg'd stools, like homely daughters of an hospital,
To knit socks for their cloven feet.
    ELD. PAL. And when these tyrant husbands, too,
      grow old,
As they have still th' impudence to live long,
Good ladies, they are fain to waste the sweet
And pleasant seasons of the day in boiling
Jellies for them, and rolling little pills
Of cambric lint to stuff their hollow teeth.
    LUCY. And then the evenings, warrant ye, they
Spend with Mother Spectacle, the curate's wife,
Who does inveigh 'gainst curling and dyed cheeks;
Heaves her devout impatient nose at oil
Of jessamine, and thinks powder of Paris more
Prophane than th' ashes of a Romish martyr.
    AMP. And in the days of joy and triumph, sir,
Which come as seldom to them as new gowns,
Then, humble wretches ! they do frisk and dance
In narrow parlours to a single fiddle,
That squeaks forth tunes like a departing pig.
    LUCY. Whilst the mad hinds shake from their
      feet more dirt
Than did the cedar roots, that danc'd to Orpheus.
    AMP. Do they not pour their wine too from an
Ewer, or small gilt cruce, like orange-water kept
To sprinkle holiday beards ?
    LUCY. And when a stranger comes, send seven
Miles post by moon-shine for another pint !
    ELD. PAL. All these indeed are heavy truths ;
      but what
Do you, th' exemplar madams of the town ?
Play away your youth, as our hasty gamesters
Their light gold, not with desire to lose it,
But in a fond mistake that it will fit
No other use.

THWACK.  And then reserve your age,
As superstitious sinners ill-got wealth,
Perhaps for th' church, perhaps for hospitals.
    ELD. PAL.  If rich, you come to court, there learn
        to be
At charge to teach your paraquetoes French;
And then allow them their interpreters,
Lest the sage fowl should lose their wisdom on
Such pages of the presence, and the guard,
As have not past the seas.
    THWACK.  But if y' are poor,
Like wanton monkeys chain'd from fruit,
You feed upon the itch of your own tails.
    LUCY.  Rose vinegar to wash that ruffian's mouth!
    AMP.  They come to live here by their wits, let
        them use 'em.
    LUCY.  They have so few, and those they spend
        so fast,
They will leave none remaining to maintain them.
    ELD. PAL.  You shall maintain us; a community,
The subtle have decreed of late : you shall
Endow us with your bodies and your goods;
Yet use no manacles, call'd dull matrimony,
To oblige affection against wise nature,
Where it is lost, perhaps, through a disparity
Of years, or justly through distaste of crimes,
    AMP. Most excellent resolves!
    ELD. PAL.  But if you'll needs marry,
Expect not a single turf for a jointure;
Not so much land as will allow a grasshopper
A salad.
    THWACK.  I would no more doubt t' enjoy
You two in all variety of wishes,
Wer't not for certain covenants that I lately
Sign'd to in my drink, than I would fear usury
In a small poet, or a cast corporal.
    AMP.  You would not ?

THWACK. But look to your old widows!
There my title's good, see they be rich too,
Lest I should leave their twins upon the parish,
To whom the deputy o' th' ward will deny
Blue coats at Easter, loaves at funerals,
'Cause they were sons of an old country wit.
    AMP. Why all for widows, sir? can nothing that
Is young affect your mouldy appetite?
    THWACK. No in sooth; damsels at your years are
      wont
To talk too much over their marmalade;
They can't fare well, but all the town must hear't:
Their love's so full of praises, and so loud,
A man may with less noise lie with a drum.
    AMP. Think you so, sir?
    THWACK. Give me an old widow, that commits
      sin
With the gravity of a corrupt judge;
Accepts of benefits i' th' dark, and can
Conceal them from the light.
              [AMPLE *takes* ELDER PALLATINE *apart.*
    AMP. Pray, sir, allow me but your ear aside.
Though this rude Clym o'th Clough presume,
In his desires more than his strength can justify,
You should have nobler kindness than to think
All ladies relish of an appetite,
Bad as the worst your evil chance hath found.
    ELD. PAL. All are alike to me; at least, I'll make
Them so, with thin persuasions, and a short
Expense of time.
    AMP.              Then I have cast away
My sight; my eyes have look'd themselves into
A strong disease: but they shall bleed for it.
    ELD. PAL. Troth, lady mine, I find small remedy.
    AMP. Why came you hither, sir? She, that
      shall sigh
Her easy spirits into wind for you,

Must not have hope the kindness of your breath
Will e'er recover her.
    LUCY. What do I hear?  Hymen defend!
But three good corners to your little heart,
And two already broiling on love's altar!
Does this become her, Ginet? speak.
    GIN. As age, and half a smock would become me.
    THWACK. Th'ast caught her, Pallatine: insinuate
      rogue!
    LUCY. Love him! you must recant, or the small
      god
And I shall quarrel, when we meet i' th' clouds.
    THWACK. 'Slight, see how she stands! speak to her.
    ELD. PAL. Peace, knight! it is apt cunning that
      we go:
Disdain is like to water pour'd on ice,*
Quenches the flame awhile to raise it higher.
    LUCY. Engine, shew them their way.

*Enter* ENGINE.

    ENG. It lies here, gentlemen!
    ELD. PAL. There needs small summons. We are
      gone!  But d' you hear,
We will receive no letters, we, though sent
By th' incorporeal spy your dwarf, or Audry
Of the chamber, that would deliver them
With as much caution, as they were attachments
Upon money newly paid.
    THWACK.                Nor no message
From the old widow your mother, if you
Have one, no, though she send for me when she
Is giving up her testy ghost; and lies
Half drown'd in rheum, those floods of rheum in
    which

     * I sprinkle water on her passion's fire;
      Disdain allays love's flame to raise it higher.
                        *Folio Ed.*

Her maids do daily dive to seek the teeth
She cough'd out last.

    [*Exeunt Engine, Elder Pallatine, Thwack.*
 Lucy. 'Las ! good old gentleman,
We shall see him shortly in as many night-caps
As would make sick Mahomet a turban
For the winter.

 Amp. Are they gone, Luce ?
 Lucy. Not like the hours, for they'll return again
Ere long. O, you carry'd your false love rarely !
 Amp. How impudent these country fellows are !
 Lucy. He thinks y'are caught ; he has you
   between's teeth,
And intends you for the very next bit
He means to swallow.

 Amp. Luce, I have a thousand thoughts
More than a kerchief can keep in : Quick, girl,
Let us consult, and thou shalt find what silly snipes
These witty gentlemen shall prove, and in
Their own confession too, or I'll cry flounders else ;
And walk with my petticoat tuck'd up like
A long maid of Almaineny.   *Exeunt.*


## Scene II.

*Enter* Younger Pallatine, Meager, Pert ; *the
two last being new cloath'd.*

 Y. Pal. Don Meager, and Don Pert, you neither
  found
These embroider'd skins in your mother's womb :
Surely nature's wardrobe is not thus lac'd !
 Pert. We flourish, Pall, by th' charter of thy
  smiles,
A little magnified with shew, and thought
Of our new plot.
 Mea. The chamber's bravely hung !

Pert. To thy own wish, a bed and canopy
Prepar'd all from our number'd pence.    If it
Should fail, Meager and I must creep into
Our quondam rags ; a transmigration, Pall,
Which our divinity can ill endure.
  Mea. If I have more left t' maintain a large
      stomach,
And a long bladder, than one comely shilling,
Together with a single ounce of hope,
I am the son of a carman.
  Y. Pal. Do you suspect my prophecies,
That am your mint, your grand exchequer ?
  Pert.    Pall, no supicions, Pall ; but we, that
      embark
Our whole stock in one vessel, would be glad
To have all pirates o' shore, and the winds
In a calm humour.
  Mea. How fares th' intelligence ?
  Y. Pal. I left 'em at the Lady Ample's house.
This street they needs must pass, if they reach
      home.
  Pert. O I would fain project 'gainst the old
      knight,
Can we not share him too ?
  Y. Pal. This wheel must move alone.
Sir Morglay Thwack's too rugged yet,
He'ld interrupt the course ; a little more
O' th' file will smooth him fit to be screw'd up.
  Pert. Shrink off, Pall ! I hear 'em.

Enter Thwack, Elder Pallatine.

  Eld. Pal. Th' hast not the art of patient lei-
      sure, to
Attend the aptitude of things.    Wouldst thou
Run on, like a rude bull, on every object that
Doth heat the blood ? This cunning abstinence
Will make her passions grow more violent.

THWACK. But, Pallatine, I do not find I have
The cruelty, or grace, to let a lady
Starve for a warm morsel.

      [PERT *and* MEAGER *take the* ELDER PALLA-
        TINE *aside.*

Y. PAL. [*apart and watching.*] Now, my fine Pert.

PERT. Sir, we have business for your ear; it may
Concern you much, therefore 'tis fit it be
Particular.

ELD. PAL. From whom ?

MEA. A young lady, sir.
It is a secret will exact much care
And wisdom i' th' delivery : you should
Dismiss that gentleman.

ELD. PAL. A young lady ! good !
All the best stars i' th' firmament are mine.
Our coach attends us, knight, i' th' bottom of
The hither street.   You must go home alone.

THWACK. I'll sooner kill a serjeant, choose my
    jury
In the city, and be hang'd from a tavern bush !

ELD. PAL. Will't ruin all our destinies have
    built ?

THWACK. Come, what are those sly silk-worms
    there, that creep
So close into their wool, as they would spin
For none but their dear selves ? I heard 'em name
    a lady.

ELD. PAL. You heard them say then, she was
    young ; and
What our covenants are, remember !

THWACK.               Young, how young ?
She left her worm-seed, and her coral whistle
But a month since : do they mean so ?

ELD. PAL. Morglay, our covenants is all I ask.

THWACK. May be she hath a mind to me ; for
    there's

A reverend humour in the blood, which thou ne'er
Knew'st : perhaps she would have boys begot
Should be deliver'd with long beards.  Till thou
Arrive at my full growth, thou'lt yield the world
Nought above dwarf or page.

    ELD. PAL. Our covenants still, I cry !

    THWACK. Faith, I'll stride my mule to-morrow,
And away to the homely village in the north.

    ELD. PAL. Why so ?

    THWACK. Alas, these silly covenants, you know,
I seal'd to in my drink ; and certain fears
Lurk in a remote corner of my head,
That say the game will all be your's.

    ELD. PAL. But what success canst thou expect,
      since w' have
Not yet enjoy'd the city a full day ?

    THWACK. I say, let me have woman : be she
      young
Or old, grandam or babe, I must have woman.

    ELD. PAL. Carry but thy patience like a gentle-
      man,
And let me singly manage this adventure.
It will to-morrow cancel our old deeds,
And leave thee to subscribe to what thy free
Pleasure shall direct.

    THWACK. We'll equally enjoy
Virgin, wife, and widow ; the younger kerchief
      with
The aged hood.

    ELD. PAL. What I have said, if I had leisure
      now
I'd ratify with oaths of thy own choosing.

    THWACK. Go, propagate ! fill the shops with thy
      notch'd
Issue, that, when our money's spent, we may
Be trusted, break, and cozen in our own tribe.

    ELD. PAL. Leave me to fortune.

Thwack. D' you hear, Pallatine?
Perhaps this young lady has a mother.—
    Eld. Pal. No more : good night !

                    [*Exit Thwack.*

I have obey'd you, gentlemen ; no ears
Are near us, but our own.   What's your affair?
    Mea. We'll lead you to the lady's mansion, sir ;
'Tis hard by.
    Eld. Pal. Hard by !
    Pert.      So near, that if your lungs be good,
You may spit thither.   That is the house.
    Eld. Pal. These appear gentlemen,
And of some rank.   I will in !
                    [*Exeunt Elder Pallatine, Meager, Pert.*
    Y. Pal. So, so ! the hook has caught him by
        the gills ;
And it is fasten'd to a line will hold
You, sir, though your wits were stronger than your
        purse.
Sir Morglay Thwack's gone home : his lodging I
Have learn'd, and there are certain gins prepar'd
In which his wary feet may chance to be
Insnar'd, though he could wear his eyes upon his
        toes.
I must follow the game close.   He is enter'd,
And, ere this, amaz'd at the strange complexion
Of the house ; but 'twas the best our friendship
And our treasure could procure.            [*Exit.*


## Scene III.


*Enter* Elder Pallatine, Meager, *and* Pert, *with
        lights.*


    Eld. Pal. Gentlemen, if you please, lead me no
        further !
I have so little faith to believe this

The mansion of a lady, that I think
'Tis rather the decays of hell : a sad
Retirement for the fiend to sleep in
When he is sick with drinking sulphur.
   PERT. Sir, you shall see this upper room is
     hung.
   ELD. PAL. With cobwebs, sir, and those so large
     they may
Catch and ensnare dragons instead of flies,
Where sit a melancholy race of old
Norman spiders, that came in with th' Conqueror.
   MEA. This chamber will refresh your eyes, when
     you
Have cause to enter it.
            [*Leads him to look in 'tween the hangings.*
   ELD. PAL. A bed and canopy !
There's shew of entertainment there indeed :
There lovers may have place to celebrate
Their warm wishes, and not take cold.  But, gentle-
     men,
How comes the rest of this blind house so nak'd,
So ruinous, and deform'd ?
   PERT. Pray, sir, sit down !
If you have seen aught strange, or fit for wonder,
It but declares the hasty shifts to which
The poor distressed lady is expos'd
In pursuit of your love.  She hath good fame,
Great dignity, and wealth, and would be loth
To cheapen these by making her dull family
Bold witnesses of her desires with you :
Therefore t' avoid suspicion, to this place
Sh'ath sent part of her neglected wardrobe.
   MEA. And will, ere time grows older by an hour,
Gild all this homely furniture at charge
Of her own eyes ; her beams can do it, sir.
   ELD. PAL. My manners will not suffer me to
     doubt.

Pert.   We hope so too.   Besides, though every
        one
That hath a heart of's own, may think his pleasure;
We should be loth your thoughts should throw
        mistakes
On us, that are the humble ministers
Of your kind stars : for sure, though we look not
Like men that make plantation on some isle
That's uninhabited, yet you believe
We would teach sexes mingle, to increase men.
    Mea. Squires of the placket * we know you
        think us.
    Eld. Pal. Excuse my courage, gentlemen; good
        faith
I am not bold enough to think you so.
    Pert.  Nor will you yet be woo'd to such mistake.
    Eld. Pal. Not all the art nor flattery you have,
Can render you to my belief worse than myself;
Panders and bawds !   Good gentlemen,
I shall be angry, if you persuade me to
So vile a thought.
    Pert.                         Sir, you have cause,
And, in good faith, if you should think us such,
We would make bold to cut that slender throat.
    Eld. Pal. How, sir ?
    Pert. That very throat, through which the lusty
        grape,
And savoury morsel in the gamester's dish,
Steal down so leisurely with kingly gust.
    Mea. Sir, it should open wide as th' widest
        oyster
I'th' Venetian lake.

* " Deliro, playing at a game of racket,
    Far put his hand into Florinda's placket ;
    Keep hold, said shee, nor any farther go.
    Said he, just so, the placket well will do."
                *Select Collection of Epigrams,* 1665.

ELD. PAL. Gentlemen, it should.
It is a throat I can so little hide
In such a cause, that I would whet your razor for't
On my own shoe.
PERT. Enough, you shall know all!
This lady hath a noble mind, but 'tis
So much o'ermaster'd by her blood, we fear
Nothing but death, or you, can be her remedy.
ELD. PAL. And she is young!
MEA. O, as the April bud.
ELD. PAL. 'Twere pity, faith, she should be cast
away.
PERT. You have a soft and blessed heart, and to
Prevent so sad a period of her sweet breath,
Ourselves, this house, the habit of this room,
The bed within, and your fair person, we
Have all assembled in a trice.
ELD. PAL. Sure, gentlemen,
In my opinion more could not be done,
Were she inheritrix of all the east.
PERT. But, sir, the excellence of your pure fame,
Hath given us boldness to make suit, that if
You can reclaim her appetite with chaste
And wholesome homilies, such counsel as
Befits your known morality, you will
Be pleas'd to save her life, and not undo her honour.
MEA. We hope you will afford her med'cine by
Your meek and holy lectures, rather than
From any manly exercise; for such,
In troth, sir, you appear to our weak sight.
ELD. PAL. Brothers and friends, a style more
distant now
Cannot be given: though you were in compass
Thick as the Alps,* I must embrace you both—
Y' have hit the very centre, unto which
The toils and comforts of my studies tend.

* The quarto reads *aspus.*

Pert. Alas, we drew our arrow but by aim.

Eld. Pal. Why, gentlemen, I have converted
    more
Than ever gold or Aretine* misled :
I've disciples of all degrees in nature,
From your little punk in purple, to your
Tall canvas girl ; from your satin slipper,
To your iron patten and your Norway shoe.

Pert. And can you mollify the mother, sir,
In a strong fit ?

Eld. Pal. Sure, gentlemen, I can,
If books penn'd with a clean and wholesome spirit
Have any might to edify.  Would they
Were here !

Mea. What, sir ?

Eld Pal. A small library,
Which I was wont to make companion to
My idle hours ; where some, I take it, are
A little consonant unto this theme.

Pert. Have they not names ?

Eld. Pal. A pill to purge phlebotomy,—A bal-
    samum
For the spiritual back.—A lozenge against lust ;
With divers others,† sir, which, though not penn'd
By dull platonic Greeks, or Memphian priests,
Yet have the blessed mark of separation
Of authors silenc'd, for wearing short hair.

Pert. But, sir, if this chaste means cannot re-
    store
Her to her health and quiet peace, I hope
You will vouchsafe your lodging in you bed,

* An Italian poet, whose works were accompanied by lewd
prints of which he was the inventor.  They are mentioned in
*Randolph's Muse's Looking Glass.* C.

† In the folio edition these lines are altered in this manner :
    "A pill to purge the pride of pagan patches,
    A lozenge for the lust of loytring love,
    And balsoms for the bites of Babel's beast :
    With many," &c.

And take a little pains.     [*Points to the bed within.*
   ELD. PAL. Faith, gentlemen, I was
Not bred on Scythian rocks : tigers and wolves
I've heard of, but ne'er suck'd their milk ; and sure
Much would be done to save a lady's longing.
   MEA. 'Tis late, sir, pray uncase !
                         [*They help to uncloathe him.*
   PERT. Your boot ; believ't, it is my exercise.
   ELD. PAL. Well, 'tis your turn to labour now,
      and mine
Anon.   For your dear sakes, gentlemen, I profess—
   PERT. My friend shall wait upon you to your
      sheets,
Whilst I go and conduct the lady hither ;
Whom, if your holy doctrine cannot well
Reclaim, pray hazard not her life ; you have
A body, sir.
   ELD. PAL. O think me not cruel.
                  [*Exeunt Meager, Elder Pallatine.*


*Enter* YOUNGER PALLATINE.

   PERT. Pall ! come in, Pall.
   Y. PAL. Is he in bed ?
   PERT. Not yet !
But stripping in more haste than an old snake
That hopes for a new skin.
   Y. PAL. If we could laugh
In our coflin, Pert, this would be a jest
Long after death.   He is so eager in
His witty hopes, that he suspects nothing.
   PERT. O, all he swallows, sir, is melting conserve,
And soft Indian plum.   Meager, what news ?


*Enter* MEAGER.

   MEA. Laid, gently laid ! he is all virgin sure,
From the crown of's head to his very navel.

Y. PAL. Where are his breeches? speak! his
    hatband too;
'Tis of grand price, the stones are rosial, and
Of the white rock.
    MEA. I hung 'em purposely
Aside, they are all within my reach; shall I in?
    Y. PAL. Soft! softly my false fiend: remember,
    rogue,
You tread on glasses, eggs, and gouty toes.—
    [*Meager takes out his hat and breeches: the pockets
    and hatband rifled. They throw them in again.**
    MEA. Hold, Pall! th' exchequer is thine own:
    we will
Divide when thou art gracious and well pleas'd.
    Y. PAL. All gold! the stalls of Lombard-street
    pour'd into a purse!
    PERT. These, dear Pall, are thy brother's goodly
    herds.
    Y. PAL. Yes, and his proud flocks; but you see
    what they
Come to; a little room contains them all
At last. So, so, convey them in again:
Because he is my elder brother,
My mother's maidenhead and a country wit,
He shall not be expos'd to bare thighs, and a
Bald crown. What noise is that;
        [*Knocking within; Pert looks at the door.*
    PERT. Death! there's old Snore
The constable, his wife, a regiment of halberbs,
And mistress Queasy too, the landlady
That owns this house.
    MEA. Belike, th' ave heard, our friend
The bawd, fled hence last night; and now they come

---

* The stage direction of "they throw them in again," above
inserted, is obviously in the wrong place, as the hat and breeches
of the Elder Pallatine ought not to be returned until the
Younger Pallatine has given the order for doing so.   C.

To seize on moveables for rent.

    Y. PAL. The bed within, and th' hangings that
      we hired
To furnish our design are all condemn'd :
My brother too, they'll use him with as thin
Remorse, as an old gamester would an alderman's
      heir.
    PERT. No matter! our adventure's paid. Follow,
Pall, and I'll lead you a back way, where you
Shall climb o'er tiles, like cats when they make love.
    Y. PAL. Now I shall laugh at those that heap up
      wealth
By lazy method and slow rules of thrift :
I'm grown the child of wit, and can advance
Myself, by being votary to chance.     [*Exeunt.*

### ACT III. SCENE I.

*Enter* SNORE, MISTRESS SNORE, QUEASY, *and*
WATCHMEN.

    M. SNORE. Days o' my breath, I have not seen
      the like ?
What would you have my husband do ? 'tis past
One by Bow, and the bell-man has gone twice.
    QUE. Good master Snore, you are the constable,
You may do it, as they say, be it right or wrong.
'Tis four years' rent, come Childermas-eve next.
    SNORE. You see, neighbour Queasy, the doors are
      open ;
Here's no goods, no bawd left ; I'ld see the bawd.
    M. SNORE. Aye, or the whores : my husband's
      the king's officer,
And still takes care, I warrant you, of bawds
And whores ; shew him but a whore at this time
O'night, good man, you bring a bed i'faith.

Que. I pray, mistress Snore, let him search the
    parish.
They are not gone far, I must have my rent.
I hope there are whores and bawds in the parish.
    M. Snore. Search now! it is too late; a woman
     had
As good marry a colestaff * as a constable,
If he must nothing but search and search, follow
His whores and bawds all day, and never comfort
His wife at night.   I pr'ythee, lamb, let us to bed.
    Snore. It must be late; for gossip Nock, the
    nailman,
Had catechis'd his maids, and sung three catches
And a song, ere we set forth.
    Que. Good mistress Snore, forbear your husband
    but
To-night and let the search go on.
    M. Snore. I will not forbear; you might ha' let
    your house
To honest women, not to bawds.   Fie upon you!
    Que. Fie upon me! 'tis well known I'm the
    mother
Of children! scurvy fleak !† 'tis not for naught
You boil eggs in your gruel: and your man Sampson
Owes my son-in-law, the surgeon, ten groats
For turpentine, which you have promis'd to pay
Out of his Christmas box.
    M. Snore.                    I defy thee.
Remember thy first calling; thou set'st up
With a peck of damsons and a new sieve;
When thou brok'st at Dowgate corner, 'cause the
    boys
Flung down thy ware.
    Snore. Keep the peace, wife; keep the peace!

* A strong pole on which men carried a burden between
them.
   † *Scurvy*, mean. *Fleak*, a flounder  a little insignificant person.

M. Snore. I will not peace: she took my silver
    thimble
To pawn, when I was a maid; I paid her
A penny a month use.
    Que.                              A maid! yes, sure;
By that token, goody Tongue, the midwife,
Had a dozen napkins o' your mother's best
Diaper, to keep silence, when she said
She left you at Saint Peter's fair, where you
Long'd for pig.*
    Snore. Neighbour Queasy, this was not
In my time: what my wife hath done since I
Was constable, and the king's officer,
I'll answer; therefore, I say, keep the peace!
And when w' have search'd the two back rooms.
I'll to bed.  Peace, wife! not a word.      [*Exeunt.*

*Enter* Eld. Pallatine, *cloathing himself in haste.*

    Eld. Pal. 'Tis time to get on wings and fly:
Here's a noise of thunder, wolves, women, drums,
All that's confus'd, and frights the ear.  I heard
Them cry out bawds! the sweet young lady is

---

* Formerly the chief entertainments at fairs were *pigs* roasted
in booths erected for that purpose.  The practice continued
until the beginning of the present century, if not later.  It is
mentioned in Ned Ward's *London Spy*, 1697; and when, about
the year 1708, some propositions were made to limit the duration of Bartholomew Fair to three days, a poem was printed,
intitled, " *The Pigs' Petition against Bartholomew Fair with
their humble thanks to those unworthy preservers of so much innocent
blood.*"  In Ben Jonson's play of *Bartholomew Fair*, Mrs
Ursula, the *Pig-woman*, is no inconsiderable character.
    See *D'Avenant's poem on the long vacation in London.* fo.
edit. 290.

   " Now London's chief, on sadle new,
    Rides into Fare of Bartholomew:
    He twirles his chain, and looketh big.
    As if to fright the head of *pig*,
    That gaping lies on greasy stall,
    Till female with great belly call.

Surpris'd sure, by the nice slave her husband,
Or some old frosty matron of near kin ;
And the good gentlemen sh' employ'd to me
Are tortur'd and call'd bawds.   If I am ta'en,
I'll swear I purpos'd her conversion.

*Enter* SNORE, MISTRESS SNORE, QUEASY, *and*
WATCHMEN.

SNORE. Here's a room hung, and a fair bed
    within :
I take it there's the he-bawd too.
    QUE.             Seize on the lewd thing !
I pray, master Snore, seize on the goods too.
    M. SNORE. Who would not be a bawd ?   they've
    proper men
To their husbands ; and she maintains him
Like any parish deputy.
    ELD. PAL. What are you ?
    SNORE. I am the constable.
    ELD. PAL. Good ; the constable !
I begin to stroke my long ears, and find
I am an ass : such a dull ass, as deserves
Thistles for provender, and saw-dust too
Instead of grains : O, I am finely gull'd.
    M. SNORE. Truly, as proper a bawd, as a woman
Would desire to use.
    ELD. PAL. Master constable,
Though these your squires o' th' blade and bill,
Seem to be courteous gentlemen, and well taught,
Yet I would know why they embrace me.
    SNORE. You owe my neighbour, Mistress Queasy,
    four years' rent.
    QUE. Yes, and for three bed ticks, and a brass pot
Which your wife promis'd me to pay this term ;
For now, she said, sh' expects her country customers.
    ELD. PAL. My wife ! have I been led to the
    altar too,

By some doughty deacon? ta'en woman by
The pretty thumb, and given her a ring,
With my dear self, for better and for worse,
And all in a forgotten dream?   But for whom
Do you take me?
    SNORE. For the he-bawd.
    ELD. PAL. Good faith, you may as soon
Take me for a whale, which is something rare,
You know, o' this side the bridge.
    M. SNORE. 'Tis indeed;
Yet our Paul was in the belly of one,
In my Lord Mayor's show; and, husband, you
      remember,
He beckoned you out of the fish's mouth,
And you gave him a pippin, for the poor soul
Had like to have choak'd for very thirst.
    ELD. PAL. I saw it, and cry'd: out
O' th' city, 'cause they would not be at charge
To let the fish swim in a deeper sea.
    M. SNORE. Indeed! why I was but a tiny girl
      then;
I pray how long have you been a bawd here?
    ELD. PAL. Again! how the devil
Am I chang'd since my own glass rendered me
A gentleman?   Well, master constable,
Though every stall's your worship's wooden throne,
Here you are humble, and o' foot, therefore
I will put on my hat; pray reach it me!
               [*Misses his diamond hatband.*
Death! my hatband! a row of diamonds
Worth a thousand marks! nay, it is time then
To doubt, and tremble too.   My gold! my gold!—
And precious stones!        [*Searches his pockets.*
    M. SNORE.      Do you suspect my husband?
He hath no need o' your stones, I praise Heaven!
    ELD. PAL. A plague upon your courteous mid-
      night leaders!

Good silly saints, they are dividing now,
And ministering, no doubt, unto the poor.
This will decline the reputation of my wit,
Till I be thought to have a less head
Than a justice o' peace.   If Morglay hear't,
He'll think me dull as a Dutch mariner.
No med'cine now from thought?   Good; 'tis de-
    sign'd.
    SNORE. Come along! 'tis late.
    ELD. PAL. Whither must I go?
    QUE. To the compter, sir, unless my rent be
    paid.
    SNORE. And for being a bawd!
    ELD. PAL.       Confin'd in wainscot walls too,
Like a liquorish rat, for nibbling
Unlawfully upon forbidden cheese!
This, to the other sauce, is aloes and myrrh.
But, master constable, do you behold this ring?
It is worth all the bells in your church-steeple,
Though your sexton and side-men* hung there too,
To better the peal.
    SNORE. Well, what's your request?
    ELD. PAL. Marry, that you will let me go to fetch
The bawd, the very bawd that owes this rent;
Who being brought, you shall restore my ring,
And believe me to be an arrant gentleman,
Such as, in's scutcheon, gives horns, hounds, and
    hawks,
Hunting nags, with tall eaters in blue coats,
*Sans* number.
    QUE. Pray let him go, Master Snore.
We'll stay and keep the goods!
    M. SNORE. Yes, let him, husband;

* *i.e.*, Sidesmen :—Unpaid Assistants to the Churchwardens,
and elected from among the congregation.   The sexton is
a paid servant.   To couple the two classes is somewhat out
of order.

For I would fain see a very he-bawd.

SNORE.        Come, neighbours, light him out !

          *[Exeunt.*

## SCENE II.

*Enter* YOUNGER PALLATINE, LADY AMPLE, PERT,
  LUCY, GINET, ENGINE, *with lights.*

AMP.   A forest full of palms, thy lover, Luce,
Merits in garlands for his victory.
I'm wild with joy ! why, there was wit enough
In this design to bring a ship o' fools *
To shore again, and make them all good pilots.

Y. PAL. Madam, this gentleman deserves to share
In your kind praise : he was a merry agent
In the whole plot, and would exalt himself
To your ladyship's service.   If you please,
For my humble sake, unto your lip too.

        *[Pert salutes her.*

AMP. Sir, you are friend to Pallatine,
And that entitles you unto much worth.

PERT. The title will be better'd, madam, when
I am become a servant to your beauty.

LUCY. Why, your confederate Pert is courtly too,
He will out-tongue a favourite of France !
But didst thou leave thy brother surfeiting
On lewd hopes ?

Y. PAL. He believes all womankind
Dress'd and ordain'd for th' mercy of his tooth,

AMP. And now lies stretch'd in his smooth
  slippery sheets ?

---

* Alluding to an allegorical poem, translated from the Dutch
by Alexander Barclay, priest and chaplain in the College of
St Mary, Otery, in the County of Devon—Published by Pynson
—Folio, 1508.   A reprint has just been completed under the
editorship of Thomas Hill Jamieson, Esq., keeper of the Library of the Faculty of Advocates.

Y. PAL. O, like a wanton snake on camomile ;
And rifled to so sad remains of wealth,
That, if his resolution still disdain
Supplyment from his lands, and he resolve
To live here by his wits, he will, ere long,
Betroth himself to raddish-women for their roots,
Pledge children in their sucking-bottles,
And, in dark winter mornings, rob small school-
    boys
Of their honey and their bread.
PERT. Faith, Meager and I us'd him with as much
Remorse as our occasions could allow.
'Las, he must think we shreds of time
Have our occasions too !
Y. PAL.        What, madam, need he care ?
For let him but prove kind unto his bulls,
Bring them their heifers when their crests are high ;
Stroke his fair ewes, and pimp a little for
His rams, they straight will multiply ; and then
The next great fair prepares him fit again
For th' city's view, and our surprise.
AMP. Why this, young gentleman, hath relish
    in't :
Yet when you understand the dark and deep
Contrivements which myself, Engine, and Luce,
Have laid for this great witty villager,
To whom you bow, as foremost of your blood ;
You will degrade yourselves from all prerogatives
Above our sex, and all those pretty marks
Of manhood, your trim beards, singe off with tapers,
As a just sacrifice to our supremacy.
LUCY. If Sir Tyrant Thrift, your phlegmatic
    guardian,
Leave but this mansion our's till the next sun,
We'll make your haughty brother tremble at
The name of woman, and blush behind a fan,
Like a yawning bride, that hath foul teeth.

Eng. Madam, 'tis time you were abed ; for sure,
        besides
The earnest invitation which I left,
Writ in his chamber, these afflictions will
Disturb his rest, and bring him early hither
To recover his sick hopes.

*Enter* MEAGER.

Y. Pal. Meager? what news ? Madam, the
        homage
Of your lip again : a man o' war, believ't ;
One that hath fasted in the face of's foe ;
Seen Spinola* intrench'd ; sometimes hath spread
His butter at the State's charge ; sometimes too
Fed on a salad that hath grown upon
The enemy's own land : but, pardon me,
Without or oil, or vinegar.
    Amp.    Sir, men in choler may do any thing.
    Mea. Your ladyship will excuse his new plenty;
It hath made him pleasant.
    Y. Pal. Meager ! what news ? how do our spies
        prosper ?
    Mea. Sir, rare discoveries ! I've trac'd your
        brother :

---

* The Marquis of Spinola conducted the celebrated siege of
Ostend.   In 1611 there was published at Cologne "Sumpti-
bus Joannis Kinckij." Engravings of the Victorious progres
of Spinola under the title "Victoriæ auspiciis excellentissimi
Ambrosii Spinulæ Marchionis a Benafero, Equitis Velleris
Aurei, &c., Ducis Universi Exercitus, Regis, Hispaniæ Potentis-
simi Philippi III. et Serenissimi Archiducis Alberti ab Austria
Belgii Principis. Tabulis Æneis delineata." Small 4to with fold-
ing plates.   The second engraving in this very rare collection is
of Ostend, with the date 1604, and the last is a splendid and beautifully engraved print of the arrival of Spinola at the Hague, 7th
February 1608, containing a representation of his reception by
the " Graff Mauritz." The engravings are seventeen in number.   He invested Bergen in 1623, but without success, for after
remaining before it for some time he found himself obliged to
raise the siege.

You shall hear more anon.

GIN.      Your ladyship forgets how early your
Designs will waken you.

ENG.                              Madam, I'ld fain be
Bold too, to hasten you unto your rest.

AMP. 'Tis late, indeed ; the silence of the night
And sleep be with you, gentlemen !
                      [*Exeunt Ample, Ginet, Engine.*

Y. PAL. Madam, good night ! but our heads
            never were
Ordain'd to so much trivial leisure
As to sleep.   You may as soon entreat
A sexton sleep in's belfry when the plague reigns ;
An aged sinner in a tempest, or
A jealous statesman when his prince is dying.

LUCY. Pray, dismiss your friends.  I would speak
            with you.

Y. PAL. Men o' the puissant pike, follow the
            lights !                [*Exeunt Meager, Pert.*

LUCY. Pall, you are as good-natur'd to me, Pall,
As the wife of a silenc'd minister
Is to a monarchy * or to lewd gallants,
That have lost a nose.

Y. PAL. And why so, Dame Luce ?

LUCY. So many yellow images at once
Assembled in your fist, and jewels too of goodly
            price ;
All this free booty got in lawful war,
And I no tribute, Pall ?

Y. PAL. What need it, Luce ? a virgin may live
            cheap ;
Th' are maintained with as small charge, as a wren
With maggots in a cheesemonger's shop.

LUCY.  Well, Pall, and yet you know all my
            extremes :
How for a little taffeta to line a mask,

* Qy. Monarch.

I'm fain to mollify my mercer
With a soft whisper, and a tim'rous blush ;
To sigh unto my milliner for gloves,
That they may trust, and not complain unto my
    aunt,
Who is as jealous of me as their wives ; and all
Through your demeanour, Pall : whose kind-
    ness, I
Perceive, will raise me to such dignity,
That I must teach children in a dark cellar,
Or work coifs in a garret for crack'd groats
And broken meat.

    Y. PAL. Luce, I will give thee, Luce, to buy—
    LUCE. What, Pall?
    Y. PAL. An ounce of ars'nic to mix in thy aunt's
    caudles.
This aunt I must see cold and grinning, Luce,
Seal'd t' her last wink, as if she clos'd her eyes
T' avoid the sight of feathers, coaches, and short
    cloaks.
    LUCY. How many angels of your family
Are there in heaven ? but few, I fear ; and how
You'll be the first that shall entitle them
To such high calling, is to me a doubt.
    Y. PAL. Why, is there never a pew there, Luce,
But for your coughing aunt and you ?
    LUCE. Hadst thou eyes like flaming beacons,
    crook'd horns,
A tail three yards long, and thy feet cloven,
Thou couldst not be more a fiend than thou art now ;
But to advance thy sins with being hard,
And costive unto me !
    Y. PAL. You lie, Luce ! you lie !
                   *[Flings her a purse.*
There's gold ; the fairies are thy mintmen, girl ;
Of this thou shalt have store enough to make
The hungry academies mention thee

In evening lectures, with applause and prayer.
A foundress thou shalt be.
  LUCY. Of hospitals,
For your decayed self, Meager and Pert,
Those wealthy usurers, your poor friends.
    Y. PAL. A nunnery, Luce, where all the female
      issue
Of our decayed nobility shall live
Thy pensioners : it will preserve them from
Such want, as makes them quarter arms with th'
      city,
And match with saucy haberdashers' sons,
Whose fathers lived in allies and dark lanes,
    LUCY. Good night, Pall ! your gold I'll lay up,
      though but
T' encounter the next surgeon's bill ; yet know.
Our wits are ploughing too, and in a ground
That yields as fair a grain as this.
    Y. PAL. Farewell, and let me hear thy aunt is
      stuck
With more bay leaves and rosemary than a
Westphalia gammon.                       [*Exeunt.*

## SCENE III.

*Enter* ELDER PALLATINE, *and* THWACK *dressing
himself.*

  ELD. PAL. Quick, dispatch, knight ! thou art as
      tedious in
Thy dressing as a court bride : two ships might
Be rigg'd for the Straits in less space than thou
Careenest that same old hulk.   Can it be thought
That one so fill'd with hope and wise designs
Could be subdu'd with sleep ? what ! dull, and
      drowsy ?
Keep earlier hours than a roost hen in winter ?

THWACK. Pallatine, the designs grew all dream,
      magic,
And alchymy to me.  I gave it lost !
Clove to my soft pillow like a warm Justice,
And slept there with less noise than a dead lawyer
In a monument.
      ELD. PAL. This is the house ; dispatch, that I
      may knock.
      THWACK. 'Slight, stay ; thou think'st I've the
      dexterity
Of a spaniel, that with a yawn, a scratch
On his left ear, and stretching his hind legs,
Is ready for all day.   O, for the Biscayn sleeve,
And Bulloign hose I wore when I was shrieve
In eighty-eight !
      ELD. PAL. Faith, thou art comely, knight ;
And I already see the town girls melt,
And thaw before thee.
      THWACK. We must be content.
Thou know'st all men are bound to wear their limbs
I' th' same skin that nature bestows upon them,
Be it rough or be it smooth ; for my part,
If she to whom you lead me now like not
The grain of mine, I will not flea myself
T' humour the touch of her ladyship's fingers.
      ELD. PAL. Well, I had thought t' have carried
      it with youth ;
But, when I came to greet her beauties with
The eyes of love and wonder, she despis'd me,
Rebuk'd those haughty squires, her servants, that
Convey'd me thither in mistake, and cried,
She meant the more authentic gentleman,
The rev'rend monsieur, she !
      THWACK. The rev'rend monsieur ?
Why, does she take me for a French Dean ?
      ELD. PAL. Her confessor, at least : her secrets
      are

Thine own ; but, by what charms attain'd,
Let him determine that has read Agrippa.*
   THWACK. Charms ! yes, sir, if this be a charm !
    or this—                [*Leaps and frisks.*
Or here again, t' advance th' activity
Of a poor old back !
   ELD. PAL. No ape, Sir Morglay,
After a year's obedience to the whip,
Is better qualified.
   THWACK. Limber and sound, sir !
Besides, I sing Little Musgrove ; and then
For the Chevy Chase,† no lark comes near me :
If she be ta'en with these, why at her peril be't.
   ELD. PAL. Come, sir, dispatch ! I'll knock, for
    here's the house.
   THWACK. Stay, stay ! this lane, sure, has no
    great renown ;
The house too, if the moon reveal't aright,
May, for it's small magnificence be left,
For aught we know, out of the city map.
   ELD. PAL. Therein consists the miracle ; and
    when
The doors shall ope, and thou behold how lean
And ragged every room appears, till thou hast
Reach'd the sphere where she, illustrious, moves,
Thy wonder will be more perplex'd ; for, know,
This mansion is not her's, but a concealed
Retirement, which her wisdom safely chose
To hide her loose love.
   THWACK. Give me a baggage that has brains !
    But, Pallatine,
Did not I at first persuade thee, those two
Trim gentlemen, her squires, might happily

* Cornelius Agrippa, who wrote *De Occulta Philosophia
Libri tres.* Col. 1533. He was born at Cologne 14 September
1486, and died either at Lyons or Grenoble 1535.
   † See both ballads in Bishop Percy's *Reliques of Ancient
Poetry.*

Mistake the person unto whom the message was
Dispos'd, and that myself was he?
   ELD. PAL. Thou didst! and thou hast got,
      knight, by this hand,
I think, the Mogul's niece: she cannot be
Of less descent, the height and strangeness of
Her port denote her foreign, and of great blood.
   THWACK. What should the Mogul's niece do here?
   ELD. PAL. 'Las, thy ears are buried in a wool sack;
Thou hear'st no news! 'tis all the voice in court
That she is sent hither in disguise to learn
To play on the guitar, and make almond-butter.
But whether this great lady that I bring
Thee to, be she, is yet not quite confirm'd.
   THWACK. Thou talk'st o' th' high and strange
      comportment that
Thou found'st her in.
   ELD. PAL. Right, sir! she sat on a rich Persian
      quilt,
Threading a carcanet of pure round pearl,
Bigger than pigeons' eggs.
   THWACK. Those I will sell.
   ELD. PAL. Her maids, with little rods of rose-
      mary,
And stalks of lavender, were brushing ermines'
      skins.
   THWACK. Furs for the winter! I'll line my
      breeches with them.
   ELD. PAL. Her young smooth pages lay round
      at her feet,
Cloath'd like the Sophy's sons, and all at dice:
The caster six wedges* a cubit long,
Cries one; another comes a tun of pistolets,†
And then is cover'd with an argosy
Laden with indigo and cochineal.
   THWACK. This must be the great Mogul's niece.

* Gages.         † Spanish pistoles.

ELD. PAL. As for her grooms, they all were
    planted on
Their knees, carousing their great lady's health
In perfum'd wines ; and then straight qualified
Their wild voluptuous heats with cool sherbet,
The Turk's own julep.

THWACK. Knock, Pallatine !
Quick, rogue ! I cannot hold.　Little thought I
The Thwacks of the north should inoculate
With the Moguls of the south.　　[*Pallatine knocks.*

*Enter* SNORE.

ELD. PAL. Speak softly, master constable ; I've
    brought
The very he-bawd.

SNORE. Blessing on your heart, sir !
My watch are above at Trea Trip* for a

---

* Sometimes spelt Tre-trip and usually Tray-trip.　A game
the nature of which is by no means clear.　Stevens imagined it
a game at cards, and Tyrwhitt a game at tables.　Hawkins was
of opinion that it was what was called Scotch Hop, an amusement of the lower classes, and he refers to Twelfth Night, Act
II., Scene 5.　Tyrwhitt's conjecture is the best, as it is verified
by the following extract from Machivell's Dogge, 1617, small
4to, signature B :—
  " But leaving cardes, lett's go to dice awhile
    To passage, trei-tripe, hazard, or mum-chance,
    But subtill mates will simple minds beguile
    And blinde their eyes, with many a blinking glaunce
    Of cogges and stoppis, and such like devilish trickes,
    Full many a purse of gold and silver pickes
    And therefore first for Hazard, hee that list
    And passeth not, puts many to a blanke,
    And trippe without a traye makes hard I wist,
    To sitte and mourne among the sleeper's ranke
    And for mum-chance, howe'er the chance doe fall,
    You must be mum for fear of marring all."
Halliwell, in his dictionary of Archaic Words, referring to
"Taylor's Motto," 1622, confirms Tyrwhitt in his supposition,
that "Tray-Trap" means "a game at dice."—See Jasper
Mayne's "City Match," 1639, Act II., Scene IV.— *Dodsley's Old
Plays*, Vol IX., p. 260, London 1825, 8vo.　In the fifth act of
the present drama, Tea-Trap is again referred to as played all

Black pudding and a pound o' Suffolk cheese ;
They'll ha' done straight : pray fetch him to me,
I'll call them down, and lead him to a by-room.
   THWACK. Pallatine ! what's he ?
   ELD. PAL.          The lady's steward, sir,
A sage philosopher, and a grave pander.
One that hath writ bawdy sonnets in Hebrew,
And those so well, that if the rabbins were
Alive, 'tis thought he would corrupt their wives.
Follow me, knight !
   THWACK.           Pallatine,
Half the large treasure that I get is your's.
   ELD. PAL. Good faith, my friend, when you are
     once possess'd
Of all, 'tis as your conscience will vouchsafe.
   THWACK. Dost thou suspect ?  I'll stay here till
     thou fetch
A bible and a cushion, and swear kneeling.
   ELD. PAL.  My faith  shall  rather  cozen  me.
     Walk in
With this philosopher.—No words, for he's
A Pythagorean,* and professes silence.
My ring, master constable.——
     [SNORE *gives him his ring, then exit with Thwack.*
Here yet my reputation's safe : should he
Have heard of my mischance, and not accompanied
With this defeat upon himself, his mirth
And tyranny had been 'bove human sufferance.
Now for the Lady Ample ; she, I guess,
Looks on me with strong fervent eyes : she's rich,
And, could I work her into profit, 'twould
Procure my wit immortal memory.
But to be gull'd ! and by such trifles too,
Dull humble gentlemen, that ne'er drunk wine

night with a lanthorn on a stall, for "ale, cheese, and pudding."
See page 202.

   * Alluding to the seven years' silence imposed by Pythagoras
on his disciples.

But on some coronation-day, when each
Conduit pisses claret at the town charge.
Well, though 'tis worse than steel or marble to
Digest, yet I have learn'd, one stop in a career
Taints not a rider with disgrace;
But may procure him breath to win the race.

[*Exit.*

## ACT IV.  SCENE I.

*Enter* YOUNGER PALLATINE, ENGINE, MEAGER,
PERT; *Pallatine richly cloath'd.*

ENG. Your brother's in the house; the letter
  which
I sent to tempt him hither wrought above
The reach of our desires.  My lady, sir,
He does believe is sick to death, and all
In languishment for his dear love.

Y. PAL. Pert and Meager, though you have both
  good faces,
They must not be seen here: there is below
A brother o' mine, whom, I take it, you
Have us'd not over tenderly.

MEA. 'Slight, he must needs remember us.

PERT. We'll sooner stay t' outface a basilisk.*

* "A distinction must be taken between the basilisk (or
cockatrice) of Scripture, and that which is so-called by modern
naturalists.   Under the name of basilisk is at present de-
signated a genus of reptiles of the *Saurian* order, which exhibit
many affinities with the *iguanes* and *monitors*.  No animal,
perhaps, has been the subject of so great a number of preju-
dices as the one now under consideration.  The most ancient
authors have spoken of the basilisk as of a serpent which had
the power of striking its victim dead by a single glance,
others have pretended that it could not exercise this faculty
unless it first perceived the object of its vengeance before it
was itself perceived by it.  Aldrovandus, and several other
writers, have given figures of it.  They have represented it
with eight feet, a crown on the head, and a hooked and re-
curved beak.   Pliny assures us that the serpent named Basilisk

Whither shall we go?

    Y. PAL. To Snore, the constable: Morglay is
      still
A prisoner in his house; take order for's
Release, as I projected; but, d' you hear?
He must not free him till I come.

    PERT. Pall, will the dull ruler of the night, Pall,
Obey thy edict?

    Y. PAL. His wife will, and she's his constable;
Name me but to her, and she does homage.

    MEA. Enough, we will attend thee there.

    ENG. This way, gentlemen.

                [*Exeunt Engine, Pert, Meager.*

*Enter* ELDER PALLATINE.

    ELD. PAL. What's this? an apparition, a ghost
      embroider'd?
Sure he has got the devil for his tailor.

    Y. PAL. Good morrow, brother, morrow!

    ELD. PAD. You are in glory, sir; I like this
      flourishing!
The lily, too, looks handsome for a month;
But you, I hope, will last out the whole year.

    Y. PAL. What flourishing? O sir, belike you
      mean
My cloathes: th' are rags, coarse homely rags,
      believ't;
Yet they will serve for th' winter, sir, when I
Ride post in Sussex ways.

    ELD. PAL. This gaiety denotes
Some solitary treasure in the pocket,
And so you may become a lender too.

has a voice so terrible, that it strikes terror into all other species—that it thus chases them from the spot which it inhabits,
and of which it retains the sole and undisputed dominion."
—*Cuvier's Animal Kingdom*, vol. ix. p. 226. *Basilisk*, in
Greek, signifies "Royal."

You know I'm far from home.
   Y. PAL. I'll lend nothing but good counsel and wit.
   ELD. PAL, Why sure you have no factors, sir, in
     Delph,
Leghorn, Aleppo, or th' Venetian Isles,
That by their traffick can advance you thus;
Nor do you trade i' th' city by retail
In our small wares : all that you get by law
Is but a doleful execution after arrest;
And, for your power in court!
I know, your stockings being on, you are
Admitted in the presence.
   Y. PAL. What does this infer, brother?
Men of design are chary of their minutes;
Be quick and subtle.
   ELD. PAL. The inference is
You prosper by my documents; and what
You have achiev'd must be by your good wits.
   Y. PAL. If you had had a sibyl to your nurse,
You could not, sir, have aim'd nearer the truth.
I saw your ears and bags were shut to all
Intents of bounty, therefore was enforc'd
Into this way : and 'twas at first somewhat
Against my conscience too.
   ELD. PAL. If not to vex
The zealous spirit in you, I would know why?
   Y. PAL. Good faith I've search'd records, and
     cannot find
That Magna Charta does allow a subject
To live by his wits : there is no statute for't.
   ELD. PAL. Your common lawyer was no anti-
     quary.
   Y. PAL. And then, credit me, sir, the canons of
The church authorize no such thing.
   ELD. PAL. You have met with a dull civilian too.
   Y. PAL. Yet, brother, these impediments cannot
Choke up my way; I must still on!

ELD. PAL. And you believe the stories of young
    heirs
Enforc'd to sign at midnight, to appease
The sword-man's wrath, may be out-done by you ?
    Y. PAL. I were unkind else to my own good parts.
    ELD. PAL. And that your wit has power to tempt
        from the
Severe, grave bench, the aldermen themselves ;
To rifle where you please, for scarfs, feathers,
And for race nags ?
    Y. PAL. It is believ'd, sir, in a trice.
    ELD. PAL. And that your wit can lead our
        rev'rend matrons,
And testy widows of fourscore, to seal,
And in their smocks, for frail commodities*
To elevate your punk.
    Y. PAL.                    All this, sir, is so easy,
My faith would swallow 't, though 't had a sore
        throat.
    ELD. PAL. Give me thy hand ! This day I'll
        cut off the entail
Of all my lands, and disinherit thee.
    Y. PAL. Will you, Sir ? I thank ye.
    ELD. PAL. But mark me, brother: for there's
        justice in't
Admits of no reproof: what should you do
With land, that have a portion in your brain
Above all legacies or heritage ?
    Y. PAL. I conceive you.
    ELD. PAL. O, to live here i' th' fair metropolis
Of our great isle, a free inheritor

* Wares taken in payment by needy persons, who borrowed
money of usurers. "Commodity" also means "interest."
The interpretation of this sentence may be that "even during
the night, Palatine could cause the old ladies to rise from bed
to lend him money on his personal bond, or to seal a bond in
security to a low, unconscientious money-lender, for the advantage of his temporary mistress.

Of ev'ry modest, or voluptuous wish
Thy young desires can breathe ; and not oblig'd
To th' plough-man's toils, or lazy reaper's sweat ;
To make the world thy farm, and ev'ry man,
Less witty than thyself, tenant for life ;
These are the glories that proclaim a true
Philosophy and soul in him that climbs
To reach them with neglect of fame and life.
   Y. PAL. He carries it bravely ! As he had felt
Nothing that fits his own remorse : but know,
Sir Eagle, th' higher that you fly, the less
You will appear to us, dim-sighted fowl,
That flutter here below.  Brother, farewell !
They say the lady of this house groans for
Your love : the tame sick fool is rich, let not
Your pride beguile your profit.       [*Exit.*
   ELD. PAL. I suspect him.  Not all the skill I
      have,
In reason or in nature, can pronounce
Him free from the defeat upon my gold
And jewels ; 'twas like a brother.  But for
His two confederates, though I should meet
Them in a mist, darker than night, or southern
      fens
Produce, my eyes would be so courteous sure,
To let me know them.


   *Enter* LADY AMPLE, *carried in as sick on a couch ;*
      LUCY, ENGINE, GINET.


   ENG. Room ! more air ! if heavenly ministers
Have leisure to consider or assist
The best of ladies, let them shew it now !
   LUCY. How do you, madam ?  Oh, I shall lose
The chief example of internal love,
Of gentle grace and feature, that the world
Did ever shew, to dignify our sex.

Eng. Work on! I must stand centinel beneath.
                                        [*Exit.*

Eld. Pal. Is her disease grown up to such ex-
        tremity?
Then it is time I seem to suffer too,
Or else my hopes will prove sicker than she.
    Lucy. More cruel than the panther on his prey!
Why speak you not? No comfort from your
        lips?
You, sir, that are the cause of this sad hour.
    Gin. He stands as if his legs had taken root;
A very mandrake.*
    Eld. Pal. How comes it, lady, all these
Beauties that but yesterday did seem to teach
The spring to flourish and rejoice, so soon
Are wither'd from our sight?
    Amp. It is in vain t'inquire the reason of
That grief, whose remedy is past. Had you
But felt so much remorse, or softness in
Your heart, as would have made you nobly just
And pitiful, the mourners of this day
Had wanted then their dead to weep upon.
    Eld. Pal. Am I the cause? Forbid it, gentle
        Heaven!
The virgins of our land, when this is told,
Will raze the monumental building where
My buried flesh shall dwell, and throw my dust
Before the sportive winds, till I am blown
About in parcels, less than eye-sight can
Discern.
    Lucy. She listens to you, sir.
    Eld. Pal. If I am guilty of neglect,
Give me a taste of duty, name how far
I shall submit to love: the mind hath no
Disease above recovery, if we have courage
To remove despair.

* *A very mandrake.* See vol. i., p. 39.

Amp. O, sir, the pride and scorns with which
    you first
Did entertain my passions and regard,
Have worn my easy heart away : my breast
Is emptier than mine eyes, that have distill'd
Their balls to funeral dew.   It is too late.
   Lucy. Ginet, my fears have in them too much
    prophecy ;
I told thee she would ne'er recover.
   Gin. For my poor part, I wish no easier bed
At night, than the cold grave where she must lie !
   Amp. Luce, Luce! intreat the gentleman to sit.
   Lucy. Sit near her, sir ; you hear her voice
    grows weak.
   Amp. That you may see your scorns could not
    persuade
My love to thoughts of danger or revenge,
The faint remainder of my breath I'll waste
In legacies ; and, sir, to you, you shall
Have all the laws will suffer me to give.
   Eld. Pal. Who, I ? sweet saint, take heed of
    your last deeds ;
Your bounty carries cunning murder in't :
I shall be kill'd with kindness, and depart
Weeping, like a fond infant, whom the nurse
Would soothe too early to his bed.
   Lucy. Nay, sir, no remedy; you must have all.
Though you procur'd her death, the world shall not
Report she died beholden to you.
   Gin. Go to her, sir, she'll speak with you again.
   Amp. Sir, if mine eyes, in all their health and
    glory,
Had not the power to warm you into love,
Where are my hopes, now they are dim, and have
Almost forgot the benefit of light ?
   Eld. Pal. Not love! lady! Queen of my heart!
What oaths or execrations can persuade your faith

From such a cruel jealousy?

AMP.        I'd have some testimony, sir; if but
T' assure the world, my love, and bounty at
My death; were both conferr'd on one that shew'd
So much requital, as declares he was
Of gentle human race.

ELD. PAL.                        What shall I do!
Prescribe me dangers now, horrid as those
Which midnight fires beget in o'ergrown cities.
Or winter's storms produce at sea; and try
How far my love will make me venture to
Augment th' esteem of your's.

AMP.  That trial of your love which I request,
Implies no danger, sir: 'tis not in me
T' urge any thing, but what your own desires
Would chuse.

ELD. PAL.  Name it! like eager mastiffs, chain'd
From the encounter of their game, my hot
Fierce appetite diminisheth my strength.

AMP.  'Tis only this: for fear some other should
Enjoy you when I'm cold in my last sleep,
I would entreat you to sit here, grow sick,
Languish, and die with me.

ELD. PAL.  How! die with you?
                        [*Takes Lucy aside.*
'Twere fit you hasten'd her to write down all
She can bestow, and in some form of law.
I fear she's mad; her senses are so lost,
She'll never find them to her use again.

LUCY.  I pray, sir, why?

ELD. PAL.  Did you not hear what a fantastic suit
She makes, that I would sit and die with her?

LUCY.  Does this request seem strange?  You will
Do little for a lady, that deny to bring her
Onward her last journey; or is't your thrift?
Alas, you know, souls travel without charge.

ELD. PAL.  [*Aside*]  Her little skull is tainted too.

Amp. Is he not willing, Luce?

Eld. Pal. My best, dear lady, I am willing to
Resign myself to any thing but death.
Do not suspect my kindness now: in troth,
I've business upon earth will hold me here
At least a score or two of years; but, when
That's done, I am content to follow you.

Amp. If this persuasion cannot reach at your
Consent, yet let me witness so much love
In you, as may enforce you languish and
Decay for my departure from your sight.

Lucy. Can you do less than languish for her death?
Sit down here, and begin.  True sorrow, sir,
If you have any in your breast, will quickly
Bring you low enough.

Eld. Pal. Alas, good ladies, do you think my
     languishment
And grief is to begin upon me now?
Heaven knows how I have pined and groan'd, since
     first
Your letter gave me knowledge of the cause.

Lucy. It is not seen, sir, in your face.

Eld. Pal. My face! I grant you; I bate* inwardly:
I'm scorch'd and dry'd, with sighing, to a mummy:
My heart and liver are not big enough
To choke a daw.  A lamb laid on the altar for
A sacrifice, hath much more entrails in't.

Lucy. Yet still your sorrow alters not your face.

Eld. Pal. Why no; I say, no man that ever was
Of nature's making, hath a face moulded
With less help for hypocrisy than mine.

Gix. Great pity, sir!

Eld. Pal. Though I endur'd the diet† and the flux,

* Contend.  Diminish—
    "Hys countenance did he never bate
     But kept hym stylle in a state."
                     *Archæologia*, xxi. 74.

† See ante. p. 5.

Lay seven days buried up to th' lips, like a
Diseas'd sad Indian, in warm sand,* whilst his
Afflicted female wipes his salt foam off
With her own hair, feeds him with buds of guacum†
For his salad, and pulp of salsa‡ for
His bread: I say, all this endur'd, would not
Concern my face.    Nothing can decline that.

    AMP. Yet you are us'd, sir, to bate inwardly?
    ELD. PAL. More than heirs unlanded, or unjoin-
      tur'd wives.

Enter ENGINE.

    ENG. What shall we do? Sir Tyrant Thrift's
      come home!
    ELD. PAL. Sir Tyrant Thrift!
    LUCY. My lady's guardian, sir.
    AMP. He meets th' expected hour just to my wish.
    LUCY. What! hath he brought a husband for my
      lady?
    ENG. There is a certain one-legg'd gentleman,
Whose better half of limbs is wood; for whom
Kind nature did provide no hands, to prevent
Stealing; and, to augment his gracefulness,
He's crooked as a witch's pin.

    LUCY. Is he so much wood?

    ENG. So much, that if my lady were in health,
And married to him, as her guardian did propose,
We should have an excellent generation
Of bed-staves.

    LUCY. When does he come?

    ENG. To-night, if his slow litter will consent;
For they convey him tenderly, lest his

* Dr. Graham, a celebrated quack of the end of last century, adopted " Earth-bathing " for the cure of various diseases. He was also famous for his " Celestial bed," a bed in which water took the place of feathers, and which was intended to counter-act sterility.

† *Guaiacum.* -A physical wood, attennant and aperient.

‡ Query, Sassafras? -A tree, the wood of which is medicinal.

Sharp bones should grate together.   Sir Pallatine,
I wish you could escape my master's sight.
    ELD. PAL.                 Is he coming hither?
    ENG. He's at the door!   My lady's sickness was
No sooner told him, but he straight projects
To proffer her a will of his own making :
He means, sir, to be heir of all.   If he
Should see you here, he would suspect my loyalty,
And doubt you for some cunning instrument,
That means to interrupt his covetous hopes.
    ELD. PAL. Then I'll be gone.
    ENG. No, sir ; he needs must meet you in
Your passage down : besides, it is not fit
For you, and your great hopes, with my dependency
On both, to have you absent when my lady dies :
I know you must have all.   Sir, I could wish
That we might hide you here.—
Draw out the chest within ! that's big enough
To hold you.   It were dangerous to have
My lady's guardian to find you, sir !
                          [*They draw in a chest.*
    ELD. PAL. How ! laid up like a brush'd gown,
        under lock
And key !   By this good light, not I.
    LUCY. O sir, if but to save the honour of
Your mistress' fame !   What will he think to see
So comely, and so straight a gentleman
Converse here with a lady in her chamber ?
And in a time that makes for his suspicion too,
When he's from home.
    ELD. PAL. I hate inclosure, I ;
It is the humour of a distress'd rat.
    GIN. It is retirement, sir ; and you'll come forth
Again so sage !
    AMP. Sir Pallatine !
    LUCY. Your lady calls, sir ! To her, and be kind.
    AMP. Will you permit the last of all my hours

Should be defil'd with infamy, proclaim'd
By lewder tongues to be unchaste, ev'n at
My death?   What will my guardian guess to find
You here?
   ELD. PAL. No more, I'll in! but think on't,
     gentle lady;
First to bate inwardly, and then to have
My outward person shut thus and enclos'd
From day-light, and your company; I say,
But think, if't be not worse than death.
                    *[He enters the chest.*
   AMP. Lock him up, Lace, safe as thy maidenhead.

       *Enter Sir* TYRANT THRIFT.

   THRIFT. Engine, where's my charge, Engine, my
     dear charge?
   ENG. Sick, as I told you, sir; and lost to all
The hope that earthly med'cine can procure.
Her physicians have taken their last fees,
And then went hence, shaking their empty heads,
As they had left less brain than hope.
   THRIFT. Alas, poor charge! come, let me see
     her, Engine.
   LUCY. At distance, sir, I pray; for I have heard
Your breath is somewhat sour with overfasting, sir,
On holiday eyes.
   THRIFT. Ha! what is she, Engine?
   ENG. A pure good soul, one that your ward desir'd,
For love and kindred's sake, t' have near her at
Her death; she'll outwatch a long rush candle,
And reads to her all night "the Posie of
Spiritual flowers."
   THRIFT. Does she not gape for legacies?
   ENG. Fie, no! there's a cornelian ring, perhaps,
She aims at, cost ten groats; or a wrought smock
My lady made now 'gainst her wedding, sir;
Trifles, which maids desire to weep upon

With funeral tales, after a midnight posset.

THRIFT. Thou saidst below, she hath made me
    her heir.

ENG. Of all, ev'n to her slippers and her pins.

AMP. Luce, methought, Luce, I heard my guar-
    dian's voice !

ENG. It seems her senses are grown warm again ;
Your presence will recover her.

THRIFT. Will it recover her ? then I'll be gone.

ENG. No sir ; she'll straight grow cold again.
On ! on ! she looks that you would speak to her.

THRIFT. Alas, poor charge ! I little thought to see
This doleful day.

AMP. We all are mortal, sir.

THRIFT. I've taken care and labour to provide
A husband for thee ; he's in's litter now,
Hastening to town : a fine young gentleman,
Only a little rumpled in the womb,
With falls his mother took after his making.

AMP. Death is my husband now ! but yet I
    thank
You for your tender pains, and wish you would
Continue it ; in quiet, governing my legacies.
When I am past the power to see it, sir,
You shall enjoy all.

THRIFT. This will occasion more church building,
And raising of new hospitals : there were
Enow before ; but, charge, you'll have it so.

AMP. I'll make, sir, one request ; which I have
    hope
You'll grant, in thankfulness to all my bounty.

THRIFT. O, dear charge ! any thing : your cousin
    here
Shall witness the consent and act.

AMP. Because I would not have my vanities
Remain, as fond examples, to persuade        ,
An imitation in those ladies that

Succeed my youthful pride i' th' town ; my plumes,
Fantastic flowers, and chains, my haughty rich
Embroideries, my gaudy gowns, and wanton jewels,
I have lock'd within a chest.

   LUCY. There, sir, there the chest stands!

   AMP. And I desire it may be buried with me.

   THRIFT. Engine, take care, Engine, to see it done.

   AMP. Now sir, I beseech you leave me ; for 'twill
But make my death more sorrowful, thus to
Continue my converse with one I so much love,
And must forsake at last.

   THRIFT. Alack, alack! bury her to-night, Engine.

   ENG. Not, sir, unless she dies.  Her ancestors
Have sojourn'd long here in St Barthol'mew's,
And there's a vault i' th' parish church, kept only
For her family : she must be buried there.

   THRIFT. Ay, Engine, ay ! and let me see ; the
     church,
Thou know'st, joins to my house : a good prevention
From a large walk ; 'twill save the charge of torch-
     light.

   ENG. What funeral guests ? the neighbours, sir,
     will look
To be invited.

   THRIFT. No more than will suffice
To carry down the corpse ; and, thou know'st,
     Engine,
She is no great weight.

   ENG. And what to entertain them, sir ?

   THRIFT. A little rosemary, which thou mayst steal
From th' Temple garden ; and as many comfits
As might serve to christen a watchman's bastard :
'Twill be enough.

   ENG. This will not do ; your citizen
Is a most fierce devourer, sir, of plums :
Six will destroy as many as can make
A banquet for an army.

THRIFT. I'll have no more, Engine,
I'll have no more! nor, d'ye hear, no burnt wine.
I do not like this drinking healths to th' memory
O' th' dead ; it is prophane.

ENG. You are obey'd :
But, sir, let me advise you now, to trust
The care and benefit of all your fate
Presents you in this house, to my discretion ;
And get you instantly to horse again.

THRIFT. Why, Engine? speak !

ENG. In brief, you know, that all
The writings which concern your ward's estate
Lie at her lawyer's, fifteen miles from hence.
Your credit, he not knowing, sir, she's sick,
Will eas'ly tempt them to your own possession :
Which, once enjoy'd, y' are free from all litigious
    suits
His envy might incense her kindred to.

THRIFT. Enough, Engine ; I am gone !

ENG. If you should meet the crooked lover in
His litter, sir, as 'tis in your own road,
You may persuade him move like a crab, backward ;*
For here's no mixture but with worms.

THRIFT. 'Tis well thought on, Engine ! farewell,
    Engine !
Be faithful, and be rich.

ENG. My breeding and
Good-manners, sir, teach me t' attend your bounty.

THRIFT. But, Engine, I could wish she would
Be sure to die to-night.

ENG. Alas, good soul ! I'll undertake
She shall do any thing to please you, sir.

　　　　　　　　　　　　*[Exit Thrift.*

AMP. Engine, thou hast wrought above the power

* " You yourself, sir, should be as old as I am,
　If, like a crab you could go backward."
　　　　　　　　　　*Shakespeare.*
Crabs move, not backward but sideways.

N

Of accident, or art.
          ENG. If you consider't with a just
And lib'ral brain : first, to prevent
Th' access and tedious visits of the fiend,
His love-sick monster ; and then rid him hence
Upon a journey, to preserve this house
Empty, and free to celebrate the rest
Of our designs.
          LUCY. This, Engine, is thy holiday.
                         [*Lucy knocks at the chest.*
What hoa ! Sir Pallatine, are you within ?
          ELD. PAL. Is Sir Tyrant Thrift gone ? open,
               lady, open !
          LUCY. The casement, sir I will ; a little to
Increase your witship's allowance of air ;
                    [*Opens a wicket at the end of the chest.*
But th' troth, for liberty of limbs, you may
As soon expect it in a galley, sir,
After six murders and a rape.
          ELD. PAL. How, lady of the lawn !
          LUCY. Sir Launcelot,
You may believe't, if your discreet faith please.
This tenement is cheap ; here you shall dwell,
Keep home and be no wanderer.
          ELD. PAL. The pox take me if I like this ! Sure,
               when
Th' advice of th' ancients is but ask'd they'll say
I am now worse than in the state of a bawd.
          ENG. D' you know this lady, sir ?
          ELD. PAL. The Lady Ample !
Her veil's off too, and in the lusty garb
Of health and merriment.   Now shall I grow
As modest as a snail, that in's affliction
Shrinks up himself and's horns into his shell,
Asham'd still to be seen.
          AMP. Could'st thou believe,
Thou bearded babe, thou dull engenderer !

Male rather in the back than in the brain ;
That I could sicken for thy love ? for th' cold
Society of a thin northern wit.
    ELD. PAL. [*Sings.*] *Then Trojans wail, with great*
        *remorse,*
*The Greeks are locked i' th' wooden horse.**

      *Enter* YOUNGER PALLATINE.

    LUCY. Pall, come in, Pall, 'tis done ! the spacious
      man
Of land is now contented with his own length.
    AMPLE. Your brother's come to see you, sir.
    ELD. PAL. Brother ! Mad girls these ! could'st
      thou believe't, sirrah ?
I am coffin'd up, like a salmon pie,
New sent from De'nshire, for a token. Come,
Break up the chest!
    Y. PAL. Stay, brother ! whose chest is it?
    ELD. PAL. Thou'lt ask more questions than a
      constable
In's sleep: pr'ythee dispatch !
    Y. PAL Brother, I can
But mark the malice and the envy of
Your nature : I am no sooner exalted
To rich possessions and a glorious mien,
But straight you tempt me to a forfeiture
Of all :—to commit felony, break open chests !
    ELD. PAL. O, for dame Patience, the fool's
      mistress !
    Y. PAL. Brother, you have pray'd well; Heaven
      send her you !
You must forsake you own fair fertile soil,
To live here by your wits !
    LUCY. And dream, sir, of
Enjoying goodly ladies, six yards high,
With satin trains behind them, ten yards long.

    * Two lines of an ancient ballad.

AMP. Cloth'd all in purple, and embroidered with
Embossments wrought in imag'ry ; the works
O' th' ancient poets drawn into similitude,
And cunning shape.
    GIN. And this attain'd, sir, by your wits !
    Y. PAL. Nothing could please your haughty
      palate
But the muskatelli, and Frontiniac grape !
Your Turin and your Tuscan veal, with red
Legg'd partridge of the Genoa hills.
    ENG. With your broad liver o' th' Venetian goose,
Fatten'd by a Jew ; and your aged carp,
Bred i'th' Geneva lake.
    AMP. LUCY. GIN. All this maintain'd, sir, by
      your wits.
    ENG. And then your talk'd, sir, of you snails
      ta'en from
The dewy marble quarries of Carrara,
And sous'd in Lucca oil; with cream of Switzerland,
And Genoa paste.
    Y. PAL. Your angelots of Brie ;*
Your Marsolini, and Parmasan of Lodi ;
Your Malamucka melons, and Sicilian dates ;
And then to close your proud voluptuous maw,
Marmalade made by the cleanly nuns of Lisbon.†
    AMP. LUCY. GIN. And still thus feasted by your
      wits !
    ELD. PAL. Deafen'd with tyranny ! is there no
      end ?

* Skinner, in his Etymologicon, voce *angelot*, says, that the
cheese known by that name is brought from Normandy, and
he supposes it to have been so called from some person of the
name of *Angelot* or *Angelo*, who first made, and perhaps
impressed it with his own name or mark.

† This obtains still. The manufacture, however, has always
been confined to one convent at Lisbon, which, until Napoleon's
invasion, had long been celebrated for its antique gates of pure
silver. A prize of such value was too attractive to escape the
rapacity of the avaricious Corsican.

AMP.  Yes, sir, an end of you: you shall be now
Convey'd into a close dark vault; there keep
My silent grandsire company, and all
The music of your groans engross to your own ears.
  ELD. PAL.  How! buried, and alive!
  Y. PAL.  Brother, your hand!
Farewell, I'm for the north: the fame of this,
Your voluntary death, will there be thought
Pure courtesy to me; I mean to take
Possession, sir, and patiently converse
With all those hinds, those herds, and flocks,
That you disdain'd in fullness of your wit.
  LUCY.  Help, Pall, to carry him! he takes it
    heavily.
  ELD. PAL.  I'll not endure't:—fire! murder! fire!
Treason! murder! treason! fire!
  AMP.  Alas, you are not heard!
The house contains none but ourselves.
            *[Exeunt, carrying out the chest.*

## SCENE II.

*Enter* THWACK, PERT, MEAGER.

  PERT.  We bring you, sir, commends from
    Pallatine.
  THWACK.  I had as lieve y' had brought it from
    the devil,
Together with his horns boil'd to a jelly,
For a cordial against lust.
  MEA.  We mean the younger Pallatine; one, sir,
That loves your person, and laments this chance,
Which his false brother hath exposed you to.
  PERT.  And, as we told you, sir, by his command,
We have compounded with the constable;
In whose dark house y' are now a prisoner.
But, sir, take't on my faith, you must disburse,
For gold is a restorative, as well

To liberty as health.*

THWACK. And you believe,
It seems, that your small, tiny officer
Will take his unction in the palm, as lovingly
As your exalted grandee, that awes all
With hideous voice and face ?

PERT. Even so the moderns render it.

THWACK. But, gentlemen, you ask a hundred
    pounds ;
'Tis all I've left.

PERT. Sir, do but think
What a prodigious blemish it will be
Both to your ingenuity and fame,
To be betray'd by one that is believ'd
No wittier than yourself, and lie imprison'd
For a bawd.

THWACK. Sir, name it not ! you kill me through
    the ear.
I'd rather, sir, you'd take my mother from
Her grave, and put her to do penance in
Her winding-sheet.   There is the sum !

MEA. I'll in, sir, and discharge you. [*Exit Meager.*
THWACK. These carnal mulcts and tributes are
    design'd
Only to such vain people as have land.
Are you and your friend landed, sir ?

PERT. Such land as we can share, sir, in the map.
THWACK. Lo' you there now ! These live by
    their wits.
Why should not I take the next key I meet,

* Anthony Wood says, that Dr. William Butler, the great
physician of Cambridge, coming to visit Francis Tresham "*as
his fashion was, gave him a piece of very pure gold to put in
his mouth ;* and upon taking out that gold, Butler said he was
poisoned." I. Athenæ Oxon. 329. Potable gold appears to
have been a considerable article in the Materia Medica. In
*Baker's Practise of the new and old physick*, 1599, p. 440. &c., it
is esteemed a specific in a vast number of disorders.—See note
page 72 of vol. i.

And open this great head, to try if there
Be any brains left, but sour curds and plum-
    broth?
Cozen'd in my youth! cozen'd in my age!
Sir, do you judge, if I have cause to curse
This false inhuman town.  When I was young,
I was arrested for a stale commodity
Of nut-crackers, long-gigs, and casting-tops: *
Now I am old, imprison'd for a bawd.
    PERT. These are sad tales.
    THWACK. I will write down to th' country, to
      dehort†
The gentry from coming hither, letters
Of strange dire news; you shall disperse them, sir.
    PERT. Most faithfully.
    THWACK.                That there are Lents,
Six years long, proclaim'd by th' State:
That our French and Deal Wines are poison'd so
With brimstone by the Hollander, that they
Will only serve for med'cine to recover
Children of the itch; and there is not left
Sack enough to mull for a parson's cold.
    PERT. This needs must terrify.
    THWACK. That our theatres are raz'd down; and
      where
They stood, hoarse midnight lectures preach'd by
      wives
Of comb-makers, and midwives of Tower-wharf.
    PERT. 'Twill take impregnably.
    THWACK. And that a new plantation, sir, mark me,
Is made i' th' Covent Garden, from the sutlery
O' th' German camps and the suburbs of Paris;
Where such a salt disease reigns, as will make

* Query.—May not this mean?—" for a common prostitute
who had stood in the Pillory, convicted of snaring birds with
a 'gig' (or decoy made of goose feathers), and of cheating
at dice play."
  † Dissuade.

Sassafras dearer than unicorn's horn.*
   PERT. This cannot chuse but fright the gentry
     hence,
And more impoverish the town, than a
Subversion of their fair of Barthol'mew,
The absence of the terms and court.
   THWACK. You shall, if my projections thrive,
In less, sir, than a year,
Stable your horses in the new exchange,
And graze them in the old.

   *Enter* YOUNGER PALLATINE, MEAGER, QUEASY,
     SNORE, MISTRESS SNORE.

   PERT. Jog off! there's Pall, treating for your
     liberty.
   Y. PAL. The canopy, the hangings, and the bed,
Are worth more than your rent: Come, y' are over-
     paid!
Besides, the gentleman's betray'd; he is no bawd!
   SNORE. Truly a very civil gentleman;
'Las, he hath only roar'd, and sworn, and curs'd,
Since he was ta'en: no bawdry, I'll assure ye.
   M. SNORE. Gossip Queasy, what a good 'yer †
     would ye have?
   QUE. I am content, if you and I were friends.
   Y. PAL. Come, come, agree; 'tis I that ever
     bleed,
And suffer in your wars.
   M. SNORE. Sweet Master Pallatine, hear me but
     speak!
Have I not often said, Why, neighbour Queasy,
Come to my house; besides, your daughter Mall,
You know, last pompion-time, dined with me
     thrice!
When my child's best yellow stockings were miss-
     ing,

   * See vol. 1, p. xxix.         † *Goodyer*—A devil.

And a new pewter porringer, mark'd with P. L.
    SNORE. Ay! for Elizabeth Snore.
    M. SNORE. The pewterer that mark'd it was my
      uncle.
    QUE. Why, did my daughter steal your goods?
    M. SNORE. You hear me say nothing; but
      there is
As bad as this, I warrant you, learnt at
The bakehouse. I'll have an oven o' mine own
    shortly.
    Y. PAL. Come, no more words! there's to recon-
      cile you,
In burnt wine and cake. Go, get you all in!
I'm full of business and strange mystery.
          [*Exeunt Snore, Mistress Snore, Queasy.*
    MEA. A hundred, Pall: 'twas all his store: it lies
Here, my brave boy, warm and secure in pouch.
    PERT. We'll share't anon.—What need you
      blush, Sir Morglay,
Like a maid newly undone in a dark
Entry? There are disasters, sure, as bad
As your's recorded in the city annals.
    THWACK. Your brother is a gentleman
Of a most even and blessed composition, sir;
His very blood is made of holy-water,
Less salt than almond-milk.*
    Y. PAL. My silly reprehensions were despis'd;
Y' would be his disciple, and follow him
In a new path, unknown to his own feet.
Yet I've walk'd in it since, and prosper'd, as
You see, without or land or tenement.
    THWACK. 'Tis possible to live b' our wits! that is
As evident as light; no human learning
Shall advise me from that faith.
    Y. PAL. Sir Knight, what will you give worthy
      my brain

* See ante, p. 120.

And me, if, after a concealment of
Your present shame, I can advise you how
T' achieve such store of wealth and treasure as
Shall keep you here, th' exemplar glory of the town,
A long whole year, without relief or charge
From your own rents?   This, I take it, was
The whole pride, at which, some few days since,
Your fancy aim'd.

    THWACK. This was, sir, in the hours of haughti-
        ness
And hope; but now—

    Y. PAL. I'll do 't, whilst my poor brother, too,
Low, and declin'd, shall see and envy it.

    THWACK. Live in full port?   observ'd and
        wonder'd at;
Wine ever flowing in large Saxon romekins *
About my board? with your soft sarsnet smock
At night, and foreign music to entrance?

    Y. PAL. All this, and more than thy invention
Can invite thee to.

    THWACK. I'll make thee heir of my estate!
Take my right hand, and your two friends
For witnesses.

    Y. PAL. Enough! hear me with haste :—
The Lady Ample's dead!   Nay, there are things
Have chanc'd since your concealment far more fit
For wonder, sir, than this.   Out of a silly piety,
T' avoid a thirst of gold and gaudy pride
I' th' world, sh'ath buried with her in a chest,
Her jewels and her clothes : besides, as I'm
Inform'd by Luce, my wise intelligence,
Five thousand pounds in gold ; a legacy,
Left by her aunt, more than her guardian knew.

    THWACK. Well, what of this?

    Y. PAL. Yourself and I, join'd, sir, in a most
    firm

* Drinking cups —goblets.

And loyal league, may rob this chest.

THWACK. Marry, and will !

Y. PAL. Then, when your promise is but ratified,
Take all the treasure for your own expense !

THWACK. Come, let us go ! my fingers burn till
    they
Are telling it ; the night will grow upon's !
Only you and I, I'll not trust new faces.
Dismiss these gentlemen!

Y. PAL. At the next street, sir.

THWACK. This is at least a girn * of fortune, if
Not a fair smile.   I'm still for my old problem ;
Since the living rob me, I'll rob the dead.

Y. PAL. On, my delicious Pert ; now is the time
To make our purses swell, and spirits climb.

[Exeunt omnes.

---

## ACT V. SCENE I.

*Enter* YOUNGER PALLATINE, AMPLE, LUCY,
ENGINE, *with a torch.*

Y. PAL. Engine, draw out the chest, and ope the
    wicket ;
Let us not hinder him the air, since 'tis
Become his food.

ELD. PAL. Who's there ? what are you ? speak !

AMP. A brace of mourning virgins, sir, that had
You died in love, and in your wits, would now
Have brought roses and lilies, buds of the brier,
And summer pinks, to strew upon your hearse.

ELD. PAL. Then you resolve me dead !

---

* "Girn" in Scotland and in the northern parts of England,
is nearly equivalent to "grin," although a "girn" is more
broadly expressed ; such as that a caged wild beast, when dis-
turbed or near starvation point, might indicate.  "Girn," in
Scotch, also means "a snare for birds."

Lucy. 'Twere good that you would so resolve
yourself.

Y. Pal. She counsels you to wise and severe
thoughts :
Why, you are no more mortified* than men
That are about to dance the morrice.†

Eld. Pal. Ladies, and brother too, whom I
begin
To worship now for tenderness of heart,
Can you believe I am so leaden, stupid,
And so very a fish, to think you dare
Thus murder me in bravery of mirth ?
You have gone far : part of my suff'rance I
Confess a justice to me.

Amp. O, do you so ?
Have your heart and brain met upon that point,
And render'd you silly to your own thoughts ?

Eld. Pal. Somewhat mistaken i' th' projection of
My journey hither.   Three hours in a chest,
Among the dead, will profit more than three
Years in a study, 'mongst fathers, school-men,
And philosophers.

Y. Pal. And y' are persuaded now, that there
is, relative
To th' maintaining of a poor younger brother,
Something besides his wits ?

Eld. Pal. 'Tis so conceiv'd.

Amp. And that we ladies of the town, or court,
Have not such waxen hearts, that ev'ry beam
From a hot lover's eye can melt them through
Our breasts !

* Teazed.

† The Morris is a very ancient dance, in which the performers were accustomed to be dressed in grotesque costume,
with bells, &c., each having a short stick which was used in the
various evolutions of the dance.  It is, even now, danced in some
provincial villages, where old customs have not yielded to
"progress," and some relics of happiness may still be stumbled
on.

Eld. Pal. Faith, 'tis imagin'd too!

Lucy. That though th' unruly appetites of some
Perverted few of our frail sex have made
Them yield their honours to unlawful love,
Yet there is no such want of you male sinners,
As should constrain them hire you to't with gold.

Eld. Pal. Y' have taught me a new music.  I am all
Consent and concordance !

Eng. And that the nimble packing hand, the swift
Disorder'd shuffle, or the slur ; or his more
Base employment, that with youth and an
Eternal back, engenders for his bread ;
Do all belong to men, that may be said
To live, sir, by their sins, not by their wits ?

Eld. Pal. Sir, whom I love not, nor desire to love,
I am of your mind too.

Y. Pal. Madam, a fair conversion : 'tis now fit
I sue unto you for his liberty.

Amp. Alas, he hath so profited in this
Retirement, that I fear he will not willingly
Come out.

Eld. Pal. O lady, doubt it not ; open the chest !

Amp. A little patience, sir.

*Enter* Ginet.

Gin. Madam, we are undone ; your guardian is
At door, knocking as if he meant to wake
All his dead neighbours in the church.

Amp. So soon return'd ! It is not midnight yet.

Eng. I know the bait that tempts him back with such
Strange haste ; and have, according to your will,
Provided, Madam, to betray his hopes.

Amp. Excellent Engine !

Eng. This key conveys you through the chancel to
The house gallery : my way lies here ! I'll let
Him in, and try how our design will relish.

         [*Exit Engine.*

 Amp. Come, sir, it is decreed in our wise counsel,
You must be laid some distance from this place.
  Eld. Pal. Pray save your labour, madam ! I'll
   come forth.
  Amp. No, sir, not yet.
  Eld. Pal. Brother, a cast of your voice.
  Y. Pal. She hath the key, brother : 'tis but au
   hour's
Dark contemplation more.
  Eld. Pal. Madam, hear me speak.
  Amp. Nay, no beginning of orations now ;
This is a time of great dispatch and haste :
We have more plots than a general in a siege.

      [*Exeunt, carrying out the chest.*

*Enter* Thrift, Engine.

 Eng. None of the writings, sir ! and yet perplex
Yourself with so much speed in a return?
  Thrift. The lawyer was from home ; but, En-
   gine, I
Had hope to have prevented by my haste,
Though not her fun'ral, yet the fun'ral of
The chest. Ah, dear Engine, tell me but why
So much pure innocent treasure should be
Thus grown into a dark forgetfulness.
  Eng. I thought I had encounter'd his intents.
All, sir, that law allow'd her bounty to
Bestow, is your's ; but for the chest, trust me,
'Tis buried, sir : the key is here, sir, of no use.
  Thrift. Hah, Engine, give it me !
  Eng. And, sir, to vex your meditation more,
Though not with manners, yet with truth ; know
   there

Is hidden in that chest a plenteous heap
Of gold, together with a rope of most
Inestimable pearl, left by her late
Dead aunt, by will, and kept from your discovery.
 THRIFT. Is this true, Engine?
 ENG. That precise chit, Luce, her cousin puritan,
Was at th' interring of't; conceal'd it till
The fun'ral forms were past, and then, forsooth,
She boasted that it was a pious means
To avoid covetous desires i' th' world.
 THRIFT. These fun'ral tales, Engine, are sad
  indeed;
Able to melt an eye, though harder than that heart,
Which did consent to so much cruelty upon
The harmless treasure.
 ENG. I mourn within, sir, too.
 THRIFT. Give me the key that leads me from
  my house
Unto the chancel door.
 ENG. 'Tis very late, sir; whither will you go?
 THRIFT. Never too late to pray. My heart is
  heavy.
 ENG. Where shall I wait you, sir?
 THRIFT. At my low gall'ry door; I may chance
  stay long.
 ENG. This takes me more than all the kindness
  fortune
Ever shew'd me; a decent transmutation.
I am no more your steward, but your spy. [*Exeunt.*

## SCENE II.

*Enter* YOUNGER PALLATINE, PERT, MEAGER, SNORE,
and WATCHMEN.

 Y. PAL. There, there's more money for your
watch. Methinks

Th' have not drunk wine enough ; they do not chirp.
   SNORE. Your wine mates* them, they understand
      it not ;
But they have very good capacity in ale ;
Ale, sir, will heat 'em more than your beef brewis.†
   Y. PAL. Well, let them have ale, then.
   SNORE. O sir, 'twill make 'em sing like the silk-
      knitters
Of Cock Lane.
   Y. PAL. Meager ! go you to Sir Tyrant Thrift's
      house.
Luce and the lady are alone.  They will
Have cause to use your diligence ; make haste !
   MEA. Your dog tied to a bottle shall not out-run
      me.                                                      [*Exit.*
   Y. PAL. Pert, stay you here with master constable;
And, when occasion calls, see that you draw
Your lusty bill-men forth, bravely advanc'd
Under the colours of queen Ample and
Myself, her general.
   PERT. If ale can fortify, fear not.  Where's Sir
      Morglay ?
   Y. PAL. I'm now to meet him i' th' church-yard.
      Th' old blade
Skulks there like a tame filcher, as he had
Ne'er stol'n 'bove eggs from market-women ;
Robb'd an orchard, or a cheese loft.
   SNORE. We'll wait your worship in this corner.
   Y. PAL. No stirring, till I either come or send.
   SNORE. Pray, sir, let's not stay long : 'tis a cold
      night,
And I have nothing on my bed at home,
But a thin coverlet, and my wife's sey‡ petticoat :

* Stupifies ; confounds ; puzzles.
† The liquor in which meat is boiled, with bread soaked in it.
So *Geta* in *The Prophetess,* " What an inundation of *brewis* shall
I swim in !"—S.   Called in Scotland "breu."
‡ Silk.  Also, a kind of woollen stuff.

She'll ne'er sleep, poor soul, till I come home
To keep her warm.
    Y. PAL. You shall be sent for straight.
Be merry, my dull sons o' th' night, and chirp.
[Exit.

    SNORE. Come, neighbour Runlet! sighing pays
      no rent,
Though the landlady be in love. Sing out!
They sing a catch in four parts.
With lanthorn on stall; at Trea Trip* we play
For ale, cheese, and pudding, till it be day :
And for our breakfast, after long sitting,
We steal a street pig, o' th' constable's getting.

Enter ENGINE.

    ENG. Sir, draw down your Watch into the church
And let 'em lie hid close by the vestry-door.
    PERT. Is he there already?
    ENG. Fat carriers, sir, make not more haste to
      bed
Nor lean philosophers to rise. I've so
Prepar'd things, that he'll find himself mistaken.
    PERT. Close by the vestry-door?
    ENG. Right, sir!
I'll to my lady, and expect th' event of your surprize.
    PERT. Follow master constable! one and one,
All in a file.
[Exeunt.

Enter THRIFT, with a candle.

    THRIFT. I cannot find where they have laid her
      coffin ;
But there's the chest. I'll draw it out, that I
May have more room to search and rifle it.
The weight seems easy to me, though my strength
Be old. How long, thou bright all-powerful mineral,

* See page 171.
O

Might'st thou lie hid, ere the dull dead, that are  
Entomb'd about thee here, could reach the sense  
To turn wise thieves, and steal thee from oblivion?—  
				[*Opens it, and finds a halter.*  
How! a halter! what fiend affronts me with  
This emblem? Is this the rope of orient pearl?

*Enter* PERT, SNORE, WATCHMEN.

PERT. Now I have told you, Master Constable,  
The entire plot.   Mark but how like that chest  
Is to the other, where the elder Pallatine  
Lies a perdu.   Engine contriv'd them both.  
  THRIFT. Ha! what are these? the constable and  
    watch?  
  PERT. Seize on him for no less than sacrilege.  
  THRIFT. Why, neighbours, gentlemen!  
  PERT. Away with him!  
  SNORE.   We shall know now who stole the  
    wainscot cover  
From the font, and the vicar's surplice.  
  PERT. Alas, grave sir, become a forfeiture  
To th' king, for sacrilege!  
  THRIFT. Hear me but speak.  
  SNORE. No, not in a cause against the king.  
  Pert. Lead to's own house! he shall be pris'ner  
    there,  
And lock'd up safe enough.  
  THRIFT. Undone for ever!			[*Exeunt.*

*Enter* YOUNGER PALLATINE, THWACK, *with an iron  
				crow and dark lanthorn.*

THWACK. Why, this was such a firk of piety,*  
I ne'er heard of: bury her gold with her!  
'Tis strange her old shoes were not interr'd too,  
For fear the days of Edgar should return,  
When they coin'd leather.  
       * Trick or quirk;—freak.

Y. PAL. Come, sir, lay down your instrument!

THWACK. Why so?

Y. PAL. I'm so taken with thy free, jolly nature,
I cannot for my heart proceed to more
Defeat upon thy liberty; all that
I told thee were rank lies.

THWACK. How! no treasure trovar?*

Y. PAL. Not so much as will pay for that small
    candle light
We waste to find it out.

THWACK. I thank you, sir.
                           *[Flings down the crow of iron.*

Y. PAL. You shall have cause, when you hear
    more. To this
Dark region, sir, solemn, and silent, as
Your thoughts must be ere they are mortified,
Have I now brought you, to perceive what an
Immense large ass—under your favour, knight—
You are to be seduc'd to such vain stratagems,
By that more profound fop, your friend, my brother.

THWACK. How had I been serv'd, if I had
    brought my scales
Hither to weigh this gold? But on! Your brother,
Whose name, let me tell you first, sounds far worse
To me than does a serjeant to a young
Indebted lover, that's arrested in his coach,
And with his mistress by him.

Y. PAL. You are believ'd. But will you now
    confirm
Me to your grace and love, if I shall make't

* Or more properly *treasure trove,* " derived," as the excellent commentator Blackstone observes, " from the French word *trover,* to find, and called in Latin *Thesaurus inventus;* which is, where any money or coin, gold, silver, plate, or bullion, is found hidden in the earth, or other private place, the owner thereof being unknown; in which case the treasure belongs to the king: but if he that hid it be known, or afterwards found out, the owner, and not the king, is entitled to it."—*Commentaries,* vol. 1., p. 295.

Appear, that, in a kind revenge of what
You suffer'd, sir, I've made this false, and great
Seducer of mankind, to suffer more ?

THWACK. The Legend, Talmud, nor the Alcoran,*
Have not such doubtful tales as these : but make't
Appear ; I would have evidence.

Y. PAL. Then, take't on my religion, sir, he was
Laid up in durance for a bawd, before
He betray'd you to the same preferment.

THWACK. Shall this be justified when my disgrace
Comes to be known ? wilt thou then witness it ?

Y. PAL. With a deep oath !   And, sir, to tempt
    more of
Your favours on poor me, that ever mourn'd
For all your sufferings, know you shall now
See him enclos'd in a blind chest ; where he
Lies bath'd, sir, in a greater sweat than ere
Corneliust took in his own tub.

THWACK. Here, amongst sepulchres and melan-
    choly bones,
Let me but see't, and I will die for joy,
To make thee instantly my heir.

Y. PAL. You shall ! and yet, ere the sun rise,
    find him
Enthrall'd too in a new distress.

THWACK. Dost want money ? bring me to parch-
    ment and
A scriv'ner, I'll seal out two pound of wax.
                    [*Young Pallatine knocks at the chest.*
Y. PAL. You, sir, my near'st ally, are you asleep?
ELD. PAL. O brother, art thou come ? quick, let
    me forth !

* *The Legend* is the well-known golden Legend : *The Talmud*
is a book of the Jewish law, devised by their rabbins, and of
great authority among them.

† The inventor of the sweating-tub used in the cure of the
Lues Venerea.   See in " Platonic Lovers," p. 57, ante.

Y. PAL. Here is a certain friend of yours, presents
His loving visit, sir.                  [*Opens the wicket.*

ELD. PAL.               Sir Morglay Thwack!
I had rather have seen my sister naked.

THWACK. What, like a bashful badger, do you draw
Your head into your hole again? come, sir,
Out with that sage noddle that has contriv'd
So cunningly for me, and your dear self.

ELD. PAL. Here! take my eyelids, knight, and
      sew 'em up :
I dare not see thy face.

THWACK. But what think you
Of a new journey from the north, to live
Here by your wits ; or midnight visits, sir,
To the Mogul's niece ?

ELD. PAL. I have offended, knight !
Whip me with wire, headed with rowels of
Sharp Ripon spurs :* I'll endure any thing
Rather than thee.

THWACK. We have, I thank your bounteous brain,
Been entertain'd with various concerts, sir,
Of whispering lutes, to soothe us into slumbers ;
Spirits of Clare † to bathe our temples in ;
And then the wholesome womb of woman too,
That never teem'd : all this for nothing, sir!

Y. PAL. Come ! I'll let him forth.

THWACK. Rogue ; if thou lov'st me !
Nay, let him be confin'd thus, one short month,
I'll send him down to country fairs for a
New motion ‡ made b' a German engineer.

* *Ripon* is a town in the county of York, still celebrated for
the excellence of the *spurs* made there. *Ripon spurs* are also
mentioned in *Ben Jonson's Staple of News*, A. I. S. 3.
      " Your box ? why there's an angell ; if *my spurs*
        Be not right *Ripon*."
† Clarry. A wine made with grapes, honey, and aromatic
spices. Halliwell observes : " Wine mixed with honey and
spices, and afterwards strained, was called *clarré*."
‡ Puppet.

Y. PAL. 'Las, he is my brother.

THWACK. Or for a solitary ape,
Led captive thus by th' Hollander, because
He came aloft for Spain, and would not for the
    States.*

Y. PAL. Sir Morglay, leave your lanthorn
    here, and stay
My coming at yon door; I'll let him out!
But for the new distress I promis'd on
His person, take it on my manhood, sir,
He feels it strait.

THWACK. Finely ensnar'd again, and instantly?

Y. PAL. Have a good faith, and go.
                            *[Exit Thwack.*

ELD. PAL. Dear brother, wilt thou give me
    liberty?

Y. PAL. Upon condition, sir, you kiss these
    hilts;
Swear not to follow me, but here remain
Until the Lady Ample shall consent
To' th' freedom I bestow.       *[He kisses the hilts.*

ELD. PAL. 'Tis done! a vow inviolate!
            *[He opens the chest and lets him out.*

Y. PAL. Now silence, brother! not one curse,
    nor thanks.        *[Exit Younger Pallatine.*

* These sort of tricks are still taught to horses, dogs. and
monkeys, and are publicly exhibited.  So in *Ram Alley*, Will
Smallshanks says to Captain Face.

    "————————————————Now, sir,
    What can you do for the great Turk:
    What can you do for the Pope of Rome?
    Hark! he stirreth not, he moveth not, he waggeth not:
    What can you do for the town of Geneva, sirrah!"

Again, in D'avenant's Poem *On the Long Vacation*, describing
the diversions of Bartholomew Fair, he mentions the

    " Ape led captive still in chaine,
    Till he renounce the Pope and Spaine."

Induction to *Bartholomew Fair*—" nor a juggler with a well-
educated ape, to come over the chain for a King of England,
and back again for the prince, and sit still for the Pope and the
King of Spain."

ELD. PAL. Fate and a good star speed me!
  though I have
Long since amaz'd myself e'en to a marble,
Yet I have courage left to ask, what this
Might mean? Was ever two-legg'd man thus us'd?

*Enter* PERT, SNORE, *and* WATCHMEN.

PERT. Pall and his friend are gone: I must not
  stay
His sight; but after you have seized upon him
Lead him a prisoner to the lady too.     [*Exit Pert.*
  SNORE. Warrant ye, though he were Gog or
    Hildebrand.*           [*They lay hold on him.*
ELD. PAL. How now! what mean you, sirs?
SNORE. Yield to the constable!
ELD. PAL. 'Tis yielded, sir, that you are con-
    stable,
But where have I offended?
  SNORE. Here, sir; you have committed sacrilege,
And robb'd an alderman's tomb, of himself
And his two sons kneeling in brass.
    ELD. PAL. How! flea monuments of their brazen
      skins!
  SNORE. Look; a dark lanthorn, and an iron crow;
Fine evidence for a jury!
    ELD. PAL. I like this plot; the Lady Ample and
My brother have most rare triumphant wits.
Now, by this hand, I am most eagerly
In love with both. I find I have deserv'd all,
And am resolv'd t' hug them and their designs,
Though they afflict me more and more. Whither
      must I go?
  SNORE. Away with him! Saucy fellow! Examine
The king's constable?                 [*Exeunt.*
          * Pope Gregory the Seventh.

## Scene III.

*Enter* Younger Pallatine, Thwack, Ample,
Lucy, Meager.

Mea. I am become your guardian's gaoler, lady;
He's safe lock'd in the parlour, and there howls,
Like a dog that sees a witch flying.

Thwack. I long to hear how my wise tutor
thrives
I' th' new defeat.

Amp. 'Tis well you are converted;
Believe't, that gentleman deserves your thanks.

Thwack. Lady, seal my conversion on your lip;
'Tis the first leading kiss that I intend
For after chastity.　　　　　　　[*Kisses her.*

Y. Pal. Luce, see you make the proposition
good,
Which I shall give my brother from this lady,
Or I'll so swaddle your small bones.

Lucy. Sweet Pall, thou shalt. Madam, you'll
please to stand
To what I lately mention'd to your own desire?

Amp. To every particle and more.

### *Enter* Pert.

Pert. Your brother's come! this room must be
his prison.

Y. Pal. 'Way, Luce, away! stand in the closet,
madam,
That you may hear us both, and reach my call.

Thwack. I'll stay and see him.

Y. Pal. No, knight! You are decreed Sir Tyrant's
judge:
Go that way, sir, and force him to compound.

Thwack. I'll fine him soundly.
Till's purse shrink like a bladder in the fire.
　　　　[*Exeunt Ample, Lucy, Thwack, Meager, Pert.*

*Enter* SNORE, ELDER PALLATINE.

SNORE. Here, sir! This is your gaol; too good
   for such
A great offender.

ELD. PAL. Sacrilege! very well:
Now all the pulpit-cushions, all the hearse-clothes
And winding-sheets, that have been stol'n about
The town this year, will be laid to my charge.

Y. PAL. Pray leave us, master constable, and
   look
Unto your other bondman in the parlour.

                        [*Exit Snore.*

ELD. PAL. This is the wittiest offspring that our
   name
E'er had; I love him beyond hope or lust.
My father was no poet, sure; I wonder
How he got him.

Y. PAL. I know you curse me now.

ELD. PAL. Brother, in troth, you lie! and whoe'er
   believes it.

Y. PAL. Indeed you do; conjurors in a circle,
That have rais'd up a wrong spirit, curse not
So much, nor yet so inwardly.

ELD. PAL. I've a great mind to kiss thee.

Y. PAL. You have not, sure?

ELD. PAL. I shall do't, and eat up thy lips so far,
Till th'ast nothing left to cover thy teeth.

Y. PAL. And can you think all the afflictions you
Endur'd were merited? First, for misleading
Morglay, your old friend; then, neglect of me,
And haughty overvaluing yourself?

ELD. PAL. Brother, I murmur not; the traps
   that you
Have laid were so ingenious, I could wish
To fall in them again.

Y. PAL. The Lady Ample, sir,

There, is the great contriver, that hath weav'd
These knots so intricate and safe : 'las, I
Was but her lowly instrument.
    ELD. PAL. Ah, that lady !  Were I a king, she
      should
Sit with me under my best canopy ;
A silver sceptre in her hand, with which
I'd give her leave to break my head for ev'ry fault
I did commit.
    Y. PAL. But say I bring this lady, sir, unto
Your lawful sheets ; make her your bosom wife :
Besides the plenty of her heritage,
How would it sound, that you had conquer'd her
Who hath so often conquer'd you ?
    ELD. PAL. Dear brother, no new plots.
    Y. PAL. Six thousand pounds, sir, is your yearly
      rent ;
A fair temptation to a discreet lady.
Luce hath fill'd both mine ears with hope ; besides,
I heard her say, she ne'er should meet a man,
That she could more subdue with wit and govern-
      ment
    ELD. PAL. That I'll venture.
    Y. PAL. Well, my first bounty is your freedom,
      sir ;
For th' constable obeys no law but mine.
And now, madam, appear !

Enter AMPLE, LUCY.

    AMP. Y'are welcome 'mongst the living, sir.
    ELD. PAL. Lady, no words.  If y'have but so
      much mercy
As could secure one that your eyes affect——
    AMP. Why, you're grown arrogant again ; d'you
      think
They are so weak to affect you ?
    ELD. PAL. I have a heart so kind unto myself,

To wish they could ; O we should live——
   AMP. Not by our wits.
   ELD. PAL. No, no ; but with such soft content ;
Still in conspiracy how to betray ourselves
To new delights : keep harmony with no
More noise than what the upper motions* make ;
And this so constant too ; turtles themselves,
Seeing our faith, shall slight their own, and pine
With jealousy.
   AMP. Luce, the youth talks sense now !
No med'cine for the brain, like to captivity
In a dark chest.
   Y. PAL. O madam, you are cruel!
   AMP. Well, my sad convertite, joy yet at this :
I've often made a vow to marry on
That very day my wardship is expir'd :
And two hours since that liberty begun.
   LUCY. Nay, hear her out! Your wishes are so
      saucy, sir.
   AMP. And, know, my glory is dispatch. My
      ancestors
Were of the fiery French, and taught me love
Hot eagerness and haste.
   ELD. PAL. Let me be rude a while ;
Lie with your judgment, and beget
Sages on that. My dearest, chiefest lady.
   AMP. Your brain's yet foul, and will recoil again.
   ELD. PAL. No more ! I'll swallow down my
      tongue.
   AMP. If, sir, your nature be so excellent,
As your kind brother hath confirm'd to Luce
And me, follow, and I'll present you straight
With certain writings you shall seal to, hood-wink'd,
And purely ignorant of what thy are.
This is the swiftest, and the easiest test,
That I can make of your bold love : do this,

       * The orbs in their courses. S.

Perhaps I may vouchsafe to marry you.
The writings are within.

   ELR. PAL. Lead me to trial ; come !

   AMP. But, sir, if I should marry you, it is
In confidence, I have the better wit,
And can subdue you still to quietness,
Meek sufferings, and patient awe.

   ELD. PAL. You rap* me, still a-new.

   Y. PAL. In, Luce !  Our hopes grow strong and
     giantly.                    [*Exeunt.*

*Enter* THRIFT, SNORE, MISTRESS SNORE, QUEASY,
                GINET.

   GINET. To him, Mistress Snore ; 'tis he has kept
Your husband from his bed so long, to watch
Him for a church-robbery.

   M. SNORE, Ah, thou Judas ! I thought what
     thou'ldst come to !
Remember the warrant thou sent'st for me
Into Duck-lane, 'cause I call'd thy maid, Trot,
When I was fain t' invite thy clerk to a Fee pie,
Sent me b' a temple cook, my sister's sweetheart.

   QUE. Nay, and remember who was brought to
     bed
Under thy coach-house wall, when thou denied'st
A wad† of straw, and would'st not join thy halfpenny
To send for milk for the poor chrisome.‡

   SNORE. Now you may sweeten me with sugar-
     loaves
At new-year's-tide, as I have you, sir.

    *Enter* THWACK, PERT, MEAGER, ENGINE.

   THWACK. We'll teach you to rob churches !
     'slight, hereafter
We of the pious shall be afraid to go
To a long exercise, for fear our pockets should

---

   * Enrapture.       † Bundle.      ‡ Babe. See vol. I., p. 79.

Be pick'd.  Come, sir ; you see already how
The neighbours throng to find you ; will you con-
    sent ?
'Tis but a thousand pounds apiece to these
Two gentlemen, and five hundred more t' Engine ;
Your crime is then conceal'd, and yourself free.
    MEA. No, he may choose ; he'll trust to th' kind-
    hearted law.
    PERT. Let him, and to dame Justice too ; who,
    though
Her ladyship be blind, will grope hard, sir,
To find your money-bags.
    ENG. Sir, you are rich ; besides, you know what
    you
Have got by your ward's death ; I fear you will
Be begg'd at court,* unless you come off thus.
    THRIFT. There is my closet key ; do what you
    please.
    ENG. Gentlemen, I'll lead you to it ; follow me !
    THWACK. D' you use to find such sums as these
    beneath
An oak after a long march ? I think, sure,
The wars are not so plentiful.
    PERT. We think so too.
    THWACK. Y' had better trail a bodkin, gentle-
    men,
Under the Lady Ample, than a pike

---

    * In Dekker's *Honest Whore*, Act I. Scene II., Fustigo says :
"If I feel not his guts, beg me for a fool."—Dodsley's Old
Plays, vol. III., p. 231.  Lon. 1825, 8vo.  The explanation of
this species of begging will be found in Blackstone.  By the
old common law there is a writ *de idiota inquirendo* to inquire
whether a man be an idiot or not ; which must be tried by a
jury of twelve men ; and if they find him, *parus Idiota*, the
profits of his lands and the custody of his person may be granted
by the king to some subject who has interest enough to obtain
them."  No doubt Sir Tyrant was perfectly alive to the danger
he ran from having made a fool of himself, and had no desire to
become the subject of such an enquiry.

Under a German General.

 PERT. We'll in for th' money, sir, and talk anon.
        [*Exeunt Engine, Pert, Meager.*

*Enter* ELDER PALLATINE, YOUNGER PALLATINE,
     AMPLE, LUCY.

 Y. PAL. Sir Tyrant Thrift, here is your ward
  come from
The dead, to indict you for a robbery
Upon her ghost.

 THRIFT. Hah! is she alive, too ?

 LUCY. Yes, and her wardship out before y' have
  proffer'd her
A husband sir ;* so the best benefit
Of all your guardianship is lost.

 AMP. In seven long years you could not, sir,
  provide
A man deform'd enough to offer me
For your own ends.

 THRIFT. Cozen'd of wealth, of fame! Dog,
  Engine !       [*Exit Thrift.*

 THWACK. We must have you enclos'd again : y'
  are very
Forward with the lady.

 ELD. PAL, I will be, sir,
Until she groan : this priest stays somewhat long.

---

* This refers to that power which a guardian, by law, was entitled to exercise over his ward ; it was taken away, together with all the other oppressive circumstances attending the feudal system, by the stat. 12 Charles II., c. 24. Before that time, Blackstone observes, "while the infant was in ward, the guardian had the power of tendering him or her a suitable match, without *disparagement* or inequality; which, if the infants refused, they forfeited the value of the marriage, *valorem maritagii*, to their guardian ; that is, so much as a jury would assess, or any one would, *bonâ fide*, give to the guardians for such an alliance, and if the infants married themselves without the guardian's consent, they forfeited double the value, *duplicem valorem maritagii.*"

THWACK. How's this? troth I shall forgive thee
    then heartily.
AMP. I've ta'en him i' th' behalf of health; to
    chide
And jeer for recreation sake: 'twill keep
Me, sir, in breath, now I am past growing.
    ELD. PAL. Hark, knight! here's relish for your
    ears. I chose
None of your dull country madams, that spend
Their time in studying receipts to make
March-pane * and preserve plums; that talk
Of painful child-birth, servants' wages, and
Their husband's good complexion, and his leg.
    THWACK. New wonders yet!
    ELD. PAL. What was that, mistress, which I seal'd
    to, hood-wink'd?
A simple trial of my confidence and love?
    AMP. Your brother has it; 'tis a gift to him
Of one fair manor, 'mongst those many that you
Have in possession, sir; and in this bond
Y' are witness to three thousand pounds I give to
    Luce.
    LUCY. Yes, sir; for Pall and I must marry too.
    Y. PAL. I were an eunuch else, and th' world
    should know 't.
    ELD. PAL. Thou could'st not have betray'd me
    to a bounty
I more love. Brother, give thee joy!
              [Thwack takes Younger Pallatine aside.
    THWACK. You are the cause of all these miracles,
Therefore I desire you to be my heir:
By this good day you must; for I've ta'en order,
Though I love your wit, you shall not live by it.
    Y. PAL. My kind thanks, sir, the poor man's
    gratitude.
    M. SNORE. Give you joy, sweet Master Pallatine,

* A confection made of Pistachio-nuts, almonds, sugar, &c.

And your brother too.

QUE. And send you more such wives
Every year : as many as shall please heaven.

SNORE. 'Tis day.   I'll not to bed, sir, now ; my Watch
Shall be drunk at your worship's wedding.

Y. PAL. They shall, and there is gold enough to keep
Them so until thy reign be out.

*Enter* PERT, MEAGER, ENGINE, *with money-bags.*

PERT. Loaden with composition, Pall.

MEA. 'Tis for your sake we groan under these burdens.

Y. PALL. The offal of Sir Tyrant's trunks, Brother.
Pray know these gentlemen ; they owe you more
Money than they mean to pay now.

ELD. PAL. I remember 'em : but no words, my cavaliers,
And you are safe.   Where shall we dine to-day ?

Y. PAL. At Lucy's aunt's ; we'll make her costive beldamship
Come off * when she beholds a goodly jointure,
And our fair hopes.

ELD. PAL. First, to the church, lady ;
I'll make your skittish person sure.   Some of
Your pleasant arts upon me may become
A wise example, and a moral too ;
Such as their haughty fancy well befits,
That undertake to live here by their wits.

[Exeunt omnes.

* To *come off*, was a phrase formerly much used.  It signifies *to pay*, as is very clearly proved from the instances produced by *Steevens*, *Farmer*, and *Tyrwhitt*, in their notes to *The Merry Wives of Windsor*, A. 4, S. 3.

# EPILOGUE.

The Office of an Epilogue is now
To smooth and stroke the wrinkles from each brow:
To guide severer judgments (if we could
Be wise enough) until they thought all good,
Which they perhaps dislike ; and, sure, this were
An over-boldness, rais'd from too much fear.
You have a freedom, which we hope you'll use,
T" advance our youthful poet, and his muse,
With a kind doom ; and he'll tread boldly then,
In's best new comic socks, this stage again.

The following are the principal alterations and interpolations of " The Wits," which occur in the revived play as printed in the folio edition of 1673. The new Prologue indicates how the taste of the times, become more degenerate, required something besides mere poetry to attract an audience.

## PROLOGUE SPOKEN AT THE DUKE'S THEATRE.

Wit, which is all the gold a poet has,
Can seldom far by any standard pass.
Nor can great pow'r by any stamp enjoin
Wit to the world as universal coin.
For though most nations oft have enmity,
And in most things: yet always all agree,
And ev'n like subjects of one pow'r submit,
That all may differ in the price of wit.
'Tis by allay, like gold, more current made :
But poets, join'd with statesmen, should persuade
You, our free-states, and all great states t' agree
How much allay in gold and wit should be.
Pure wit, like ingots wrought without allay,
Will serve for hoard, but not for common pay.
Th' allay's coarse metal makes the finer last ;
Which else would in the peoples' handling waste.
So country jigs and farces mixt among
Heroic scenes make plays continue long.
But there are some who would the world persuade,
That gold is better when the stamp is bad ;
And that an ugly ragged piece of eight
Is ever true in metal and in weight:
As if a guinny* and lovis† had less
Intrinsic value for their handsomeness.
So diverse, who outlive the former age,
Allow the coarseness of the plain old stage ;
And think rich vests and scenes are only fit
Disguises for the want of art and wit.

   * Guineas were first coined in the reign of Charles II.
   † Louis d' Or, value about twenty shillings sterling.

Since wit's extrinsic value amongst all
Has seasons, money-like, to rise and fall ;
And since our poet found his did begin
To lessen, he, prince-like, did call it in.
And then he quickly melted it again :
For what is hotter than a poet's brain ?
He hopes the second stamp has brought it forth
With decoration and will raise the worth.
Or it, at least, by being mill'd, does get
Form so exact as none shall counterfeit.
For as in dearth of money, states grow bold
With laws, and suffer coiners of false gold ;
So you, our states, in want of wit, he says,
Permit some public coiners of false plays.
If glist'ring shows, or jingling sounds you pass
For current plays, we justly pay you brass.
Well, gentlemen ! let him to others give
His wit for gold ; I by your silver live.
I'm of your party and these shifts abhor :
Poets are princes but are very poor.
He may, at last, endeavour to enjoin
You, as his subjects, to take leather coin.

The Younger Pallatine's Soliloquy at close of the
first Act is thus altered in the folio :—

Sure neither of these wondrous wits were born
To more than to five senses, yet they aim
To do far greater things and newer in
The world than I.   Well, they are strangely wise,
And I am but the Lady Fortune's fool,
Whom she, perhaps, does for her pride or sport,
Keep gaudily sometimes ; and then condemns
Me to her usual livery ; and yet,
Though but her fool, if my design succeeds,
I'll turn to solid gold their airy dream :
They by their wits shall live, and I by them.

The following is introduced immediately after
Lady Ample and Lucy go out, at the end of the
first Scene of the second Act.

*Enter* SNORE, Mrs SNORE, Mrs QUEASY.

QUE. Master Snore, pray hear me! you are Constable.
SNORE.  Lord, neighbour Queasy, what need this?  D'ye think
I do not know my own office?
  QUE.  Who you?  I warrant you,
As well as the proudest of 'em, and no man
Is more hearty to the poor; for no man
Gives 'em more good counsel, to forbear coming
Near the parish, for the good of us all.
  SNORE.  Well, well, be brief;
I protest I'm so full of weighty matters,
That my head grows e'en too big for my hat.
You must be brief, neighbour Queasy, I say,
In short, you must be brief.
  M. SNORE.  My husband has but too much of the king's business.
  QUE.  Alas, I know't! but you being as I said,
In your office.
  SNORE.  Again?  will you still go a mile about
To my office, before you come next door
To the matter?  where is the warrant?
Come, give me the warrant.
  QUE.  Pray stay; 'tis wrapt up
In a clean handkerchief, and I'll be sworn
'Tis of the best sort of warrants; the justice's
Own hand is to't.  I scorn but t' have the best,
And from the best.  I am sure it cost me
A round shilling.
  SNORE.  Let me see, let me see.  Well! 'twill serve turn.
  QUE.  My rent has been long due, and you must get
Into the house to search for harlotry people——
Nay but gossip, hear me a little.
  SNORE.  O wretched authority! must thou ever
Have thy ears open, and thy eyes ne'er shut?
Still all noise and no sleep? no rest in office?
  M. SNORE.  Bodikins! Can't you hear a neighbour speak?
  QUE.  You may say to the old houswife; why, mistress,
(For you must give good words) my neighbour Queasy
Has forborne you day after day; she has
Children and you have none.  The baggages

About you are able to earn their own living,
And, to say truth amongst our selves,
Too easily ; the more's the shame.

SNORE. What's all this to the matter?

M. SNORE. Gossip Queasy, had I my husband's office,
I would not for the versal world endure you.
Truly, truly you have too many words.
Husband, you only need to say, Mistress,
(For the truth is, she goes like any Lady)
You know that my neighbour Queasy has still
Forborne and forborne, and has had good words
After good words ; but where is the money to make
The pot boil ? her husband is a weak
And sickly man with getting many children :
And you are able to work for your living :
Nay, they say your maids work day and night ;
And for my part——

SNORE. Your part is too long.

M. SNORE. How ? what a murrain ails you, trow ? may not
One make use of one's own tongue for a neighbour?
I knew what's what before you were my husband.

SNORE. O parish, parish ! how art thou mistaken ?
Thou buildst schools to breed poor children to Latin,
The Pope's language ; but I say, and say't again,
Come, fall to work ; and build me schools to breed
Old women to speak no language.

QUE. Truly, gossip, your husband's in the right ;
There's no care taken of women in years.

M. SNORE. Faith they shall never breed me to be old
Whilst I live, nor to be dumb till I'm dead.

SNORE. Wife, wife, be patient, wife ! D'you think
I am to serve no more warrants but this ?  I have
Four more for searches, impossible searches :
I am to search for four of the most dangerous
And the most invisible knaves that ever
Carried a dark lanthorn.

M. SNORE. Nay, thou hast a hard task, that's the truth of't !

SNORE. One of 'em (somewhat deaf, as I am told,
For I have spies) has lodg'd above twelve months
In a belfry.  The second has corrupted

A tankard-bearer, and lies in a conduit.
The third to change his complexion is turn'd
Chimney-sweeper, and skulks all days in chimneys,
And at night trains horse and foot under ground.
The fourth (if spies may be believ'd) does lye
At anchor in a sculler on the Thames :
I shall know where ; and will prove to his face
(In spite of Sathan) that he lies not there
To bob for griggs, but to bob for the people.
    M. Snore. Nay, for those under ground, or on the
        water,
I know not what to think ; but if there be
Any knaves above ground, thou'lt find 'em out
I'faith ; that I'll say for thee.
    Que. If any man in town can do't, he'll do't ;
And bring 'em face to face, alive or dead,
To make their answer to the law.
    M. Snore. Well gossip ; if the harlot pays no rent,
Shall my husband carry her to prison ?
    Que. In truth I know not what to say.   I would
Be loth to be too cruel ; for the woman
(Bating her overcourteousness in bringing
Youth together) does seem an honest woman,
And keeps a very orderly house.
    M. Snore. Berlady, and that's a good thing.
    Que. No flesh comes there o' Sundays ; powder'd or
Not powder'd : no I warrant ye, though ne'er
So brave : nor apprentices but on holidays,
When their hands are rid of their masters' business.
    M. Snore. And none can live without some recreation.
    Snore. She shall have recreation too in Bridewell.
    Que. Nay, pray Master Snore, let her labour on
In her calling, else she can't pay her rent.
    M. Snore. Husband, that's very true ; rent must be
        paid.
    Snore. Well, neighbour Queasy, go home with my
        wife,
And when 'tis late and dark I'll serve the warrant.
                                [Ex. several ways.


In Act three, Scene one, after " We'll search
the two back rooms, and then to bed," instead of

Snore saying: "Peace, wife! not a word," and making his exit with Mrs Snore, Mrs Queasy, and Watchmen, the Scene is still continued with the same characters, thus:

M. SNORE. Well, I'll make thee know that none
But a sow would have thought of that pig.
   SNORE. Bunting, in very deed,
You are too blame, she's an honest man's wife;
'Twas ever said Christopher Queasy was
An honest man. He takes pains to get children
For the good of the Common-wealth.
   M. SNORE. Marry come up!
There be others take pains as well as he.
   SNORE. Prithee be quiet, wife! I do confess
Thou art a great pains-taker.
   M. SNORE. Takes pains, quoth he?
   SNORE. I say, go to! no more words! go to, I say.
   M. SNORE. I will not go to! bid me go to?
   SNORE. How now, housewife? do you slight au-
     thority?
Behold this staff! in very truth, I shall
Swaddle you with the king's wand of office.
   M. SNORE. Strike a married woman! I defy thee!
For though thou art my husband, thou shalt know
That I'm a married woman.
   SNORE. What, quarrel with the king's watch, Goody-
     Hector?                 *[Goes to strike her.*
   QUE. Woe to us, when constables break the peace!
   SNORE. I'll make her know authority.
   QUE. Neighbour Snore, pray hear reason; would you
     have
Authority over your own wife?  *[He makes at his wife*
                                   *again.*
   M. SNO. Do, do! kill the child I mean to go withal!
   QUE. Hold, hold, neighbour Snore!
   MRS. SNO. Thou a husband? bear witness, Gossip
     Queasy,
That he strikes a married woman.
   QUE. Nay I hope, he has murder'd you. If there
Be law in the land I'll follow't against him
When you are dead; therefore take comfort.

M. Snore. Nay, I've my death's wound.

Que. Out. alas! where is it?

M. Sno. Truly, gossip, I think——in my crupper.

Que. You a constable? y'are a cuckoldly cut-throat!
How do you, gossip? Th'art a murderer!
I ever said, that if cruel Cain were
A constable, he look'd like thee.

Snore. Will you turn traitor too against authority?

Que. Do, tyrant, do! kill thy whole parish!

Snore. In truth, I shall also find out your crupper.

Que. Mine? do thy worst for all thy power! my
  crupper?

Snore. I shall find it, if thou provokest me more.

Que. Out tyrant! strike thy wife? The comfort is
That thy reign lasts but a year.

Snore. Thou she-satan! wilt thou tempt authority?

Que. Do, kill me too! th'ast a Judas face. My husband
Compar'd to thee, looks like any justice.

M. Sno. Your husband, goodly tripe, compar'd to mine?

Que. How now, mistress! i' faith I cry you mercy!
Are you so quickly come to life again?

M. Sno. Yes, seeing how ill you would use me
After my death. My husband look like a constable,
And yours like a justice? I will try, housewife,
How your face will look, when I've flea'd off
Your tawny mask: my nails are whetted for't.

Que. Are they so sharp!
'Tis well I'm provided for a good occasion.
You'll find mine have not been pared
This twelve month.                    [*They fight at arms length.*

M. Snore. Why husband! art not asham'd not to
  part us?

Snore. During my reign, I'll sometimes be for the
  peace,
And sometimes for the liberty of
The subject. They shall be mad if they please.

                              [*Exit* Snore.

M. Snore. Hold, Gossip Queasy, hold! By my consent
Let's not be mad, because he'd have us so.

Que. Beshrew your heart for putting me out of breath.
But I'll follow him as fast as I can,
That he may help me to my rent.

Again, after the exit of the Elder Pallatine, which closes the third Act in the original edition, this Scene is tacked on, and with it the Act is made to end.

*Enter* CONSTABLE, *and* EIGHT WATCHMEN.

SNORE. Here has been goodly care taken to-night
Of the king's bus'ness. Eight of our Watch are missing.
Call 'em over!

   1. Francis Fumble!

   2. Here.

   1. Barnaby Belch!

   3. Here.

   1. Simon Sleep!

ALL. Not here.

SNORE. Put down Simon Sleep. There have been
   complaints
Against that Simon Sleep; neighbours, he is
To blame in his own house. He snorts so loud
That he wakes half the Parish.

   1. Indeed his wife has often told him of it,
With tears in her eyes, but, alas
'Twould not do.

SNORE. I've excus'd him because he is my kinsman;
Yet, under the rose, the kindred comes only
By a bastard daughter of my grandmother's.

   1. Bryan Bumm!

   4. Here.

   1. Anthony Ale!

   5. Here.

   1. Timothy Tost!

   6. Here.

   1. Leonard Lazy!

   7. Here.

   1. Gregory Grumble!

   8. Here.

   1. Nathanael Nod!

ALL. Not here.

SNORE. Nathanael Nod's too ancient to look after
State-matters in winter nights. He must e'en
Give up his lanthorn.

   1. He has been a good Watchman :

The parish should maintain him now he's old.

Snore. The Common-wealth should do't; for I am sure
That the last Coronation day he drunk
Out an eye heartily in the king's service.

1. Old Nat Nod is a very hearty man;
And will be loth to give over a loser:
He may perhaps drink out another winter.

Snore. No, no, he's gone, he's gone! and neighbours
We must all go; for when we have drunk
Our full measure, as they say, we must e'en
Lye down and sleep with our forefathers.

1. He has yet an eye left.

Snore. An ill one, poor man. He sleeps as he walks.
'Tis not long since he lighted his young wife,
And led her so much out of the right way,
That she came not home above a week after.

1. But truly, sir, he often asked her pardon.

Snore. You always excuse Nod: the Common-wealth
Must be better serv'd; he shall watch no more.

1. Then farewell a true subject! Old as he is,
He will ring all night, once every year, for
Queen El'zabeth's birth-day; and he had like
To have been hang'd for't.

Snore. Come, come, 'twas his own fault: he wore his
    beard
Too long, and the bell rope caught hold of it.

Enter ELDER PALL.

Who goes there?

Eld. Pal. Master constable, you'll excuse my care
Which wakes me for the Common-wealth; I could
Not chuse but come back and enquire a little
After your pris'ner; who I hope is safe.

Snore. I've chosen for his guard four men of blood,
The leanest of our watch, and youngest too,
Whose wrath ne'er lets 'em sleep but at a sermon.

Eld. Pal. My man shall be at your house in the
    morning
With a med'cine of money lest you should
Be sick with watching.

Snore. E'en what you please, as a means of prevention;
If your man pass that way, or so; but, sir, I would

Be loth to trouble him.   I think I'm well.
I've known the time when my poor Watch and I
Danc'd a round with our rug-gowns, in the snow,
Till we lookt like a cluster of white bears.
   ELD. PAL. You and your Watch were the Dutch
      painter's sketch
Who drew the Berwood and his dancing bears ;
For I remember all those beasts were white.
   SNORE. What are these ?

   *Enter* FIDDLERS *with Instruments under their Cloaks.*

   ELD. PAL. By the long spreading of their cloaks
I take 'em for men of melody loaden with music.
   SNORE. Stand ! stand !
   ELD. PAL. What are you ?
   SNORE. Peace, sir, a whole age
Of experience is short enough t' examine
Some kind of shrewd fellows.   Sir, they may be
Most dang'rous thieves ?
   ELD. PAL. How sir, thieves ?
   SNORE. Yes. for aught I know.
   ELD. PAL. If these are thieves, 'tis but in stealing
Tunes from the Theatres which they spoil in taverns.
   SNORE. What are you ? whence come you ? whither
      go you ?
Answer all this together, and at once :
For I shall quickly trap you if you falter
In long speeches.
   FIDLER. We have been playing at a wedding.
   SNORE. The bold knave avoids my questions :
And tells me what he has been doing, as if we men
Of justice, ever tir'd with business, would be troubled
With what he has been doing.
   ELD. PAL. Sir, these are the firkers of the city fiddles.
   SNORE. Say you so, sir ? well boys, I hope to see
Old England merry again.   Look, look, my wife
And my neighbour Queasy !

   *Enter* MRS SNORE, QUEASY.

   ELD. PAL. They come to chide you and your rambling
Watch for keeping late hours.
   M. SNORE. Truly, my mouse, I cannot sleep without
'Tis better to be wife to three justices,            [thee.

Than to one constable.

QUEAS. Ay, ay, constables sit in the cold streets
To do justice to wanderers; but justices
Do it to their wives in warm beds.

M. SNORE. Alack-a-day! here are fiddlers! poor souls!
They put me in mind of my wedding night.

SNORE. And me of a dance.   I'll dance presently.

ELD. PAL. Well spoken, though but seldom done, by
    men
Of your long staff.

ELD. PAL. Y'ave a hopeful old husband, he deserves
A singular patent for all the profits
Belonging to the myst'ry of the morrice.
After this dance you need no other charm:
Make haste, take him to bed whilst he is warm.
            [*Exeunt Eld. Pal. one way, they the other way.*

And, as if "the groundlings" could not have
enough of these popular characters—Snore, his wife,
and Mrs Queasy, the following dialogue comes in
in the last Scene of the 4th Act, just after Mrs
Snore has said, "I'll have an oven of my own!"

QUE. Will you prove this before the Widow Bran,
Our baker's mother?

M. SNORE. I prove? what should I prove? Lord what
    a fending
And proving there is in your company!

SNORE. Your tongue cuts out more bad work in a
    minute,
Than these hands of authority can make up in a month.

M. SNORE, Why, what have I said?

QUE. You said, my girl, Mary Queasy by name,
Did find your uncle's yellow stockings in
A porringer: nay, and you said she stole them;
And by the same good token that your uncle
Was a pewterer: and of this I'll take
My book-oath: and I've a clerk to my cousin,
And mayhaps can have law without money.

SNORE. What say you? hah! can you have law with-
    out money?
Do you rob young clerks of their masters' fees?

That's fine, i'faith.    You have law without money?
Come now before my staff, and swear to that.
    QUE. What shall I swear? I scorn to swear untruths.
And I'd have you know I'm of the law's side.
    SNORE. You! who you? when you speak slightingly
        of it,
As if 'twere a poor thing which may be had without
        money?
    QUE. Did I say so? y'are in authority
And may speak what you please for a year, but,
If you die out of office you will dearly
Answer this in th' other world.
    M. SNORE. Ay, you wish my poor husband in heaven.
    QUE. Know, I scorn to be so uncharitable.
    Y. PAL. Come, gossips must agree! the very mention
Of law and money does ever breed quarrels.
    SNORE. Sir, we who sit in office
All night, must never hear of money, lest
We should be tempted in the dark.
    QUE. Who should tempt you in the dark? d'you mean
        me?
I am an honest woman, and tempt nobody.
    Y. PAL. Make peace, Mistress Snore! Be you the
        constable.
    M. SNORE. Neighbour Queasy! pray hear me.
'Troth thou art as froward with sitting up late
As any child.  I said your daughter came
Too much to the bake-house, whereby there was
Something missing, whereby, nay prithee mark,
I said your daughter was to blame to keep
Evil company, for I love Mary, I
Care not who knows it, not I: and I'd fain
Give her good counsel.
    SNORE. My wife tells you the very words she spoke.
    M. SNORE. Come prithee send Mary to me.
    QUE. Why truly I am somewhat thick of hearing:
But if that which you said were all, my daughter
Can take good counsel as well as another.
    Y. PAL. Come, no more words! there's to reconcile
        you——
In burnt wine and cakes.  Go, get you all in!
                    [*Ex.* SNORE, Mrs SNORE, QUEASY.

With this quatrain the Younger Pallatine concludes the Act :—

Methinks blind fortune ushers me too fast ;
But if she finds the way to bring me rich
From thence where this imagined treasure lies,
The poets shall confess that she has eyes.

Once more; in the fifth Act, after the Watch have sung the Catch, " With Lanthorn on stalls," Snore has this Scene :—

*Enter* YOUNGER PALLATINE.

Y. PAL. Chirping my birds of night? who could ex-
    pect
So sweet a concert of old nightingales ?
You sing as if you percht in tavern bushes.
    SNORE. Sir, we can sing, and sing without a fiddle ;
And we can cough in tune too.   I have seen
Mad boys in my days, and have sung all night
With them, when Bounce the bell-man has kept time.

*Enter* MUSICIAN.

SNORE. Who goes there? stand! stand still, and come
    before me.
MUS. Your pleasure, sir?                    [*He advances.*
SNORE. Did not I bid you stand still ?
MUS. Yes, sir.
SNORE. Why did you stir then ?
MUS. Because, sir, you bid me come before you.
SNORE. I did bid you stand still and come before me.
MUS. You did, sir.
SNORE. And could you do both together ?
MUS. No, sir.
SNORE. How dare you then presume to make your
    choice,
Which to do first, before my pleasure's known ?
    MUS. Why truly, sir——
    SNORE. O, are you caught?   There's one of my new
    tricks
To make you know the wit of a constable.

PERT. And a shrewd one.

SNORE. From whence come you?

MRS. Who, I sir?

SNORE. You, sir? who else, sir? what, is there another
Knave behind you? or is the devil your
Companion? I fear, Master Pallatine.
We shall find more of the pack. Well, I ask
Again, whence come you?

MRS. I come, sir——

SNORE. Quick, quick! are you consid'ring what to say?
Speak, and speak quickly, ere y' have time to think.

MRS. Sir, if you please to have patience——

SNORE. Patience? pray note him, Master Pallatine,
He tells me of patience, who have been held
The very lamb of Ludgate. Sirrah! sirrah!
But that I'm loth to break my staff of office
Ere my year's out, I'd make your coxcomb know
That I have patience. Come, where have you been?

MRS. Where have I been, sir? why, where have I
been?
I'm sure I ha'nt been far.

SNORE. D'you mark him, sir?
Here's an answer which might stagger a horse!
I do protest that I grow weary of
Authority, because night after night,
I meet such intricate and cunning knaves.

PERT. Shall his reply scape thus?

SNORE. In truth I had forgot. O, the knave answer'd
Where have I been? which does repeat my question.
Then, why where have I been; which is his question
To my demand; and then he said, I'm sure
I ha'nt been far. O most intricate varlet!

Y. PAL. For my part, I think it half charm, half riddle.

SNORE. Observe how he ends like a subtle devil.
I'm sure I ha'nt been far; as who should say,
That I must take his bare assurance for some
Place which he maliciously conceals.
But come, sirrah,
You'll not confess where you have been?

MRS. An't please your worship——

SNORE. Worship! that softens the cake into custard.

MRS. I have been at a wedding.

SNORE. Thou knave, why did'st not tell me so before?
MUS. Your worship would not let me.——
SNORE. How, would not I let thee go to a wedding?
Y. PAL. Of what profession are you?
MUS. A poor musician, sir.
SNORE. Still where there are weddings there will be
  music.
Y. PAL. Alas, the married stand in need of comfort.
SNORE. Stay, stay! can you sing the constable's catch?
MUS. I can sing my part, sir.
SNORE. Master Pallatine, I profess by yea
And nay we'll have that catch: 'twas made of me.
Y. PAL. The songster Snore will never be forgotten.

*The second Catch is sung, and acted by them in
Recitative Burlesque.*

**1.**

1. Stand, who goes there! stand, who goes there?
  Come over the kennel, now come near.
        Hey ho! I hear a great noise
        Like that of the angry boys.
3. There's one you may think him as well
            A hector of hell
  By the brawling and roaring he makes,
  Stand, stand! now stay till the constable wakes.

**2.**

A coach! ho, a coach! it is gone by;
The coachman drives till the horses fly!
Hush, hush, and lye still! lye still! hark! hark!
        Newgate's black dog
        Has worried a hog;
I hear his brother of Dowgate bark!

**3.**

Another coach it drives from the Strand!
Then have at the harness; stand ho, stand!
Ha ha, young gallant, bring forth your wench,
And now come before the bill-men's bench.
His hat is soon off, and his mistress quakes,
But stay, sir, stay, till the constable wakes.

Y. PAL. Well sung, old boys! he who likes sighing
   better
Is much more the sexton's friend than his own.
Engine, your coming hastens me away.

*Enter* ENGINE.

Dispatch! give your directions to my friend.     [*Exit.*

Further on in the same Act the Scene, where
the Elder Pallatine is taken up by Snore, is thus
altered:

*Enter* SNORE, PERT, WATCHMEN.

PERT. Pall and his friend are gone, I must not stay
To be seen, but after you have seiz'd on him,
Lead him a pris'ner to the lady too——
   SNORE. I'll do't, though he were Gog or Heildebrand.
                               [*Exit Pert.*
   ELD. PAL. What mean you, sirs?
   SNORE. Yield to the constable.  [*They lay hold on him.*
   ELD. PAL. 'Tis yielded that you are a constable;
But where have I offended?
   SNORE. Here, sir, you have committed sacrilege,
And rob'd an alderman's tomb of himself,
And of both his children kneeling in brass.
   ELD. PAL. How, flea monuments of their brazen skins?
   SNORE. Nay, I believe, if we should search the tomb
Within, we should find somewhat else missing.
   ELD. PAL. Why, did the good alderman bury money,
To buy alms-custards, for posterity?
   SNORE. No, sir, but one of his dead daughters
Had a fine head of hair, and I am sure
Yours is none of your own.
   ELD. PAL. I see you are scandalized at periwigs;
But the sexton, being a diligent man,
Was before me at that work.
   SNORE. O, did you come too late? bear witness that
The gentleman confesses, he was there
With a felonious intent.
   ELD. PAL. Master constable,
When you walk in the night you need no lanthorns;
Y'are quick-sighted, and can find truth without 'em.

Q

Snore. Look! a dark lanthorn, and an iron crow;
Fine evidence for a jury.
    Eld. Pal. And all this preparation in the church
Was to dig for departed periwigs.
    Snore. Say you so, sir? what shifts young gallants use
To get hair from others, and yet they take
More pains to lose their own.
    Eld. Pal. I like this trick.  The lady Ample, and
My brother, have triumphant wits; I grow
In love with both.  Well, whither must I go?
    Snore. Away with him! Examine
The king's constable?  Away with him!          [*Exeunt.*

In the last Scene of the fifth Act, Snore, after
saying "Now, you may sweeten me with sugar
loaves, &c.," is followed up thus, before Thwack,
Meager, Pert, and Engine enter:—

    M. Snore. And now, sir, we may tell you, how you
        imprisoned
The rich bawd, for offering to corrupt justice
With half her old gold, and mill-money, left
Under your desk; and you never released her
Till she sent you the other half.
    Queas. And you examined her
Thrice over too, that you might hear enough
Young wickedness: there your worship seemed angry,
And called out for more stark naked truth,
    Snore. Two of your clerks lye buried in the church,
Who held a long siege out of seven years' famine
In your worship's house; and, at last, died bravely
Of a surfeit of chippins.*
    M. Snore. Ay, ay, French chippins!
His clerks were turned gallants for they
Would eat in the mode, as they call it,
And have broths made of shells of new-laid eggs
And skins of silver eels.
    Que. Ah, these French! many an honest woman's son
Has been poisoned by their kickshaws.
    M. Snore. Well fare old Islington for wholesome dainties!
Who ever heard of poison in stewed prunes?

* Fragments of bread.

The two concluding lines of the play are thus rendered :—

To shew that their design but seldom hits,
Who aim to live in splendour by their wits.

EPILOGUE SPOKEN AT THE DUKE'S THEATRE.

I am so constant to you, gentlemen,
That, in pure kindness, I am come again.
I'll tell you now my judgment of the Play,
And not ask yours ; for yours the poets say,
If poets can speak truth, is very small :
Lord! how I've heard them swear y've none at all !
All Prologues cry, the critics are undone !
Nay, I my self was offer'd to be one ;
But, since so many write, I did eschew
Th' uncivil pow'r of judging some of you.
'Tis strange that you are thus turn'd back again
To infant stature from gigantic-men.
The time has been you threw great poets down,
But now are by small poets overthrown.
Ours boasted that he felt your strength decline
Since he made war ; but this he said in wine :
I mean in fumes of such a frantic fit
As poets have, when poems do not hit.
I think, like women, they grow choleric,
And scold because they hurt not whom they strike.
Long have the poets made rebellious war
Against the senates, who their princes are.
And, though the poets have still losers been,
Yet, after loss, reserves are still brought in.
Such is our Play ; consisting of a few
Old rallied forces, with as many new.
He's weary of this war ; and, being near
The danger of his climateric year,
Does parley, and would urge, since he must treat,
How little you will gain by his defeat.
He will not of his weakness more declare
To those, with whom he held so long a war ;
The conquer'd, who too much themselves debase,
Do rudely then the victor's pow'r disgrace.

### AMBER.    CAUDLES.    Page 121.

*Amber.*    Some have poetically imagined it to be a concretion
of the tears of birds ; others, the urine of a beast ; others, the
scum of the lake Cephisis, near the Atlantic ; others, a congela-
tion formed in the Baltic Sea, and in some fountains where it
is found swimming like pitch.

Amber is reputed of some medicinal efficacy, being used in
suffumigations to remove defluxions, and in powder, as an
alterant, absorbent, sweetener, and astringent.

In times of plague, those who work in amber at Koningsberg
are said to be never infected ; whence it is held a preservative.
It is esteemed a lithonthriptic, diuretic, and promoter of mas-
turbation.

Caudles are thus described in " Warner's Antiquitates
Culinariæ :"—

" *Caudel rennying.*    Take vernage, or other gode swete wyne,
and zolkes of eyren beten, and streyned, and put therto suger,
and colour hit with saffron, and sethe hit tyl hit begyn to boyle,
and strawe pouder of ginger theron : and serve hit forthe."

" *Caudel ferres.*    Take chekyns and choppe hom, and cast
hom in brothe of beef, and cast therto clowes, maces, pynes,
and reisynges of corance, and a lytel wyne and saffron ; for
X mees, take the zolkes of 40 eyren beten and streyned ; and
take saunders and canel drawen, and put in the same pot : and
then take half a quartron of pouder of ginger, and bete hit with
the zolkes ; and in the settyng doune put hit into the same pot,
and stere hit wel togeder, and make hit rennynge and sumqwat
standynge ; and dresse hit, and serve hit forthe.    Or elles take
conynges instede of chekyns, and do on the same wyse."

*Britannia Trivmphans, a Masque. Presented at White Hall by the Kings Majestie and his Lords, on the Sunday after Twelfth-night, 1637. By Inigo Iones, Surveyor of his Majesties Workes, and William D'Avenant, her Majesties Servant. London, printed by John Haviland for Thomas Walkley, and are to be sold at his Shop at the flying Horse, neere Yorke house.   1637.*

The masque of " Britannia Triumphans " is unnoticed
by Langbaine, and it is not printed in the folio edition of
our author's works.   It appeared in quarto immediately
after having been acted, and is believed to have been suppressed, from having excited great clamour on account
of its being represented on the Sabbath day.   The author
of " The stage condemned, 1698," has devoted nineteen
pages to an account of this masque, and states that at
that period it was very scarce.   In Kippis' Biographia,
folio, Lond. 1789, an edition is mentioned, very lately
printed in Ireland," but this we have never seen, nor
does the Biographia Dramatica take cognizance of it.

On the title page, Britannia Triumphans bears to have
been written " by Inigo Jones, surveyor of His Majesty's
works, and William D'avenant, Her Majesty's servant."

To Inigo Jones is given credit for the introduction,
not only of scenery and machinery of a superior order,
but of designs for character-costume.   He had been for
some years in Italy whither " he had been sent to study
the art of design " for which he had early evinced a
decided taste.   " He was," says his pupil and executor,
Webb, in his vindication of Stonehenge, "Architect-
General unto four mighty kings, two heroick queens, and
that illustrious and never-to-be-forgotten Prince, Henry.
Christianus the fourth, king of Denmark, first engrossed
him to himself, sending for him out of Italy, where,
especially at Venice, he had many years resided."   He is
said to have assisted in the building of the palace
of Fredericksburg, the principal court resembling that of
Heriot's Hospital, Edinburgh, the design of which is
understood to have been his.   He was appointed Surveyor of Works for Prince Henry, which office terminated
at the Prince's death, 6 Nov. 1612.   He then visited Italy
once more, and during his absence, one " M. Constantine,
an Italian," is mentioned as " Architect to our late Prince
Henry," he undertaking the machinery for the masque at
the Earl of Somerset's marriage.   This must have been an
honorary appointment as there was no such office in the
Prince's household.   On the return of Inigo Jones to
this country, he, in 1615, received the appointment of

Surveyor of Works, with a yearly stipend of eight shillings a-day for his entertainment, eighty pounds per annum for his "recompense of availes," and two shillings and eightpence a-day for his riding and travelling charges, besides £12 15s 10d yearly for livery. Of this office, which had been held by Simon Basil, the king had granted Jones the reversion.

The first recorded notice of Inigo Jones' inventions for the stage is given by Ben Jonson in his introduction to "the masque of Blackness," which he had prepared by command of the Queen of James I., for performance at Whitehall, on twelfth-night, 1604-5. It was the first entertainment her majesty had given, and, at her suggestion, the characters were to be Blackamoors.

Jones was again engaged to prepare the stage accessories incident to three Latin plays represented before the King in the Hall of Christ Church, Oxford, towards the end of August 1605. He appears to have received £50 for his trouble, but his employers seem to have thought that he had promised more than he performed, or rather than they had expected. From the description, that is questionable. Thus it was:—" The stage was built close to the upper end of the hall, as it seemed at the first sight; but, indeed, it was a false wall, faire painted, and adorned with stately pillars, which pillars would turn about, by reason whereof, with the help of other painted cloths, their stage did vary three times in acting of one tragedy."—*Leland's Collectanea—Malone's Shakespeare*.

The next occasion on which his talents in the scenic department were called into exercise was Twelfth Night 1605-6, when the masque of Hymen, also the product of Ben Jonson's Muse, was presented in honour of the nuptials of the young Earl of Essex with Frances Howard, a daughter of the Earl of Suffolk, the Lord Treasurer. The dresses were most superb, and Inigo Jones tried to excel himself. Jonson thus notices what was considered novel: " Here the upper part of the scene, which was all of clouds, and made artificially to swell, and ride like the rack, began to open, and the air clearing, in the top thereof was discovered Juno sitting in a throne supported by two beautiful peacocks; above her, the region of fire, with a continual motion, was seen to whirl circularly, and Jupiter standing in the top, (figuring the Heaven) brandishing his thunder." Jonson was highly commendatory of Jones' work. "The design and art," he says, "together with the devices and their habits, belong properly to the merit and reputation of Master Inigo Jones, whom I take modest occasion, in this fit place, to remember, lest his own worth might accuse me of an ignorant neglect, from my silence." The poet himself was present, and assisted in turning a globe wherein the masquers sat, which was so contrived that it "stood, or rather hung, for no axle was seen to support it."—*Gifford's Life of Ben Jonson*, vol. vii.

Jones appears to have been employed in other matters for his majesty, for in June 1609 he is entered in the books of the treasurer of the chamber to the King as the recipient of £14 6s 8d, "for carreinge letters for his majesties servyce into Fraunce." Both prior to this, and afterwards, he was engaged with Ben Jonson in several masques, Ben always chronicling his praises of his co-mate. At Christmas 1610-11 they devised another masque for the Queen, for which they both received a like reward for their "invention," viz. £40 each.

Inigo Jones invented the structure for Chapman's masque of the two honourable Houses or Inns of Court; the Middle Temple and Lincoln's Inn; performed before the king at Whitehall on Shrove Monday at night, being the 15th Feb. 1613  Also for Cœlum Britannicum, a masque at Whitehall in the Banquetting House, on Shrove Tuesday night. 18th Feb. 1633.

"It was attributed to our author, though the machinery, which was very fine, was contrived and executed by Inigo Jones, and part of the piece itself written by Tho. Carew (*Ath Oxon.*, vol ii., col. 413). The King himself wore a mask in this piece, and the rest of the performers were men of the first quality in the three nations. This we find omitted in Langbaine's Catalogue." *Memoir of Davenant* in Kippis' Biographia.

As Surveyor of Works. Inigo Jones was not idle. He erected, with unprecedented rapidity, the new Banquetting House at Whitehall, on the scite of the old Banquetting House, which had been destroyed by fire on 12th January,

1618-19; he was requested to make a drawing "by way of map or ground plot," to enable a commission appointed by the Crown, "to plant and reduce to uniformity Lincoln's Inn Fields," and, among numerous other things, "received his Majesty's commands to produce, out of his own practice in architecture, and experience in antiquities, whatever he could possibly discover concerning Stonehenge." The result attending the last was not very satisfactory. A folio volume, published three years after his death, contains "some few undigested thoughts" upon the subject. His later works were the great west portico of Old St. Paul's, the Queen's House at Greenwich, the Theatre of the Hall of the Barber Surgeons, in Monkwell Street, London. He was also employed in planning the great square or piazza of Covent Garden, for the Earl of Bedford. The arcade or piazza was carried along the whole of the north and east sides; the church completed the west; and the south was girt by a grove of trees, and the garden-wall of Bedford House in the Strand.

Although Ben Jonson had been lavish of his praise of Inigo Jones, still Jones thought fit to take umbrage at him. The cause of this is not known, but the quarrel appears to have been kept up for a considerable time. From Jonson's "Conversations with Drummond, of Hawthornden," 1619, we learn that "he said to Prince Charles, of Inigo Jones, that when he wanted to express the greatest villaine in the world, he would call him ane Inigo," and he further stated that "Jones having accused him for naming him, behind his back, a fool, he denied it; but, says he, I said, he was ane arrant knave, and I avouch it." A reconciliation appears to have taken place, for they again worked together as before, but it was of short duration, a second and fiercer quarrel having ensued. The reason seems to have been that Jones from the popularity he had acquired as a distinguished architect, began to persuade himself that he was a better man than Ben, and was consequently entitled to greater credit in the preparation of the masques on which they were jointly engaged, and in particular because "rare Ben" had placed his own name first on the title of a masque named "Chlorida," 1630, thus:

" The Inventors, Ben Jonson, Inigo Jones." This led to Jones taking advantage of his power at court, and introducing, as poets of the court entertainments, Townshend, Carew, Shirley, Heywood, and Sir Wm. D'avenant, who were exceedingly courteous towards him, willingly yielding the palm to his mechanical skill. D'avenant affably acquaints the public that " The inventions, ornaments, scenes, and apparitions, with the descriptions, were made by Inigo Jones, Surveyor-General of his Majesty's Works; what was spoken or sung, by William D'avenant, his Majesty's servant." Heywood, also, bowing to the stage carpenter, thus observes :— " So much for the subject itself, but for the rare decorements which now apparell'd it, when it came the second time to the Royall viewe, (her gracious majesty then entertaining his highnesse at Denmark House, upon his birth-day), I cannot pretermit to give a due character to that admirable artist, Mr. Inego Jones, master surveyor to the King's work, &c., who to every act, nay, almost to every sceane, by his excellent inventions, gave such an extraordinary lustre; upon every occasion changing the stage, to the admiration of all the spectators; that, as I must ingenuously confesse, it was above my apprehension to conceive ; so to their sacred majesties, and the rest of the auditory, it gave so general a content, that I presume they never parted from any object, presented in that kind, better pleased or more plenally satisfied."

Like the modern melodramas of the sensational order, and those very dreary pieces, rejoicing in a plentiful display of female legs, stilted verse, and nigger melodies, dignified by the erroneous title of burlesque.

" Painting and carpentry are the soul of masque."

This Ben Jonson satirically remarked at the time when Inigo Jones gained the ascendant.

Still those adjuncts to the attractiveness of stage entertainments were not adopted in the public theatres, the plays of Shakespeare and others of the day relying upon their plot and action, and needing no accessories. Strange contrast, when now a-days those very plays, which then stood and even now could stand upon their own merits, fail to command an audience, unless aided by the artist's brush, an unlimited supply of Dutch metal, and the employment of mechanical appliances.

As Ben Jonson lived up to, or rather beyond his income, the circumstance of his not being called upon to prepare a masque for the subsequent year, " by reason of the predominant power of his antagonist, Inigo Jones," was a deep source of regret, broken in health and necessitous as he then was. By Jones' malicious influence was the poet not only then set aside, but during the rest of his melancholy existence. The ire of Jonson rose to such a degree that he was induced to pen a satire entitled "An Expostulation with Inigo Jones," or " Iniquo Jones," as he otherwise called him. In this, he laughs at the architect's "velvet suit," and twits him with

"Thy twice conceived, thrice paid for imagery."

Gifford, while adopting the view that Jonson himself takes of Inigo Jones "to be the Dominus do-all of the work and to engross all the praise," adds, that, as now with the Christmas Pantomine openings, "an obscure ballad-maker, who could string together a few rhymes, to explain the scenery, was more acceptable to him than a man of talent, who might aspire to a share of the praise given to the entertainment."

————" O shows, shows, shows !
The eloquence of masques ! what need of prose—
Or verse, or prose to express," &c.

On the production of Ben's play of the Magnetic Lady, in October, 1632, Inigo Jones was present. and amiably " made himself remarkable by his boisterous ridicule of it." Langbaine says, " It was generally esteemed an excellent play, though in the poet's days it had some enemies."

This conduct, no doubt, determined Jonson to crucify Jones in a greater degree than previously, and so the "Master Surveyor" was dragged into his next new play, " The Tale of a Tub," 1633. Inigo incensed, got the part suppressed, as appears from this entry in the office book of the Master of the Revels :—

" R [ceived] for allowinge of the Tale of the Tubb, Vitruvius Hoop's part wholly struck out. and the motion of the tubb, by commande from my lorde chamberlin ;

exceptions being taken against it by Inigo Jones, Surveyor of the King's Workes, as a personal injury unto him.   May 7, 1633—£2, 0s 0d."

"The motion of the tub," referred to, was a ridiculous piece of mechanism intended to caricature some machinery which Jones had once contrived.

Although Vitruvius Hoop was forbidden as well as the motion of the tub, Jonson still insisted upon introducing Jones in a more subdued form under the appellation of " In-and-In Medlay of Islington, corpus and head borugh."   Throughout this character two favourite words of Jones' are employed—" feasible" and " conduce." As a specimen the following dialogue will suffice :—

"SQUIRE TUB. Can any man make a masque here, in
        this company ?
    TO-PAN. (*A Tinker*). A masque!   What's that ?
    SCRIBEN. (*The great writer*).  A mumming or a show,
With Vizards and fine clothes.
    CLENCH (*the farrier*).  A disguise, neighbour,
Is the true word.   There stands the man can do't, sir ;
Medlay, the joiner, In-and-In of Islington,
The only man at a disguise in Middlesex.
    SQUIRE TUB.  But who shall write it ?
    HILTS.  Scriben, the great writer.
    SCRIBEN.  He'll do it alone, sir ; he will join with no man.
Though he be a joiner, in design he calls it,
He must be sole inventor.   In-and-In
Draws with no others in's projects ; he will tell you
It cannot else be feasible, or conduce :
Those are his ruling words, please you to hear'em ?
    SQUIRE TUB.  Yes ; Master In-and-In, I have heard of
        you.
    MEDLAY.  I can do nothing, I.
    CLENCH.  He can do all, sir.
    MEDLAY.  They'll tell you so.
    SQUIRE TUB.  I'd have a toy presented,
A Tale of a Tub, a story of myself,
You can express a Tub ?
    MEDLAY.  If it *conduce*
To the design, whate'er is *feasible ;*
I can express a wash-house, if need be,
With a whole pedigree of Tubs.

SQUIRE TUB. No; one
Will be enough to note our name and family.
Squire Tub of Totten, and to shew my adventures
This very day.   I'd have it in Tub's Hall,
At Totten-Court, my lady-mother's house ;
My house, indeed, for I am heir to it.

MEDLAY. If I might see the place, and had surveyed it
I could say more ; for all invention, sir,
Comes by degrees, and in the view of nature ;
A world of things concur to the design,
Which makes it *feasible*, if art *conduce*."

The last of the works of Inigo Jones was the church in Covent Garden, which was finished and consecrated 27th September 1638.   The civil war interposed and all peaceful occupations were set aside.   Inigo Jones, like the rest, joined the King's standard, and was taken, along with Robinson the actor, Hollar, Peake, and Faithorne the engraver, with arms in their hands at the siege of Basing.   The last twelve years of his life present merely a history of anxieties and disappointments.   He was not only imprisoned but fined for his loyalty.   He had saved some money, which, in these perilous times, he was anxious to preserve.   This he effected in unison with Nicolas Stone, the sculptor.   They first buried their treasure in a private place in Scotland Yard, whence, lest workmen they had employed should, in accordance with an order published by Parliament, give the information, they removed it privately, and with their own hands buried it in Lambeth Marsh.

A Life of Inigo Jones, edited by Peter Cunningham, was printed for the Shakespeare Society, 1848, accompanied by " Remarks on some of his sketches for Masques and Dramas, by J. R. Planché : and five Court Masques, edited from the original MSS. of Ben Jonson, John Martin, &c., by J. P. Collier, with fac-similes of drawings applicable to these, by Inigo Jones, selected from innumerable designs in the possession of his Grace the Duke of Devonshire.

Inigo Jones was the son of a cloth-worker, and was born in West Smithfield in 1573.

The following anecdote in reference to his Christian name is authentically related :—

Lady Northington, attending a Levee during the indisposition of her husband,—the Earl, Lord High Chancellor of England,—held a colloquy with his Majesty George II., who, among other things, made enquiry as to the Earl's country residence, the Grainge in Hampshire. After nearly exhausting the fullest particulars she just remembered, for his Majesty's information, that it had been originally built by (as she termed him) Indigo Jones,—" Ay, ay," said the King, " I know. Indigo Jones—Yes—I've often heard of him. I believe he made a fortune as an architect somewhere in the Indies." On her return home, she, in the course of conversation with her husband, retailed the circumstance. " Well! of all the idiots," exclaimed the Earl with an oath, " it puzzles me to know whether you or the King was the greater."*

" The blunders about the period of Jones's death," observes Peter Cunningham, " are almost beyond belief. Antony Wood says he died 21st July 1651 ; Kennet, 22d May 1651 ; Walpole copies Wood, and Walpole's editor (Dallaway), correcting his author, says he was buried 26th June 1632. Allan Cuningham says he died

* The indisposition under which Lord Northington so frequently laboured was a fit of the gout induced by his convivial revelry in early life, while a student in the Temple. Many a severe twinge was the result of his early indulgencies. When suffering from its effects, he was once overheard in the House of Lords to mutter, after some painful walks between the Woolsack and the Bar, " If I had known that these legs were one day to carry a Chancellor, I'd have taken better care of them when I was a lad." Lord Northington's judicial talents were of the first order : " he was a great lawyer," said Lord Eldon, a high authority, " and very firm in delivering his opinion. He was fond of literature, and throughout life kept up his acquaintance with the Greek and Latin classics. He was also skilled in Hebrew. He married in 1743, Miss Huband, the daughter and co-heiress of Sir John Huband of Ipsley in Warwickshire, who survived him many years. His circumstances were not of the best, but shortly after his marriage his brother Anthony Henley died without issue, and on him devolved the paternal estates in Hampshire and Dorset, together with a mansion in Lincoln's Inn Fields. His own death occurred on the 14th January 1772, and he was succeeded in the title and estates by his only surviving son Robert, who subsequently was appointed Lord Lieutenant of Ireland, and died in 1786 at the early age of 39 without issue, whereby the title became extinct.

in June 1653. I have examined the register of St Bennet's, and find that he was buried 26th June 1652. The errors about Webb's relationship to Inigo are equally absurd. Some call him his nephew, others, his son-in-law. He was neither." His death occurred at Somerset House, Strand, London.

Jones was never married. The bulk of his property he devised to John Webb, his executor, the husband of "Ann Jones, my kinswoman." Webb had been a pupil of Jones, and succeeded to his master's collection of designs. He wrote " a vindication of Stonehenge restored." His death occurred 24th Oct. 1672 at Butleigh in Somersetshire.

Vandyck painted a portrait of Jones. The finished picture went, with the Houghton collection, to St Petersburg, but the sketch *en grisaille*, engraved by Hollar in 1655, for the first edition of " Stonehenge restored," was in the possession of a descendant, Major Inigo Jones, 11th Hussars, who, at his own expense, had it re-engraved to illustrate Cunningham's Life of the Architect.

The residence of Inigo Jones was in Scotland Yard. He was a Roman Catholic, and paid periodical fines to the overseers of the poor of St Martin's-in-the-Fields for the privilege of eating flesh in Lent, by reason of some unknown necessity.

A small collection of his plans for shifting scenery in masques is preserved among the Lansdowne MSS. in the British Museum.

There were some rambling MS. notes about Jones in a copy of the first edition of " Stonehenge restored," formerly in the Harleian Library, but since lost. They were supposed by Horace Walpole to have been written by Philip Herbert, fifth Earl of Pembroke and Montgomery, but, as Mr Peter Cunningham justly remarks, that was an impossibility, as the Earl died five years before the book was published, He rather suspects that the notes were the production of Sir Balthazar Gerbier, in some degree a rival of Jones.

There is a unique little volume, numbering 36 pages, in the library of one of the editors of the present work entitled " a Manifestation by Sir Balthazar Gerbier,

Knight, London, printed for the Authour. 1651," 18mo,
to prove that certain scandalous reports concerning himself and family, which he asserts had been spread by certain individuals, among whom was Sir William D'avenant,
were without foundation. He has this motto on the title
page. " Job xiii. 18. Behold now I have ordered my
cause, I know that I shall bee justified." He commences his " Manifestation " thus :—" Socrates and
many other famous men being abroad remained silent.

" Petrarch and several others made use of their best
eloquence in their own justification ; for that occasions
and times permit not all men to imitate some *Anabaptists*,
who, for the most part, will rather suffer themselves to
bee beaten then to make any resistance.

" Did not Paul speake in his owne defence and challenge the right of a Roman that his enemies might not
take any advantage against him ?

" And why should I not defend my selfe, since some
men have past their verdits on mee, for having made
my application to the late King's Court ?

" Others againe have hatcht and practised mischiefe
against me, beleeving that I inclined to popularity ; and
deemed that though I was a Courtier in show, yet I was
not so in effect.

" A third party hath been possest with a most injurious opinion, that I was untrue to either.

" And others have been apt to suffer scandalous dis-
famations to take place with them, on impossible sugges-
tions touching the profession of my Religion, and my
manner of life.

" Now these are the four branches which referre themselves to your judicious consideration ; whereon I shall
proceed with that sincerity, and plainnesse, as you may
justly expect.

" And to the end that I may give the greater satisfac-
tion to such as are lovers of truth, I shal first mention
my origine."

He then goes on to give his pedigree from the time
of his great grand-father,—and how it was predicted
" by a learned astronomer," that he was to be a great
traveller. His narrative proceeds thus :—

" My father being deceased, my mother permitted me

to accompany one of my brothers into France, wher I attained unto languages and sciences, so that at my returne home, though I was but a ladde, yet I had pretty good insight in severall arts and sciences, and I excelled not a little in writing, limning, drawing, and in mathematickes, as geometry, architecture, fortifications, and in the framing of warlike engines, all which brought me to bee considered of by Prince Maurice of Orange, who thought well of me. I was by him recommended unto Noel Caron, the then States Generall Ambassadour, who was comming for England, and who afterwards presented me to King James." But, he tells us, "all the allurements, promotions of Courts, nor worldly favours, were not capable to put me from my continuall care for my soules salvation, which I was taught to preferre before all things." At Court, "in the first twelve yeares of my attendance, I was employed in messages to forreigne Princes abroad,—and during my being at home I was made use of for my languages, my pen, and knowledge in other sciences."

"Now as for my skill in arts and sciences," he continues, "and particularly in architecture, these I employed in the contriving of some of the Duke of Buckingham's houses, and in the adorning of them."

He takes some pains to disabuse the reader's mind of his actions having been guided by mercenary motives :—

"I did also contrive some mines, massoned up in ships, which were to have blown up the Dycke at Rochell, for all which I never so much as touched a penny of the King's, nor of the Duke of Buckingham's monies, which I refused to meddle withall at my very first application to him, when as the said Duke (happily to try me), had left five hundred pounds under his bolster, which he commanded me to take as I waited on him at his rising, willing me to dispose of the same to the workmen ; but on the contrary, I called for the Duke's Steward, and wisht him to lock up the said monies for to bee delivered upon account.—Moreover, to prove that I never handled any of the Duke's monies, I doe referre my selfe to the testimony of Master Auditor Hill, in whose office it will be found upon record, that when as after the Duke's death, some malicious persons thought to have laid strange things to my charge, pretending that I could not have had the managing of affaires in the Duke's time, but that vast sums must needs have past through my hands; it was as then by the said Auditor proved, that I never had the disposing of the Duke's monies; and, therefore, could not be accountable for one single penny of the same; nor could I be accused to have made a fortune, which was sufficiently evidenced, by my never having purchast so much as an inch of ground, nor a thatcht House whilst my attendance. And besides all this, it is an unquestionable truth, that during the whole space of my thirty yeares' application to the Court of England, I never accepted of any present, lesse of a bribe, though it is manifest that I have obliged a number of men by my good offices."

After detailing how, after the Duke of Buckingham's death, he was sent to Spain to endeavour to effect a reconciliation between that country and England, and afterwards to reside in the Court of Bruxels in Brabant, but he further alleges that Cottington and those of his faction sought to compass his destruction, and, " finally, the said Cottingtonian faction prosecuted me, even at my returne into England, so that I could not obtaine the payment of one penny of my disbursements for my twelve yeares' residency abroad." "Then was my returne into Brabant impedited, M.<sup>r</sup> Du Vic knighted, and appointed to be resident in my stead; nay, I was not so much as permitted to return to Bruxels to get off my wife and children." He therefore passed into France, being " threatned to be stabbed by the Cottingtonians," when another grievance occurred; " Mr. Clement Cotterell, who was but my adjoynct, was knighted, and the Master of Ceremonies' place settled on him, though it is mine under the Great Seale during life." He goes on to say : " Neither did the Court's resent against me cease here. I was not only set upon in my owne person, but those of my family were likewise assaulted, and, finally, my fame was impaired; as also, endeavours were used to make me passe throughout all the world for a monster amongst men to all posterity."

At the French Court he " had a great deal of right to claim favour, for that by an advertisement, which I sent from Bruxels. to King Louis the 13th, I saved his life ; a certain Burgignian, named Triboulet, having been set on to kill him, by a wicked misrule, one Chantelouve, a priest who attended the then Queen mother" : on his appearance at Court, therefore, he was well received by the Queen Regent, the Princes of the blood, the Ministers of State, and he was consulted by M<sup>r</sup>. D'Emery, "the Chiefe of the Finances," as to the means of increasing the revenue and mitigating the taxes. He was encouraged by the Duke of Orleans and the Princes "to proceed on an establishment," which would have been worth to him and his colleagues,—the Count D'orvall, the Marquis de la Ferte Imbant, and Monsieur Montavron, a grand partizan—thirty thousand pounds sterling. "This was granted unto me under the Great Seale of France, and I was actually proceeding in the said establishment, putting myself to vast charges."

At this time, it would seem, "a secret cabale, which envied me, moved against me," the Bishop of Puis presenting a petition to the Queen Regent, commencing thus :—" How that *ipso facto* she was an excommunicated person, for having conferred such a charge as the general superintendency of that office which was conferred on me ; for, said he, I am an Heretick, such a one as the Papists terme all Protestants. Whereupon, Will. Crafts immediately whipt in, and alleged to the French Queen Regent, how that I was the man, who he supposed to have destroyed all the King of England's affaires. And to make me passe for a greater monster than ever there was on the earth, he not only said, that I was not the father of those children which were in my family, that I had squandered their means away, but worse than this ; that I had ravisht them, and that I used violence on their soules, for that they would be Papists, if they could but get loose from me." This so incensed the Queen that she commanded the Chancellor of France and the Attorney-General of the French King in the Parliament of Paris, " to put an absolute stoppe on the establishment which by Patent I was to make in three hundred Townes in that kingdom." He further complains that three of his daughters were abducted from his house, and without his consent, placed in a nunnery. " Finally, the said

Caball, not yet satisfied with the rape of soules, with the depradation of my estate, with the scandals, and the horrid falsehoods which they had vented, proceeded to a further plot to drive me out of France, pretending that I was a friend to the Spaniards, and that therefore I was an unfit person to breath on that soyle." So leaving for England " they dogged me and the rest of my family, and caused seven cavaliers to set upon me between Rovan and Deepe, where in the highway they tooke from me all my papers, and all the money which I had, leaving me nought but one French farthing; insomuch as that I might have starved, if Sir William Bicher at Rovan had not supplied me with ten pound in money, besides what other persons lent me at that time, among which I am bound to note the Lady Marquise of Moupay, then a venerable godly aged lady of the Protestant religion, who sent this message, " Have a care of your person, and looke not after those that stripped you, for they are here at court too mighty for you to wrestle withall." Accompanying this were fifty pistols in gold. He received another letter from " one Jaques D'Eldime, a merchant, wherein he did advertise me that if I would but turn a Roman Catholique, that then I should have mine own heart's desire, and thus he said he was commanded to write to me from one La Bernardierre, the chiefe of a new order stiled, that of the Sacrament of Miracles."

We have been thus particular in quoting so largely from Sir Balthazar's curious " manifestation," in order that his complaints and grievances may be exhibited in his own words, and the proper value be set on them. And this more for the reason that he drags in Sir William D'avenant as one of those who maligned him, although, whether true or false, the offence of which the poet stands accused is a very venial one, he simply having been incredulous, but Sir Balthazar seems to have attached the highest importance to every passage concerning himself.

Immediately following the previous quotation, the manifestation thus continues :—" And notwithstanding this public matter of fact, the malice of men was so great, as they that endeavoured to make the world

beleeve that the disaster which then befell me, between
Roan and Deepe was but a fixion; and who should
be the authour of this abominable falsehood, but William
Crafts and Davenant the poet, who reported it frequently
at the Louvre, and up and down Paris. Neither were
they contented to disperse the said calumny throughout
France, but they published it into all other parts by their
letters, insomuch as that Westminster Hall was filled with
the same, and it was the common talk about London,
how that I had committed horrid things with some of
my own family, and not only in these latter times but
even during my attendánce on the Duke of Buckingham;
which false brute was so cunningly disperst and insinu-
ated into men, as that even persons of honour and judgment did not know what to make of it, whereon they
exprest the sence, by the return of their letters to their
friends, of which letters one was shewed unto me at
Paris, by the late Sir Edmond Stafford, Kt., which said
letter mentioned all those horrid abominable scandals
which were uttered of me."

Further than asserting that Sir Balthazar's adventure
between Rouen and Dieppe was a fiction, nothing is laid
to the charge of D'avenant, for the letters just-mentioned
are not alleged to have emanated from him or any of his
friends, and Sir Balthazar seems to have been, as is usual
in cases of the kind, somewhat perplexed as to who was
the actual author of the insinuations against him which
he seems to have taken so much to heart.

He goes on to state that there was residing at the
Louvre a Mrs Sanderson,* whose husband lived in London,
and from whom she received "the said scandalous
reports," he "being said to be the authour of them, and
that he did make it his ordinary discourse among men
to blaze the same. Wherefore at my return hither I
thought it necessary to use all proper diligence for to
discover the true authour of this infamous scandal. And
having surmised the said William Sanderson to have been
the man," Mr. Sanderson was induced to make a declara-
tion of his innocence.

Sir Balthazar winds up by stating that he was not to

* Probably the mother of the lady who subsequently became
the wife of Betterton.

blame for the abduction of his three daughters, and for their becoming Roman Catholics, when he had "used all possible endeavours to instruct them even from their infancy in the true profession of the Protestant Religion," and how after they had been taken from him he "omitted not anything that could be thought of or practised to reclaim them."

He then proceeds to glorify himself further by saying that he did not deserve "to be ranked under the censure of those who have followed the disapproved courses of the court," that secondly, "with the open face of a free man borne," he "from his very infancy was taught to observe, next unto the increase of God's kingdom, the publick welfare, advantage, and good," and therefore was a courtier not in show but in effect. And thirdly, that even in opposition to the Duke of Buckingham, for whom he "would willingly have laid downe his life in any just cause;" he was a mortal enemy to "those things which proved grievances to the people," declaring also "that I loved the king's person in such a degree as that had it been possible for me to have delivered him from those causes which lost him in the opinion of the people, and have prevented those evils which overwhelmed them, I would willingly have laid down my neck on the block, and have died both for him and them, so it had been God's pleasure." "Wherefore as I could never persuade myself that there was a possibility of disuniting the king and people's interest, I doe therefore maintaine that I have been true to both. The which being conceived to be satisfactory, these will not need any addition at all, for that this manifestation is addrest to the judicious, who, moreover, cannot be thought to mistake themselves so farre, as to conclude, that anything which is by me alleged on this subject should rather proceed from a particular resentment of the injustices which have been done to my owne person and family, and the ingratitude to my long and faithfull services, then from a just and laudable zeale for the publick good, unto which all other considerations ought to give place."

"Sir Balthazar Gerbier and his family" formed the subject of a picture painted by Anthony Van Dyck, which was engraved and published by Boydell, 1st Feb.

1766, the original picture being then in the collection of Her Royal Highness the Princess Dowager of Wales, to whom the print is dedicated. The picture is seven feet by ten feet in length. The subject consists of Sir Balthazar leaning on the back of a chair, on which Lady Gebrier sits with an infant lying across her knees, while their other eight children are partly grouped around her and partly distributed throughout. The engraving is now exceedingly scarce.

PRINCES of sweet and humane natures have ever, both amongst the ancients and moderns in the best times, presented spectacles and personal representations, to recreate their spirits wasted in grave affairs of State, and for the entertainment of their nobility, ladies, and courts.

There being now past three years of intermission that the King and Queen's Majesties have not made Masques with shewes and intermedii, by reason the room where formerly they were presented having the ceiling since richly adorn'd with pieces of painting of great value, figuring the acts of King James of happy memory, and other enrichments, lest this might suffer by the smoke of many lights his Majesty commanded the surveyor of his works that a new temporary room of timber, both for strength and capacity of spectators, should be suddenly built for that use ; which being performed in two months, the Scenes for this Masque were prepared.

### THE SUBJECT OF THIS MASQUE.

Britanocles, the glory of the western world hath by his wisdom, valour, and piety, not only vindicated his own, but far distant seas, infested with pirates, and reduc'd the land, by his example, to a real knowledge of all good acts and sciences. These eminent acts, Bellerophon, in a wise pity, willingly would preserve from devouring time, and therefore to make them last to our posterity gives a command to Fame, who hath already spread them abroad that she should now at home, if there can be any maliciously insensible awake them from their pretended sleep, that even they with the large yet still increasing number of the good and loyal may mutually admire and rejoice in our happiness.

The Queen's Majesty being seated under the State and the room filled with spectators of quality, at the lower end of the room was a stage raised of a convenient height, and an oval stair down into the room.   That which first presented itself to the eye was the ornament that enclosed the scene.

In the under part of this were two pedestals of a solid order, whereon captives lay bound, above sate two figures in neeches; on the right hand a woman in a watchet* drapery, heightened with silver, on her head a *Corona Rostrata*,† with one hand holding the rudder of a ship, and in the other a little winged figure with a branch of palm, and a garland: this woman represented Naval Victory.   Opposite to this on the other neech sate the figure of a man bearing a sceptre with a hand and an eye in the palm, and in the other hand a book, on his head a garland of *Amaranthus*,‡ his cuirass was of gold with a *Palludamentum*§ of blue and antique bases‖ of

* Pale blue.

† *Rostrata Corona*—A Garland given to a captain for a victory at sea.—*Plin*. 16, 3, and 4.   A crown with a peak like the stem of a ship.

‡ Everlasting flower.

§ "*Paludamentum*—A cote armour.   *Sallust: Val. Max.*— A souldier's garment."  *Cooper's Thesaurus*. 1578, folio.   Used also by Pliny and Cicero.

"He dyd of his surcoat of pallade."—*Isenbras*, 124.

*Pallade*—Palle, or rich cloth.—*Halliwell*.

‖ That part of any ornament which hangs down, such as housings :—

"Phalastus was all in white, having his bases and caparison embroidered."—*Sidney*.

Also, may mean stockings, or armour for the legs,—

"Nor shall it ere be said that wight
With gauntlet blue and bases white,"
*Butler's Hudibras.*

crimson, his foot treading on the head of a serpent.
By this figure was signified right government;
above these were other composed ornaments cut
out like cloth of silver, tied up in knots with
scarfings all touch'd with gold.

These pillasters bore up a large freize with a
sea triumph of naked children, riding on sea horses
and fishes, and young tritons with writhen trum-
pets and other maritime fancies.  In the midst was
placed a great compartment of gold, with branches
of palm coming out of the scrolls, and within
that a lesser of silver with this inscription :—
VIRTUTIS OPUS, proper to the subject of this
Masque, and alluding to that of Virgil : *sed fam-
am extendere factis, &c.*  From this came a drapery of
crimson, which tied up with great knots in the
corners hung down in folds on the sides of the
pillasters.

A curtain flying up discovered the first Scene
wherein were English houses of the old and newer
forms, intermixt with trees, and afar off a prospect of the City of London and the river of
Thames, which, being a principal part, might be
taken for all Great Britain.

From several parts of the Scene came Action and
Imposture.  Action a young man in a rich habit
down to his knees with a large guard * of purple
about the skirt wherein was written with silver
letters MEDIO TUTISSIMA, on his head a garland of
laurel, and in one hand a branch of willow.  Imposture in a coat with hanging sleeves and great skirts,
little breeches, a high crowned hat, one side pinned
up, a little ruff, and a formal beard, and an
angling rod in his hand with a fish at the hook,
with a bag and a horn at his girdle.

* An ornamental hem, lace, or border.  *Now obsolete.*

### ACTION.

My variable sir ! I'th' name of Heaven
What makes your falsehood here where fame
    intends
Her triumphs all of truth ?   Her trumpet she
Hath chosen new and clean, lest it should taint
Her breath.   Thou art so useless to the world,
That thou art impudent when thou dost share
What is most cheap, and common unto all,
The air and light.   I do beseech thee, my
Fine false artificer, hide both thy faces,
For thou art double everywhere.   Steal hence,
And I'll take care thou shalt no more be miss'd
Than shadows are at night.

### IMPOSTURE.

Be patient, sir !
This valiant humour of disdain works not
So powerfully as you believe.   I hide myself.
The reasons must be strong that shall persuade
Me under ground.   The badger loves his hole,
Yet is not so bashful but dares look out
And shew himself when there is prey abroad :
Then strangely arrogant, I pity thee
As politics do men too humble for
Their care, much more for their redress ; that is,
I smile at thee, the graver way of scorn,
For should I laugh I fear t'would make thee
    think
Thy impudence had somewhat in't of wit.
Didst ever hope to be so useful in
The manage and support of human works
As I ?

### ACTION.

Proceed ! proceed ! make up your history.

### IMPOSTURE.

Wisely the jealous sceptics did suspect
Reality in every thing, for every thing but seems,
And borrows the existence it appears
To have! Imposture governs all—even from
The gilded Ethnick* mitre, to the painted staff
O' th' Christian constable; all but pretend
Th' resemblance of that power which inwardly
They but deride, and whisper merry questions to
  themselves,
Which way it comes.

### ACTION.

Y' have cunningly observ'd
This is a pleasant new philosophy :

### IMPOSTURE.

Right, sir! and what is pleasant unto all
Is generally good.   Troth, I could wish
Our reason were as certain as our sense
Would alter in dispute, as little be
As soon confirm'd.   But since it is not so,
That universally shall take which most
Doth please, not what pretends at profit and
Imaginary good.   Is it not fit
And almost saf'st to cosen all, when all
Delight still to be cosen'd ?

### ACTION.

These lectures would
Subdue a numerous sect, wert thou to preach
To young soft courtisans, unpractis'd heirs,
Of over practis'd usurers, silken
And fine feathered gallants, whose easy ears
Still open to delights, and shut at truths.
But fate takes not so little care of those
* Heathen—Pagan.

For whom it doth preserve the elements,
That what is chief within us should be quite
Deprav'd, as we were only born to aim
At trifles here, like children in their first
Estate of using legs, to run at sight
Of bubbles, and to leap at noise of bells.

### IMPOSTURE.

Even so believ'd, and in their chiefest growth
They beat my Grandsire Mahomet's
Divinity ; who doth allow the good, a handsome
    girl
On earth, the valiant, two in Paradise.

### ACTION.

Thou art so read in human appetites
That, were the devil licensed to assume
A body, thou might'st be his cook ; yet know,
If you endeavour it, you may persuade
Yourself there are some few 'mongst men
That, as our making is erect, look up
To face the stars, and fancy nobler hopes
Than you allow ; not downward hang their heads
Like beasts to meditate on earth, on abject things
Beneath their feet.

### IMPOSTURE.

T'is a thin number sure,
And as much disperst, for they would hardly meet
In councils and in synods to enact
Their doctrine by consent, that the next age
May say they parted friends.

### ACTION.

'Tis possible,
'Less you steal in amongst them to disturb
Their peace, disguis'd in a canonick weed,

Nor are these such, that by their reasons strict
And rigid discipline, must fright nice court
Philosophers from their belief, such as impute
A tyrannous intent to heavenly powers,
And that their tyranny alone did point
At men, as if the fawn and kid were made
To frisk and caper out their time, and it
Were sin in us to dance, the Nightingale
To sing her tragic tales of love, and we
To recreate our selves with groans, as if
All perfumes for the tiger were ordained
'Cause he excels in scent: colours, and gaudy
    tinctures for
The Eastern birds, whilst all our ornament
Are russet robes, like melancholy Monks.

#### IMPOSTURE.

There are, sir, of this rigid sect, and much
They govern too that think the godwit* and
The rail† were meant the eagles' food, and men
Design'd to feed on salads in a mead,
As if it were created but a great
And larger kind of frogs.

#### ACTION.

It is confess'd
There are some sullen clerks that love
To injure and to scant themselves, yet you
May find a few whose wisdoms merit greater sway
That will allow us pleasures 'bove our cares,
Yet these we must not compass with our guilt,
But every act be squared by virtue's rule.

---

  * A bird of particular delicacy.
    " No ortolans nor godwits crown his board."—*Cowley.*
  † " Of wild birds, Cornwall hath quail, rail, partridge, and
pheasant."—*Carew.*

### IMPOSTURE.

Virtue ! 'Tis a mere name.   Virgins that want
A dowry learnt by rote, to raise the price
Of old unhandsome looks, admit there's one
Or two allow in nature such a thing
And that it is no dream : these mighty lords
Of reason have but a few followers,
And those go ragged too : the prosperous, brave
Increasing multitude pursue my steps.
The great devourer of mysterious books
Is come ! Merlin, whose deep prophetic art
Foretold that at this particle of time
He would forsake's unbodied friends below
And waste one usual circuit of the moon
On earth, to try how nature's face is chang'd
Since his decease.

Merlin the prophetic magician enters apparel'd
in a gown of light purple down to his ankles,
slackly girt, with wide sleeves turned up with
powdered ermines, and a roll on his head of the
same, with a tippet hanging down behind; in
his hand a silvered rod.

### ACTION.

Your eyes encounter him
As you would make great use of's visit here.

### IMPOSTURE.

With reason, sir, for he hath power to wake
Those that have many ages slept, such as
When busy in their flesh were my disciples.
Hail thou most ancient prophet of this Isle !
I, that have practised superstitious rites
Unto thy memory, beg thy immortal aid
To raise their figures that, in times forgot,
Were in the world predominant : Help to
Confute this righteous fool, that boasts his small

Neglected stock of wisdom comes from Heaven,
    and show
How little it prevailed on earth, since all
The mighty here are of my sect.

### MERLIN.

'Tis long
Since this my magic rod hath struck the air,
Yet loss of practice can no art impair
That soars above the reach of nature's might.
Thus then I charm the spirits of the night,
And unto hell conjure their wings to steer,
And straight collect from dismal corners there
The great seducers of this Isle, that by
Their baits of pleasure strove to multiply
Those sad inhabitants, who curse that truth below
Which, here on earth, they took no pains to know.
Appear ! appear ! nimbly obey my will
T'express I died t' increase my magic skill.

———

The whole Scene was transformed into a horrid
hell, the further part terminating in a flaming
precipice, and the nearer parts expressing the
suburbs, from whence enter the several Antimasques.

### 1. ENTRY.

*Of mock music of 5 persons.*

One with a viol, the rest with
Tabor and pipe,
Knackers and bells,
Tongs and key,
Gridiron and shoeing horn.

### 2. ENTRY.

A ballad singer his } with their Auditory,
    companion

II.                         S

A porter laden,
A vintner's boy,
A kitchenmaid with a hand-basket,
A sailor.

### 3. ENTRY.

A crier of mouse-traps ⎱ bearing the engines be-
A seller of tinderboxes ⎰ longing to the trades.
The master of
Two baboons and
An ape.

### 4. ENTRY.

A mountebank in the habit of a grave doctor,
A zany ⎱
A harlekin ⎰ his men,
An old lame charewoman.
Two pale wenches presenting their urinals,* and he
    distributing his printed receipts out of a budget.

### 5. ENTRY.

Four old-fashioned Parasitical Courtiers.

### 6. ENTRY.

Of rebellious Leaders in war :
        Cade,
        Kett,
        Jack Straw, and
            their soldiers.

The apparel of these in part shewed their base
professions, mixt with some soldier-like accoutre-
ments.

These Antimasques being past, Bellerophon
entered riding on Pegasus, in a coat armour of
silver scales, and on his head an antique helm

* Bottles in which water is kept for inspection.
"These follies shine through you, like the water in an
urinal."—*Shakespeare.*

with plumes, his bases watchet with lables of gold,
a golden javelin in his hand, the point of lead.

The Pegasus was covered all with white close to
his skin, his main and tail of silver, with large
white wings, his reins and saddle of carnation
trim'd with silver.  He, riding up into the middle
of the room with an attendant, alighted.

### Action.

Bellerophon !  That th' off-spring art of heaven,
Most timely, and by inspiration sure,
Thou com'st to help me to despise and scorn
These airy mimic apparitions, which
This cosening prophet would present as great
Examples for succeeding times to imitate.

### Bellerophon.

Through thick assembled clouds, through mists
    that would
Choke up the eagle's eye, I, in my swift
And sudden journey through the air, have seen
All these fantastic objects, which but shew
How dull the impious were to be so sillily
Misled, and how the good did ever need
But little care, and less of brain, to scape
Th' apparent baits of such gross fools.

### Imposture.

Ay, Sir,
T'were easy to subdue if choleric scorn
Might make up confutation without help
Of arguments.  The virtuous, Sir, of late
Have got a fine feminine trick to rail
At all they will dislike, refer what is
Not easily understood unto a kind
Obedient faith, and then call reason but
A new and saucy heretic.  Those that

My reverend prophet rais'd which you, Sir, in
A virtuous fury have called fools, I'm sure
Did govern when alive, and by
Imposture made their estimation thrive.

### BELLEROPHON.

Monster ! thou know'st 'tis not thy strange defence
Of reason that provokes my rage, but thou
Would'st cunningly disguise thy sense
In reason's shape, cosening thy willing self,
And giving seeming pleasures real attributes :
These taking tunes, to which the numerous world
Do dance, when your false-sullenness shall please,
You may compare to th'dangerous music of
The swan, a merry preparation still
To melancholy death.

### IMPOSTURE.

Cry mercy, Sir !
You are Heroic virtue, who pretend
An embassy from heaven, and that y'are sent
To make new lovers here on earth ; you will
Refine the ways of wooing, and prescribe
To valour nobler exercise than what
The ancient knights' adventurers taught.   But first
See these of the old Heroic race.   Merlin
Assist me once more with thy charming rod,
To shew this strict corrector of delights,
What ladies were of yore, and what their knights,
Although their shapes and manners now grow
     strange,
Make him admire what he would strive to change.

### BELLEROPHON.

Alas ! how weak and easy would you make
Our intellectual strength, when you have hope
It may be overcome with noise and shows.

### IMPOSTURE.

Yes! and this moral magistrate ; your strict
O'er solemn friend, that in such comely phrase
Disputes for active virtue, and declares
Himself the mark of all unrighteous opposites.
His magnanimity shall yield at last,
Straight take my angle in his hand, then bait
The hook with gilded flies, to fish in troubled
    seas :
For all the world is such, and, in a storm,
Where the philosopher, that still swims in
Profoundest depths, will, Sir, as easily
Be snapt, as fools that float on shallow streams,
And taken with a line no stronger, sir, than what
Will tear a little gudgeon's jaws.

### ACTION.

The knight adventurer that you intend
To raise, must then adventure far, and make
His valour captivate, surer and soon
As his lamenting lady's looks.  I'll not
Be taken else.

### IMPOSTURE.

Most reverend lord of dark
Unusual sciences ! begin thy charm.

### MERLIN.

Like furious rivers meeting underground,
So hollow and so dismal is the sound
Of all my inward murmurs, which no ear
But with a mild astonishment can hear ;
Though not so loud as thunder, thunders are
A slower noise, and not amaze so far.
Which to express, that distant spirits hear
And willingly obey : Appear ! appear !

At this the hell suddenly vanisheth, and there
appears a vast forest, in which stood part of an old
castle kept by a giant, proper for the scene of the
mock Romanza which followed. Out of this
forest comes running and affrighted a dwarf and
damsel. The dwarf in blue and white, and the
damsel in a straight bodied gown and wide
sleeves of changeable,* with a safeguard† of silver
stuff, and a past and partlet‡ like a moral figure in
old paintings. To these a knight in old fashioned
armour, with spear and shield, his squire apparel'd in a yellow coat, with wide sleeves and
strossers§ cut in panes of yellow and watchet.
After them a giant in a coat of mail, his bases red
and silver, with a faulchion hanging in a chain :
and in his hand an iron mace, a great roll of black
and white on his head ; a Saracen's face with great
black mustachoes.

## THE MOCK ROMANZA.

### Dwarf.    Squire.

Dwar. Fly from this forest, squire ! Fly, trusty
    spark !
I fear like child whom maid hath left i'th' dark.
    Squire. O coward base ! whose fear will never
    lin ‖

---

* Now the taylor make thy doublet of changeable taffeta ;
or thy mind is a very opal.—*Shakespeare.*

† See "Guard," *ante*, p. 267.

‡ *Partlet*—A ruff, or band for the neck.—The term sometimes applied to the habit-shirt. " Wyth gay gownys and gay
kyrtels, and mych waste in apparell, rynges, and owchis, wyth
partelettes and pastis garneshed wyth perle."—*More's Supply-
cacyon of Soulys,* Sig. L. ii.

§ Tight drawers. The word is corrupted into " strouces " in
Sir John Oldcastle, p. 71.

‖ Cease.

Till't shrink thy heart as small as head of pin !
Lady, with pretty finger in her eye,
Laments her lamkin knight, and shall I fly ?
Is this a time for blade to shift for's self,
When giant vile calls knight a sneaking elf ?
This day, a day as fair as heart could wish,
This giant stood on shore of sea to fish
For angling rod he took a sturdy oak,
For line a cable that in storm ne'er broke ;
His hook was such as heads the end of pole,
To pluck down house ere fire consumes it whole.
This hook was bated with a dragon's tail ;
And there on rock he stood to bob for whale,
Which straight he caught and nimbly home did
    pack
With ten cart load of dinner on his back :
Thus homward bent, his eye too rude and cunning
Spies knight and lady by an hedge a funning.
That modicum of meat he down did lay,
For it was all he eat on fasting day.

Enter GIANT, KNIGHT, and DAMSEL.

DWARF.

They come !  In's rage he spurns up huge tree roots,
Now stick to lady, knight, and up with boots.

GIANT.

Bold recreant wight ! what fate did hither call thee
To tempt his strength that hath such power to
    maul thee ?
How durst thy puling damsel hither wander ?
What was the talk you by yond' hedge did maunder ?

DAMSEL.

Patience, sweet man of might !  Alas heaven knows
We only hither came to gather sloes,

And bullies two or three ; for, truth to tell ye,
I've long'd six weeks with these to fill my belly ;
I'feeks, if you'll believe 't, nought was meant sure
By this our jaunt, which errants call adventure.

### GIANT.

Shall I grow meek as babe when ev'ry trull is
So bold to steal my sloes and pluck my bullyes ?*

### KNIGHT.

Fear not!  Let him storm on, and still grow rougher,
Thou art bright as candle clear'd by snuffer,
Canst ne'er endure a blemish or eclipse
From such a hookt nose, foul mouth'd, bobber† lips?
Ere he shall boast, he us'd thee thus to's people
I'll see him first hang'd high as any steeple.

### GIANT.

If I but upward heave my oaken twig,
I'll teach thee play the Tom-boy,‡ her the Rig§
Within my forest bounds.  What doth she ail
But she may serve as cook to dress my whale ?
In this, her damsel's tire and robe of sarsnet,
She shall souse bore, ‖ fry tripes, and wild hogs'
    harsnet.¶

### KNIGHT.

O, monster vile ! thou mighty ill bred lubber !
Art thou not mov'd to see her whine and blubber ?
Shall damsel fair, as thou must needs confess her,
With canvass apron, dress thy meat at dresser ?
Shall she, that it is of soft and pliant mettle,
Whose fingers silk would gall, now scour a kettle ?

---

* Bullace.   A small black and tartish plum of wild growth.
† Saucy.              ‡ A mean fellow.              § A wanton.
‖ Pickle cabbage.
¶ Query *Harslet ?*  "A haggise, a chitterling, a hog's hars-
let."—*Nomen.*, p. 87.

Though not to scuffle given, now I'll thwart thee,
Let Blowze, thy daughter, serve for shillings forty.
'Tis meeter, I think, such ugly baggages
Should in a kitchen drudge for yearly wages,
Than gentle she who hath been bred to stand
Near chair of Queen with island shock in hand,
At questions and commands all night to play,
And amber possets* eat at break of day,
Or score out husbands in the charcoal ashes.
With courtly knights, not roaring country swashes,†
Hath been her breeding still, and's more fit far
To play on virginals and the guitar
Than stir a seacoal fire or scum a cauldron
When thou shalt break thy fast on a bull's chaudron.‡

### GIANT.

Then I perceive I must lift up my pole,
And deal your love-sick noddle such a dole
That ev'ry blow shall make so huge a clatter,
Men ten leagues off shall ask, Hah! what's the
    matter?

### DAMSEL.

Kind grumbling youth! I know that thou art able,
And want of breeding makes thee prone to squabble.
Yet, sure thy nature doth compunction mean,
Though, 'las, thy mother was a sturdy Quean:
Let not meek lovers kindle thy fierce wrath,
But keep thy blustering breath to cool thy broth.

---

* *Posset*—A drink of wine or treacle boiled with milk, usually taken before retiring to rest. *See* Merry Wives of Windsor, v. 5. "The wines be lusty, high, and full of spirit, and amber'd all."—*Beaumont and Fletcher. i.e.,* scented with ambergris. See ante, p. 211.

† Halliwell, in his Archaic and Provincial Dictionary, illustrates "Swash: a roaring blade, a swaggerer," with these identical two lines, but without marking D'avenant as his authority.

‡ Entrails.

#### KNIGHT.

Whine not, my love, his fury straight will waste him,
Stand off a while and see how I'll lammbaste* him.

#### SQUIRE.

Now look to't, Knight! this such a desp'rate blade is
In Gaul he swinged the valiant Sir Amadis!

#### DWARF.

With bow, now Cupid, shoot this son of punk,
With Crossbow else, or pellet out of trunk!

#### GIANT.

I'll strike thee till thou sink where the abode is
Of wights that sneak below, called Antipodes.

#### MERLIN.

My art will turn this combat to delight,
They shall, unto fantastic music, fight.
[They fall into a dance and depart.

#### BELLEROPHON.

How trivial and how lost thy visions are!
Did thy prophetic science take such care,
When thou wert mortal, with unlawful power
To recollect thy ashes 'gainst this hour,
And all for such import?  Surrender straight
This usurpation of thy warmth and weight,
And turn to air, thy spirit to a wind!
Blow thine own dust about! until we find
No small remainder of ill gather'd thee
And like to it; so waste thy memorie.

#### ACTION.

Thou Imposture, to some dark region steal!
The light is killing, cause it doth reveal

* Beat soundly.

Thy thin disguise, i'th dark thou ne'er wilt fade,
For dismal plants still prosper in the shade;
Thou art a shadow, and observe how all
Vain shadows to our eyes stretch and grow tall,
Just when the sun declines to bring in night,
So thou dost thrive in darkness, waste in light.

### BELLEROPHON.

Away! Fame, still obedient unto fate,
This happy hour is call'd to celebrate
Britanocles, and those that in this Isle
The old with modern virtues reconcile.
Away! Fame's universal voice I hear,

                        *[a trumpet within.*
'Tis fit you vanish quite when they appear.
                    *[Exeunt Merlin, Imposture.*

---

In the further part of the Scene, the earth open'd and there rose up a richly adorn'd palace, seeming all of Goldsmiths' work, with porticoes vaulted on pillasters running far in: the pillasters were silver of rustic work, their bases and capitols of gold. In the midst was the principal entrance, and a gate; the doors' leaves of bass-relief, with jambs and frontispiece all of gold. Above these ran an architrave, freize, and cornice of the same; the freize enricht with jewels; this bore up a ballestrata,* in the midst of which, upon a high tower with many windows, stood Fame in a carnation garment trim'd with gold, with white wings and flaxen hair; in one hand a golden trumpet, and in the other an olive garland.

In the lower part leaning on the rail of the ballesters were two persons, that, on the right hand, personating Arms with a cuirass and plum'd helm. and a broken lance in his hand.

* Balustrade.

On the left hand, a woman in a watchet robe trim'd with silver, on her head a bend,* with little wings like those of Mercury, and a scroll of parchment in her hand, representing Science.

When this palace was arrived to the height, the whole scene was changed into a Peristilium† of two orders, Doric and Ionic, with their several ornaments seeming of white marble, the bases and capitals of gold; this, joining with the former, having so many returns, openings, and windows, might well be known for the glorious Palace of Fame.

The Chorus of poets enter'd in rich habits of several colours, with laurels on their heads, gilt.

[Music.

### FAME SINGS.

#### 1.

Breake forth! thou treasure of our sight,
    That art the hopeful morn of every day,
Whose fair example makes the light,
    By which heroic virtue finds her way.

#### 2.

O thou, our cheerful morning rise!
    And straight these misty clouds of error clear,
Which long have overcast our eyes,
    And else will darken all this hemisphere.

#### 3.

What to thy power is hard or strange?
    Since not alone confined unto the land;

---

* Query, Band?

† A place set about with pillars—a cloister.—*Cooper's Thesaurus.*

"The Villa Gordiana had a peristyle of two hundred pillars." —*Arbuthnot.*

The sceptre to a trident change !
And straight unruly seas thou canst command !

4.

How hath thy wisdom rais'd this Isle ?
　　Or thee, by what new title shall we call ?
Since it were less'ning of thy style,
　　If we should name thee Nature's Admiral.

5.

Thou universal wonder, know !
　　We all in darkness mourn till thou appear,
And by thy absence dull'd may grow,
　　To make a doubt if day were ever here !

The Masquers came forth of the Peristilium, and stood on each side, and at that instant the gate of the Palace open'd, and Britanocles appeared.

The habit of the Masquers was close bodies of carnation, embroidered with silver, their arming sleeves of the same ; about their waist two rows of several fashioned leaves, and under this their bases of white reaching to the middle of their thigh ; on this was an under basis with labels of carnation embroidered with silver, and betwixt every pane were puffs* of silver, fastened in knots to the labels ; the trimming of the shoulders was as that of the

* The origin of the word "puff" is said to be this : —In France, at one time, the *coiffure* most in vogue was called *pouff*. It consisted of the hair raised as high as possible over horse-hair cushions, and ornamented with objects indicative of the tastes and history of the wearer. The Duchess of Orleans, for example, on her first appearance at court after the birth of her son and heir, had on her *pouff* a representation, in gold and enamel, most beautifully executed, of a nursery. There was the cradle and the baby, the nurse, and a number of play-things. Madame d'Egmont, daughter of the Duc de Richelieu, after her father had taken Port Mahon, wore on her *pouff* a little diamond fortress, with sentinels keeping guard.

basis ; their long stockings set up were carnation with white shoes, and roses ; their bands and cuffs made of purls* of cut work ; upon their heads little carnation caps, embroidered as the rest, with a slit turned up before, out of the midst came several falls of white feathers diminishing upwards in pyramidal form.

This habit was beautiful, rich, and light for dancing, and proper for the subject of this Masque.

[*Music.*

The Palace sinks, and Fame, remaining hovering in the air, rose on her wings singing, and was hidden in the clouds.

### CHORUS.

Britanocles, the great and good appears,
His person fills our eyes, his name our ears,
His virtue every drooping spirit cheers !

### FAME.

Why move these princes of his train so slow,
As, taking root, they would to statues grow ?
But that their wonder of his virtue turns them so.

'Tis fit you mix that wonder with delight,
As you were warm'd to motion with his sight,
To pay the expectation of this night.

### CHORUS.

Move then in such a noble order here,
As if you each his governed planet were,
And he mov'd first to move you in each sphere.

### CHORUS.

O with what joy you'll measure out the time !

* Purl—an embroidered and puckered border. "Himself came in next after a triumphant chariot made of carnation velvet, enriched with purl and pearl."—*Sidney.*

Each breast like his still free from every crime,
Whose pensive weight might hinder you to climb.

### THE MASQUERS DESCEND INTO THE ROOM.

The song ended, the scene turns to that of
Britain.

### THE MASQUERS DANCE THEIR ENTRY.

Which ended, a new chorus of our own modern
poets raised by Merlin, in rich habits diff'ering from
the rest, with laurels on their heads gilt, make
their address to the Queen.

### 1.

Our eyes, long since dissolv'd to air,
To thee for day must now repair,
   Though rais'd to life by Merlin's might ;
Thy stock of beauty will supply
Enough of sun from either eye,
   To fill the organs of our sight.

### 2.

Yet first thy pity should have drawn
A cloud of cypress or of lawn,
   To come between thy radiant beams ;
Our eyes, long darkened in a shade,
When first they so much light invade,
   Must ask and sicken with extremes.

### 3.

Yet wiser reason hath prevail'd
To wish thy beauties still unveil'd,
   'Tis better that it blind should make us
Than we should want such heavenly fire,
That is so useful to inspire
   These raptures which would else forsake us.

### 4.

Who knows but Homer got his flame
From some refulgent Grecian dame
　　Whose beauty gave his Muse supplies;
And would not trust in humble prose
His noble thoughts, but rather chose
　　High numbers, though with loss of eyes?

Here the scene changed, and in the farthest part
the sea was seen, terminating the sight with the
horizon; on the one side was a haven with a
citadel, and on the other broken grounds and
rocks; from whence the sea-nymph Galatea came
waving forth, riding on the back of a dolphin, in
a loose snow white garment; about her neck chains
of pearl, and her arms adorn'd with bracelets of
the same; her fair hair disheveled and mixt with
silver, and in some part covered with a veil which
she with one hand graciously held up. Being arrived
to the midst of the sea, the dolphin stayed, and
she sung, with a Chorus of music,

### GALATEA'S SONG.

### 1.

So well Britanocles o'er seas doth reign,
　　Reducing what was wild before,
That fairest sea-nymphs leave the troubled main,
　　And haste to visit him on shore.

### 2.

What are they less than nymphs since each make
　　shew
Of wondrous immortality,
And each these sparkling treasures wears that
　　grow
Where breathless divers cannot pry?

### 3.

On ever moving waves they us'd to dance
    Unto the whistling of the wind ;
Whose measures hit and meet by erring chance,
    Where music can no concord find.

### 4.

But now for their majestic welcome try
    How ev'n and equally they'll meet,
When you shall lead them by such harmony,
    As can direct their ears and feet.

Which done, she gently past away, floating on
the waves as she came in. After this, some ships
were discern'd sailing afar off several ways, and
in the end a great fleet was discovered, which,
passing by with a side wind, tackt about, and with
a prosperous gale entered into the haven, this con-
tinuing to entertain the sight whilst the dancing
lasted.

### THE VALEDICTION.

### 1.

Wise nature, that the dew of sleep prepares
To intermit our joys and ease our cares,
    Invites you from these triumphs to your rest !
May ev'ry whisper that is made be chaste,
Each lady slowly yield, yet yield at last ;
    Her heart a pris'ner to her lover's breast.

### 2.

To wish unto our royal lover more
Of youthful blessings than he had before,
    Were but to tempt old nature 'bove her might,
Since all the odour, music, beauteous fire,
We, in the spring, the spheres, the stars, admire
    Is his renew'd and better'd ev'ry night !

II.               T

3.

To bed, to bed ! may every lady dream
From that chief beauty she hath stolen a beam,
  Which will amaze her lover's curious eyes !
Each lawful lover, to advance his youth,
Dream he hath stolen his vigour, love, and truth ;
  Then all will haste to bed but none to rise !

<hr>

THE KING'S MAJESTY.

| | |
|---|---|
| Duke of LENNOX. | Lord LODOWICK STUART. |
| Lord WILLIAM HAMILTON. | Earl of DEVONSHIRE. |
| Earl of CARLILE. | Earl of NEWPORT. |
| Earl of ELGIN. | Lord ANDEVOR. |
| Lord PHILIP HERBERT. | Lord PAGET. |
| Lord RUSSELL. | Lord WHARTON. |
| Mr FRANCIS RUSSELL. | Mr THO. HOWARD. |

In the list of performers in Britaunia Triumphans,
LORD WILLIAM HAMILTON is placed below the Duke of
Lenox, and above the Earl of Carlisle. The youngest
son of the second marquis, he was created Earl of
Lancrick or Lanark, in Scotland, 31st March 1639. In
the next masque of Salmacida Spolia, the ignorance of
the printer converted him into an Irish peer as Earl of
Leimerick, in which blunder he is followed by Chetwood.
His only brother James, whom he succeeded, was created
12th April 1643, Duke of Hamilton.

Clarendon asserts, and probably with truth, that his
grace " had more out-faced the law in bold projects and
pressures upon the people than any other man durst have
presumed to do, as especially in the projects of wine and
iron, about the last of which, and the most gross, he had
a sharp contest with the Lord Coventry, who was a good
wrestler too, and at last compelled him to let it pass the
seal, the entire profit of which always reverted to himself, and such as were his pensioners."* Coventry was
Lord Keeper of the Great Seal, " and enjoyed this place,
with an universal reputation—and sure justice was never
better administered for the space of about sixteen years,
even to his death some months before he was sixty years
of age."†

As heir of his father the Marquis succeeded to the
Earldom of Cambridge which had been created 16th
June 1619. The succession to this honour was by that
illegal court, called the High Court of Justice, held as
sufficient to exclude his grace from the benefit of availing
himself of the laws of Scotland, which being an inde-
pendent kingdom, having a separate government author-
izing the levying of an army to relieve the King of
Scotland, he asserted on his capture that he was entitled
to be dealt with as a prisoner of war. He was informed
that not as Duke of Hamilton, but as Earl of Cambridge,
the Court would sit in judgment upon him. Accordingly
he was tried as an English Peer—convicted and sentence

* Clarendon, vol. i., p. 263. Oxford 1826, 8vo.
† Clarendon, vol. i , p. 80.

of death was passed upon him. He was executed upon the 9th of March 1648-9, and his body carried by sea to Hamilton where it was interred in the Parish Church.

The first Duke of Hamilton exhibited more dignity when he suffered than he had previously done. He was much esteemed by the King, but he was not a faithful councillor to his majesty. His dealings with the saints of the solemn league and covenant were, to say the least, questionable. He was one of the most distrusted of his majesty's advisers. Of his rapacity, Clarendon has spoken distinctly. After his death a pamphlet, now, it is believed, of rare occurrence, entitled *Digitus Dei* was published, in which his grace was accused of treasonably plotting with the Scotish rebels in order to secure the Crown to himself.

THOMAS BRUCE FIRST EARL OF ELGIN, was the second son of Edward Lord Bruce of Kinloss, Master of the Rolls to James I., by whom he was raised to the peerage. He died in 1609 in the sixty-second year of his age, and was interred in the Rolls Chapel, where a memorial was erected to his memory. By his wife Magdalen, daughter of Sir Alexander Clerk of Balbirny, he had two sons, Edward and Thomas, and a daughter Christian, who, upon her union with William Earl of Devonshire, was presented by the King with a portion of no less a sum than ten thousand pounds.

Edward his eldest son, the second Baron, was made a Knight of the Bath at the creation of Henry Prince of Wales. He was never married, and was slain in a duel with Sir Edward Sackville, afterwards Earl of Dorset. Clarendon, referring to the latter, observes, "He entered into a fatal quarrel upon a subject very unwarrantable with a young nobleman of Scotland, the Lord Bruce, upon which they both transported themselves into Flanders, and attended only by two chirurgeons placed at a distance, and under an obligation not to stir, but upon the fall of one of them, they fought under the walls of Antwerp, when the Lord Bruce fell dead upon the place, and Sir Edward Sackville, for so he was then called, being likewise hurt, retired into the next monastery, which was at hand."* Thomas, his brother, thus

* Vol. I., p. 106, Oxford 1826, 8vo.

became the third Lord Bruce of Kinloss. He was not only raised to the Earldom of Elgin in Scotland, 21st June 1633. but was created Baron Bruce of Whorlton in the county of York, 2d August 1641. He died upon the 19th day of December 1663, and was buried in the family mausoleum in the churchyard of the parish of Moulden, Bedfordshire. His Lordship was twice married, his first wife, Anne Chichester, was Anne, daughter of Sir Robert Chichester by Frances, daughter and co-heir of Sir John Harrington, by whom he had one son created Earl of Ailesbury in 1664. This branch of the family of Bruce became extinct in the male line upon the death of Charles Bruce fourth Earl of Elgin and third Earl of Ailesbury, who, though thrice married. had only one son, who died in 1739 without issue. He was offered a dukedom in 1746 according to Horace Walpole,—See letters vol. iii.,—but having no issue male declined the honour. He, however, obtained in that year a patent as Lord Bruce of Tottenham, with a remainder to his nephew Thomas Bruce Brudenell, who was created Earl of Ailesbury in 1776, and died in 1814. In 1821 his son Charles was made Marquis of Ailesbury. in which honour and the inferior ones he was succeeded by the present Peer.

The Barony of Kinloss under the charter of 1601 being to Edward Bruce "*suisque heredibus et assignatis*," was claimed recently by the present Duke of Buckingham as heir of the original patentee through Lady Mary Bruce, who married Henry Duke of Chandos. the only one of the three daughters of Charles fourth Earl of Elgin who left issue. This dignity, unclaimed for more than a century, was adjudged 21st July 1868 to his grace by a Committee of privileges.

LORD PHILIP HERBERT was the fourth son of the Earl of Pembroke and Montgomery. His three elder brothers dying without issue, the succession opened to him upon the demise of his father in January 1649-50. Earl Philip was twice married. He died 11th December 1669, and was succeeded by his son William.

Mr FRANCIS RUSSELL was the immediate younger brother of William Lord Russell, and died according to Collins, "a month before his father in France, unmarried."

This must, therefore, have been in April 1641, as the Earl died on Sunday the ninth of May of small-pox "and was buried at Cheyneys."* Archbishop Laud in the account of himself says, "This Lord was one of the main plotters of Strafford's death; and I know where he and other Lords, before the Parliament sat down, resolved to have his blood. But God would not let him live to take joy therein, but cut him off in the morning, whereas the bill for the Earl of Strafford's death was not signed till night." Collins, referring to Clarendon, says, "this statement is malicious and unchristian like," but the Chancellor's statement comes only to this, that the Earl promised the King to save Strafford's life; but he did not do so. He never says that Bedford and the other Lords did not conjointly plot to take away Strafford's life.

The execution of Strafford was to speak plainly a murder under colour of law—a crime in which both the King and his Parliament equally shared.

WILLIAM LORD PAGET was the son and heir of his father, also named William, who died upon the 29th of August 1629, and who married Lettice daughter and co-heir of Henry Knowles of Kingsbury, Warwickshire. When the succession opened to him he was between nineteen and twenty years of age. He had previously been made a Knight of the Bath. Upon the coronation of Charles I., at the commencement of the civil war, he joined the Parliament, but having come to a belief of its evil intentions abandoned its service and sought pardon from his majesty for his temporary absence from his service. His wife Frances was eldest daughter of Henry Earl of Holland, who was beheaded by the Parliament, and by her was father of three sons and seven daughters. His Lordship died October 19th, 1678. His successor William was much employed by the British Ministers in foreign Embassies, and when acting as Ambassador to Turkey he helped materially to bring about the peace of 1698-9, "whereby all Europe was in tranquillity." He died 25th Feburary 171$\frac{2}{3}$, and was succeeded by his only surviving son Henry, who was

* Collins, vol. i., p. 112, London 1751, 8vo., quoting from Peck's Desiderata Curiosa, vol. ii., p. 76.

created Earl of Uxbridge. His elder son, Thomas Lord Paget predeceased his father. He was possessed of great poetical talent, and his " Essay on Human Life," now so little known, was thought so much of, that upon the first appearance of Pope's Essay on Man, which was published anonymously, the authorship was ascribed to his lordship.

The Earldom of Uxbridge became extinct in the male line; but the Barony of Paget being one constituted by writ was adjudged to the heir of line who carried it to the family of Bayly of Plancenywyd in the Island of Anglesey, who thereupon took the name of Paget, and the Uxbridge Earldom was thereafter revived, and still subsists although merged in the Marquisate of Anglesey.

The founder of the family was a man of extreme prudence and sagacity. In a common-place book which was some years since in the possession of his descendant, Lord Boston, are the following maxims :—

| | |
|---|---|
| Fly the Courte. | Lerne to spare. |
| Speeke little. | Spend in measure. |
| Care less. | Care for home. |
| Devise nothing. | Pray often. |
| Never earnest. | Little better. |
| In answer coole. | And dye well. |

These rules may be supposed to have steered his course safely through the perilous reigns of Henry VIII., Edward VI., Mary, and Elizabeth.

PHILIP, FOURTH BARON WHARTON.—The Wharton family although one of considerable antiquity, do not appear to have attained the dignity of the peerage, until the latter part of the reign of Henry the Eighth, or commencement of that of Edward the Sixth. After flourishing as Barons, Earls and Marquises, the honours came to an end in the person of the only Duke, Philip, the last male of the race, whose eccentric career closed in the year 1731, at the early age of thirty-two at a Benedictine Convent in a small Spanish village, where he had been charitably entertained by the monks. Not having been attainted, the out-lawry of his grace did not extinguish the Barony, accordingly the out-lawry having been reversed by a judgment of the Court of King's Bench, upon the claim of the co-heirs, it was held 24th July 1845. that the Barony of Wharton having been created by writ, was descendible to heirs general, and was then in abeyance.

At the date of the masque, Philip, the fourth Baron, was under age, probably between seventeen and eighteen, as he did not obtain his writ of summons to the House of Peers until April 1640. His father Sir Thomas Wharton, was the younger of the two sons of Philip, the third Lord. The elder son Sir George, was killed in a duel with Sir James Stewart. eldest son and heir-apparent of Walter, first Lord Blantyre, in which both parties were killed. Sir George was a high spirited young man, haughty, insolent. and quarrelsome. He was a favourite of James 1., and married the Lady Anne Manners, a daughter of the Earl of Rutland. The other combatant was a godson of the King and highly regarded by him. According to the old ballad, printed by Ritson in his ancient songs from a black letter copy of the period, the encounter arose from a gambling dispute. There is a Scottish version in the "Minstrelsy of the Scottish border," and a third edition will be found in "Scotish Ballads and Songs, Historical and Traditional," with copious introductory observations. They were before the quarrel intimate friends, and were by Royal order buried in one grave at Islington, 10th November 1609. As Sir George left no children. his brother Sir Thomas became apparent-heir to the Barony, but he died on the 17th of April 1622, leaving Philip, who on the death of his grandfather 26th of March 1626, thus became fourth Baron Wharton.

It is a singular fact, that this youth honoured by his Majesty as a companion in the present masque, should after attaining majority, take part with the enemies of Charles, and be numbered with those who pursued Strafford, and Archbishop Laud to the death. Lord Wharton was thrice married, first to Elizabeth, daughter of Sir Rowland Wandesford, by whom he had one daughter, who became the wife of Lord Willoughby of Eresby, Lord Great Chamberlain of England : secondly to Jane, heir of Arthur Goodwyn of Upper Wichendon, by whom he had Thomas, afterwards first Earl of Wharton and Goodwyn, who died without issue, and four daughters; and thirdly, Anne, daughter of William Carrgroom, of the Bedchamber to James I., the only offspring of which union was William who died young. His Lordship departed this life at an advanced age, shortly after the execution of his last will, on the 1st of February, " in the seventh year of the reign of King William the Third, and in the year of our Lord one thousand six hundred and nynty five."*

Upon the 24th of February 1695-6. Thomas. fifth Lord Wharton, took his seat in the House of Peers. He had previously married Anne, one of the two daughters and co-heiresses of Sir Henry Lee of Ditchley, in the County of Oxford, by whom he had no children. Park in his edition of Walpole's " Royal and Noble Authors" has raised her to the peerage as a Marchioness, although she had not even attained the rank of a Baroness. She lived and died the wife of a Commoner. Mrs Wharton had a fondness for the muses, and some of her poetical productions have considerable merit. She was authoress of a tragedy called " Love above Crowns" still existing in manuscript. The original MS. clothed in exquisite old morocco, and dedicated in her own beautiful handwriting to her beloved friend Mrs Howe. was purchased at the distribution of the Strawbery Hill treasures for Charles Kirkpatrick Sharpe. Esq., and is now deposited in the Library of the British Museum.

By his second wife, Lucy, daughter of Lord Lisburn, his Lordship had Philip born December 1698, and two daughters Jane and Lucy. On the 2d December 1706, he was created Viscount Winchendon and Earl of Wharton, and in March 1714, was raised to the higher dignity of Marquis of Wharton and Malmesbury: Honours which he enjoyed for a brief period, as he died during the succeeding year.

The Marquis was a remarkable man. He was a powerful promoter of the revolution, and was generally understood to have been the author of the ballad of " Lilibulero." with which he was accustomed to boast he sang the last monarch of the Stewart dynasty out of his three

* Scotish Ballads and Songs.   Edinburgh, 1868, 8vo., vol. 2. p. 159.

kingdoms. That this somewhat dull performance had a very great influence on the public mind is unquestionable, but it would have met with little attention had it not been for the unpopularity of James, and his undisguised efforts to re-establish popery, which had alarmed the nation, and revived the memory of the Smithfield burnings of Mary and the Protestant massacres of Catherine de Medicis. The ballad singers might have bawled Lilibulero about the streets until they were hoarse, had James only amused himself and his wife with Popery, and not attempted to force his subjects to join in their amusement. This famous ballad was occasioned by the appointment of Talbot Earl of Tyrconnel, as Viceroy of Ireland, in 1657, in consequence of his being a Roman Catholic. Wharton is said by Bishop Warburton to have been translator of a pretended letter of Machiavel to Zenobius Buodelmontius, in vindication of himself and his writings appended to the English translation of Machiavel, 1680.—Folio. See Park's edition of Lord Orford's "Catalogue," vol. 4, p. 68, London 1806, 8vo.

The religious hypocrisy and open profligacy of Wharton was admitted by his friends who extenuated it by referring to his eloquence, his sagacity, his courage, his consistency as a Whig, and as a man upon whom his party could rely. He was deemed consequently a fitting ruler for Ireland, whither he went in 1708. In 1710, England was favoured with his portraiture by that skilful painter Dean Swift.*

The Dean whilst conceding that the Viceroy possessed talents of the highest order, held him up to public scorn as not possessed of a single virtue ; a profligate husband, a false friend, a sensualist, a liar, a hypocrite and an atheist, whilst pretending a love of religion. There is not perhaps in the English language, a more bitter and scurrilous libel. Wharton did not pay any attention to it ; but continued to enjoy the emoluments of his high office until his return from Ireland. His pickings must have been considerable, as he was, it is said, embarrassed

* Short character of his Excellency Thomas, Earl of Wharton, Lord-Lieutenant of Ireland, 1710, 12mo, price 4s. Reprinted in Scott's Swift, vol 4, p. l.

when he left England, but quite comfortable when he came back. Swift's bitter attack will be found in the fourth volume of Scott's edition of his works.

Both the wives of the Marquis loved the muses. Anne was worthy of a better husband. Their marriage was dissolved on the 29th of October 1685.* Lucy his second spouse was celebrated in the following verses as a toast by the Kit-cat Club, in 1693—

> When Jove to Ida did the gods invite,
> And in immortal toasting passed the night,
> With more than bowls of nectar they were blest
> For Venus was the Wharton of the feast.

Three stanzas of an address to Cupid have been held by Park a sufficient authority to give her ladyship a place in his edition of Lord Orford's Catalogue. She did not outlive her husband long. Her will bears date the ninth day of December 1715. She desired to be buried at Winchendon, "in a private but decent manner, as my late husband Thomas, Lord Marquis of Wharton and Malmesbury was." It was proved upon the 20th day of February following, whilst the testament of her husband bears date the 8th of April 1715, and was proved the 13th September thereafter. Two eminent physicians were witnesses, Sir Samuel Garth, author of the "Dispensary," and Sir Hans Sloane, both of whom were attending professionally when it was executed.

The Marquis had for some years been deaf, so much so, that he latterly delegated the duty of saying grace before and after meat to his son Philip, first and last Duke, then a precocious youth of from fifteen to sixteen years of age. Upon one occasion when a large dinner party—gentlemen only it is presumed—were assembled, having been called upon by his father to discharge the duty, the obedient son rising slowly, uttered the following lines in a regular canting tone :—

> Pray heaven to shorten
> The days of Lord Wharton,
>     And set up his son in his place ;
> He'll drink and he'll ——
> And a thousand things more
>     With the same puritanical face.

* Parish Register of Winchendon, referred to in Park's edition of Walpole's Catalogue of "Royal and Noble Authors," vol. 3, p. 267, London 1806, 8vo.

Whereupon the Marquis solemnly ejaculated Amen, to the infinite amazement of those present.

Philip was under age when his father died, and therefore could not take his seat in the House of Peers as Marquis of Wharton. His elevation to a Dukedom before he attained majority prevented him ever doing so, and it was not until the 21st August 1719, that, introduced by the Dukes of Kingston and Bolton, and producing his writ of summons, he took the oaths, and was placed next before "The Duke of Portland."

With the Duke ended the race of the Lords Wharton, in the male line.

He was a man who, as Lord Orford remarks, "threw away brightest profusion of parts on witty fooleries, debaucheries. and scrapes. which may mix graces with a great character. but never can compose one." "With talents to govern any party, this lively man changed the free air of Westminster for the gloom of the Escurial, the prospects of King George's Garter for the Pretender's; and with indifference to all religion, the frolic lord who had writ the ballad on the Archbishop of Canterbury, died in the habit of a capuchin,"* at the age of thirty-two.

His Grace married Anna Theresa, daughter of Major-General Holmes. by whom he had no issue. The two daughters of the Marquis were Lady Jane, who married first John Holt, Esq. of Redgrave Hall, and second Robert Coke, Esq. of Longford, and died a widow before the 19th January 1761. Her sister, Lady Lucy, who had been divorced by Act of Parliament, from her husband Sir William Morrice, Bart., for adultery with Lord Augustus Fitzroy, predeceased her sister. As neither of these ladies left children, all the issue of Thomas. Marquis of Wharton, failed, and the representation of the family devolved upon the female issue of Philip, the fourth Lord, who appeared as a performer in the masque. By a decision of a Committee of Privileges, dated 24th July 1848, confirmed by the House of Lords, the Barony of Wharton was declared to be in abeyance between the representatives of Elizabeth. Mary, and Philadelphia, his three daughters.

* Orford's Catalogue, by Park, vol. 4. p. 121-2.

# SALMACIDA SPOLIA.

SALMACIDA SPOLIA.

*Salmacida Spolia. A Masque presented by the King and Queen's Majesties, at Whitehall. On Tuesday the 21st day of January 1639. London. Printed by I. M. for Thomas Walkley and are to be sold at his shop at the Signe of the flying Horse neere Yorke House* 1639.

*Salmacida Spolia. A Masque presented by the King and Queens Majesties at Whitehall on Tuesday, the 21 day of January, 1639—Dublin. Printed and sold by the Editor, W. R. Chetwood in the Four-court-Marchalsea; Messrs G. and A. Ewing, P. Wilson, H. Hawker, and S. Price, in Dame Street; G. Faulekner, and A. Long in Essex-street, J. Esdale, on Cornhill, Booksellers.* M.DCCL. 12mo. This formed one of a " Select Collection of Old Plays."

Chetwood in reprinting Salmacida Spolia observes in his prefatory brief notice to the reader that it was presented by king Charles the first, his Queen and the chief nobility that attended the Court. "Sir William Davenant and that great architect Inigo Jones, Esq., were the inventors. By the description in the Masque, we may easily imagine the habits, scenes, and machinery were set forth with the utmost magnificence. The painting was designed by the inimitable Peter Paul Rubens."

"This Masque," he goes on to say, "is not in the works of Sir William Davenant in folio 1673; which was my chief motive for printing it; more for its curiosity than entertainment; and I do not expect any but the curious will be entertained by it.

"The music was composed by Mr Lewis Richards, master of His* Majesty's band, who may be supposed to be eminent in his profession, since many songs and sonnets of those times, with an anthem on the birth of Prince Charles, King Charles the second, were composed by him." After remarking that the text stands "as it does in the original," he concludes thus: "here imagination must assist the reader; and as the poet writes on fancy

> Round her all nature's various species stand,
> And follow her unlimited command,
> A sea rouls on with harmless fury here;
> Strait 'tis a field, and trees and herbs appear,"

Salmacida Spolia literally interpreted means the Spoils of the Fountain Salmacis, in Caria. The following fragment of Ennius preserved by Pompeius Festus gives this account of the Fountain.†

"Salmacis nomine nympha Cæli et Terræ filiä, fertur causa fontis Halicarnasi aquæ appellandæ fuisse Salmacidis, quam qui bibisset vitio impudicitiæ mol-

---

* A mistake- Richards was Master of Her Majesty's band—the songs, sonnets, and anthem referred to by Chetwood have escaped the researches of Dr Burney in his History of Music.

† Pompeius Festus in Usum Delphini, Amst. 1699, 4C., L. xii., p. 475.

lesceret, ob eam rem, quod ejus aditus augustatus par-
ietibus occasionem largiter juvenibus petulantibus
antecedentium puerorum puellarumque violandarum
quia non patet refugium. Ennius". ' Immediately after
this extract Festus adds " Salmacis da spolia sine sanguine
et sudore."

This addition gave rise to a learned contest in which
Joseph Scaliger insists that the first word should be
joined to the second—whilst Dacier contends that the
words should stand separate as above.

Whatever side his Royal Highness the Dauphin took
in the controversy. it is obvious that D'avenant was a
convert to Scaliger—for he says :—

" SALMACIDA SPOLIA.

The ancient *Adages* are these—
Salmacida Spolia sine sanguine sine sudore, potius quam,
Cadmia victoria, ubi ipsos victores pernicies opprimit."

" This piece," observes Campbell in Kippis, " is
omitted in Mr Langbaine's catalogue, and in the col-
lections of D'avenant's works, which, however, is a
point of injustice : for though no question can be made
that Inigo Jones was a man of exalted genius, yet
convincing evidence might be brought to prove. that
in matters of this nature few people had a more lively
imagination, or a taste more correct than our author."*

This Masque was probably the last of those magnificent pageants wherein Charles and his Queen so much
delighted, and in which their courtiers thought it an
honour to perform.   The unhappy disputes which were
gradually ripening into a defiance of the existing government suspended these and other court gaieties, and gave
place to matters of serious moment. commencing with
the executions of Strafford and Laud and not terminating
even with the murder of the Sovereign.

The state of the metropolis antecedent to the repub-
lican explosion shows the pains that had been taken to
stimulate the people to acts of violence. which, from
London, their centre, spread over the whole nation.   The
editor of the " Account of the Proceedings against the
EARL OF STRAFFORD, 1641," says, " You may hereby
understand the constitutions of the two kingdoms, which

* Biographical Dictionary—voce Davenant.

were then in a most strange and preternatural fermenta-
tion, a sick stomach nauseating at pleasant and wholesome meat, the body politick growing hot and feavour-
ish, in strange jactations and unquietnesses, wilfully
refusing and scorning the advice of a most skilful
Æsculapius."

This, though a quaint, is unquestionably a true picture
of the times, of which there is an interesting record
extant, in a paper which coolly proscribes those
who, in either house of parliament, were eminent for
their loyalty.

A Copy of a Paper posted up at the Wall of Sir William
Brunkard's House, in the Old Palace Yard, in Westminster, Monday, May 3, 1641.

The Names of the Straffordians posted.

1. Lord Digby.
2. Lord Compton.
3. Lord Buckhurst.
4. Sir Robert Hatton.
5. Sir Thomas Fanshawe.
6. Sir Edward Alford.
7. Sir Nicholas Slanning.
8. Sir Thomas Danby.
9. Sir George Wentworth.
10. Sir Peter Wentworth.

And 35 other gentlemen therein named.
At the bottom is this HINT :—
" This, and more, shall be done to the enemies of justice
afore-written."

In the Anti-masque it is not easy to separate the real
from the unreal performers. Some names are evidently
fictitious such as Pert, Arpe, Rimes, and Tartareon—
perhaps Pert may mean the representative of that
character in the Wits. Skipwith probably was one
of a loyalist race still existing as Baronets—Slingsby
might possibly be a relation of that excellent man
Sir Henry Slingsby of Scriven, Bart., who suffered
death for his Sovereign. His memoirs published twice
in the present century indicate rather a marked disin-
clination to these courtly gaieties and make it somewhat
questionable whether any very near relative would take a
part in them. There were however other landed pro-

prietors of the same name. Chumley or Cholmondely may have been Thomas Cholmondely of the Vale Royal, Cheshire, now represented by the Lords Delamere.

One person deserves more than a mere notice—the "little swine who play'd with his two countrymen as they slept," "acted by Mr Jeffrey Hudson." On this very diminutive little gentleman Davenant wrote "Jeoffreidos, on the captivity of Jeffery," a poem in two cantos— a very amusing production which will be found in the volume of his poems termed Madagascar, 12mo, and is included in the folio edition of his works, 1673. Sir Walter Scott in the present century brought Sir Jeffery —for he was knighted—under the notice of the public by introducing him in the latter portion of the romance of Peveril of the Peak with another remarkable person of the opposite sex, Margaret Lucas, the second and famous Duchess of Newcastle. Both Jeffery and the Duchess are described with infinite felicity.

Geoffrey Hudson was the son of a labourer. He was born at Okeham in 1619. At the age of seven he was not eighteen inches high—at which period of his exis- tence he was taken into the family of the Duke of Buck- ingham, at Burleigh on the Hill, and had there the honour of being introduced to royalty then on a progress, through the medium of a cold pie, in which he was served up to table to create a surprise to the court.* On the marriage of Charles I. he was presented to the service of the Marquis of Hamilton ; and was so far trusted as to be despatched to France to bring over Her Majesty's midwife. In his passage he was taken by a pirate and carried into Dunkirk. His captivity gave rise to Sir William Davenant's Jeoffreidos, a poem on his duel with a turkey-cock. His diminutive size did not prevent his acting in a military capacity ; for during the civil wars he served as captain of horse. In following the fortunes of his royal mistress into France, he engaged in a quarrel with a Mr Crofts, who contemptuously came into the

---

* It was a common device at the feasts of the old English, in the times prior to Charles Second's reign, when the nobility dispensed their hos- pitality in the ancient halls of their ancestors, instead of nestling in Lon- don, to have an extensive pie served up at table, from which on being opened, a flock of living birds flew forth to the no small surprise and amusement of the guests.

field armed only with a squirt; a second meeting was appointed on horseback, when Geoffry killed his antagonist at the first shot. For this he was expelled the Court, and putting to sea he again was captured by a Turkish rover, and sold into Barbary. On his release he was made a captain in the Royal Navy ; and on the final retreat of Henrietta, attended her to France, where he remained until the Restoration. In 1682, this little gentleman was made of that importance as to be supposed to be concerned in the popish plot, and was committed to the Gatehouse, where he ended his life at the age of sixty-three.

Of Lewis Richard by whom the music was composed nothing has been ascertained beyond the fact that he was "Master of *her* majesties Musicke," and not of *his* Majesty's, as Burney asserts in his General History of Music, vol. iii., p. 385. London 1789, 4to—In a note he adds, "This musician's name has occurred nowhere else in my researches."

DISCORD, a malicious fury, appears in a storm, and by the invocation of malignant spirits, proper to her evil use, having already put most of the world into disorder, endeavours to disturb these parts, envying the blessings and tranquillity we have long enjoyed.

These incantations are expressed by those spirits in an Antimasque : who on a sudden are surprised, and stopt in their motion by a secret power, whose wisdom they tremble at, and depart as foreknowing that Wisdom will change all their malicious hope of these disorders into a sudden calm, which after their departure is prepared by a disperst harmony of music.

This secret Wisdom, in the person of the King attended by his nobles, and under the name of Philogenes or Lover of his people, hath his appearance prepared by a Chorus, representing the beloved people, and is instantly discovered, environed with those nobles in the throne of Honour.

Then the Queen personating the chief heroine, with her martial ladies, is sent down from Heaven by Pallas as a reward of his prudence, for reducing the threat'ning storm into the following calm.

In the border that enclosed the scenes and made a frontispiece to all the work, in a square niche on the right hand stood two figures of women, one of them expressing much majesty in her aspect, appareled in sky colour with a crown of gold on her head, and a bridle in her hand, representing Reason : the other, embracing her, was in changeable silk with wings at her shoulders, figured for Intellectuall Appetite, who while she embraceth Reason, all the actions of men are rightly governed. Above these, in a second order, were winged children, one riding on a furious lion, which he seems to tame with reins and a bit : another bearing an antique ensign : the third hovering above with a branch of palm in his hand, expressing the victory over the perturbations.  In a niche on the other side stood two figures joining hands, one a grave old man in a robe of purple, with a heart of gold in a chain about his neck, figured for Counsel ; the other a woman, in a garment of cloth of gold, in her hand a sword with a serpent winding about the blade, representing Resolution, both these being necessary to the good means of arriving to a virtuous end.

Over these and answering to the other side was a round altar raised high, and on it the bird of Pallas, figured for Prudence ; on either side were children with wings, one in act of adoration, another holding a book, and a third flying over their heads with a lighted torch in his hand, representing the intellectual light accompanied with Doctrine and Discipline, and alluding to the figures below, as those on the other side.

Above these ran a large freize, with a cornice-ment: in the midst whereof was a double compart-ment rich and full of ornament: on the top of this sate Fame with spreaded wings, in act, sound-ing a trumpet of gold: joining to the compart-ment, in various postures lay two figures in their natural colours as big as the life; one holding an anchor representing Safety; the other representing Riches, with a cornucopia; and about her stood antique vases of gold. The rest of this freize was composed of children, with significant signs to ex-press their several qualities; Forgetfulness of injuries, extinguishing a flaming torch on an armour; Commerce, with ears of corn; Felicity, with a basket of lillies; Affection to the country, holding a grasshopper; Prosperous success, with the rudder of a ship; Innocence, with a branch of fern: All these expressing the several goods, fol-lowers of Peace and Concord, and fore-runners of human felicity: so as the work of this front consisting of Picture qualified with moral Philoso-phy, temper'd delight with profit.

In the midst of the aforesaid compartment in an oval table was written: SALMACIDA SPOLIA.

The ancient adages are these:

Salmacida Spolia sine sanguine sine sudore, potius quam. Cadmia victoria, ubi ipsos victores pernicies opprimit.

But, before I proceed in the descriptions of the Scenes, it is not amiss briefly to set down the histories from whence these proverbs took their original.

For the first Melas and Arevanius of Argos, and Troezen conducted a common colony to Halicar-nassus in Asia, and there drave out the barbarous Carie and Lelegi, who fled up to the mountains; from whence they made many incursions, robbing and cruelly spoiling the Grecian inhabitants, which could by no means be prevented.

On the top of the right horn of the hill which surrounds Halicarnassus, in form of a theatre, in a famous fountain of most clear water, and exquisite taste called Salmacis : It happened that near to this fountain one of the colony, to make gain by the goodness of the water, set up a tavern, and furnish'd it with all necessaries, to which the barbarians resorting, enticed by the delicious taste of this water, at first some few, and after many together in troops, of fierce and cruel natures, were reduced of their own accord to the sweetness of the Grecian customs.

### The other Adage is thus derived.

The city of Thebes, anciently called Cadmia, had war with Adrastus, the Argive king, who raised a great army of Arcadians and Missenians, and fought a battle with them near Ismenia, where the Thebans were overthrown, turned their backs, and fled into their city ; the Peloponesians, not accustomed to scale walled towns, assaulting furiously, but without order, were repulst from the walls by the defendants, and many of the Argives slain : at that instant the besieged, making a great sally, and finding the enemy in disorder and confusion, cut them all in pieces, only 'Adrastus excepted, who was saved by flight : but this victory was gotten with great damage and slaughter of the Thebans, for few of them returned alive to their city.

The allusion is, that his Majesty out of his mercy and clemency approving the first Proverb, seeks by all means to reduce tempestuous and turbulent natures into a sweet calm of civil concord.

A curtain flying up, a horrid scene appeared of storm and tempest; no glimpse of the sun was seen, as if darkness, confusion, and deformity, had possest the world, and driven light to heaven, the trees bending, as forced by a gust of wind, their branches rent from their trunks, and some torn up by the roots: afar off was a dark wrought sea, with rolling billows, breaking against the rocks, with rain, lightning and thunder: in the midst was a globe of the earth, which at an instant falling on fire, was turned into a Fury, her hair upright, mixt with snakes, her body lean, wrinkled, and of a swarthy colour, her breasts hung bagging down to her waist, to which with a knot of serpents was girt red bases, and under it tawny skirts down to her feet: in her hand she brandisht a sable torch, and looking askance with hollow envious eyes, came down into the room.

## FURY.

Blow winds! until you raise the seas so high,
That waves may hang like leaves in the Sun's eye,
That we, when in vast cataracts they fall,
May think he weeps at Nature's funeral.
Blow winds! and from the troubled womb of earth,
Where you receive your undiscover'd birth,
Break out in wild disorders, till you make
Atlas beneath his shaking load to shake.
How am I griev'd, the world should every where
Be vext into a storm, save only here?
Thou over-lucky too much happy isle,
Grow more desirous of this flatt'ring style!
For thy long health can never alter'd be,
But by thy surfeits on Felicity:
And I to stir the humours that increase
In thy full body, over-grown with peace,

Will call those Furies hither, who incense
The guilty, and disorder innocence,
    Ascend! ascend! you horrid sullen brood
Of evil spirits, and displace the good!
The great make only wiser, to suspect
Whom they have wrong'd by falsehood, or neglect ;
The rich, make full of avarice as pride,
Like graves, or swallowing seas, unsatisfied ;
Busy to help the State, when needy grown,
From poor men's fortunes, never from their own.
The poor, ambitious make, apt to obey
The false in hope to rule whom they betray :
And make religion to become their vice,
Nam'd, to disguise ambitious avarice.

The speech ended, three Furies make their entry
presented by M. Charles Murray, M. Seymor, M.
Tartureau.

This antimasque being past, the scene changed
into a calm, the sky serene, afar off Zephyrus
appeared breathing a gentle gale : in the landskip
were corn fields and pleasant trees, sustaining
vines fraught with grapes, and in some of the
furthest parts villages, with all such things as might
express a country in peace, rich, and fruitful.
There came breaking out of the heavens a silver
chariot, in which sate two persons, the one a woman
in a watchet garment, her dressing of silver mixt
with bulrushes, representing Concord : somewhat
below her sate the good Genius of Great Britain,
a young man in a carnation garment, embroidered
all with flowers, an antique sword hung in a scarf,
a garland on his head, and in his hand a branch of
platan* mixt with ears of corn : these in their
descent sung together.

* The plane tree.

### 1. Song.

*Good Genius of Great Britain, Concord.*

#### CONCORD.

Why should I hasten hither, since the good
I bring to men is slowly understood?

#### GENIUS.

I know it is the people's vice
To lay too mean, too cheap a price
On ev'ry blessing they possess,
Th' enjoying makes them think the less.

#### CONCORD.

If then, the need of what is good,
Doth make it lev'd,* or understood,
Or 'tis by absence better known,
I shall be valued, when I'm gone.

#### GENIUS.

Yet stay! O stay! if but to please
The great and wise Philogenes.

#### CONCORD.

Shall dews not fall, the sun forbear
His course, or I my visits here?
Alike from these defects would cease
The power and hope of all encrease.

#### GENIUS.

Stay then! O stay!  If but to ease
The cares of wise Philogenes.

#### CONCORD.

I will! and much I grieve, that though the best
Of kingly science harbours in his breast,

* Believed.

Yet 'tis his fate to rule in adverse times,
When wisdom must awhile give place to crimes.

Being arrived at the earth, and descended from
the chariot, they sing this short dialogue, and then
departed several ways to incite the beloved
people to honest pleasures and recreations, which
have ever been peculiar to this nation.

### BOTH.

O who but he could thus endure
   To live, and govern in a sullen age,
When it is harder far to cure,
   The People's folly than resist their rage ?

After which there followed these several Entries
of Antimasques.

### I. Entry.

Wolfgangus Vandergoose, Spagrick,* Operator to
the invisible Lady, styled the Magical sister of the
Rosicross, with these receipts following, and many
other rare secrets, undertakes in short time to cure
the defects of nature, and diseases of the mind :—

1. Confection of hope and fear to entertain
    Lovers.
2. Essence of dissimulation to enforce love.
3. Julip of fruition to recreate the hot fevers of
    love.
4. Water of dalliance to warm an old courage.
5. A subtle quintessence drawn from mathe-
    matical points and lines, filtered through a
    melancholy brain, to make eunuchs en-
    gender.
6. Pomado of the bark of comeliness, the sweet-

* *Spagyrist*—a chymist.

ness of wormwood, with the fat of gravity, to anoint those that have an ill mind.

7. Spirit of Saturn's high capers and Bacchus' whirling vertigo to make one dance well.

8. One drachm of the first matter, as much of the rust of Time's scythe, mixt with the juice of Medea's herbs; this, in an electuary, makes all sorts of old people young.

9. An opiate of the spirit of muskadine taken in good quantity to bedward, to make one forget his creditors.

10. Powder of Menippus tree, and the rind of hemp to consolate those who have lost their money.

11. Treacle of the gall of serpents, and the liver of doves to initiate a neophite courtier.

12. An easy vomit of the fawning of a spaniel, Gallobelgicus, and the last coranto, hot from the press, with the powder of some lean jests, to prepare a disprover's welcome to rich men's tables.

13. A Gargarism* of Florio's first-fruits, Diana de monte Major, and the scraping of Spanish Romanzas distilled in balneo,† to make a sufficient Linguist without travelling, or scarce knowing himself what he says.

14. A Bath made of a catalogue from the mart, and common places, taken in a Frankfort dryfat; in his diet he must refrain all real knowledge, and only suck in vulgar opinions, using the fricasce of confederacy, will make ignorants in all professions to seem and not to be.

* A liquid form of medicine to wash the mouth with. " Apophlegmatisms and gargarisms draw the rheum down by the palate." - *Bacon*.

† Synonymous with bagnio a bath.

### 2. ENTRY.

Four old men richly attired, the shapes proper to the persons, presented by { M. Skipwith. M. Brough. M. Pert. M. Ashton

### 3. ENTRY.

Three young soldiers in several fashioned habits, but costly, and presented to the life, by } M. Hearne. M. Slingsby. M. Chumley.

### 4. ENTRY.

A nurse and three children in long coats, with bibs, biggins,* and muckenders.†

### 5. ENTRY.

An ancient Irishman, presented by   M. Jay.

### 6. ENTRY.

An ancient Scotishman, presented by M. Atkins.

### 7. ENTRY.

An old-fashioned Englishman, and his mistress, presented by } M. Arpe. M. Will. Murray.

These three Antimasques were well and naturally set out.

### 8. ENTRY.

Doctor Tartaglia and two pedants of Francolin, presented by { M. Rimes. M. Warder. M. Villiers.

### 9. ENTRY.

Four Grotesques or drollities, in the most fantastical shapes that could be devised.

* Caps.                    † Dirtied handkerchiefs.

### 10. ENTRY.

The invisible lady, magical sister of the Rosicross.

### 11. ENTRY.

A shepherd, presented by M. Charles Murray.

### 12. ENTRY.

A farmer and his wife, presented by M. Skipwith.

### 13. ENTRY.

A country gentleman, his wife, and his bailiff, presented by } M. Boroughs. M. Ashon. M. Pert.

### 14. ENTRY.

An amorous courtier, richly ap-pareled, presented by } M. Seymor.

### 15. ENTRY.

Two roaring boys, their suits answering their
profession.

### 16. ENTRY.

Four mad Lovers, and as madly clad.

### 17. ENTRY.

A jealous Dutchman, his wife, and her Italian Lover presented by } M. Arpe. M. Rims. M. Tartareau.

### 18. ENTRY.

Three Swiss, one a little Swiss, who played the wag with them as they slept, presented by } M. Cotterell. M. Newton. M. Jeffrey Hudson.

## 19. ENTRY.

Four antique Cavaliers, imitating a manage and tilting.*  } M. Arpe.<br>M. Jay.<br>M. Atkins.<br>M. Tartarean.

## 20. ENTRY.

### A Cavaleritro and two Pages.

All which Antimasques were well set out and excellently danced, and the tunes fitted to the persons.

The Antimasques being past, all the Scene was changed into craggy rocks and inaccessible mountains, in the upper parts where any earth could fasten, were some trees, but of strange forms, such as only grow in remote parts of the Alps, and in desolate places; the farthest of these was hollow in the midst, and seemed to be cut through by art, as the Pausilipo† near Naples, and so high as the top pierced the clouds, all which represented the difficult way which heroes are to pass ere they come to the throne of Honour.

The Chorus of the beloved people came forth, led by Concord and the good Genius of Great Britain, their habits being various and rich : they go up to the State and sing.

* " In thy slumbers
I heard thee murmur tales of iron wars,
Speak terms of manage to the bounding steed."
*Shakespeare.*

† *Pausilypus*—A mountain near Naples, so called from the beauty of its situation. The tomb of Virgil is there. The mountain is famous for a subterranean passage nearly half a mile in length, and twenty-two feet in breadth, affording a safe and convenient passage to travellers.-- *Sut.* 4.- *Syle.* 4, v. 52.— *Plin.* 9, c. 53.— *Strab.* 5.— *Senec.* ep. 5 and 57.

## II. Song.

*To the Queen Mother.*

### 1.

When, with instructed eyes, we look upon
  Our blessings that descend so fast,
From the fair partner of our Monarch's throne,
  We grieve they are too great to last.

### 2.

But when those growing comforts we survey,
  By whom our hopes are longer liv'd,
Then gladly we our vows, and praises pay
  To her, from whom they are derived.

### 3.

And since, great Queen, she is derived from you ;
  We here begin our offerings
For those, who sacrific'd to rivers, knew
  Their first rights due unto their springs.

### 4.

The Stream, from whence our blessings flow, you
    bred ;
  You, in whose bosom, even the chief, and best
Of modern Victors laid his weary head,
  When he rewarded victories with rest,
Your beauty kept his valour's flame alive ;
Your Tuscan wisdom taught it how to thrive.

*Inciting the King's Appearance in the Throne of*
*Honour.*

*To be printed, not sung.*

Why are our joys detain'd by this delay ?
  Unless, as in a morning overcast,

We find it long ere we can find out day;
  So, whilst our hopes increase, our time doth
    waste.

Or are you slow 'cause th' way to Honour's throne,
  In which you travel now, is so uneven,
Hilly, and craggy, or as much unknown,
  As that uncertain path which leads to Heaven?

O, that philosophers, who, through those mists
  Low nature casts, do upper knowledge spy,
Or those that smile at them (o'er-weening Priests)
  Could, with such sure, such an undoubted eye,

Reach distant Heaven, as you can Honour's throne,
  Then we should shift our flesh t'inhabit there,
Where we are taught, the Heroes [all] are gone;
  Though now content with earth, 'cause you are
    here.

The song ended they return up to the stage,
and divide themselves on each side; then the
further part of the scene disappear'd, and the
King's Majesty and the rest of the Masquers were
discovered, sitting in the throne of Honour, his
Majesty highest in a seat of gold, and the rest of
the Lords about him. This throne was adorned
with palm trees, between which stood statues of
the ancient heroes; in the under parts on each
side lay captives bound in several postures, lying
on trophies of armours, shields, and antique
weapons, all his throne being fayned of Goldsmiths'
work. The habit of his Majesty and the Masquers
was of watchet, richly embroidered with silver,
long stockings set up of white; their caps silver with
scrolls of gold, and plumes of white feathers.

II.                              X

### III. SONG.

*To the King, when he appears with his Lords in the
Throne of Honour.*

#### 1.

Those quar'ling winds, that deafned unto death
  The living, and did wake men dead before,
Seem now to pant small gusts, as out of breath,
  And fly to reconcile themselves on shore.

#### 2.

If it be kingly patience to out last
  Those storms the people's giddy fury raise,
Till like fantastic winds themselves they waste,
  The wisdom of that patience is thy praise.

#### 3.

Murmur's a sickness epidemical;
  'Tis catching, and infects weak common ears;
For through those crooked, narrow alleys, all
  Invaded are, and kill'd by whisperers.

#### 4.

This you discern'd, and by your mercy taught;
  Would not, like monarchs that severe have bin.
Invent imperial arts to question thought,
  Nor punish vulgar sickness as a sin.

#### 5.

Nor would your valour, when it might subdue,
  Be hinder'd of the pleasure to forgive;
Th' are worse than overcome, your wisdom knew,
  That needed mercy to have leave to live.

#### 6.

Since strength of virtues gain'd you Honour's throne:
  Accept our wonder, and enjoy our praise!

He's fit to govern there, and rule alone,
　Whom inward helps, not outward force doth
　　arise.

———

Whilst the Chorus sung this song, there came softly from the upper part of the heavens, a huge cloud of various colours, but pleasant to the sight, which descending to the midst of the scene open'd, and within it was a transparent brightness of thin exhalations, such as the gods are feigned to descend in : in the most eminent place of which her Majesty sate, representing the chief heroine, environed with her martial ladies ; and from over her head were darted lightsome rays that illuminated her seat, and all the ladies about her participated more or less of that light, as they sate near or further off : this brightness with many streaks of thin vapours about it, such as are seen in a fair evening sky, softly descended : and as it came near to the earth, the seat of Honour by little and little vanished, as if it gave way to these heavenly Graces. The Queen's Majesty and her ladies were in Amazonian habits of carnation, embroidered with silver, with plumed helms, bandrickes* with antique swords hanging by their sides, all as rich as might be, but the strangeness of the habits was most admired.

### IV. Song.

*When the Queen and her Ladies descended.*

1.

You that so wisely studious are,
To measure, and to trace each star,
How swift they travel, and how far,
　Now number your celestial store,

* Baldricks.

Planets, or lesser lights, and try,
If in the face of all the sky,
   You count so many as before.

### 2.

If you would practise how to know
The chief for influence, or show ;
Level your perspectives below !
   For in this nether orb they move !
Each here, when lost in's doubtful art,
May by his eyes advance his heart ;
   And through his optic learn to love !

### 3.

But what is she that rules the night,
That kindles ladies with their light,
And gives to them the power of sight ?
   All those who can her virtue doubt,
Her mind will in her face advise,
For through the casements of her eyes,
   Her soul is ever looking out.

### 4.

And, with its beams, she doth survey
Our growth in virtue, or decay ;
Still lighting us in honour's way !
   All that are good she did inspire !
Lovers are chaste, because they know
It is her will they should be so ;
   The valiant take from her their fire !

When this heavenly seat touched the earth, the King's Majesty took out the Queen, and the lords the ladies, and came down into the room, and danc't their entry, betwixt which and the second dance was this song.

## V. Song.

### *After the First Dance.*

#### 1.

Why stand you still, and at these beauties gaze
    As if you were afraid,
    Or they were made
Much more for wonder than delight ?
Sure those whom first their virtue did amaze,
    Their feature must at last invite.

#### 2.

Time never knew the mischiefs of his haste !
    Nor can you force him stay
    To keep off day :
Make then fit use of triumphs here ;
It were a crime 'gainst pleasant youth, to waste
    This night in overcivil fear.

#### 3.

Move then like Time, for Love, as well as he,
    Hath got a kalender,
    Where must appear,
How evenly you these measures tread ;
And, when they end, we far more griev'd shall be,
    Than for his hours when they are fled.

The second dance ended, and their Majesties
being seated under the State, the scene was
changed into magnificent buildings composed of
several selected pieces of architecture : in the
furthest part was a bridge over a river, where
many people, coaches, horses, and such like were
seen to pass to and fro : beyond this, on the
shore were buildings in prospective, which shooting

far from the eye shewed as the suburbs of a great
city.

From the highest part of the heavens came forth
a cloud far in the scene, in which were eight
persons richly attired representing the spheres;
this, joining with two other clouds which appear'd
at that instant full of music, covered all the
upper part of the scene, and, at that instant
beyond all these, a heaven opened full of deities,
which celestial prospect with the Chorus below
filled all the whole scene with apparitions and
harmony.

### VI. Song.

*To the King and Queen, by a Chorus of all.*

So musical as to all ears
Doth seem the music of the spheres,
Are you unto each other still;
Tuning your thoughts to eithers' will.

All that are harsh, all that are rude.
Are by your harmony subdu'd;
Yet so into obedience wrought.
As if not forc'd to it, but taught.

Live still, the pleasure of our sight !
Both our examples and delight,
So long until you find the good success
Of all your virtues, in one happiness.

Till we so kind, so wise, and careful be,
In the behalf of our posterity,
That we may wish your sceptres' ruling here.
Lov'd even by those, who should your justice fear.
When we are gone, when to our last remove
We are dispatch'd to sing your praise above.

After this song the spheres passed through the air, and all the deities ascended, and so concluded this Masque: which was generally approved of, especially by all strangers that were present, to be the noblest and most ingenious that hath been done here in that kind.

*The invention, ornament, scenes and apparitions, with their descriptions, were made by* INIGO JONES, *Surveyor General of his Majesty's works.*

*What was spoken or sung, by* WILLIAM D'AVENANT, *her Majesty's servant.*

*The subject was set down by them both.*

*The music was composed by* LEWIS RICHARD, *Master of her Majesty's Music.*

FINIS.

---

THE NAMES OF THE MASQUERS.

| | |
|---|---|
| The KING'S MAJESTY. | The QUEENE'S MAJESTY. |
| Duke of LENOX. | Dutchesse of LENOX. |
| Earle of CARLILE. | Countesse of CARNARVON. |
| Earle of NEWPORT. | Countesse of NEWPORT. |
| Earle of LEIMRICKE. | Countesse of PORTLAND. |
| Lord RUSSELL. | Lady ANDOVER. |
| Lord HERBERT. | Lady MARGARET HOWARD. |
| Lord PAGET. | Lady KELLYMEKIN. |
| Lord FIELDING. | Lady FRANCIS HOWARD. |
| Master RUSSELL. | Mistris CARY. |
| Master THOMAS HOWARD. | Mistris NEVILL |

As the Duke of Lenox, the Earls of Carlisle and Lords Paget, Herbert, and Russel have been already noticed, it is not necessary to say anything further about them as actors in *Salmacida Spolia*. The Earl of LEIM-RICKE, in the list of masquers, is an evident misprint. Chetwood makes him the Earl of Limerick, a title which did not exist in the year 1639, nor for more than a century afterwards. The word should have been LANERICK, or in more modern parlance LANARK, the younger brother of the first Duke of Hamilton, having been created Earl of Lanerick or Lanark by Charles I. His Lordship was born at Hamilton on the 11th December 1616, and his father dying 3d of March 1624, his guardianship devolved on his elder brother, who placed him in the University of Glasgow, and after he had finished his education there, sent him abroad with an equipage suitable to his rank. After having travelled some years on the continent he took up his residence in France, where he was much esteemed, and had offers of high offices which he declined to accept, and preferred returning home, which he did in 1637, being then twenty-one years of age.

"His great merits and accomplishments caused him to be received at court with the highest distinction, and he became a great favourite both with the king and queen."* His being selected as one of the masquers affords ample proof of the estimation in which he was held by them. After the execution of his brother in 1649, he obtained the Dukedom of Hamilton, and was invested by Charles II. with the order of the Garter. He accompanied that monarch to Scotland, but, not being acceptable to the

* Anderson's " Memoirs of the House of Hamilton." page 111. Edinburgh, 1825, 4to.

Covenanting party, retired to the Isle of Arran, still in possession of the Hamilton family. He afterwards joined Charles with such troops as he could raise, and accompanied his majesty to Worcester, where he met with his death, occasioned by a slug-shot crushing the bone of the leg, which resulted in mortification. Had amputation followed as recommended by Howard, the king's physician, it was generally believed that his life might have been saved.

Basil, Lord Fielding, was the eldest son of William, Earl of Denbigh, by Susan Villiers, sister of the first Duke of Buckingham. He was made a Knight of the Bath at the coronation of Charles I. Unlike his father, who was fighting for the king and served as a volunteer in Prince Rupert's troop, the son accepted a commission from the Parliament, which, with the Earls of Essex and Manchester, he surrendered upon the passing of the Self-denying Ordinance, 2d April 1645. At this date he was Earl of Denbigh, his father having died of wounds received in a skirmish with the Parliament troops near Birmingham, 3d April 1643.

Earl Basil had four wives, the first of whom was Anne, eldest daughter of Richard, Earl of Portland, the Lord High Treasurer. By none of these ladies had he any children, so that his honours and estates devolving on his death, in November 1675, upon his nephew, William, son of George, Earl of Desmond, the English and Irish honours united, and have so descended to the present Earl of Denbigh and Desmond.

Master Russel was Francis, a younger brother of William, Lord Russel, of whom a brief notice has previously been given.

Master Thomas Howard was the second son of Thomas, Earl of Berkshire, and upon the demise of his elder brother, Charles, Viscount Andover, without issue male, succeeded, in April 1679, to his father's Earldom. Although twice married, having only one daughter by his first wife, the honours passed to the next male heir upon his death—12th April 1706 at a very advanced age.

The LADY KELLYMEKIN was the young wife of Lewis Boyle, eldest son of Richard, Earl of Cork, who was born the 23d May 1619, upon whom, though a child, Charles I. conferred the dignity of a baron and viscount of Ireland, by the titles of Baron of Bandonbridge and Viscount Kynalmeaky. The letters patent are somewhat unusual, for the honours are granted to the boy and the heirs male of his body, whom failing, to himself and his other heirs male, " tam de corpore, quam a latere dicti comitis (de Cork)." They bear date, 26th February 1627-8. His Lordship, upon 26th December 1639, espoused Lady Elizabeth Fielding, third daughter of William, Earl of Denbigh, and sister of George Fielding, Earl of Desmond. The Viscount, at the age of thirteen, upon the third March 1629, tilted at a tournament before royalty.

As Lady Elizabeth was the youngest of the family she must have been under age when she married. She appears shortly after the event as a masquer in *Salmacida Spolia*, as performed on the 21st of January 1639-40, the year not then ending until the 24th of March.

The Viscount was of considerable service to the king in the wars of Ireland, where he was very successful. Unfortunately he was killed at the battle of Liscarroll, having been shot through the head, 3d September 1642. He left no issue, but, under the patent, his brother, as next heir male, was entitled to the honours, but did not assume them. He was at a later date created Earl of Orrery by Charles II., having, when seven years of age, been made Baron of Broghill by Charles I., with a similar remainder in his patent to that of his brother Kynalmeaky.

Lady Kynalmeaky survived her husband, and was created COUNTESS OF GUILFORD for life upon the restoration of Charles II.*

LADY ANDOVER was Dorothy, second daughter of Thomas, Viscount Savage, and wife of Charles, Viscount Andover, eldest son and successor of Thomas, first Earl of Berkshire. In 1669, upon the death of her father-in-

---

* Lodge, vol. i., p. 90. London 1754. 8vo.

law, she became a countess, and died 6th December 1691, at the age of eighty.

LADY MARGARET HOWARD, the third daughter of Theophilis, second Earl of Suffolk, married in 1640 Roger, first Earl of Orrery, whom she survived. Her sister, Lady Frances, became the wife of Sir Edward Villiers.

END OF VOLUME SECOND.

TURNBULL AND SPEARS, PRINTERS, EDINBURGH.

*In one vol., crown 8vo, price 24s.*

**ARCHIE ARMSTRONG'S JEST BOOK,** printed from the original editions of 1632 and 1640, with Life, &c., by T. H. JAMIESON, Advocates' Library.

*In one vol., crown 8vo, Roxburghe binding, 10s. 6d.*

**A PEDLAR'S PACK OF BALLADS AND SONGS,** with Illustrative Notes by W. H. LOGAN, with numerous curious wood-engravings.

"Really a welcome addition to our stock of edited English Ballads."— *Notes and Queries.*

*In two vols., post 8vo, cloth 21s.*

**ANCIENT AND MODERN SCOTTISH SONGS HEROIC BALLADS, &c.,** collected and edited by DAVID HERD, a page for page Reprint of the edition of 1776, with Memoir and Notes by SIDNEY GILPIN; with fine VIGNETTES. *185 copies printed.*

THE SAME ON LARGE PAPER, two vols., 4to cloth, 42s.
"The first classical collection of Scottish Songs."—Sir W. SCOTT.

*In one vol., small 4to, cloth, Price 12s.*

**ENGLISH METRICAL HOMILIES,** from Manuscripts of the Fourteenth Century, with Introduction and Notes by JOHN SMALL, M.A., facsimile, &c.

*Privately printed, price 6s. In one vol., 8vo.*

**THE COMMON-PLACE BOOK OF ROBERT BURNS.** Printed from the original MS.—with Introduction, &c., the impression limited to one hundred and fifty copies.

*Preparing for publication. In two vols, crown 4to, price £2, 2s.*

**THE SHYP OF FOOLES OF THE WORLDE,** translated out of Laten, Frenche and Doche, into Englysse Tonge, by ALEX. BARCLAY, Preste. Reprinted from Pynson's edition 1509, with Introduction, Notes and Glossary by T. H. JAMIESON, one hundred and twelve Woodcuts reproduced in facsimile from the Basle edition in Latin of 1497.

THE SAME, LARGE PAPER, two vols., demy 4to, price £3, 3s.

*Shortly will be published. In four vols., crown 8vo.*

**THE WORKS OF GAWIN DOUGLAS,** BISHOP OF DUNKELD, now first collected, with Introduction, Notes, Memoir, Glossary, &c., by JOHN SMALL, M.A.

*A few copies on large and thick paper to form four vols., 8vo.*